SOUTHERN SONS ~ DIXIE DAUGHTERS

BOOK TWO

RIVER RUCKUS BLOODY BAY

JOHN M. CUNNINGHAM, JR.

Southern Sons, Dixie Daughters: Book 2, *River Ruckus, Bloody Bay*
Ashland Park Books
Montgomery, Alabama

ISBN: 978-1-7322488-3-0
Cover Design: Teddi Black
Format: Megan McCullough
Back Cover Photo Credit: Lynn Tatum
Contact Information: ashlandparkbooks@gmail.com
Website: www.theauthorscove.com
Copyright 2020 by John M. Cunningham, Jr.

This is a work of fiction. Any resemblance to actual persons living or dead is purely coincidental.

In loving memory of my parents,
Dr. John Malcolm Cunningham and
Gwendolyn Owens Cunningham

ACKNOWLEDGMENTS

I'd like to thank Norma Jean Lutz and Lynne Tagawa for reading my manuscripts and advising me during the writing process.

MAIN FAMILIES

The Jessup Family

Jackson John Jessup/Miriam Rebecca Holden Jessup (deceased)

Children: Alexander Dunwoody
                  Susan Rebecca
                  Susannah Miriam (deceased)

Slaves: Dolphus
                  Huston
                  Hulda
                  Fannie

The Westcott Family

Evander Lawrence Westcott/Gertrude Anne Mills Westcott

Children: Moxley Adam

                  Benjamin Francis
                  Catherine Anne "Annie"

Slaves: Nancy/ Danny Yates
                  Alice
                  Titus
                  Jason
                  Samson
                  Jonas
                  Becky

The Soileau Family

Louis Soileau/Emerita Soileau

Children: Philippe
              Jacques (deceased)

The Hamilton Family

John Gordon Hamilton/Mary Edith Vernon Hamilton

Children: John Stephen
              Mary Agnes
              Amelia "Amy" Jane

The Evans Family

Matthew "Matt" Ryan Evans/Sarah Howard Evans

Children: Augusta Jane
              Howard
              Vivian
              Caroline (Carrie)
              Sarah (Sallie)
              Mary Elizabeth
              Randolph
              Virginia

Slaves: Minervy
              Elkanah

MAIN CHARACTERS

USS *Madison*

Captain:	Commander Charles Vincent
Lieutenants:	Johnson Buckley (executive officer, later lieutenant commander & *Madison's* captain)
	Alfred Warren (later the executive officer under Buckley)
	Felix Underwood
	Hiram Mandover
	Jonas Birdwell
Master:	Xavier Locke
Ensigns:	Christopher Rawlins
	Samuel Whitehurst
Chief Engineer:	Harold Edges
Paymaster:	Levi Upton
Ship's Surgeon:	Robert Kirby
Assistant Surgeon:	Michael Youngblood
Lieutenant of Marines:	Edward Zollicoffer
Marine Sergeant:	George Kite
Marine Private:	Arthur Quigley
Surgeon's Steward:	John Shoot
Master-at-Arms:	Duncan O'Malley
Landsman:	Danny Yates
Landsman:	Juniper Jones
Wardroom Steward:	Paul Bridges
Ship's Boys:	Jamey Roscoe
	Billy Hoag

INTRODUCTION

Although the title of this series may lead readers to assume it's a novel about Southerners fighting for the South during the Civil War, such an assumption is only half-right. Southerners also fought for the Union. One of this novel's major historical figures, David Glasgow Farragut, was a Southerner.

The former slave Danny Yates, of course, is also a Southerner. He finds freedom and service on board a Union man-of-war. Dennis J. Ringle, in his book *Mister Lincoln's Navy* published by the Naval Institute Press, says that at the outset of the conflict 2 ½ per cent of the United States Navy's enlisted men were black. Not long after shots were fired the Union navy, he says, recruited black sailors by the hundreds to fill its expanding squadrons' muster roles. Some were free, and others escaped slaves.

These books, then, tell the stories of Southern sons and Dixie daughters on both sides of the conflict – white Southerners, black Southerners, and French-speaking Creoles.

INTRODUCTION

CONTENTS

1862

MAY 25TH
–
AUGUST

1

As the British steamer *Bahama* rounded forested Hog Island, she entered Nassau's harbor, and Master Alexander Jessup, Confederate States Navy, widened his eyes. Side-wheelers and sailing sloops, screw steamers of every length and tonnage, hundreds it looked like, crowded it. British, Yankee. And blockade-runners, easily recognized by their low profile, squat masts, and bluish-white or lead color meant to blend in with the dawn's light. Designed for speed, Alex had seen some of them under construction in Scotland during his recent stay in London.

Sails furled, they gently rocked on its clear as glass swells. Several ships steamed out, their funnels streaming smoke. Warm tropical sunrays bathed Nassau's array of buildings, painted various colors, and its swaying palms. Ladies twirling parasols, their escorts alongside, strolled its nearby beach. No longer was it that sleepy little Bahamian village he'd remembered from before the war.

Thirty minutes later he and Lieutenant Stribling, who recently served with him aboard the commerce raider *Sumter*, worked their way up a curbed, people-packed walkway beneath royal poinciana trees' brilliant red-orange canopies and past colorful limestone buildings. The whole island of New Providence, Alex recalled, was mostly limestone. Buggies jostled and maneuvered up a macadamized road. Some passersby curiously eyed the cast net draping Alex's sea chest. A train of wagons carrying boxes stacked atop boxes marked "C.S.A." headed for the wharves.

"I imagine they'll be loading those crates on one of our runners," Stribling said. "They're certainly not trying to hide whose side they're on."

"Which should make our stay here most enjoyable, sir," Alex said. "Almighty remarkable how fast this place has changed. Last time I was here, fishermen mostly visited this town. This street we're on here, it didn't have curbs. Not much in the way of big fancy houses either, by my recollection." He gestured at a street lamp. "Nor lights."

"The war's the reason," Stribling said.

"One good thing about this war. It is profitable for some folks."

"I can't think of a better spot for our blockade-runners to rendezvous. Let's hope we can locate Lieutenant Maffitt quickly. Commander Bulloch said he was quartered at the Victoria Hotel."

"That's a new hotel. I hope it has a billiard room. I haven't played billiards in over a year. I could play a few relaxing games of billiards right now. I haven't touched a cue stick since this war started."

"First, we check-in at the hotel, and then we find Mister Maffitt." Alex grinned. *And billiards after that.*

They stopped a local who gave them directions. Within minutes, they turned through a gate and went up a curbed road curving toward a long building atop a rise overlooking the harbor. The Royal Victoria Hotel, with its wide piazzas, towered four stories high. The entrance projected from the rest of the building and a cupola capped its roof. More palms and shrubs marked their path.

Upon checking in, they inquired about Maffitt. The desk clerk gave them his room number.

They then wedged through the lobby's throngs, climbed the stairs to the second floor, and followed it to the fourth door on their right.

Panting from the climb, Stribling set down his chest and swiped perspiration off his brow before he knocked. "Lieutenant Maffitt. Lieutenant Maffitt."

They waited; they listened; no response.

"Maybe he's eating dinner," Alex said.

Stribling stroked his neat, brown beard. "I'd try to find him, but I have no idea what he looks like. Have you met him before?"

Alex shook his head no.

"Let's get on up to our room."

"Then play billiards, sir."

"We eat dinner first. Find out what's what around here, come back to see if Mister Maffitt's in, finish our business with him, and then you can play all the billiards you want till you can catch a blockade-runner home."

Alex rearranged his cast net gathered atop his sea chest. He followed Stribling up another flight to the third floor and their assigned quarters.

After a quick dinner at a café near the harbor, Alex and Stribling returned to the hotel. Within the next hour, Alex knocked on Maffitt's door. Again, he and Stribling got no response, so they went outside into the hotel's gardens.

Couples and individuals bustled along its broad, paved paths circling all manner of flora. Silk cotton trees, royal poincianas, other shrubs and flowers Alex couldn't identify. Children scampered about; one boy chased a dog, and a girl sat on a curb cradling a kitten. A native Bahamian balanced a basket of bread on her head, carefully moving around a parked buggy. A tree house built around a cotton tree sparked Alex's interest. Opposite this tree house, across the path, stood a small structure in front of which two ladies sat on stools, one whipping her bow across a violin's strings and the other one rapidly plucking her guitar. Behind them, a slightly-built man belted "Camptown Races" off-key. He owned thick, black wavy hair, a neat mustache, and a large beard that spanned his jaw trimmed to a sharp point at his shirt's collar. His deep-set eyes were dark.

Covering his ears, Alex winced. He and Stribling started to move on, but when they did, the music abruptly stopped.

"I guess you fellows were wondering who this fellow is over here, baying like a hound dog," the singer said behind them.

Alex and Stribling turned back. The man hastened up to them, the ladies following.

"Try singing like a coyote with a sore throat," Alex said.

"No. I say a hound dog." The man clapped Alex's shoulder. Hand outstretched, he and Alex shook. Stribling's handshake followed. The man crooked his hand around the pretty guitar player's elbow. "I haven't seen you fellows before. Have you just arrived?"

"Yes, sir," Stribling said.

"Where from?"

"England. We served on the *Sumter*. The Yanks bottled her up at Gibraltar. So we abandoned her and went there before catching a ship here."

The man's brows arched in recognition. He slipped his other hand in the violin player's. "Semmes's command. Fascinating story, what the papers all said, how y'all escaped the Mississippi's Head of the Passes below New Orleans last year and out-sailed the *Brooklyn*. Excellent. Excellent. You and your crew captured lots of Yankee ships, according to what I read. Would you fellows be looking for a blockade-runner to take y'all home?"

"That was the general reason for our coming here," Alex said.

"Hmm. I might be able to oblige."

"That's all fine and well," Stribling said. "But who are you?"

The man wheeled both ladies toward the garden gate. "Lieutenant John Maffitt's my name."

"Sorry about my previous sarcasm, sir," Alex said. "The coyote with the— "

"Forget it."

"Sir!" Stribling said. "We've been looking for you. The desk clerk gave us your room number."

Maffitt lowered his voice. "Be there, gents, at seven-thirty." Howling like a coyote, he guided his lady friends toward the hotel, their boisterous laughter drawing stares from everyone nearby.

Alex chuckled. "He has a sense of humor. Any man with a sense of humor is fine by me."

At seven-thirty in the evening, Alex and Stribling rapped on Maffitt's door.

"Come in," drawled a soft feminine voice.

A blockade-runner's wife, daughter, fiancée? Alex wondered. By her Southern accent, Alex judged she wasn't one of the island's British roses. On his way back to his room after a few games of billiards, where he'd whipped a Yankee naval officer thrice, he'd spotted the lieutenant in the hotel lobby telling who knew what story which made the bevy of females clustered around him burst into hilarity. Alex smiled to himself. *Aw, the poor rooster. All those hens fussing over him.*

He and Stribling entered. A girl who appeared no older than twenty arose from the edge of Maffitt's bed. "I am Martha Elizabeth Massingale." Her brown eyes sparkled at Alex. Her touch of admiration made his insides squirm.

"She's the daughter of a friend," Maffitt said. "Came in on a runner with her parents the day before yesterday."

"My father happens to be the captain of the blockade-runner *Eugenia Princess*," Martha said. "The best blockade-running captain there is."

Maffitt grunted.

Martha's gleeful eyes slid Maffitt's direction. "With the exception of our gallant Captain Maffitt, of course."

Laughing, Maffitt slapped his chair's arms.

"Pleased to meet you, Miss Massingale," Stribling said.

Martha fixed her sparkling browns back on Alex.

Alex fidgeted. He wished she'd quit looking at him that way. Her red hair and her eyes reminded him of his neighbor back in Mobile, his sister Susan's neighbor, Mary Hamilton.

"Thank your parents for their kind invitation, Miss Massingale," Maffitt said. "Tell them I will join their rendezvous for champagne in the gardens shortly."

Martha smiled at Alex before she glided out the door.

"Now then," Maffitt said, standing. "To the business at hand. Where are you gents from?"

"South Carolina," Stribling said.

"Alabama," Alex said. "Mobile, sir."

"My first wife was from Mobile."

"I'm sorry, sir," Stribling said.

"No need to be sorry. She's still alive. We're divorced." He cleared his throat. "You arrived on the *Bahama?*"

Stribling and Alex nodded.

"I thought so."

"A firm in my state owns her," Stribling said.

"Correction," Maffitt said. "Partly owns her. Fraser, Trenholm and Company, in Liverpool, are also her owners. She's a good ship, and is serving us well." He went to a table and poured himself a glass of water. Lifting his glass toward them as a gesture of offering them some, Alex and Stribling shook their heads. Maffitt quaffed the water. "Well then, not too long ago, I arrived here on the *Gordon* with a load of cotton and found Mister John Low at this hotel. He's British, but also a provisional master in our Navy. He brought in the *Oreto*. Fraser, Trenholm and Company built her for us."

"Yes, sir." Stribling said.

Alex knew Captain Bulloch, their agent in England, had contracted for *Oreto* and another vessel called the *290*. That was his mission, contracting for commerce raiders. This he'd learned during his brief London stay. And he was already aware of Fraser, Trenholm and Company's role in this.

"Mister Low told me privately, soon after my arrival, that the *Oreto* had attracted many suspicions with the authorities here. The Mister Yankee consul on this island, Sam Whiting, and Commander Henry Hinckley of Her Majesty's Navy, have been trying to stop her from sailing. Why, you ask? Because they suspect her warlike character, which if it can be proven, violates Britain's Foreign Enlistment Act."

"Which means we'll lose her permanently." Alex spoke this obvious statement unintentionally. It was just something that spun through his head while Maffitt explained the situation.

"I promptly gave up command of the *Gordon* and took charge of the *Oreto*. Her nominal captain is James Duguid, a Brit whom Captain Bulloch hired to disguise her intended purpose. Low commanded the ship through him on the way down, and now I command her through Low till he can get back to England as ordered. Secretary Mallory approved my decision to take charge, but I am to relinquish command if Commander North accompanied you on the *Bahama*."

"He turned down the command outright, sir," Stribling said. "That's why we were looking for you. To tell you that."

"Ah, so the *Oreto's* command is definitely mine!" Maffitt quickly sobered. "The truth is, I'm in a delicate and difficult situation here."

"Where is she now?" Alex asked.

"Cochrane's Anchorage."

"About nine miles east of here."

"I see you've visited this island before. Alas, I am bereft of a crew."

"What's become of the officers and crew that brought her here?" Stribling said.

"They abandoned her. Why, you ask? Consul Sam bribed some of them to quit, and others did it because they got angry after they realized they weren't informed of her true destination. They were told she was a merchant ship bound for Palermo so the Yankee spies in England wouldn't get wind of her true nature and intent. They felt betrayed."

"Have you any officers yet?" Stribling stroked his beard thoughtfully.

"Secretary Mallory sent me a mere two, if you care to call them officers. There's a provisional master, Mister Otey Bradford. Not what I'd call impressive. A 'jack of all trades and good at none,' that one. And then there's Acting Midshipman George Sinclair, Jr. The only time he's been to sea was when he was on the blockade-runner that brought him here."

"Mister Jessup and I have a barrelful of sea duty behind us. Count me in." Stribling nudged Alex.

"Me too." Though eager to go, Alex was also mildly disappointed at having to leave the hotel's billiard tables.

Maffitt clasped their hands. "Welcome aboard. But heed this warning. Avoid Cochrane's Anchorage at all costs and maintain silence concerning the *Oreto*. Why, you ask? Because Queen Victoria's ships watch her night and day. And a whole Yankee squadron has sailed down, some twelve ships, to keep an eye on her. Hinckley's already boarded her, so he knows her warlike construction."

"Understood, sir," Stribling said.

"As far as everyone on this island knows, I'm the captain of a blockade-runner and nothing more."

"A blockade-runner captain," Alex said. "Yes, sir."

"Sir," Stribling said. "There is one other urgent matter. We have arms and munitions aboard the *Bahama* intended for the *Oreto*. If the Yankees discover this, it might prove another threat to the *Oreto's* freedom."

"Secretary Mallory sent me word of her cargo. I'll inform Mister Low immediately. We'll transfer everything to a bonded warehouse. That way, they can't get their hands on anything." Maffitt turned pensive. Lifting his gaze, he dreamily uttered a poetic line. "But where is he, the Pilgrim of my song. The being who upheld it through the past?" He flashed a smile. "Lord Byron. Do you like poetry?"

"Mister Jessup likes catching and eating mullet," Stribling said. "He never goes anywhere without his cast net. Billiards, too, if we could have such a table aboard a ship."

"Forgive me. Quoting poetry's a habit. A pastime. Sort of." He grabbed a sheet of stationery off his chest of drawers and jotted something down. He thrust it in Stribling's hand. "This is Bradford and Sinclair's room number. Find them and teach them a few things. Some lessons on seamanship would be nice."

"We'll do our best, sir," Stribling said.

2

AFTER BREAKFAST, ALEX and Stribling sat in the Royal Victoria's lobby surveying its crowds. A tall girl, around age twelve, Alex guessed, cornered two smaller girls against a near wall. Though he couldn't hear what the tall girl was saying, her words muffled by the lobby's din, he noted her body language, her upraised fist, and her posture. Amused, he chuckled silently. *Moody females, bunch of mother hens.*

One of the small girls suddenly looked away, her expression bored, as she pretended not to hear her nemesis. Her action reminded him of Susanna. Susanna had a knack for ignoring people, like their neighbor Mary Hamilton, when they mocked her. Ignoring was how she fought back, whereas Susan always delivered full verbal broadsides at her foes. Identical twins they might have been but quite the opposites in personality.

Susan was his family's pit bull. But this time, his silent chuckle wasn't amused; it was sad. She'd better be keeping up Susanna's and their mother's graves like he'd asked her before he shipped out for New Orleans with Commander Semmes. Before he'd gone off to the Naval Academy, that duty had always fallen on him and his father. It wasn't that Susan didn't want to help; it was because her visiting the cemetery dredged up too many painful memories. But since he and his father were both at war…*painful or not, Susan, it's your duty to care for their gravesites. How do you think I felt when I went there? Every time I did it, I had to keep my big trap shut in front of Father while my heart tore itself to pieces.*

The tall girl stalked off.

"What do you think of Sinclair?" Stribling asked.

Thankful for the distraction, Alex said, "I showed him a picture of a ship and its masts, then I explained what each mast and sail was called. He still gets them confused sometimes."

"He doesn't understand the difference between a fore, main, and mizzenmast? That's basic."

"He understands that part. It's the sails he gets confused. Heaven knows what'll happen when I start teaching him a ship's rigging. Standing rigging, running rigging." He paused, cocked an ear, and then laughed. "I can hear him right now, asking me this question. 'Mister Jessup, what makes a rigging run?'" He laughed again. "How did it go with Bradford?"

"Captain Maffitt's right," Stribling said. "He has some knowledge of seamanship, but it's limited. Guess what he did when I asked him what to do if a messenger started to part? He gave me a blank stare. He said he thought I was talking about a person. 'Look here, Bradford,' I said. 'All a messenger is, is a line we use to haul a heavier line between ships. And if a sailor sees it starting to part, he puts a stopper on it, and if it breaks, he either knots or splices it."

"Does he know how to splice a line?"

"He claims he does. We'll have to wait and see. I'd say we have our work cut out for us. If I knew an appropriate line of poetry I could quote about them in honor of Captain Maffitt, I would."

"He's a little eccentric, but I like him."

"He's a far sight more sociable than Old Beeswax."

"Colder than a flounder on ice, our former Captain Semmes."

"Good wonderful morning!"

Alex recognized the cheerful voice behind him and when he looked up, he hit upon the lovely oval face that provoked an inward groan. Martha Massingale and a female friend. That dang girl wouldn't leave him be. He and Stribling stood.

"Morning, ladies." Stribling tipped his tweed cap.

"Mister Stribling, may I present to you my very good friend, Lydia Stiles," Martha said.

"How do you do." Stribling's mild blue eyes took in Lydia's soft, gentle face.

Martha's fixed gaze on Alex made him fidget and stare at the wall behind her.

"What's your first name, Mister Stribling?" The trace of a British accent laced Lydia's question.

"John."

"Lydia's father commands a blockade-runner also," Martha said. "He's from London, but his wife's from South Carolina."

"I am also South Carolina-born," Stribling said. "What part of that state is your mother's home, Miss Stiles?"

"Martha." Lydia brushed aside Stribling's question. "You were quite right. These chaps are quite the lookers." She closed on Stribling; Martha on Alex.

His gaze glued on the wall, Alex stammered.

Stribling smiled. "I'm happily married, miss."

"Oh." Lydia blushed and retreated.

"Are you married, Mister Jessup?" Martha said.

Blast it! "I'm engaged."

"Since when?" Stribling grinned at him.

Martha moved in front of Alex, blocking his wall-staring, "You're not engaged, Mister Jessup? To anybody?"

Stribling thinks this is all funny. Ha, ha.

"Please take us to the beach, sirs." Lydia said. "The weather's so jolly good!"

"Uh…I'm going to my r-room." Alex moved past Martha. "I'm getting my…uh…my c-cast net."

"There's no mullet in these waters," Stribling said. "Ladies, my friend and I will be delighted to escort you down to the beach."

"Marvelous!" Martha said.

Dandy. Alex swore. Just almighty grand and dandy and every other marvelous word he couldn't remember.

3

SOME TEN YARDS ahead of Stribling and Lydia, Alex and Martha strolled the beach. A tropical breeze brushed Alex's cheeks; fiddler crabs scuttered sideways into their holes. He wished he'd turn into one of them, that he'd have a dark, sandy hole all by his lonesome; a refuge, a means of escape. Females. Dang complicated creatures. Years ago, he'd hoisted the white flag trying to unravel their riddles. While Stribling and Miss Stiles chattered their tongues off Martha ceased her aggressiveness as quickly as she'd started it. *Dang mysterious, changing her behavior all of a sudden.* Whatever her reason, it was irrational—all females were irrational— but there was a reason nonetheless. *Complicated.* He picked up a conch shell and flung it into the water. Females. They were all just too dang complicated.

Martha cleared her throat.

She'd seen what he'd done.

Dang it! Dang it! Dang it! She was just like Mary, waiting for him to start their conversation. How could he start a conversation with Mary? Miss Massingale's hair was the same dark red as Mary's, but she wasn't Mary. Even if she was Mary, he couldn't start a conversation. Every time he saw Mary back home, she'd smile at him and paste his tongue inside his head.

Martha cleared her throat a second time.

Alex muttered under his breath and mustered his courage. His question stammered off his tongue. "Where might you be from, Miss Massingale?"

15

"The Southern Confederacy."

"I figured that much. I meant the state."

"Mississippi."

"Where in Mississippi?"

"Biloxi. And you?"

"Mobile. Both Gulf Coast folks, it seems."

"Southern sons and Dixie daughters we are. Nothing like growing up in the Deep South."

"Does your family own slaves?"

"Father abhors slavery."

"So why is he on our side?"

"He believes a state has the right to decide its own affairs and dislikes the North's attitudes toward us."

Their walk continued while he groped for another question.

Martha picked up two conch shells, one of which she handed him. "Let's see who can throw farthest."

Alex let his shell drop.

She smiled wryly. "Scared I'll throw farther than you?"

Alex let Stribling and Lydia pass, and then he spoke the lie. "Nothing scares me."

"I'll bet there's one thing that does scare you."

"Name it."

She pointed at herself.

"Nonsense."

"Do all girls frighten you?"

"No girl frightens me."

"Well, you took you long enough to start our conversation, and when you finally did, you stammered. You also lied about being engaged."

"You're almighty blunt with your nonsense, aren't you? I have a sister. She does not scare me. Nor does any girl. I like girls. I am quite fond of them, actually."

Martha reached for his sleeve. "Will you let me throw your cast net?"

"You know how to do that?"

"I've seen my uncles and my father do it, and I'm willing to learn if you'll teach me."

"It's not easy. It takes lots of practice."

"I realize that. I said I'm willing to learn."

"Then let your father teach you." Alex pulled back, and when he did so he realized what his action had proven. Martha did frighten him. A man his age, afraid of her like a little boy? No, it wasn't girls. He did like them immensely. That, at least, was true. He'd thoroughly enjoyed the Academy's dances. Girls with whom he'd danced there didn't pose a threat. No, something deeper. An internal alarm warned him to watch out for Martha. "I'm heading back to my room."

"And leave me out here all alone?"

"Stribling's gone on up ahead. You still have time to catch him and Lydia."

"But…I didn't mean… I was only…!"

Alex hastened out of earshot. That female touched a sore spot. *Confound them all.*

In the Royal Victoria's lobby, he soon found Maffitt encircled by six chatty, fan-fluttering, eyelash batting, admiring ladies. Maffitt's amused face darted around them; his brows bounced comically; his humor and wit sparked their peels of high-pitched laughter. Upon spying Alex, his jokes stopped. Rolled newspapers in hand, he gestured him to approach.

"Sir?" Alex said.

"Have you seen Martha?"

"She's with Lieutenant Stribling and Lydia, sir. They're walking the beach. They'll be fine. Stribling's a first-rate Christian gentleman. He's also married."

"Martha spoke highly of you," a lady beside Maffitt said.

"Ma'am?"

"I'm Mrs. Massingale, Martha's mother. After she met you and Mister Stribling last night, she came straight to our room and told my husband and me all about you."

"I don't figure she could've said much," Alex said. "She hardly knows me."

Maffitt slapped the newspapers against Alex's chest. "Here. Mrs. Stiles's husband brought these in yesterday. Read them. Catch up on the war news if you've a mind to." He patted another lady's hand, at rest on his forearm. "We're all meeting him in the garden for a spot of tea." He mimicked "spot of tea" with a proper British accent.

The ladies' laughter erupted.

Alex smiled broadly. Nectar to hummingbirds was their jovial Captain Maffitt. Seeing no unoccupied chair or sofa, Alex considered continuing to his room as planned. Suppose he encountered Bradford or Sinclair, though? They'd pelt him with questions while he was trying to read. He hated being bothered while reading. Let those fellows save their curiosities for tonight. He threaded thick clusters of humanity to a vacant spot. Cross-legged, he sat on the floor against a wall.

He riffled through the newspapers. Most were from the Virginia front, and they cited events from other war fronts which they took from other papers. The first one atop the stack, dated the first of May, said Yorktown teetered on the brink of defeat. If it fell, Alex expected Norfolk's navy yard would fall next, thus dealing a mortal blow to the South's ability to build adequate ships. Fort Macon, North Carolina, a shorter article said, had fallen the previous month.

The next paper summarized a big battle in Tennessee, at a place called Pittsburg Landing. He read the details of the battle around the Shiloh Meeting House and realized how close they'd come to a victory. General Albert Sidney Johnston had surprised Grant. According to this report it was a fierce, bloody affair. Thousands on both sides were killed. Johnston's forces drove Grant's army toward the Tennessee River the first day. Johnston suffered a leg wound, possibly mortal, and Beauregard assumed command. During the night, another Yankee force arrived and reversed Confederate fortunes.

He tossed the paper aside. The next paper's words, set in large type, screamed in his ears: "FORTS JACKSON AND ST. PHILLIP CAPTURED! NEW ORLEANS TAKEN!" Stunned, he devoured the account. Thankfully, Ben served on *McRae*. He, too, was on the high seas. *Huh?* The next long paragraph described the action at the forts and *McRae's* role. He set the paper in his lap. Poor Ben. He'd never made it out.

He recalled that day just over a year ago before the war started, on his native Alabama's beach, when he served as Ben's second in a duel against their shipmate and sworn enemy, Master Xavier Locke, while they were serving aboard USS *Madison*. Thankfully, Alabama seceded the day of their duel. Its secession saved both him and Ben from a court-martial since it led them to resign from the Navy. With Captain Vincent's well wishes, he'd sent them ashore in one of *Madison's* boats.

Then they caught a lighter which took them to Mobile, about thirty miles up Mobile Bay. Within minutes after their arrival, he and Ben arrived at his home. They'd been close friends since their Naval Academy days, and Locke their sworn enemy just as far back.

Once the war began, Alex rejoined Ben in Ben's home city of New Orleans. Alex served aboard CSS *Sumter*, a successful commerce raider under the command of Raphael Semmes till Union ships finally bottled her up at Gibraltar. *McRae* was supposed to have been a commerce raider as well, but something must've happened which prevented her escape from New Orleans.

"Is something wrong, sir?"

"It looks like we're losing the war, Sinclair. Have a seat."

Sinclair sat beside him, Bradford beside Sinclair.

"My closest friend was aboard the *McRae*," Alex said. "Her captain was killed. It appears she got the worst end of Yankee shells."

"Your friend may still be alive, sir," Bradford said.

"Or he might have been transferred somewhere else before the battle," Sinclair said.

"Y'all might be right. There is one other comforting thing. I've never read a newspaper yet that's gotten all its facts straight. Things may not be as bad as these papers claim."

"Maybe not," Bradford said.

"Sir," Sinclair said, "since you're not doing anything at this particular moment in time, I was wondering if could you each me how to throw a cast net."

Alex slapped his knees decisively. "Sinclair, that's a mighty fine suggestion. Stay here. I'll be back. We'll catch a boat to Hog Island, and I'll teach you."

"Pardon me, sir," Sinclair said, "but isn't the beach closer?"

"Hog Island's a mere jump across the harbor. I said we'll go there." He headed for his room to get his net. No worries about Hog Island. Martha wouldn't be there.

4

HIS LONG TRIP finally at an end, ex-newspaper editor Moxley Westcott yawned as he debarked his train in Mobile. For ten miserable hours, he'd traveled in one of its two packed passenger cars, the remaining cars laden with cannon and equipment bound for Confederate troops. That trip took a toll on his body. He needed to hire a hack to take him to a hotel. Hopefully, it had an unoccupied room.

That tomfool flag officer, David Farragut, and his ships had captured his hometown, New Orleans, back in April. When General Butler's Yankees shut down his newspaper, it forced him to escape that city via Louisiana's swamp roads before cutting north into Mississippi. After selling his horse to a farmer near Jackson, who also let him scrub himself clean in his bathhouse and change clothes, he continued to Meridian, where he purchased passage down the Mobile & Ohio Railroad.

He proceeded up the street. Ever since he'd escaped New Orleans, he'd berated himself for his foolishness there. Outsmart General Butler, the city's military governor? Threaten him like he'd done, over his brother Ben's wound suffered in the naval battle below the city? What a fool he was. A genuine tomfool. He didn't stand a chance against that Yankee. At least he saw Ben, a prisoner on a Yankee ship in Farragut's squadron, before he left the city. He seemed to be under the care of a competent Yankee naval surgeon. "Brother, you better not die on me. You hear?"

Recent events galloped through his head—his threatening not to print Butler's General Order if he didn't help him learn his wounded brother's whereabouts, which resulted in his newspaper's closing, which led to the confiscation and possible destruction of his house, which landed him in this present unpleasant situation, his owning nothing save a razor, a pistol, a few threadbare clothes, and the small sum of cash he'd gotten for selling his horse. Never in his life had he felt so poverty-stricken.

Finally, he reached a livery stable where a hackney cab was available.

"The Battle House Hotel's a fine establishment, mister," its driver said. "I'll take you there."

Moxley assessed the driver, a white man sporting a heavy brown mustache. "How much?"

The driver's gray saucer eyes looked kindly down from the driver's box. "I don't mean to offend, but you look a mite rough. Where might you be from?"

"New Orleans."

"You're a refugee from that place, are you, mister?"

"Yes."

"In that case, I'll charge nothing. Climb in. The hotel's over on the corner of Royal and St. Francis Streets. Not far."

Moxley climbed in and set his bedroll beside him.

The driver popped his whip and whistled shrilly, urging his horses into a trot.

Moxley grimaced, thankful the driver only whistled once. Whistling never failed to irritate him.

"A fine establishment the Battle House is. Finest in the whole entire Confederacy. Five stories way high, made of brick, and a big beautiful lobby on the second floor. On the first floor, the stores are, 'cepting these days they're only open for business when a blockade-runner brings in a decent cargo. Shower-baths are available in its bathroom."

Moxley realized his unkempt appearance sparked that comment. "Lots of soap handy, I hope."

"A refugee, huh?" The driver drove the rest of the way silently. Moxley settled back in his seat and shut his eyes till they arrived.

Moxley tossed his bedroll on the floor, pulled out his wallet, and thumbed through his dwindling cash. Eight dollars a day was what this fine and fancy hotel charged. He may have enough left for two weeks' room and board. He sat in a chair and pulled off his battered shoes. He wiggled his left big toe, poked out of a hole in his tattered black sock. He needed new socks, new shoes. A shop on the first floor advertised some. That kind of purchase, though, would severely diminish his finances. Better to suffer what he had till he found a job.

He started unbuttoning his shirt. Tomorrow he'd visit Mobile's famous author, Augusta Jane Evans. He'd promised his sister Annie he'd get her to autograph Annie's copy of her book, *Beulah*. "Maybe she'll advise me on a newspaper job. A writer of her prominence probably knows all the editors in this city." He flopped on his bed, his arms behind his head. "Me, Moxley Adam Westcott, asking a lady for help. Never thought I'd see the day I did that. Hate asking a lady for any kind of anything." His eyes closed, he slept.

After a bath, a shave, and a meager breakfast, Moxley hired a hackney cab that carried him to Miss Evans's home on the city's outskirts. It seemed everyone in Mobile knew where this literary beacon lived. As they turned off Spring Hill, onto a wide lane penetrating massive live oaks, a white, single-story cottage awaited them at its end. A mere single-story cottage? With a wing on each side? An author of her prominence, whose *Beulah* sold one-hundred thousand copies before the war, lived in a small home, at least by his standards. No, it wasn't really small, but neither was it a mansion. It was, however, a far sight smaller than he'd imagined. He'd expected to see a house large as or larger than his home, provided the Yankees hadn't burned his home like they'd threatened to do back in New Orleans.

He went up the front porch steps and yanked its doorbell's small cord.

A pale youth peered at him out the right sidelight. Cautiously, he cracked open one of its double doors. "Who are you?"

Moxley stared down at him. "You go first."

"Randolph Evans, sir. Sallie's not here. She's at Camp Beulah with Mary Elizabeth."

"I'm looking for Miss Augusta Evans."

A black man with a pencil-thin mustache stepped up behind Randolph. "Beg your pardon, sir, but Miss Evans isn't receiving visitors today."

"She can't," Randolph said, "'cause she's walking round her room worrying about my brothers. Our parents are gone to Corinth to see one of them, and she's having coughing fits."

Miss Evans's footsteps sounded down the hall. Her constant coughs sounded painful. "She's ill?"

"Yes, sir," the butler said. "Come back tomorrow, next day maybe, maybe she'll be feeling better. Who do I tell her called?"

"Moxley Adam Westcott, a former newspaperman from New Orleans."

"She'll receive you sure 'nough, sir, when she's feeling better."

"Give her my regards, and tell her I hope she recovers soon. I'll call again."

Moxley sprinted after the hack ambling back down the lane. "Wait. Wait. Take me back to town!"

5

DESPITE HIS BATTERED shoes, Moxley devoted the next day to wandering Mobile's streets. Much of the city resembled New Orleans. Gas street lamps, billiard halls, oyster saloons and other restaurants, pillared houses, iron-laced verandahs, fences and gates, flagstone banquettes, and a few streets paved with oyster shells.

Immaculate their sidewalks were, and it didn't take long to realize why. Practically everyone worked outside their homes or businesses sweeping, sweeping, sweeping. They paid him no mind as he dodged their swift brooms.

Gone the fashions from before the war. Top hats, caps, and fancy bonnets, displaced by palmetto hats for the most part, worn by men and women. Few ladies, he noticed, wore kid gloves; many hoopskirts suffered ragged hems and fading colors; other women wore homespun dresses minus hoops. Nor did much jewelry dangle from their necks or ears, or bracelets adorn their wrists.

Daylight waned. He sauntered in and out of stores not far from his hotel when he came upon an establishment advertising newly-arrived guitars via blockade-runner. He went inside.

"What gives you the right to dress like that, lady?" a small-statured, heavily bearded man boomed from behind a counter.

"It's my right to wear what I want when I want," the lady said. "I'll take that guitar behind you. One-hundred fifty dollars on the barrelhead."

Though Moxley understood he was no judge of craftsmanship, the guitar on the shelf behind the man didn't look that expensive.

"If my wife were here, she'd yank those pretty pearls off your big ears, your nabob ladyship. Why, I've a mind to do it myself."

Moxley's eyes slid toward the customer. Her chin held high, she stood at the counter in all her so-called glory, decked out in a fine silk dress overwhelmed by large pink flounces swallowing the floor between the counter and an empty shelf behind her. Huge pearl earrings dangled from her ears and a ruby necklace hung from her skinny neck.

"Will you sell me that guitar or not?" The lady was growing agitated.

The man lowered his voice. "No, can't say that I will. You got a load of nerve, prancing in here like her almighty highness better'n us normal folks whose wallets and reticules are hurting so much. Have you forgotten there's a war on, Miss Queen Victoria? You probably don't care how hard things are to come by these days. How'd you come by those fancy clothes, anyhow? Why are you wearing such foolish things during these tragic times?"

"None of your business. And sir, I will have you know here and now, this very instant, that I will never, ever shop here again."

"Please, lady. You can do better'n that. I've heard that one a thousand times."

"And I will tell all my friends about the abominable service I get here, you rude little man."

The shopkeeper blew her a sarcastic kiss. "Good-bye and good riddance, your ladyship. Pardon me for not bowing."

Huffing, the lady departed.

"Forgive me for blowing off at her." The man addressed Moxley. "Folks who act like that lady, flaunting themselves around us poorer folks, are starting to get my dander up. The name's Joseph Browne, proprietor of this store."

"Moxley Westcott."

"I've never seen you in here before."

"Never visited Mobile before."

"Where are you from?"

"New Orleans. That guitar costs a hundred fifty dollars?"

"Actually, it's eighty-five. But I wouldn't sell anything for any amount of money to that prima donna who just waltzed in here. Do you play?"

Moxley shook his head. "Sister does. Considering purchasing her a new one for, whenever this tomfool war ends, for whenever I get back home."

Browne handed him the instrument.

Moxley strummed it. Sounded fine to him, but he knew nothing about music, much less guitars.

"How does fifty dollars sound to you?"

Moxley set it down. "Sure about that?"

"If I weren't, I never would have made the offer. You're a refugee, you're thinking more about your family than yourself. I have a good first impression of you, Westcott."

"Thanks. Not such a bad fellow yourself."

Moxley paid for the guitar. A good first impression? Thinking of others more than himself? *Bah!* He hadn't changed that much.

Late next morning, Miss Evans's *Beulah* tucked under his arm, Moxley visited the author's home and introduced himself to her siblings.

"My apologies, Mister Westcott. She's at Camp Beulah," Caroline Evans said. She coughed into her pale fist.

A frail girl, Caroline. Moxley pitied her. He started. Why did he pity her? He was the one who was suffering.

"It's an old house on our land we've turned into a hospital," Sallie Evans said. "Gusta's in charge of all the female nurses."

"We work in shifts," Mary Elizabeth Evans said. "Some of us stay here and help mother do chores and help look after Randolph and Virginia. At the moment, Minervy's watching them for us."

"The elderly slave I saw taking them around back."

"She's been with our family for years, even went out west with us when father tried making a life in Texas."

"I don't see how Gusta does it," Sallie said. "She spends longer hours at Camp Beulah than anyone, and for all those big, fancy words she knows, there's one simple one she doesn't understand....*Rest*."

"Make no mistake. Gusta does understand its meaning." Caroline's voice also sounded weak. "She just hasn't learned how to do it yet." Coughing again, Caroline led him into the front parlor.

"Mary Elizabeth and I are due there within the hour," Sallie said. "Would you be so kind as to escort us?"

"'Course I will. My pleasure."

"Do please excuse us," Mary Elizabeth said. "My sister and I must collect a few necessary items before we go."

"'Course."

As the ladies' footsteps faded down the main hallway, Moxley stirred. Breath swooshed out of him. Sitting on a sofa staring absently out a jib window was a thing of beauty, an exquisite physical specimen, a sable-haired female of the most extraordinarily perfect features—high cheekbones, flawless alabaster skin.

"Who are you?" she said, still staring out the window.

"Moxley Adam Westcott," he said. "You are one of Miss Evans's sisters, I presume?"

"You've presumed wrong. You're Benjamin Westcott's brother, I presume, who is my brother Alex's closest friend. Little Randolph told me you were in town. I didn't believe him."

"You know my brother? How?"

"I happened to have met him the day after he and some stupid man named Locke fought their foolhardy duel. Over the bay, on the beach near Mobile Point a few hours before Alabama seceded."

"Interesting."

"Why?"

"Are you sure you won't change your mind about accompanying us, Susan?" Sallie returned to the parlor.

"Stop asking me," Susan said. "I'll never set foot in that hideous place again."

"Have it your way."

"I always do."

Sallie headed back down the hall.

"Miss Jessup, since hospital work doesn't suit you, why did you come here today?" Moxley said.

"Miss Evans came to my house early this morning and pestered me worse than mosquitoes till I gave in. I only came here to make her shut up."

"Her house. No further."

"She finally gave up trying to make me go with her! She lost, I won. So there! I always have my way. I want to go home!"

She's pretty, and pretty childish, shouting how she wants to go home. "Where do you live?"

"On Government Street. Up Spring Hill Road too. Take me up Spring Hill Road. That's where I live during the summer."

"This house is on Spring Hill Road."

"Wait. No. Take me back to my house on Government Street first."

Perplexed by Susan's behavior, Moxley sighed. "Miss Jessup, just tell me, and I'll escort you wherever you want to go, but only after Miss Evans autographs my sister's book."

"First to my house on Government Street, where I'll pick up my servants and next to my home in Spring Hill."

"'Course."

Moxley followed Sallie and Mary Elizabeth into Camp Beulah. Soft moans greeted him, above which rose a harmonica's soothing music. On a stool in the hallway sat a bandaged soldier, moving the instrument back and forth across his mouth playing a tune Moxley liked—"Aura Lee." To his left, a ward filled with beds and soldiers, who lay on their backs or stomachs or sides while doctors examined them. To his right, another ward. This one held a smattering of patients and several empty cots. No beds here. Ladies sat on stools beside them, wrapping bandages around arms or legs or feet, and spreading wet towels across feverish heads. A doctor flipped pages, notes on patients' conditions, he supposed.

"Wait here," Sallie said. "I'll find Gusta."

A tiny, willowy lady approached minutes later.

"Miss Augusta Evans?" Moxley said.

Face grave, Miss Evans nodded. "Shall we repair outside where we can converse?"

With a long sweep of his arm, Moxley gestured her to move ahead.

Outside, beneath the cool canopy of a nearby live oak tree, he handed her Annie's copy of *Beulah*. The author dashed her name across the title page and handed it back.

"Thanks," he said.

"You are quite welcome."

"Sister'll be excited to get it."

"Did I hear correctly, that you are from New Orleans?"

"Yes."

"Have you a place to stay?"

"Battle House for the time being."

"Several weeks ago, one of our newspapers reported the Philistines as firing on your city."

"Philistines? Oh, you mean the Yankees. Report got it wrong. I ran a newspaper myself, but Butler shut it down because I refused to print one of his orders."

"Splendid!" Miss Evans clapped loudly. "Standing up to the Yankees! Hurrah for you! Since you're a journalist, would you by chance know Mister Randall?"

"Know someone named Randall, but that's his first name."

"I'm talking about James Ryder Randall. He wrote that wonderful song 'Maryland, my Maryland.' He's a refugee from New Orleans just like you. He visited me last month."

"No, Miss Evans, can't say I ever met him. Truth is, I didn't come to you just for an autograph. Need employment. Will you help me get on with a newspaper here?"

The author's thumb and forefinger touched her strong chin. "I will write a letter of recommendation for you. Whether they hire you or not will be their decision."

"Understood. Thanks."

"My parents telegraphed me yesterday that they're leaving Corinth. They were visiting one of my brothers. He's in the Army. They might be home by evening. Maybe you'll be able to meet them."

"Your brother's safe?"

"He is, thank the good Lord. My parents said Beauregard began abandoning Corinth on the evening of the twenty-ninth. They're uncertain of his army's destination. Stop by my house tonight, and I shall have those letters ready for you. What was the name of your newspaper?"

"The *New Orleans Sentinel*. I was both its editor and publisher." He tipped his cap at her. "Till tonight, Miss Evans. Escorting Miss Jessup back to her house."

The author touched his arm. "Be careful, Mister Westcott. She's a troubled lady. I trust you're aware of what you're getting yourself into by taking her home."

"I've a good suspicion."

"Wait here. I'll be back."

Within minutes, she thrust a sheet of brown wrapping paper into his hands. "Doctor Ryan wrote his coachman a pass. He's outside with a maroon coach. He'll take you back into town."

"Again, Miss Evans, thank you."

Keeping his manners, Moxley sat opposite Susan in the coach during their ride back to her house. He fired one question after another as though interviewing her. She, however, dodged most of his questions, thus thwarting his efforts to know her better. When he queried about other siblings, her silent glance snapped back. All he got out of her was that Mobile had gone through a series of commanders and work on its defenses continued. The city's present commander was a general named John Forney.

Of her personal life he uncovered nothing, save that her father was recently promoted to colonel and served in the Shenandoah Valley under Stonewall Jackson. Her brother had written her from England and that he was well. For some inexplicable reason, she attracted him. He sensed her rude manner and sometimes loud voice was an act. An attractive perplexity was what she was. He determined to discover everything about her, why she behaved the way she did, and figure out how to change her. It'd at least get his mind off how Butler's men had humiliated him. He shook his head. The notion of changing her sneaked into his brain unbidden. Why did he want to do that? Because she was physically pretty, even beautiful? *Can't lie to myself. True.* He pondered his recent generosity, buying Annie that guitar and the store owner's comment about his thinking of others more than himself. He hadn't changed. He would never, ever change.

They halted at her home.

"Thank you, Mister Westcott," she said once he assisted her out of Doctor Ryan's coach. "I've decided against going to Spring Hill. I'm tired. Maybe another day. I do need to go up there this time of year, what with the fever season and all."

"Be happy to escort you." He noticed a slave whistling and rocking on her front porch. *Stop that whistling!* "That's the Fannie you were telling me about?"

"A headache of the first order. She's taken away my only means of controlling her, a stupid toy fife her dead papa made her years ago. My father always took it from her when she misbehaved, and he'd keep it till she did like she was told. She's found a good hiding place for it. I've looked everywhere I can think of, but without any luck. No one but her knows its whereabouts."

"Permit me to make an attempt."

"Good-bye, Mister Westcott."

"But— " Moxley grunted. "Well…Good-bye."

The boots he'd spotted in one of the Battle House's stores cost seventy-five dollars. Before he set out for Mobile's newspaper offices, Moxley purchased them and a new pair of black socks with most of what remained in his wallet. His feet ached, but he wanted to make the best impression possible when he contacted editors. He'd have bought new clothes if he could've afforded them and if stores had some on hand. He was glad Mister Evans loaned him one of his suits, and Sallie Evans took up the trousers in the waist and legs so they'd fit him better. Walking became more comfortable.

Miss Evans's letters of recommendation folded neatly in his pocket, he headed down two flights of stairs. How much would her letters help him? Would they hire him out of sympathy because he was a refugee, or because his writing was good? Was he good? Could he write as well as Longfellow or Irving? He hit the staircase's first landing. Maybe he wasn't smart enough to earn literary fame. Miss Evans was famous. So why couldn't he be more famous than her? He hit the final landing before crossing the hotel's lobby and then plodded down another flight and out onto the street. He could write better than any female.

6

OXLEY KNOCKED ON the Evanses' door and waited all of a
minute before their butler answered.

"Step right on inside here, sir," the butler said. "The Evanses were
just wondering about you and wondering whether or not you found
yourself employment."

Moxley joined the family in the parlor. Mister Evans set aside
his newspaper, Mrs. Evans, her Bible. Sitting cross-legged on the
floor, Randolph and Virginia read books while in a wing chair, Mary
Elizabeth patched a sleeve in a dress draped over her lap.

"Gusta's in her study working on her new novel," Mrs. Evans said.
"Let me tell her you're here."

"How did everything go?" Mister Evans said.

"Papers aren't hiring," Moxley said. "Not making enough profit. A
former editor myself, I understand that. Half-expected it."

"Good evening, Mister Westcott." Miss Evans spoke from the dining
room adjoining the parlor. "I overheard what you said. I am deeply sorry."

"Not your fault. Had it not been for the war's effect on Mobile's
economy, they'd have hired me on your recommendation alone. All told
me that." He pulled out his wallet. "Almost broke. Enough for another
night or two at the Battle House, maybe another meal or two. That's all."

"I sympathize with you."

"What's your next move?" Mister Evans said.

"Been pondering that. My brother Ben was in the Navy. Fought
at New Orleans." He recounted the battle of New Orleans, Ben's

potentially fatal wound and capture. As he described each detail, Miss Evans uttered one angry word under her breath: "Philistines. Philistines." He didn't mention Locke, though. "Well, sir," he concluded, "decided my next best move is to enlist in the Army."

Miss Evans clapped. "Hurrah! When?"

"Tomorrow. Next day. Must visit Miss Jessup again first."

"Why?" Miss Evans said.

"She intrigues me."

"She bites," Mary Elizabeth said.

"Shush that talk, Mary E," Mrs. Evans said.

"Please, Mister Westcott," Miss Evans said. "Follow me." She led him into the dining room and through a door into her study.

Moxley marveled at the books cramming her floor-to-ceiling bookcases. Hundreds of them, a library twice the size of his own. At one case, he scanned the books' spines.

"Are you searching for a specific title?" She nudged aside a stack of papers on her desk.

He whirled on her. "I'll wager you attended the Judson Female Institute. I know you're of a religious bent, and I heard Judson's a good religious school up in Marion, Alabama."

"That is a Baptist school, and I am Methodist." She looked directly at him. "Besides, my formal education is limited. I attended a private school in Mobile for a brief time, but it is my mother who provided most of my education, and I have also tutored myself as well as my siblings. All these books in this room, sir, are my textbooks. I have read and studied them all."

Moxley's jaw dropped. "All? Every last one?"

"I'm a fast reader. I don't understand why my brain works the way it does, except that the Lord has enabled me to comprehend things quickly and retain everything I've read word for word. To Him be the glory for the gifts He's given me. But sir, I did not bring you in here to show off my library. I brought you here to discuss Susan confidentially, out of Randolph's and Virginia's earshot."

"My sister Annie's had no formal education either, and she enjoys reading."

"Mister Westcott, I'm trying hard not to be petulant. Please, sir, do sit down."

Moxley worked out of its spot *The Last Days of Pompeii* by Edward Bulwer-Lytton. He thrust it at her. "What's this about? Recite a passage from it."

Miss Evans set it on her writing desk beside her thickening manuscript. Moxley picked up a page, words on brown wrapping paper.

"Sir." Miss Evans's voice turned stern.

Startled, Moxley let the page drop.

"My time is too precious to have it wasted with trifling chitchat. That chair over in that corner. Please, sir. Again, I do not mean to sound petulant, but I beg of you sit down, hush up, and listen."

Amused, Moxley did like he was told.

Miss Evans pulled up her desk chair opposite him. "We had a patient in Camp Beulah several weeks ago who demonstrated an interest in Susan. That makes you the second man who's taken an interest in her within a short period of time. The first gentleman is no longer in Mobile. His regiment has gone to fight under General Beauregard."

"Nonsense. I'll wager that before the war, men called on her all hours of the day."

"Trust me when I tell you. True, other men have admired her, but only from a distance. She has this unsociable reputation, understand. That's why most men avoid her. She never shouted or misbehaved around him or any other patient in the hospital because I laid down the law in that regard."

"She does talk loud as a trumpet sometimes. That much I'll give you. Bah! An act. Her rudeness as well. Saw right through it the minute we started our conversation. My wanting to spend time with her is purely intellectual. What I want to understand is this. Why does she behave the way she does? It intrigues me."

"Do you believe in God?"

"Attend church with other hypocrites whenever I get the urge." He noted the author's eyes flash briefly. His comment made her mad.

"I didn't always believe in God," Miss Evans said. "During my youth, I read books which questioned His existence. My mother never worried about me, nor did she ever argue with me when I shared with her my doubts. She firmly believed my convictions would turn back toward Christ. She was right. They did. Ever since I put my faith in Him, my soul has enjoyed perfect peace. But Susan, sir, has never doubted God's existence."

"So you believe in God and enjoy peace of mind, Miss Jessup believes in God but doesn't. Thought all you real believers were a happy lot."

"Mister Westcott. Please listen to me. Susan's trouble is this. She questions His love, whereas I don't. She doesn't believe God is a God of love, and therefore she hates Him."

"I'll change her."

"I've tried helping her. Although I still consider myself her friend, she no longer likes me. Or, as you might say, pretends she doesn't like me. My sense tells me it's time to back off, at least temporarily. Perhaps you ought to be careful how you approach her. She's been grievously hurt. She doesn't care to get close to anyone anymore, especially not to any man."

"Why?"

Before Miss Evans could answer, the front door slammed shut.

A merry, masculine voice echoed from the hallway. "Is Carrie home, Mister Evans? Or Miss Gusta?"

Miss Evans gestured at Moxley to follow her. "We'll discuss this more later. The good Captain Whittaker's come all the way up the bay from Fort Morgan, a full day's journey."

Moxley followed her. Perhaps the good captain needed another good man like him in his unit.

Whittaker bowed in greeting. Miss Evans introduced Moxley, explained his situation, and his desire to become a soldier.

Whittaker stroked his brown walrus mustache. "I don't doubt you'd pass a surgeon's examination, Westcott."

"In fine health," Moxley said.

Whittaker followed Miss Evans and her sisters into the parlor.

Though Moxley wanted to continue their conversation, he reconsidered. Probably best wait till Whittaker ended his visit. That way, he and Whittaker could discuss things privately. He did want to join the Army, seeing it as his only option, except he didn't care to get sent to the front, not because fighting in Virginia or elsewhere frightened him, but because his interest in Susan encouraged him to stay here. She was one beautiful puzzle. He didn't know exactly why he wanted to figure her out, except that of all the ladies he'd ever known, he thought her the prettiest, save for her personality.

Upon Whittaker's departure, Moxley took his leave a minute later and caught him at the end of the Evanses' carriageway touching Spring Hill Road.

They strode toward the city.

"Say I do sign up, Captain?" Moxley said. "Is there a guarantee I can join a unit stationed here, you think?"

"Our army here's small," Whittaker said. "Mobile's a vital city, though, important for its two railroads, and our bay's still open for blockade-runners. We'll get attacked one day. The question is, will we be able to repel the Yanks when they come?"

"I'd like to stay here," Moxley said. "Don't need much training. Seen it all done at Fort Jackson lots of occasions. I can handle musket and pistol. Shot quite a few deer and squirrel in my time."

"Let me warn you about this, that ever since our government passed its conscription law, conscripts aren't very popular with our volunteers."

"Not a conscript. I'm also a volunteer. Second, what other people think about me is their problem, not mine."

They strolled past the Sisters of Visitation Convent some several minutes later. A mile or so up ahead, men who'd been laying a railroad climbed into wagons to head home. On the opposite side of Spring Hill Road spread Ashland Estate, waning sunlight slanting through the oak trees flanking the mansion's private lane. Owned by a prominent businessman named Lorenzo Wilson, it filled acres stretching clear down to the Shell Road. The railroad, Moxley had read in a newspaper, was one of his business ventures.

"We can use every man we can get," Whittaker said at last. "But you'll get sent to a camp of instruction first. Here in our state, in either Talladega or Notasulga."

"Don't want to go to either one. Said that just before."

"You'll have to go there for training, Mister Westcott. You have no other option."

"How long is the training?"

"At least a month. Maybe longer."

"I'll get sent back here."

"You'll go wherever the War Department wants you to go."

"Suppose you need more men here?"

"I've a two-day pass. I'm staying in town at a friend's home. The conscription officer's a friend, and since you're still a civilian and a friend of Miss Evans and he owes me a favor, well, let's meet at the Diamond Coffee Saloon tomorrow evening, say, six o'clock. Let me speak with him first. I'll also need to discuss things with my superiors. Maybe we can work out something. You'll still have to go to a training camp. I can't make any guarantees."

They resumed their long walk toward town, Whittaker giving Moxley directions to the saloon and talking about other subjects.

While Whittaker talked, Moxley's thoughts meandered back to the lovely Miss Susan. Perhaps he'd have a chance of staying close to her after his military training. Nice thing that would be. Very nice.

7

ANNIE'S GUITAR SLUNG over his shoulder, Moxley hired a horse and rode to Susan's home up Spring Hill, her refuge during the fever season, Miss Evans told him. The author had given him her address and directions.

Her black brows fierce, she confronted him on her gallery. "Leave."

"After I rode all this way for us to spend time together?" Moxley said.

"That's your fault. Go back where you came from."

This beauty wouldn't discourage him. She'd miscalculated his determination. Moxley rested one foot atop the lowest step. "I'm coming inside."

"No."

"Realize you're at your prettiest when you're angry?" He went up the steps, slipped off Annie's guitar, and sat in a rocker. The guitar, he laid across his lap.

Susan slammed the door behind her.

He started rocking, sensing her presence through the open window behind him. He wagered she was playing a game to see whether or not he'd leave. *Miss Jessup, a lady of your fine physical features? I'd wait an eternity.* He shut his eyes and rocked a little faster, enjoying the pleasant breeze caressing his cheeks.

Susan came back outside.

His eyes opened.

"I said 'leave.'"

"No you didn't. Said go back to where I came from. Came to this city all the way from New Orleans. Probably get arrested if I went back there, means I have to stay here."

"Get off my property, or else I'll have you arrested for trespassing."

"Not trespassing. Here on legitimate business."

"We have no legitimate business to conduct."

"You, Miss Jessup, are mistaken." Gripping Annie's guitar by its neck, Moxley rose and seized Susan's hand, which he closed around it. "Bought this for my sister. Keep it for me till I can get it to her."

She thrust it back at him. "You bought it you keep it." Her voice bordered on shouting.

"Can't do that, miss. Joined the Army. Some fellow might steal it. It's safer in your hands."

The angry red in Susan's face receded. "Why did you go off and do something stupid like join the Army? You might get killed."

"Yanks shut down my newspaper. Can't find work here. Army's my only option, provided I want to live."

"If you want to live, sir, you'll stay away from me and quit the Army."

Moxley pulled in his grin. He wasn't used to smiling, but this girl highly amused him.

"You are dumb as an ox and an irresponsible idiot. I want nothing to do with you."

A huge laugh welled up inside Moxley, but he managed to contain it. "Insult me till the cows come home. Makes no matter to me. Folks' opinions don't faze me one way or other. Why, even Brother Ben knows that, Miss Susan."

"You will address me as Miss Jessup."

"Susan, Miss Susan, that's how I'll address you this time forward."

Susan clutched her head and screamed. "Leave!"

Moxley sat back down in the rocker. "Provided you'll tell me— "

"I don't have to tell— "

"Tell me why you're so angry all the time and why you like shouting and shattering folks' eardrums off. A beautiful lady like yourself oughtn't to have so much hate pent up inside her."

"That's none of your business."

"Haven't enlisted yet, just plan on doing it. Yes, indeed, Miss Susan. Believe I have a world of time to rock and wait till you tell me."

He eyed Susan, her face buried in her hands, her shoulders trembling. "Miss Jessup? Miss Susan?"

Susan fled inside the house.

Moxley pursued. "What's this? What's happened? What's going on?" Ignoring her butler and smirking Fannie, Moxley joined her in the drawing room.

Fists clenched at her sides, her eyes seemed to snap. "All right. All right. I will tell you what happened, and after I tell you, I want you out of my house. It's not because I dislike you, it's because I don't want to get close to anyone anymore. I don't want to suffer anymore hurt."

Moxley listened to the story of her twin sister's untimely death. He started toward her, surprised by his selfless desire to comfort and encourage her.

"Keep away," she said. "I am fond of you, Mister Westcott, same as I'm fond of your brother who I met before this war started, the day Alabama seceded. Do not return, though, for both our sakes."

"At least keep Sister's guitar for me, and allow me to retrieve it once this war's over."

"Go. Go. I must change my clothes. I'm going to the post office to look for employment. Uncle Will's wages aren't enough to support me anymore."

"Who's Uncle Will?"

"My father's yacht captain. Now leave. Go."

Moxley bowed gallantly and departed. After he changed her, he'd court her. He reined his horse down her dirt carriageway. On the Spring Hill Road, he pondered. *Me court her?* He was thinking stupid again. No, he would do it. Yes. No harm trying. A few hours remained before he was due to meet Captain Whittaker. Hopefully, the captain would have good news.

8

RUMORS OF BUTLER's tyranny reached Monmouth, Evander Westcott's sugar cane plantation, and other plantations along the River Road. The general's actions troubled Evander, who wondered how far the Beast's fist would stretch. Upon his and his family's arrival, his overseer, Kirk Swan, told him all his field hands had gone to New Orleans.

"That doesn't surprise me," Evander said.

During their journey upriver aboard one of Farragut's small gunboats, he'd seen slaves walking off their masters' lands in droves. Slaves or no slaves, he and his family must survive. By taking the oath of allegiance, what a bitter pill that was, he'd gotten transportation back to Monmouth and avoided imprisonment in Fort Jackson. He'd be doing business with the Yankees now, something else he loathed.

Since thousands of poor white folks in New Orleans needed work, he hit upon an idea. "We'll offer them more money than the Yankees can pay them," he told Swan. "Go into the city. Hire as many as you think we need."

Three weeks later, Swan brought back word that their slaves and hundreds of others had moved into Camp Parapet over near Carrollton, commanded by an abolitionist general named Phelps. Despite Swan's efforts to recover them, the general refused to turn them over, nor did he heed Butler's orders about returning the contrabands to their masters.

Swan proceeded into New Orleans and hired thirty unemployed white men. What tales they told! Under threats of arrest and confiscation of their merchandise, New Orleans shop owners resumed business. Reluctantly, grudgingly, they conducted business with Yankee troops. Confederate sympathizers continued getting arrested for various offenses, major and minor. Butler sentenced some to serve time on Ship Island, and others, such as Mayor Monroe, he imprisoned in Fort Jackson. Those guilty of capital offenses or former Confederate soldiers who violated their paroles soon dangled from nooses.

But it was the New Orleans ladies who caused the most difficulties for Butler's "blue boys," the new laborers said. Gleefully, they hurled insults at the soldiers, walked around them, spat at them, did anything and everything possible to express their contempt and make their lives miserable.

"It was like they was daring the Yanks to arrest 'em," one dusty-haired man said. He spat a stream of tobacco.

"That gen'l got his paws full with them girls," another man said. He showed Evander his news clipping.

Dated May 15, it proclaimed Butler's General Order 28: "As the officers and soldiers of the United States have been subjected to repeated insults from the women (calling themselves ladies) of New Orleans, in return for the most scrupulous noninterference and courtesy on our part, it is ordered that hereafter when any female shall, by a word, gesture, or movement, insult or show contempt for any officer or soldier of the United States, she shall be regarded and held liable to be treated as a woman of the town plying her avocation."

"The mayor protested this here order," the man said. "Didn't do no good. Them ladies, fer the most part, quit their cantankerous acting."

Evander sent them on up the road toward the red brick sugar house and their new quarters.

Flag Officer David Farragut slumped in his cabin's desk chair, ill and weak, his flotilla's captains seated in front of him for his specially called conference.

During May, he'd dispatched Commander Porter's mortar squadron to Ship Island in Mississippi Sound, pondering an attack on Mobile, while up the Mississippi his ships captured Baton Rouge without serious incident. Another domino, Natchez, fell quickly and bloodlessly on the thirteenth. Several days later, Farragut joined six gunboats and *Madison* three miles below Vicksburg, where his ship dropped anchor. Eight Rebel Columbiads bristled from the bastion's 200-foot high bluff, and thousands of Rebel troops defended it.

Farragut hoped to meet Flag Officer Charles H. Davis somewhere along the river. Davis was slugging his way southward some fifty miles above Memphis.

His forefinger tapped his desk as he considered Secretary of the Navy Gideon Welles's order: open the Mississippi and "effect a junction with Flag Officer Davis commanding (pro tem) the Western Flotilla." Thus, in the sweltering, mosquito-plagued summer misery, he'd kept below Vicksburg. His vessels' coal supplies were dwindling and many, including his own *Hartford,* had suffered damage from frequent groundings during their trip up. Mister Welles didn't understand his situation. His vessels were built for oceans and seas, not rivers.

"What do you think, gentleman?" Farragut's voice was weak. "Do we attack the Rebel batteries at Vicksburg, or do we not?"

"Smash them up, sir." Captain Palmer's fist smacked his palm.

"Smash up what?" Captain Wainwright said.

"The bluffs, sir," Palmer said. "We can go in and smash the bluffs beneath their guns."

"Until the earth gives way beneath their batteries and they tumble into the river, I suppose." Captain Craven wagged his head skeptically.

Captain Alden furrowed his brow and shook his head.

Farragut's eyes shifted to *Madison's* captain, Charles Vincent. He really liked Vincent. The man was one of his most capable commanders.

"I think it would be unwise to attack Vicksburg at this moment," Vincent said.

Too ill to offer counterarguments, Farragut called for a vote. Attack Vicksburg, or don't attack Vicksburg. By a majority, the captains voted "no."

"All right. It is decided." Farragut mopped sweat off his forehead. "Gentlemen, return to your ships and weigh anchor. Captain Wainwright, you give the order for the *Hartford.* The river's falling. If we don't get back to New Orleans, we're liable to be trapped here."

"Aye, sir," the captains said, almost in unison.

Madison steamed downriver as far as Baton Rouge when she met Farragut's *Hartford* steaming back upriver in early June in the van of three other ships.

Though Farragut had recalled just several of Porter's mortar boats, Porter brought his whole squadron instead.

General Butler promised Farragut seven thousand men and towboats to pull the schooners upriver. But when would they arrive?

9

BEFORE SUNRISE, ALEX learned a blockade-runner had slipped into Nassau, having penetrated Mobile's blockade. Among other things, she carried letters. Longing for news from his father and Susan, he sought out the runner's captain and soon thereafter one of his men brought in a sack of mail and, yes, one bore Susan's name.

She'd penned it on the back of several pieces of wallpaper, folded in half, sealed with wax, and addressed on the outside to the home which hosted him in England, from where he'd last written her several copies of the same letter in the hope a runner would get one of them through the blockade.

Since the hotel was noisy, he recalled a place further inland, not far away, but a decent spot where he might possibly be able to read and digest his sister's every syllable undisturbed—a great staircase someone many years ago had carved into limestone rock at the southern end of a street. He'd climbed it during a visit before the war. He hoped not many curious people were climbing it today.

Gripping the staircase's rails, Alex bounded up its steps two, three at a time. Once he reached the top he turned back, winded from his long, fast climb, and gave a quick glance at the distant buggies and buildings, and then sat on the topmost step. Two people came up behind him for a brief view of the landscape, said not a word to him, then headed back down. He slipped his finger between the letter's folds and pried off the wax. Susan had dated it the second day of June.

No mention did she make of Fannie, Hulda, or Huston. Far as she knew, their father was well, though she hadn't heard from him in weeks. Probably too busy up in the Shenandoah Valley, she'd said. The Valley had been a hotbed of fights this past May. McDowell, Front Royal, Winchester. Based upon what she'd read, Jackson was whipping the daylights out of the three enemy armies sent against him. Southern papers hailed him a hero.

McClellan must've finally made it up the Peninsula, Alex told himself during his reading. He and Joe Johnston fought somewhere called Seven Pines. General Johnston suffered a serious wound there, so Davis appointed his military adviser, General Robert E. Lee, in command. Alex questioned Davis's wisdom selecting him as Johnston's replacement, for it was Lee who'd lost western Virginia.

Several events she mentioned concerned the Navy. Just as Alex feared, the South lost Norfolk, its only shipyard, as McClellan's army bore down on it during its Peninsular advance. Two days after that, the Confederates evacuated it. *Merrimack/Virginia's* crew, without an operational base, scuttled her. Farragut, meanwhile, had steamed up the Mississippi to Vicksburg but failed to subdue it. She knew no further details.

"Well, hello!"

Alex groaned. *Martha. Great. Wonderful. Let's get up and do a jig.* She and her mother stood halfway up the steps wearing what looked like, from his vantage point, spanking new dresses.

"Hello, Mister Jessup!" Mrs. Massingale called to him. Lifting her dress's hem just shy of her ankles with one hand and gripping the staircase's rail with the other, she carefully made her way up.

Alex lowered Susan's letter. He peered past Martha's mother to see whether or not she followed.

"There is a grave matter we must discuss," Mrs. Massingale said at the top of the steps.

"How'd you find me here?" Alex scrambled to his feet, folded Susan's letter, and crammed it down his trouser pocket.

"It wasn't an easy accomplishment. We searched the town a long time. I'd say you've become pretty skilled at avoiding us since that day at the beach."

"I've had lots of practice, ma'am."

Skirt rustling and puffing from the long climb, she met him at the top step. "Before I'll allow my daughter up here, we'll have a nice, friendly little chat."

Friendly? She sounded as friendly as a rattlesnake.

10

ALEX SHRANK BEFORE Mrs. Massingale's wagging finger. That same guilty conscience which nagged him when his mother scolded him returned. He shifted his feet, gazed up at the bright blue sky and cottony clouds.

"Listen to my words, young man." She pointed at her lips, then resumed wagging her long, intimidating finger. "Martha likes you."

"She has sounded that loud as a ship's bell, ma'am."

"Last week, she asked you to teach her how to throw a cast net. Why didn't you?"

"Aw, there's no need to get your dander up, Mrs. Massingale."

"You mean to tell me you have no idea why she asked?"

"Cast nets have weights in them so they'll sink over the fish after they're thrown so they're sort of heavy and you have to wade in the surf and…and… and I don't think it's something a pretty lady like her has any business learning. You get dirty and wet and start reeking of fish. Y'all are from Biloxi. She's seen her father and uncles do it, and if she really wants to learn they can teach her."

"Dear me. My fears are confirmed. You believe her request was serious." Finger lowered, she mellowed. "You don't understand us ladies much, do you, son?"

Aw! Get it over with. "Well, not exactly, ma'am. Truth be told."

"Martha only wanted you to teach her because she knew how much you enjoyed doing it. She figured it as a way for y'all to get to know each other better, and if she took an interest in what interested

51

you, well, she was hoping maybe you two would become better friends. As for her accusing you of being scared of her, let me explain that one to you. When she did that, it didn't exactly come out the way she meant it. She merely meant to tease. She'd hoped you'd laugh with her about it. She meant no harm. She thought you had a sense of humor."

"I do. And I am not scared of your daughter either."

"She was only teasing, Mister Jessup. Nothing more. Ah, but I detect there is something about us that does scare you."

"No, ma'am."

She wagged her finger at him again. "Nuh, uh, uh! I have a sense about things like that. What is it about us that frightens you so? We don't bite."

Like barracudas you don't.

Mrs. Massingale slapped her hands on her hips, her stern expression demanding an answer.

Dang it! "Mrs. Massingale, I am defeated. I didn't swear to the whole truth." He groped for a way to express what Martha, unintentionally, helped him figure out. Dare he admit it to her mother, though? He hardly knew the lady. "Martha herself doesn't give me a scare." *Another half-truth.* "I do find her beauty downright striking." *The whole truth.* "It's something else that puts a fear in me."

"My ears are attentive."

"It…er…it begins with a…a 'k.'"

"A 'k'? That's all you'll tell me?"

"Afraid so, ma'am."

"Mister Jessup, forgive me for sounding harsh. I guess it's the mother in me, but if not for Martha, will you not answer my question for yourself?"

"I figure I've already answered it, much as I care to."

"The hotel's hosting a ball tonight. You will attend it?"

"No, ma'am."

"Why not?"

"I have an appointment with a Yankee to play billiards. I beat him a couple days ago. He wants the opportunity to redeem his honor."

"Is a Yankee's honor worth more to you than a Dixie daughter's fun?"

Alex turned at Martha's question. She stood at the top of the steps, her small, round green hat tilted forward, her matching green parasol shielding her soft, pale face from the sun. Her merry eyes seemed to dance. He stirred at her beauty, the fineness of her features, her perfect coiffure and dainty walk. *Aw, no! My "k" word. I can't do it. Wait one minute. Ah-ha! I have an idea.* "Mrs. Massingale, I will attend the ball and dance with your daughter on one condition." He shifted back to Martha. "Miss Massingale, if you will accurately tell me how many steps there are which you just climbed, I will do it."

"That's easy. There's sixty-six."

"Wrong. The number is sixty-five. I visited Nassau a couple of years before the war and counted them myself. Therefore, I will play billiards tonight."

"There are sixty-six, sir."

"All right, Miss Confident. Prove it. Say you're correct, I'll sign your dance card."

"Sixty-six times?"

"I'll sign it sixty-six times."

Martha winked at her mother before she went back down the steps.

From out of her reticule, Mrs. Massingale pulled a stubby pencil followed by a long receipt. "Wait, dear."

"Waiting, Mother," Martha yelled from the foot of the steps.

"This receipt was for my daughter's new hat and our new dresses. Turn it over, number it one through sixty-six. For each step she takes, check off a number."

Alex spread the receipt along the side of the limestone rock through which the staircase had been carved. He quickly numbered it. "Are we ready, Mother?"

"Ready, my dear. Come up nice and slow, so that we can count."

One step at a time, Martha made the ascent while calling out the numbers. "Sixty-six!" she shouted at the top of the staircase when she reached it.

Alex's face drained. He could've sworn he'd counted sixty-five steps. "Again. Do it again. Let me count 'em out loud this time."

"As you wish." Martha went back down.

Alex hadn't experienced a ball like this since his Academy days. Up in the large tree house built around the silk cotton tree in the Royal Victoria's garden, five musicians played Strauss. Dancers whirled and glided across its paths beneath soft-glowing torches, gentlemen in swallow-tailed coats and ladies in frilly ball gowns. He made certain his first partner was someone safe, Lydia Stiles, whose card he'd signed and with whom he'd danced a quadrille.

A different song, a different lady, that was Maffitt's style. Sinclair danced with girls who appeared more his age while Bradford stood behind a table quaffing glass after glass of punch and stuffing square after square of chocolate cake in his mouth, seemingly content assessing the ladies without participating. Alex double-quicked to him.

"Over there, Mister Jessup." Cake in hand, Bradford gestured at Martha. "She's dancing around that curve and heading this way. Never seen that fellow she's dancing with before."

"Is the cake good?" Alex said.

Bradford gulped his down. "Have a piece, sir." He reached for a knife to cut Alex some.

"No, thanks. You look hungrier'n me."

"Hungrier'n most everybody all the time, sir. Did you hear the *Oreto* got released?"

"Always getting seized and released."

"How many times has it been already, do you think?"

Alex shrugged. "Scuttlebutt has it the *Greyhound* seized again her today. They're trying to put her on trial in the Admiralty Court. Enjoy cramming that cake down your mouth. Oh! By the way, did anyone ever tell you your cheeks look like a squirrel's when you eat?"

Bradford chuckled as he crammed more cake into his mouth.

Moving along the table's edge, Alex fixed his eyes on Martha. Thank goodness she'd relented on his dancing with her sixty-six times. Had he done that, no telling how many rumors would fly around this place. Gentlemen usually did no more than three dances with the same girl, except in serious courting cases, such as their being engaged. Maybe he'd misjudged her. Maybe she wasn't growing that attached to him, after all. Then again, this signing her dance card business had been his harebrained idea.

Yet tonight, she'd captured his rapt attention, whirling in her indigo gown adorned with flounces and ribbons and lace. She and her brown-haired dance partner conversed. Swiftly and rhythmically, they danced his direction.

"Jessup, in the immortal words of Captain Semmes, you are a blockhead," Alex muttered.

She gazed up into her young dance partner's face. Did he detect her admiring him?

Marriage won't trap me. He crumpled a napkin. *Martha Massingale, you're torturing my mind. Don't you understand I want to die a bachelor? Chasing me everywhere I go. Leave a man alone, will you? Let me live and die in peace.* "Let her go!" Alex loosed these words before he realized he'd said them.

Startled, the man halted Martha.

"Miss Martha." Alex bowed. "May I have the honor of this next dance?"

Martha curtsied. "The pleasure is mine, Mister Jessup. But I do believe I have one more dance with this gentleman before your name comes up on my card."

The young man bowed deeply. "Sir, I defer to your wishes."

Alex led her back onto the dance floor. Being close to her during their turning and whirling set his heart racing. When the dance ended, he and Martha hastened to a quieter spot where they sat on a bench.

"Who was that man you were dancing with earlier?" Alex said.

"Are you jealous?" Martha said.

"Please, Miss Massingale, no more of those flirty little games. Who is he?"

"Laurens Read, Captain Maffitt's stepson. He arrived this afternoon."

"Miss Massingale, Miss Martha." He paused, his mind and heart suddenly atwitter. "I…uh…uh…"

Martha gave him a puzzled look.

"Forgive me."

"For what?"

"For my previous conduct. For the way I…what I am trying to say is…uh…"

Her forefinger touched his lips. "No need for that. I understand. The 'k' word."

Alex pressed his hands in his lap and nodded. What seemed like hours were only minutes; their gazes lingered. Her eyes were pretty, her chin, round and her lips, small. Lips. Her lips. Urge swelled inside him. He shoved it down. It swelled back larger. He glanced around. *No witnesses.* He leaned toward her, pulled back, but before he could stop himself he planted a quick kiss on her sweet lips.

"Why, Mister Jessup! I had no idea!"

"I know I shouldn't have done that, Miss Massingale, but I guess I finally figured out I do like you. A whole lot."

"There you two are." Mrs. Massingale's voice rang out from beside a large shrub.

Martha pouted, disgusted by the interruption. "I'll give you my address back home before I leave."

"I have two letters, one for my sister in Mobile and one for my father. Will you mail them for me when you return?"

"Definitely. When I return home. Maybe next month."

"Back, back, you two, with everyone else, where I can keep an eye on you." Mrs. Massingale poked Alex's arm playfully before shooing them toward the dancers.

"Yes, ma'am." Alex stole another glance at Martha. He wanted to slap his forehead. He'd kissed her! He'd actually done it!

11

WHILE *HARTFORD* STEAMED up the Mississippi Farragut busied himself in his cabin when his fleet captain, Henry Bell, accompanied by a gaunt man in tattered clothes, entered his cabin.

"Who is he, Captain Bell?" Farragut asked.

"He's from Vicksburg, sir," Bell said. "A deserter. He's brought us some news."

"Find Mister Gaubadan and send him to me."

"Aye, sir."

Minutes later, Farragut interviewed the man while his clerk, Edward Gabaudan, penned notes, and Captain Bell stood behind him listening.

He brought news about *Arkansas*, a Rebel ironclad under construction about which Farragut had heard rumors.

"Where is she?" Farragut said.

"She's gettin' herself fitted out in Yazoo City," the deserter said.

"How many guns does she have?"

"Twenty. But I reckon I might be wrong. That's only what I heered. She's pretty near ready fer fightin'. Men's workin' on her around the clock every day of the week and they're sleepin' in a steamer anchored close by. That's what I heered."

"What caliber guns?"

"Ain't quite teeched my finger on that there particular."

"I heard last month McBlair commands her."

"Lieutenant Isaac Brown's the big chief now," the deserter said.

"Are you hungry?"

"Could use some food, yessir."

"Captain Bell, see that this man gets fed."

Bell took him out of Farragut's cabin.

Farragut ran his hand over his balding head.

"Are you well, sir?" Gabaudan said.

Not one to divulge his true feelings about such matters, Farragut kept silent and waved off his clerk.

That's all they needed. A fully armed Rebel ironclad. They were defenseless against those vessels. He'd written Secretary of the Navy Welles about *Arkansas* when he first learned about her, but it did no good. Maybe the deserter's information wasn't entirely accurate. Perhaps he still had time to find her and sink her before she entered the Mississippi. The Yazoo was about twelve miles north. He knew a little about Lieutenant Brown, but not much. The most important thing he knew was that he was hard-driving and stubborn, a worthy opponent if they ever matched muzzles.

Rumors poured into Farragut's cabin throughout the day. Beauregard had left Corinth for Okolona. Flag Officer Davis defeated a Rebel force at Memphis, and the troops accompanying him had finally occupied it.

Late afternoon, after *Hartford* weighed anchor and her squadron steamed upriver toward Baton Rouge, she met *Itasca* coming down. That vessel had fought a skirmish at Grand Gulf. Her masts and rigging and taffrail got shot to pieces. Her captain told Farragut a Rebel battery ambushed them when they left their stations to find a coal ship. Guerillas drove off the enemy.

Porter's mortar boats were on their way up. Farragut wished his foster brother would arrive quicker, also Butler's promised reinforcements. *Arkansas* neared completion; time was crucial.

Danny followed two of *Madison's* boys, Roscoe and Hoag, aft where their ship's wardroom steward, Petty Officer Paul Bridges, awaited them. Their recent skirmish at Grand Gulf exacted no casualties. Rebel batteries, however, firing from earthworks higher than her hull, had slightly damaged *Madison's* stern. The carpenters' hammers and saws disrupted the quiet quarterdeck.

And Danny's blood warmed. The longer he'd pondered Nancy's betrayal, her and the Westcott's butler Titus getting hitched after he'd spent thirty years thereabouts searching for her, the madder he grew. He hated himself for his attitude, but the harder he tried quelling his storm the harder it blew. It'd caused clashes with shipmates in the berth deck, and close calls with the warrant and commissioned officers.

"Quit dragging your feet, Yates," Bridges snapped.

"Don't rush me," Danny snapped back.

"Belay that back talk!"

"Belay yourself."

"Yates."

Danny halted at the wardroom hatch. Captain Charles Vincent called his name, his voice an iron fist in a velvet glove.

His scowl deepening, Danny looked at the captain.

"Did Bridges tell you not to back talk him?" Vincent said.

"Yes, sir."

"Then why did you keep doing it?"

"Because I wanted to. I ain't nobody's slave no more. I ain't in the mood."

"You aren't a slave on this ship."

"I feel like one."

"Do you want a discharge? I'll be happy to arrange that if you wish. I have enough troublemakers on board without you becoming another one."

"I like your goatee." He turned back toward the hatch. As he descended it, Vincent sent for Master-at-Arms O'Malley and the ship's corporal. Before he could set down dinner plates around the officers' mess table, he found himself in shackles.

O'Malley marched him forward, down three decks into a cramped compartment in the ship's forward hold, guarded by a musket-toting Marine. The master-at-arms laughed after he shut the door behind him. Its lock clicked, loud and depressing in Danny's ears.

"Yates won't be with us much longer, Quigley," the master-at-arms told the Marine. "Our captain's had enough of him. Ever since he lost his missus, he's been a sour apple."

"He's no different than the rest of us," Quigley said. "All his religious talk is nonsense."

"He sure doesn't act like the doctor. Some hypocrite Yates turned out to be, just when I was sort of starting to like him."

"We still got Jones, and he ain't no problem. I'd say one of them aboard's plenty. I always said we ought to've sent 'em all back to Afriky, then this war we're fighting never would've happened."

"Stay here and keep guard. Sergeant Kite will send a man to relieve you in a few hours." O'Malley's steps faded.

Shackles rattling, Danny plopped down on the deck, wriggled up against the bulkhead, and bowed his head between his knees drawn up to his powerful chest. The master-at-arm's words blared through his troubled thoughts. *Oh! What's become of me?*

He lifted his head. Gradually, his eyes adjusted to the blackness. All around him, blank bulkheads. Like shadows, three barrels stood beside the compartment's door. He recalled his grandfather's stories about his passage to America on a slave ship, how he and other slaves, shackled together, were packed below the spar deck in the slaver's hold with scarcely enough room to move or breathe. He spoke of the white men who tossed them scraps of food as though they were animals and of the many captives who died during the murderous voyage. A few, his grandfather had said, killed themselves on the way over. Not once did any of them set foot on the spar deck for fresh air till they reached America.

The hold's stench. This was one detail he recalled his grandfather describing. His compartment's rancid odor provoked the memory. He did feel like a slave again now, shackled in a small compartment. He screamed.

Quigley banged on his door, shouting at him to stop.

"I wanna see Doctor Kirby! Give me Doctor Kirby!"

"Tomorrow, Yates," Quigley shouted back through the door. "Go to sleep."

"I can't."

"Shut up."

Danny slumped. Humiliation was not a good feeling, and tie that with the disrespect he'd shown Bridges and the captain, that didn't feel so good either.

Danny took the tin plate that Doctor Robert Kirby, *Madison's* surgeon, brought him. It held one slice of bread and a mug of water.

"I'm sorry," he told the doctor, who sat directly opposite him outside the compartment, a Marine nearby.

"So am I," Doctor Kirby said. "Some men have started losing respect for you."

Danny nudged back the plate. His stomach recoiled from the food.

"Talking back to an officer, Danny, especially to the captain who's a staunch abolitionist fighting to free your people, that is unacceptable."

Danny nodded. "Yes, sir. I know. I have a hard time forgiving."

"You left the captain no choice."

"Not him, sir. He did right. Titus I can't forgive for stealing Nancy from me, and Nancy I can't forgive for going with him. And Tuck, sir. He's the cause Nancy got taken from me back when we were slaves at Willow Wood, in Georgia. Tuck got me in trouble for stealing something I did not steal, something that belonged to white man Phineas. Nor can I forgive Phineas for selling Nancy to some slave traders. They all did me wrong. It's not fair."

"Life isn't always fair."

Danny scooted back against the bulkhead; his chains rattled.

"Did you know I was engaged once? She was the most beautiful girl in all Philadelphia. Anna Wilmington was her name. She had the most beautiful blond hair and the clearest blue eyes. I never saw her in a bad mood. Not ever. A fine girl she was, always smiling and laughing and speaking kind words. She came from a wealthy, prominent family. Her father was a judge. But she didn't care about society and social status. Some of her friends were poor, others middle-class, and others wealthy. I was a young medical student at the time."

Danny already regretted his conduct yesterday. So why was Doctor Kirby telling him this? He heard the answer when the doctor hesitated on his next sentence.

"The week before our wedding…" Doctor Kirby spoke softer. His voice trailed off as though he, in his mind, was wandering back to this distant time of which he spoke. "She was riding a horse on the fourth of July, going with her cousin Alfred to visit a poor farmer's wife outside the city. Right before they turned down a wooded path, a firecracker exploded. Her startled horse reared and threw her. She hit the road head first, Alfred told me. Killed in an instant."

Danny suddenly looked up and gasped. "Doctor!"

"It's true. A youth was around the path's corner exploding the firecrackers and didn't see or hear her approach. It was an accident. He felt as horrible as we did about it and said had he known she was coming he would've waited. None of us pressed charges."

Danny's spirits sagged lower. He wasn't nothing but selfish, worrying about his own problems and taking them out on others. The good Doctor Kirby worried more about others than he did himself. "I'm sorry."

"She's in heaven now. That is my solace. I won't say forgiving that boy was easy, because it wasn't. Forgiveness seldom is. Eventually, though, we all forgave him. His name was Wallace. I learned from his parents when his birthday was and bought him a present. That started my healing process. The memory of Anna's death will never leave me. Like I said, life isn't always fair." He nudged the plate back toward Danny. "Aren't you hungry?"

"Doctor, sir. Does Captain Vincent really plan on discharging me?"

"He and I discussed it this morning. I persuaded him to give you one more chance. Mind you, though. Your attitude best change fast."

Danny's stomach unknotted. He picked up a piece of bread and crammed it in his mouth.

"I have a patient scheduled in five minutes. Sore throat or something of that nature."

Danny pondered the doctor's tragedy. Everyone aboard, except for Locke and Upton, had started respecting him. Some of it he'd won, from men like Sanders, Appleton, and others. Based on what the master-at-arms said last night, that he had liked him till he'd begun acting the hypocrite, he'd probably lost all he'd worked so hard to gain.

He lifted the chain linking his ankles, then let it drop with a thud. If the doctor could forgive the boy who caused his fiancée's death, why couldn't he forgive others?

12

ANNIE WESTCOTT'S EYES followed the rugged old giant from its massive squat trunk, up its low flared base to its towering canopy of heavy limbs and green leaves spreading every which way. The oak tree stood near the corner edge where the two white stables joined forming an ell, her brothers' favorite playground when they were small. They'd crawl out along its powerful branches, then hop down atop the stables which they pretended was a fort. At first, the horses beneath them fussed in their stalls when they heard them crawling along the roof wielding wooden pistols and yelling "bang, bang" at imaginary enemies. Over time, the animals became used to it and quieted down.

Her pinto, Trotter, nudged her arm. "All right, boy. Patient. Be patient." She wanted to climb this tree once, just once in her life, she wanted to do it. "I will climb it, Mother. Reprimand me all you want for being unladylike. I see nothing wrong with girls climbing trees. Nothing at all. All I've ever seen was this big ole thing daring me for years to climb it."

Jason, their horses' groom, ambled to her.

"Trotter's nudging me," she said. "He's probably hungry. Take him inside his stall and feed him."

Jason's eyes darted between the tree and her. "Are you figurin' on doin' what I think you're figurin' on doin'?"

"My brothers climbed it all the time."

"Your mother will get mad."

"Pshaw! I love Mother, but she most certainly has some strange notions when it comes to what ladies can and cannot do. She'll let me exercise by riding Bessie or Trotter, but could I ever get dirty climbing trees when I was little? Of course not. Silly, isn't it? Ladies don't climb trees, ladies don't sweat. Why, every time I go riding I sweat." Her fingers touched her forehead; she rolled her eyes melodramatically. "Why, mercy me. I do fear I feel some awful drops of sweat beading my delicate little forehead this very second." She laughed.

"Yes, Miss Annie. Better be careful, Miss Annie."

"This tree's nothing. I've conquered harder challenges than this."

Jason led Trotter around to the front of the stables.

Annie drew a long, deep breath. "Here we go, tree. Watch me climb you. I will climb you in honor of my brothers."

Not wearing a hoop freed her arms and legs, let her stretch higher, on tiptoes, to grasp the tree's low, wide base. Upward she pulled herself, grunting and groaning, her legs and feet scraping bark till she sat in the base and caught her breath. "Take that, tree. I whipped you good." She rubbed her knees beneath her dress. One of its tiny red ribbons got torn off during her climb, but she shrugged. Her dress was getting ragged anyway. All her dresses were on account of the Yankee blockade. No fabric coming into the city to make new dresses, no needles or thread to mend old ones. Maybe all that would end, now that the Yankees had conquered the city.

The huge limb stretching over the stables tempted her beyond resistance. Lying prone like her brothers always did, she clutched both sides of the limb and dragged herself along it, toward the stables using her arms and legs. Bark dug into her body and scratched her cheeks. Higher she went. Higher and farther. She rested her head against the limb for a breather. Gasped. The sound of horses. Three, no, four men riding on the road. Men in blue uniforms. *Yankees! Turning through our gate! I'd better warn Father!* Wormlike, she wriggled down the limb quickly. Her foot touched the base of the tree. She tumbled off. Her world went black.

13

ANNIE CAME TO.

Ugh. Her head. Did Trotter kick it? Flat on her stomach, she spat out foul-tasting grass and dirt and, shaking her head, shoved herself up. The whistle of a dove's wings rose in front of her as the gentle bird fled into the treetop.

A firm hand forced her back down; two hands gripped her shoulders from behind. She squirmed against that grip.

"Stop movin', Miss Annie," Jason whispered. "Don't let the Yankees catch you. They looked mean."

"Let me go." Annie's whisper was louder, more demanding.

"Cain't do that, Miss Annie. We'll be safe, long as we stay here."

"Mother. Father. Alice."

"Too late, Miss Annie. The Yankees in the big house already."

Jason stretched out beside her. From behind the stables, they peered down the road past the smokehouse where they had a clear view of the big house some hundred yards distant. A sergeant sat astride a dun horse; another soldier held the reins of the other three horses, two black and one gray. Annie's mouth tasted like tin. She had no weapon to fight them. No gun, no knife, no cane, not even a big stick. *Father, what are they doing?*

Two soldiers exited the back door, her mother close behind shouting and gesturing wildly. Annie moved to get up. Jason jerked her back down and shook his head. Her arm, he pinned to the ground.

The soldiers stuffed silverware and expensive china plates and saucers into their saddlebags. One went back inside. Soon he returned with her mother's jewelry box which he handed to the soldier holding the reins.

"They're stealing everything," Annie said. "I can't lay here and do nothing."

But Jason's strength exceeded hers; he refused to let her up.

She had that gun her friend and neighbor Jenny Inchforth Watkins gave her the previous year. Since this was a Sunday, their overseer Mister Swan was in his house. But it was too far away. He might not realize what was happening. Her breath caught. On the gallery, her father shook his fist at the robbers. The sergeant admired her father's gold watch; he turned it over in his hand. Annie called down curses on them in angry whispers.

The sergeant whipped out his pistol and aimed it at her father's stomach.

Annie hid her face in the grass. She pounded it softly. Nothing, nothing they could do to stop them.

"Miss Westcott."

Swan's whisper sounded behind her.

Jason eased off his hand, and she managed to stand while keeping out of the Yankees' sight.

"They're stealing everything," Annie said. "Even father's watch."

Swan raised his double-barreled shotgun. "The range is too far for me to use this from here. Maybe I can ease up closer."

"There's a pistol Jenny gave me in Ben's quarters. I think I can make it if I run fast. Get on over to the kitchen. That's the shortest range. Be careful."

"Stay put and out of sight, Miss Westcott, else they're liable to hurt you."

"I will not!" Annie stifled her voice. Her whisper came out loud. "I'm going to get that pistol. When I open fire, you will open up from behind the kitchen."

"I got a better idea."

"No. You're our employee. You work for us. Do like I say."

Swan shot her an irritable look.

Annie knew he didn't like ladies telling him what to do. Well, too bad. Today he had no choice.

Swan crouched and duck-walked swiftly, pausing behind one oak tree after another on his way to the kitchen directly opposite the house.

Jason followed Annie at a sprint toward Ben's quarters.

A shot cracked from the big house. Her father fired his musket at the Yankees from the lower gallery.

"No witnesses!" the sergeant yelled, whipping out his revolver.

More shots rang out.

Annie darted through Ben's side door and up the steps.

A shot nicked the doorframe behind Jason.

"They're after us!" Jason yelled.

Two booms roared from Swan's shotgun.

Three bangs responded.

Annie threw the pillow off the pistol. How did Jenny teach her to load it? *Powder. Percussion caps.* "Help me find the gunpowder, Jason. I'll get the percussion caps."

Feet pounded up the stairs. Annie and Jason scrambled behind Ben's bed, scant space between it and the wall. A glance out the window— the sergeant sprawled on the grass, dead. So too, her parents. She stifled a sob. *And Mister Swan.*

The Yankee filled the doorway, his square chin bristling whiskers like the needles on a cactus, his lewd dark eyes glowering. "Well now, if'n it ain't a li'l black boy an' a purty li'l Rebel wench."

"Get away." Trembling, she aimed the pistol at him.

The other two Yankees came up behind him. "What have we here, Caleb?" one said.

"Ripe for the pickings, I'd say," the other Yankee said. "Everyone's dead 'cept her and the boy."

"Stay away from her!" Jason shouted.

"I'll...I'll shoot." Annie cocked back the hammer.

"Sure you will." Lust filled Caleb's dirty face. "Don't see no percussion caps on the cylinder's nipples. Doubt it'll do you much good. Keep an eye on the boy. I'll handle the wench first." His palm swiped his lips. "We'll share her."

14

LUNGING AT CALEB, Jason slugged his jaw. Caleb recoiled, seized Jason, and threw him onto Ben's bed. Caleb's friends seized his feet and jerked him to the floor; their revolvers' muzzles pressured his spine.

"No! Please!" Annie squealed. Tears streaming, she cowered in a corner.

Caleb produced a jackknife and up it swept, toward her face.

She seized his wrist, struggled mightily, shoving the blade aside.

He shoved it back at her nose and then down to the first button on her dress's bodice. "I'm going to rape you." His tone sounded calm and matter-of-fact.

Shots erupted from the steps. The two men pinning Jason collapsed, their blood splashing the wall like splattered paint.

Caleb let go Annie, drew his revolver, whirled toward the door.

Annie snatched her pistol off the bed and whacked him upside his head with such force that he staggered, which caused his shot to miss Jenny when he fired.

Jenny returned fire. He tumbled forward.

Annie tossed aside her gun.

"Mother and I were coming down the road for a visit when we heard the shooting." Jenny glared at the dead men. "When I saw the dead sergeant outside, I grabbed his pistol, and we came up fast as we could."

"It's all over with now, dear," Jenny's mother, Mrs. Inchforth, spoke from the doorway. "We've killed them all."

"Revolvers always were more reliable than derringers," Jenny said. "One, even two bullets in this situation wouldn't have been enough."

"They've killed everybody." Annie steadied her cold tremble. "Everybody. Everybody."

"'cept us," Jason said.

Hoofbeats brought them back outside. A squad of horse soldiers trotted forward, their leader a blond lieutenant.

Her tears drying, Annie recounted to them all that happened.

"I am sorry for your loss, miss." The lieutenant's tone and demeanor carried genuine sympathy. "These men were deserters. They caused several problems in Kennerville. We've been looking for them ever since, and when we recognized the sergeant's dun horse running down the River Road and heard all the gunfire on this place, I regret that we arrived too late." He gave the dead sergeant a casual glance. "You ladies are good shots."

Annie looked over at her parents. Alice, also dead, was somewhere inside the house. All the servants were, and Swan was sprawled beneath an oak tree. Numbness gripped her. Every bone in her trembling body went cold. "Sir." She choked on the word, the thought, of her family.

Workers hurried down the road from their quarters.

"Will you help me bury them?" Annie asked.

The lieutenant tipped his kepi. "Yes, miss. We'll do all and anything we can to help." He dismounted and ordered his men to do the same.

15

ANNIE LANGUISHED IN loneliness. Since Swan was dead, Annie requested that Mister Inchforth send his overseer to manage Monmouth while he managed his plantation. Mister Inchforth also promised help with the Westcott's other farm, Holly Oaks, near Baton Rouge. This lifted a huge burden off Annie, who understood nothing about managing and recordkeeping, nor could she bear looking at her parents' tombs every morning inside their small picket enclosure. Alice and the other domestics, she'd buried in a separate plot.

Not many weeks after her parents' deaths, to help heal her emotional pain, Annie and Jason returned to New Orleans. She sent Jason up the River Road to the Yankee camp at Kennerville, where he found the lieutenant whom they'd met that day the deserters killed her family. He provided her transportation back to the city.

During the ride back to New Orleans on a small steamer, courtesy of General Butler in gratitude for her and Jenny killing the deserters, her tears evaporated. Soon after she and Jason debarked the boat at Carrollton, a Yankee officer who crossed her path admired her. She awarded him an annoyed look. The ride home seemed forever.

The Garden District's floral aromas laced the odor of horses and other animals and vehicles traveling St. Charles Street. Pigeons strutted across its median or soared onto rooftops. Doves perched from trees and brown squirrels scampered across manicured lawns. At last, they turned up a road toward her Prytania Street house.

"Almost there, Miss Annie," Jason said.

Annie nodded.

"Annie! Annie!" her friend and neighbor Clara Dawson called from the Dawsons' gallery. "Mother! Father! Annie's back. Hurry!"

Annie reined in Bessie. "The Yankees killed my parents." Annie dismounted at the Dawsons' gate. "And Alice and Mister Swan and everyone, they're all dead."

"I despise every last one of them," Clara said. "They tease me because I have freckles."

Mrs. Dawson led her husband to Annie and clasped Annie's hand. "Is there anything we can do, Annie dear? May we help you unpack?"

"Yes, ma'am." She gestured Jason up ahead with her wagon. Reins in hand, she led Bessie as she walked beside her friends. Fiercely resisting the horrific images battling inside her head, she recounted events at Monmouth. Not in detail, though. She couldn't have withstood those images had she described them in detail.

Mister Dawson warned her about General Butler. "We all call him Spoons."

Annie managed a chuckle, the first time she'd laughed in weeks.

His arm circled Annie's waist. "Lots has happened since you've been away. We'll catch you up on the news on the way there, but basically, Butler thinks he's Bonaparte. As in Napoleon Bonaparte. He's also a thief."

Annie collapsed in her gallery's white wicker armchair.

While Jason and the Dawsons' two servants lugged her trunks into her home, the Dawsons sat beside her. Mister Dawson detailed more of Butler's misdeeds he'd either heard about or read. Although aware of "The Woman's Order," Annie hadn't heard the stories of shop owners getting arrested because they refused to sell to Yankees or the man sentenced to hard labor downriver in Fort Jackson because he dared shout a "hurrah" for President Davis. A week ago, thousands witnessed the hanging of one William Mumford because he hauled down the United States flag off the United States Mint's roof.

"My dear," Mister Dawson said, "Butler's brother is also here. His name's Andrew."

"Is he in the Army?" Annie said.

"Some blue-bellies refer to him as colonel, but he's no colonel. No indeed. He's not in the Army at all. He's a so-called businessman, and he and his brother the general are on the make, speculating in business ventures like monopolizing most everything which comes into the city. Groceries, medicine, things like that. They're both making a personal profit off our defeat. Word has it Butler's staff got their hands in the pot too."

"Have you any news about Nancy? Where Titus has taken her?" The Dawsons shook their heads.

"I'm afraid for her, Mister Dawson," Annie said. "I must find her."

"In this big ole city?" Mrs. Dawson said. "Where will you start looking?"

"Titus is bad. Father never should have bought him after Maxfield died. We had no idea he was so cruel till it was too late. He hid his true nature well."

"Surely Nancy will come back," Clara said. "Surely, if Titus is as evil as you say."

"I'll find her," Annie said.

"I'm your friend. You have me, Annie. Jenny and me."

Annie forced a grateful smile, not because she wasn't appreicative, for she was, but because laughing and smiling during these tragic days had grown difficult. "You two are my very closest friends, dear Clara. I don't know how I will survive my tragedy without you."

Clara brightened.

As much as she loved Jenny and Clara, she also loved Nancy. Nancy, too, was a very close friend and family, as far as she was concerned...not an escaped slave like Titus. *Titus, you'd better not hurt her.*

"He...llo...Freckles!" two passing soldiers yelled at Clara.

Red-faced, Mister Dawson bounded down the steps toward the gate, but before he could say or do anything the Yankees guffawed and sprinted off. He waved his fist at them.

Clara pulled a tiny mirror from her dress pocket. "Oh, why was I born with them. They're all over my face."

"Ignore those kinds of men, honey," Mrs. Dawson said. "When you react, it only encourages them to tease you more."

Waiting for Titus to go into their small garden out back so she could leave, Nancy dusted windows. Nothing fancy about their new house. Rectangular and narrow, its four sparsely furnished rooms joined one to the other straight back, the farthest back room their bedroom. Titus rented it from a wealthy black Creole family, its owner a doctor who hated slavery. It was in a district downriver from the French Quarter called the Faubourg Marigny. Titus had started working for them. They paid him well.

Nancy set down her duster. *This chile sure made the mistake, marrying that man.* In the next room, Titus sat on a stool tying his brown gardening boots. His sly look alerted her that he suspected she was up to something.

"Will you be coming with me?" he said.

"You know I don't like digging in dirt," Nancy said.

"I want you outside with me."

"This chile needs to go to the store. She needs needles and thread." She moved swiftly in front of her sewing machine, blocking it from his view.

He darted around her. A spool of thread whacked the wall. "There's the thread. Don't lie to me. Where are you really going?"

Her lips tightened.

He thumped her head. "Catherine Anne's way upriver. You can't get to that lily-white all by yourself." He thumped her head again, harder. "Do you have a pass to be out on that street by yourself? Suppose a policeman catches you? We're still supposed to be slaves, Stupid."

This time, she cringed.

"Since you can't be going trying to find Catherine Anne, and since I know you're lying to me about buying needle and thread, I figure you must be trying to find Danny."

"That ain't true!"

Titus slapped both her cheeks, twice, sharply, back-handed and with his palms. "Stay away from Yates, you hear me? And keep away from the Westcotts less you want me hurting you worse'n that. You don't need to keep being their slave doing everything they tell you. The Yankees are here." He popped her cheeks again with his palm. "And we got us a good deal from the Brulets. They're nice people, letting us live here like we're free."

Nancy's lips quivered. Why wouldn't that man leave her in peace? She returned to the front room and resumed dusting. *Danny, my Danny, this chile needs you. Awful bad.*

16

WHEN FARRAGUT RETURNED to Vicksburg on the twenty-fifth of June, he left his cabin for the quarterdeck and surveyed six of his squadron's ships anchored seven miles below the Rebel garrison. He lifted his binoculars to his eyes and scanned a peninsula. De Soto Point, his nautical charts called it. He shifted his attention to the garrison's river batteries, the guns bearing down on the Mississippi from towering bluffs. Vicksburg's defenses looked stronger than they'd been on his previous visit.

"Captain Wainwright, drop anchor," Farragut said.

"Aye, sir." Wainwright relayed this order to his boatswain.

The boatswain piped sailors to *Hartford's* capstan. Leaning hard on the capstan bars, the sailors walked around and around it, the flagship's hawser slowly running through her hawse pipe till her anchor splashed into the Mississippi River.

Farragut bit back his annoyance. He might've arrived sooner had not Butler reneged on his promises. Rather than the seven thousand troops he'd agreed to give General Thomas Williams, who was cooperating with his operations, he gave the general a little over three thousand instead. Instead of the tugs he'd promised Porter's schooners, Porter received nothing, and thus, more irritating delays. Farragut figured Butler did this out of spite, for he and Porter behaved like roosters at a cockfight. Further delaying matters, the flag officer's flagship had to get towed off a sandbar below Natchez by one of General Williams's steamers.

Soon after his arrival, *Brooklyn* lowered a boat carrying a young man no one on *Hartford* recognized. Once he boarded *Hartford*, an officer escorted him to the flag officer's cabin.

"Sir." The young officer saluted.

Farragut, seated at his desk, returned the salute.

"I am Medical Cadet Charles Rivers Ellet. Three other men and I crossed De Soto Point yesterday. My father, Lieutenant Colonel Alfred Ellet, is pleased to inform you that he has four rams on the other side of the Point."

"How many guns are his rams carrying, Mister Ellet?"

"None, sir. But they are fast. And Flag Officer Davis's ironclads lay farther upriver. The entire river is open between Memphis and Vicksburg. Would you like me to convey a message to him, sir?"

Farragut had little use for Alfred Ellet's unarmed rams. He cleared his throat. "Thank you for your information, Mister Ellet." He dipped his pen in an inkwell and scribbled a message, which he handed to the medical cadet. "Take this to Lieutenant Colonel Ellet. He's to break up all communication between the Yazoo River and Vicksburg."

Young Ellet snapped to attention and saluted. "Yes, sir. I will deliver it now."

"Good. Dismissed."

Another message via courier he dispatched to Davis, not an order, but a request since he held no authority over him. He asked him to bring down his ironclads.

Later in the day, Farragut paced *Hartford's* quarter deck pondering the Rebel ironclad *Arkansas*. Rampant rumors about her, warnings that she neared completion, that she was steaming into the river any day. All right, then. Where was she? He didn't give those rumors much credence.

His crews endured baking heat and biting-mosquitoes and half-rations. Thanks to their constant grounding and getting towed off bars, his ship shared their suffering. They were on a fool's errand. Mister Welles didn't understand what he did, ordering him up to this miserable place. His ships were built for deep water, not rivers.

A shout from the mainmast's lookout.

Though Farragut looked astern, his poor eyesight hindered his ability to identify all the vessels at the distance they were spotted.

"General Williams's transports, sir," Wainwright said. "The *Kennebec*, *Oneida*, and *Pinola* are escorting them."

"Soon as they're anchored, signal their captains and General Williams to come aboard. We'll make our plans and do our fighting and get this thing over with so we can get back to New Orleans. No telling when Davis will get here. I'm done waiting for him."

"Aye, sir."

The next afternoon, Farragut followed Porter's bombardment from *Hartford's* mizzen rigging above the battle smoke after he landed a division of General William's troops some two thousand or so yards below Vicksburg. Clutching the rigging with one hand, his spyglass in his other hand, he watched the arcing mortar shells shrieking and smashing the bluff below Vicksburg's batteries. Other shells landed in the town with a thud. "Bad fuses," he muttered, disappointed.

The next day, Porter's bombardment resumed. General Williams's troops, aided by over a thousand slaves brought in from nearby plantations, began the back-breaking work of digging a canal across the De Soto Peninsula's hard clay earth. Farragut hoped it'd be deep enough for his ships to pass through to Tuscumbia Bend, thereby avoiding Vicksburg's batteries and isolating that stronghold. When the river rose in June, the Mississippi would divert into it, so claimed theory and logic.

He signaled all his commanding officers and General Williams aboard his ship for a conference. Their decision was reached: "We'll have another go at passing the Rebel batteries," Farragut said. "We'll try to link up with Flag Officer Davis's batteries."

"A risky move, sir," *Madison's* Captain Vincent said.

"Very true." Farragut gestured to *Hartford's* Captain Wainwright. "I've worked out our ship's dispositions. You will have your ships in position by two o'clock tomorrow morning."

"Aye, sir," all the captains said, almost in unison.

Captain Wainwright proceeded to give the captains their ships' assignments, and by two next morning every vessel in the squadron rode at anchor in their designated stations with their divisions.

Locke lay on his cot; his restless energy regarding the pending fight kept him awake. It seemed forever till his cabin door opened, and a bull's eye lantern glared at him.

"The flag officer has hoisted the signal, sir," the quartermaster, holding the lantern, said. "Beat to Quarters, sir. Quietly, sir, so the Rebs on the hills don't hear us. Captain's orders."

Locke swung off his cot and snatched his pistol and cutlass. "About time the old man does something."

On the spar deck, tars dashed fore and aft, tossing buckets of sand across the holystoned planking, spreading it every which way with brooms lest men slip in blood. Others rolled water casks into place or removed tampions from gun muzzles or lashed hammocks along starboard rails to catch splinters. Gun carriages rumbled on their trucks. Danny hurried tourniquets toward Zollicoffer's forecastle guns.

"Yates!" Locke snapped.

Danny turned quickly.

"Give us some of those."

Danny tossed him a handful.

Seizing his frock, Locke shoved him against the funnel's casing. "Don't throw those at me."

"I didn't mean to, sir. I'm in a hurry. Doctor Kirby needs me in sick bay."

"I don't think he meant anything by it, sir," Ensign Rawlins said.

"Everything Yates does is intentional. Find O'Malley."

"Mister Locke."

"Those are my orders, Rawlins."

Rawlins hurried off in search of the master-at-arms.

Locke smoldered. He wanted Yates dishonorably discharged. He wanted him off this ship.

One hour later, while Porter's shells exploded short of Vicksburg's cannon with earsplitting fury, Farragut's squadron started toward Vicksburg.

Farragut scrambled up ratlines to *Hartford's* mizzen masthead. Flashes off the bluff. Rebel guns or Porter's shells? All they could do till sunup was shoot at flashes. The sky was like pitch; the battle smoke dense, swirling, choking.

Starboard broadsides thundering, *Richmond, Hartford*, and *Brooklyn* steamed ahead, in the van of their divisions.

At 3:45 A.M. *Hartford's* Marines, manning her bow gun, opened her battle. Shell bursts, shrapnel, rigging cut to pieces, hull struck more than once sending her into a shudder. Wainwright ordered her halted but to keep firing while her gunboats, muzzles smoking, passed. Splinters danced into hammock nettings. One man collapsed on the spar deck; a bullet whistled past Farragut's head.

"Sir! Sir!"

Farragut glanced down at the poop deck's gun captain, beneath him on the rigging.

"Sir." the gun captain said. "Please, sir. Get down. I need to aim my gun your direction."

Farragut scampered back down; a boom yanked his attention directly overhead; the rigging onto which he'd clung came crashing down.

When daylight unveiled their predicament, Locke fumed. Porter's steamers had lost all semblance of order during the battle; their bows and sterns aimed every direction, obstructing his division's route upriver. Rebel musketry and artillery booms echoed from the hills. Porter's mortars hurled shells at them. *Madison's* and other men-of-war's broadsides roared.

Madison's starboard taffrail exploded, its shattered pieces whirling and flying across her poop deck; another shot cut her bowsprit in two and a third sent Zollicoffer's Marines diving for cover behind the capstan. Some two hours later, *Brooklyn* hoisted a signal to her division: "drop downriver." Not a man aboard *Madison* suffered injury, nor any killed, at least among her gun divisions.

"I wonder how our flag officer fared," Rawlins said.

"Do you see him up ahead? Are any of our ships in sight? They made it around the bend. We didn't." He waved his fist in Rawlins's wide eyes. "I'd like to give Porter a piece of my mind and a taste of my fist for what his steamers did. Their captains are a bunch of incompetents!"

Smoke-stained, the first gun captain stepped up. "Rebs have stopped firing, sir. I think we're out of their range. Shall I secure the gun?"

"Are you stupid or something, Lumpkin?" Locke said. "Not till Vincent passes the order."

"But sir."

"Back to your station, man."

The gun captain stepped back to the starboard Dahlgren.

When Upton came on deck, he surveyed the eerily silent hills. Already, the ship's carpenter had put his men to work making repairs. He went up to the poop deck, saluted the quarterdeck, and spoke to Lieutenant Alfred Warren, the deck officer, before descending its ladder Locke's direction.

"No casualties to report?" Upton said.

"No," Locke said.

Upton's dark brows lowered; a second time, he searched the hills. "I wonder if we're getting out of this place in one piece. We're trapped. We can't elevate our guns high enough to fight back. We might die here." He swatted a mosquito. "Maybe the doctor's right."

"Don't tell me you're starting to believe all that religious nonsense of his."

"He's an educated man."

"Well, I'm smart too. I finished third in my class at the Academy, and I came close to placing second and I tell you, the doctor's been playing with your head and telling you lies. It's a charade, Upton. A game."

"Suppose we do get killed up here, what will happen to us then?"

"Quit sounding like a preacher."

"Well, I've been considering it." Upton went forward for a casualty report from Zollicoffer and Kite.

17

AUGUSTA EVANS'S GAZE followed Randolph and Virginia Evans banging out Georgia Cottage's back door, down its porch steps. They faced General Beauregard seated opposite her. She'd perched herself on the porch's cypress railing, gripping one of its square columns to steady herself.

"How many Yankees have you killed, General?" Randolph's eyes were bright, eager, his voice deepening and cracking and sounding more and more like Howard's and Vivian's.

"A hundred trillion million?" Virginia said.

The swarthy Creole smiled down at the children. "A thousand."

"A thousand?" Randolph said. "All by yourself?"

"Myself and my pistol." Eyes sparkling, he patted the revolver on his hip.

"Oh, no you didn't. I'm not that stupid."

"Randolph." Mrs. Evans spoke from the back door. "You and Virginia go on and play. Your sister and the general need to visit."

"We want to hear about the battles," Randolph said.

Mrs. Evans planted her hands on her hips. Up went her right brow, the way she warned her children of pending chastisement if their disobedience continued.

"Run, Virginia!" Randolph shouted all of a sudden.

Virginia lit out across the backyard squealing, their game of tag begun.

"Whew!" Miss Evans got off the porch railing. "Now that that's over, perhaps we can talk. Is your throat feeling better, General?"

Beauregard massaged it. "Oui, Mademoiselle. As I was saying a minute ago, when I read your *Beulah*, it brought tears to my eyes on many a page. And I am not a man given to much crying."

"I'm honored."

Determined to know the hero of Manassas better, Miss Evans devoted the next hour interviewing him. She sensed his courage, that he was a man who had his own mind about things. Against his family's wishes, he'd attended West Point, he told her. They disliked his socializing with Americans, but in his youth, he'd studied Napoleon Bonaparte's military campaigns and always admired him and thus, wanted to follow in his footsteps by becoming a soldier. Since his evacuation from Corinth, he'd suffered from exhaustion and a sore throat. His doctors advised a furlough and rest. Since no major campaign seemed imminent, he turned temporary command of his Army of the Mississippi over to Bragg and came to Bladon Springs, a resort near Mobile, for a brief rest.

"I've begun a new novel," Miss Evans said after her impromptu interview. "Would you do me the honor of reading some of it?"

"You do me great honor by asking."

They reentered the cottage. In General Beauregard, Miss Evans realized she'd made a true friend and had found in him an excellent source of information for *Macaria*. She'd spent long hours writing it every day of the week, even while nursing patients at Camp Beulah, except on Sundays. The Cause of her beloved South demanded its publication as quickly as possible.

18

SINCE HE'D PASSED Vicksburg's batteries, Farragut's frustrations multiplied. His cabin was shot to pieces; his fleet surgeon reported seven dead and thirty wounded.

Richmond's bulwarks were shattered, and one of her guns was blasted off its carriage. Another ship, struck four times, also suffered casualties.

Flag Officer Davis brought down four of his ironclads the first day of July: his flagship *Benton,* and *Carondelet, Cincinnati,* and *Louisville.* The flag officers discussed the situation and agreed they needed thousands of more troops to capture the Rebel garrison. A letter to General Halleck, commander of the Department of the Mississippi, they hoped would persuade him to send reinforcements. Meanwhile, their ships remained anchored or stayed moored to the river banks and underwent repairs. Their medical supplies dwindling, doctors did their best to aid the sick and wounded. Porter's shells continued arcing and screaming and exploding toward the town from below. Davis's mortar boats soon arrived and joined in from above.

Farragut fumed. Nothing aggravated him more than doing nothing.

On the third day of July, Farragut and Davis received Halleck's reply: "The scattered and weakened condition of my forces renders it impossible for me at the present to detach any troops to cooperate with Vicksburg."

Gabaudan lowered Halleck's response. "Do you have a reply, sir?"

Farragut ground his teeth. Slaves working on Williams's canal sang amidst crashing trees. Aboard *Hartford,* petty officers barked orders at sailors holystoning her deck. Much of his crew, felled by malaria and other illnesses, were aboard *Richmond,* his hospital ship. He constantly swatted mosquitoes harassing his sweaty ears.

"Begging the flag officer's pardon, sir." Wainwright spoke beside him. "In my opinion, we're wasting our time here. General Williams is having problems getting our canal excavated, and with the water falling faster than his men can dig, and half his men down with malaria and dysentery— "

"No, Gabaudan," Farragut said, interrupting Wainwright. "I have no reply. Transcribe that for Flag Officer Davis."

Gabaudan quickly departed to carry out the admiral's order.

Although Farragut shared Wainwright's opinion, he kept it to himself. His men were suffering, Williams's men were suffering, the river falling rather than rising, mosquitoes and sweltering heat made life almost unbearable. Every day Vicksburg grew stronger while his forces grew weaker; other batteries were being built below and more guns brought in. If they stayed here much longer, they'd have to run a much longer gauntlet of gunfire on the way back to Baton Rouge. Yet still, *Arkansas* posed a threat. Time would prove whether or not rumors regarding her were true. Davis could supply him from towns above, but he had no ironclads to fight the Rebel clad, nor could he leave the clad in his rear. Davis had the means to sink her. So why should he keep his deep-water wooden fleet up here to be blown out of the water by an enemy most of his guns couldn't reach? Farragut mopped his brow. He just may disobey Welles's orders this time. He just may go back to New Orleans, for his health and his crews'.

On the sixth day of July, a ship arrived to carry the sick and wounded to Memphis.

On the tenth day of July, at midnight, twelve of Porter's mortar schooners headed downriver again. Orders from Welles. Destination: Hampton Roads, Virginia.

On Sunday the thirteenth, shortly after divine services, a cry rang out from *Hartford's* main masthead. "Ship ahoy!"

"Where away?" *Hartford's* deck officer called back through a speaking trumpet.

"An ironclad, sir. Rounding the upper bend."

Farragut and Wainwright swapped worried glances.

Wainwright gasped. "The *Arkansas*."

Farragut lifted his binoculars to his eyes. "Not the *Arkansas*. She's flying a United States ensign."

"Glad she's one of ours," Wainwright said.

Smoke puffed out of the vessel's twin stacks situated forward atop her iron casemate, aft a rather large dome; the letters S and X, one letter per stack painted near their top, identified her as *Essex*. Her iron casemate was long and huge, dwarfing every gunboat in Farragut's squadron, and her freeboard was barely visible above the waterline. No real bows or stern did she have either, for the casemate's sloping sides spanned most of the vessel's length. As she slowly maneuvered into position, her awnings popping in the breeze, Farragut thought she resembled a gigantic, ugly, floating breadbox.

"I'd hate living in that thing," Farragut said. "Open-air, sea breezes, salt water, that's a true sailor's life. My other foster brother, Commander William Porter, commands her. David will be sorry he missed seeing him. I wonder if he has any more news on the *Arkansas*."

"I suppose we'll find out soon enough, sir," Wainwright said.

Danny hovered behind Doctor Kirby, bent over Upton. Curled up and shaking on a cot beneath the wardroom's open hatch where breezes blew in, the paymaster winced. Sweat coated his stubbly face and splotched his shirt. Its stale odor wafted into the dispensary. No one need tell him what Upton's illness was. He'd witnessed it many a time on plantations; he'd learned its symptoms through close observation. Malaria. Shortly after the fighting ended, he'd assisted the berth deck's malarial patients topside into fresh air. He realized that whenever a swamp was nearby, or stagnant water or lots of mosquitoes, so too was the disease. He figured a connection between them existed, but no one, not even doctors, knew what it was.

Fresh air contributed to the disease's remedy. Danny would also assist Upton topside and lay him amongst the other sufferers soon as the doctor finished tending him. What they really needed, though, was a hospital ship on this side of the bend. Had they made it past Vicksburg, they'd have had *Richmond's* services.

Upton's teeth clicked rapidly.

"Yates," Doctor Kirby said.

Danny slid his palm behind Upton's sweaty back and helped him sit upright.

"Am I d-dying, Doc?" Yates said.

"Without taking my medicine, yes. We haven't much left."

"Will I get well fast?"

"I certainly hope so, but I'm afraid it's not up to me."

Despite his weakened condition, Upton nearly leaped off his cot. "It is up t-to you! Y-You're a d-d-doctor!" Exhausted from his outburst, he slumped back and pulled the blankets back around him. He managed to sit upright, still shaking, without further help.

Doctor Kirby spoke softly, his tone soothing. "I'll do all I can. But ultimately, what happens to you is out of my hands. Danny, the quinine."

Danny reached for it in the medicine cabinet behind him.

"It tastes bad." Upton screwed up his face.

"Hold your nose. That way, you'll not taste it."

Malaria's cure was simple: quinine. Danny had also seen whiskey used, cod liver oil, and turpentine. So had Upton, which was why he despised Upton's childish behavior. Upton, Locke, Titus, Tuck, Phineas. That anger he'd fought so hard to kill, coiling tightly inside his head, rearing within his burning heart...No! He could not return to all his hateful thoughts. Mister Rawlins saved his bacon last time when he told Captain Vincent the truth about the tourniquet, the one he'd tossed at Mister Locke. Mister Locke was trying to get rid of him. He couldn't let that happen.

"Suppose my medicine proves inadequate and you die?" Doctor Kirby measured out the quinine. "What then? Are you ready to meet your Maker?"

"L-Let's g-get started and g-get it over with."

Danny turned back while the doctor administered the medicine, and his heart had grown so hard, he prayed...prayed for a softer heart.

Deserters who'd come down in a skiff informed Farragut and Davis that *Arkansas's* construction was finished, and she was about to steam down the Yazoo. Though Farragut's doubts lingered, he convened a conference in mid-July. In attendance were General Williams, Flag

Officer Davis, and Colonel Ellet, whose four unarmed rams lay nearest the Yazoo's mouth. After lengthy discussion they settled on reconnoitering the Yazoo and put Commander Henry Walke, Davis's squadron, in command. Walke's vessels were *Tyler*, *Carondelet*, and one of Ellet's rams, *Queen of the West*.

Farragut retired that evening unconcerned about the rumored Rebel menace. But as daylight broke, thunderous gunfire sent him racing topside.

"Sounds like Commander Walke's engaged some horse artillery." Farragut spotted Wainwright's odd expression. Then he laughed at himself. In his haste, he'd neglected to change out of his nightclothes. He hurried back into his quarters and remedied that. Within minutes, he returned.

Hartford's tars had given their attention upriver. Not one vessel had gotten up steam; no one had anticipated what was happening. And now it was too late. On Mississippi's riverbanks Farragut's squadron sat between Ellet's rams and Davis's ironclads. Opposite these squadrons, on Louisiana's riverbanks, lay transports.

Firing intensified.

Drums rolled "beat to quarters."

Tars sprang to their battle stations and cast loose their guns.

Three guns on each broadside, with two forward and two astern, *Arkansas's* ten guns blazed at her enemy. Her gun ports opened, her crews ran out the guns, fired, and then withdrew them back inside the casemate as the gun ports slammed shut. The ports opened again and the gun crews fired again, wreaking havoc on the Union's anchored warships.

Berating himself for getting surprised, Farragut observed events from the mizzen rigging. *Tyler* and *Queen of the West* had fled before the rust-red *Arkansas's* thunder and lightning while *Carondelet* ran aground. Now *Hartford* shuddered beneath shots hurled at her and though she replied in kind, her exploding shells bounded off the Rebel ironclad. Past his ships, *Arkansas* steamed, her guns booming, an incessant cacophony of death and explosions.

Davis's squadron endured much the same, except the Rebel's speed slowed.

Farragut saw the reason. She no longer had her stack. He strained for a harder look, brought his glass to his eye, and noticed serious dents in her iron casemate. *Ah.* Maybe they could go back and finish her off.

Once the Rebel battled her way past Davis she rounded De Soto Point and drew alongside Vicksburg's wharf amidst thousands of spectators' applause.

Not one to whittle away time when events demanded action, Farragut dispatched a lieutenant across De Soto Point to inform Captain Bell of his plan. The four mortar schooners David Porter left behind were to come up and bombard the lower batteries at the flag officer's signal. Meanwhile, Davis's ships would draw fire from the enemy's upper batteries. The Rebels thus distracted, he would draw alongside *Arkansas*, even board her if necessary, before the sun settled below the horizon. But like most everything else this most miserable summer, his plan misfired.

Davis delayed the attack. When the firing above and below the river finally started, the river's current carried Farragut's quiet ships downriver. They made it below the town, but due to the cloudy night they missed the ironclad.

At 8:30 P.M., *Hartford* anchored between *Brooklyn* and *Madison*. Sailors manned rails and rigging, waving caps and shouting lusty cheers.

But Farragut's frustration flushed his face. Another humiliation. This time, he blamed Davis—his insistence upon a night attack, his delays. He regretted he didn't outrank him so he could've ordered him to do what he wanted.

Further efforts to sink the ironclad came to naught. Eight days later, the flag officer received new orders from Secretary Welles: "Go down the river at your discretion. Not expected to remain up there during the season."

The next day, Farragut's squadron headed back for Baton Rouge.

And *Madison's* Master, Xavier Locke pondered what he'd do to Annie Westcott when they reached New Orleans. He'd killed her brother Ben during the battle below that city, and now the day soon approached for her demise. She'd spat in his face, she'd insulted him. Oh, yes. Not just her demise. Her death.

19

THE TROOP TRAIN squealed to a stop at the Mobile & Ohio's depot. Major Philippe Soileau welcomed the salty air swooshing into his car once its door opened and Colonel George Stevens, his brigade commander, stepped down and out into the evening's blackness. *Mobile.* They weren't far from his home, New Orleans. The salt air…he missed it. He filed out behind his fellow officers. Quickly he surveyed his dark surroundings and the street lamps' glows which guided them to the street.

Save for the clatter of couplers, the depot was quiet. He had no idea how late the hour was. He only knew their commander, General Braxton Bragg, had them moving rapidly. Their entire army, so it was rumored, was speeding toward Tennessee fast as possible to beat the Yankee General Buell, slowly slugging east through Tennessee's Cumberland Mountains, to Chattanooga. Such was the rumor, and since they traveled on trains, he assumed it true. Only the army's horse-drawn units journeyed overland. Why hadn't General Beauregard rejoined them?

Soldiers piled out of the cars behind them; sergeants and lieutenants barked orders for them to assemble with their units. The soldiers hastened to their colors and guidons and shuffled into their squads, their uniforms tattered, their faces and hands dirty, but their demeanors proud.

He clutched the rosary he'd carried in his pocket throughout every campaign. His thoughts wandered toward New Orleans, its recent Yankee occupation, his parents, and Mademoiselle Catherine

Anne Westcott. No Yankee had better lay a hand on them. Did his good friend Benjamin Westcott fight them below the city? Had his opinion of the war changed like his own opinion had?

No longer an officer in Morphy's Rifles, he'd been promoted and transferred to the Army of Tennessee and given command of an Alabama regiment. *Perhaps General Beauregard, he no longer commands us. Perhaps it is General Bragg. Yet I have not heard my Creole comrade has been given a different command.*

He wished he'd have time to visit his parents' friends, the Mont-Pierres, who lived here. He wished that through them, he could give his parents a message. Monsieur Mont-Pierre had been friends of Philippe's cousins living near Cherbourg, and it was his cousins who'd written his grandfather about their coming to this city. On numerous occasions, Philippe and his family had visited them. He knew Mobile almost as well as he did New Orleans. Had he and Mademoiselle Catherine Anne been born here their courtship, perhaps, it would not have been so difficult.

"Soon as roll call's finished, we'll be spelling here for ninety minutes, by which time a steamboat should arrive to ferry us across the bay where we'll catch the Great Northern," Stevens said. "Go tell your company commanders."

"Yes, sir," Philippe said. "May I ask of you the time, sir?"

Stevens went over to a street light and consulted his watch. "It's moving toward nine o'clock."

"Sir, with your permission, my parents, they have friends here. May I call on them?"

"Can you get back in time?"

"With your permission, sir, I will try. If I cannot, I will promptly return."

"Permission granted, but only after you relay my orders to your companies."

"Thank you, sir." Philippe joined his assembled men.

He repeated Stevens's order to his company commanders and warned his men not to wander from the depot's immediate vicinity. He gave himself forty-five minutes before reporting back. He wasn't keen on reporting back, not keen on killing any Yankees these days. Pittsburg Landing was the fiercest battle he'd participated in so far. Fighting, it was no longer fun.

Killing...he reached inside his trouser pocket and clutched his rosary...*killing no longer appeals to me. This war, is it not a sin?* Yet he could not desert his men. That, too, would be a sin, the sin of cowardice, the sin of dishonor, the sin of letting down courageous men who might, in the future, die. *I will do penance after this war has ended. If I must make a pilgrimage to Rome to do so, I will. I promise it. And then, Mademoiselle Catherine Anne and me, we will marry.* If he did penance, what would Catherine Anne think? Might that affect their chance at marriage? He'd promised her he'd become a Protestant before they wed. Too soon. It was too soon to worry about that.

He turned up a street leading to the Mont-Pierre's block. When he saw a wagon pull up behind him, he gestured for it to stop. "Monsieur."

The shaggy-haired man reined in the two black horses pulling his vehicle. "More of you boys passing through our city, I see. Must be on y'all's way to a big battle. That's what all the newspapers have been saying."

"I must find someone quickly. Monsieur. Please."

"Where you from? I take it your accent's Creole."

"From New Orleans, Monsieur. Please. I have not much time. You will take me there?"

"Look, young man. I'd be glad to oblige, but I'm really tuckered out. Me and my crew and *Lady Amber* have been out on the bay all day running errands and delivering supplies and I've just gotten back. I'm on my way to my apartment to catch up on some sleep. I've a two-day shore leave, and I intend on taking full advantage of it."

"The *Lady Amber*, Monsieur? Your name, it is Captain William Hughes?"

Surprised, Hughes almost sprang off his wagon seat.

Philippe grinned. "One of my best friends is likewise one of Alex's. His name, it is Benjamin Westcott. Benjamin, he mentioned your yacht a few times and often wished his father would purchase one."

"Climb aboard my wagon, young man. I'll take you to wherever you want to go. I…uh…maybe…."

"Monsieur? Sir?" Philippe sat on the wagon bed's opened end gate, his big feet dangling inches from the ground. The yacht captain's ominous tone disturbed him.

On the way to the Mont-Pierres' home, Philippe listened while Hughes recounted Ben's tragedy. Not once did he interrupt Hughes with a question. Rather, he digested every detail. The fight below the city, as Moxley had described it; Ben's two wounds and his grave condition aboard the Yankee *Pensacola*. Moxley, he said, had escaped the city and had joined the Army. Presently, he was learning military basics at a camp of instruction in Notasulga.

Philippe worried about his Catherine Anne and her fretting over her brothers. He wished to enfold her in his arms, to kiss her, to bring her comfort.

"Ben's a prisoner," Hughes said. "That's all we know."

A prisoner? *Non!* "Benjamin has survived his wounds, that is my hope. Here, sir. Stop here. This is the house. Wait for me, please. I shall not be long. I will need to get back to my regiment within a brief time." He climbed off the end gate.

Through the three-story home's central dormer window, a light flickered. Every other window was dark. He jiggled its iron gate. Locked. His eyes wandered down from the dormer to the front door and the black crepe draping it, and to the eight square pillars, likewise shrouded in black crepe. He made the sign of the cross. The Mont-Pierres had but one son, Clement, and six daughters. Someone inside had died. He hoped it was not him.

He jiggled the gate again. No longer was he concerned about his message, which he wished them to try and get delivered to his parents. *Non.* He wanted to console them. He looked up at the dormer again; its light went out. Turning back, he returned to Captain Hughes's wagon.

"The depot, Monsieur, *c'il vous plait*."

Hughes said nothing on the way back to the depot. The black crepe said it all.

20

"WHO'RE THOSE GIRLS in your buggy?" Susan asked.

Hughes brushed the back of his weathered hand over his mouth. "Their runner came in through the Swash Channel early this morning."

"They'd better not be wanting to stay with me overnight."

"They've rented a room at the Pattison House. The Battle House is all full."

"I am Martha Massingale, daughter of the gallant blockade-running captain, Roger William Massingale." Martha climbed down from the dusty black buggy. "And I made it clear to the polite captain here that I, my good friend Lydia Stiles, and our mothers, we were all looking for you."

"I don't know you," Susan said.

"Of course not." Lydia's mother spoke from the buggy.

"How can you know us when we've never met?" Mrs. Massingale said, also from the buggy.

"I don't like strangers calling on me."

"Oh, I'm hardly a stranger." Martha undid her bright blue reticule's drawstrings.

Susan detected a twinkle in Hughes's dark eyes.

"Your gorgeous brother Alex would recognize me in an instant." From inside her reticule, Martha produced Alex's letter. "He asked me to deliver this."

Susan came down the steps and snatched it. She scanned its contents. "He's in fine health in Nassau. Thank you, Miss Massingale."

"I prefer Martha."

"*Miss* Massingale. I suppose you found me because Alex told you where I lived."

"Because like she said, Susan, she was looking for you," Hughes said. "And since I knew you weren't working at the post office this hour and had started living on Government Street year -round to be closer to your work, I brought her straight here."

"What were you doing at the Pattison House?"

"I was on my way to a hardware store when I came upon these ladies standing outside the hotel looking lost."

"As usual, you offered your services."

"Naturally."

"Do you have any more questions I'll be happy to answer?" Martha said.

Susan folded the letter. "Is he trying to get back home?"

"We're not sure. He said he didn't want to come with us but never said why."

"He may have gotten orders we don't know anything about," Mrs. Massingale said.

"My friends and I are on our way to Biloxi in the morning," Lydia said. "I have a letter for your father too. I'll see it gets delivered."

"Give it here," Susan said. "I'll mail it."

Martha handed her the letter and as she climbed back in Hughes's buggy, this time, she allowed the yacht captain's assistance.

"Why did you call my brother gorgeous? Do you like him?"

"Why, a girl would be foolish not to feel attracted to a man with his good looks," Martha said. "Has he mentioned something to you about a 'k' word?"

"He has not. Why?"

"He told me something about a word beginning with a 'k,'" Mrs. Massingale said.

"And I am determined to find out what it is, even if I have to stay up all night reading a dictionary," Martha said.

"Why is that?"

Back in his buggy, Hughes gripped his horses' reins.

"So she can figure out why she scares him," Lydia said.

Hughes popped his whip; his horses headed out Susan's gate.

"Scare Alex?" Susan yelled back as the buggy rattled out the gate. "What did you do?"

"Nothing!" Martha waved at her; the horses moved into a trot. "He *kissed* me! He's not scared of me anymore!"

"Kissed you? My Alex? What'd he do that for?"

"Because I'm irresistible!" Martha waved again as the buggy rattled out of earshot.

Susan returned inside the house and set Alex's letter in a walnut box. It contained all his letters, all her father's, and all of Moxley's from Notasulga. She'd not responded to him. Yet he was one persistent gentleman. His letters never stopped. He mentioned that his training was nearing an end and that his regiment, like the other regiments from his training camp, were being sent to Mobile. "I look forward to our seeing each other once again," he'd written. She wasn't. Huston's footsteps pulled her from her musings.

"Are you ready to eat, Miss Susan?" the butler said.

"Eat what? A little corn?"

"Corn and oysters, Miss Susan."

"When this war's over, I'll never eat seafood again. Especially not oysters. I'll get gloriously, wonderfully fat!"

Mid-July, it slinked into Nassau and claimed its first victim, a friend of Maffitt's, a young officer in the Fourth West Indies Regiment. Yellow Jack. Diabolical Yellow Jack. Moans and delirious cries throbbed throughout the Royal Victoria's lobby, a din of the diseased and the dying. Maffitt, Stribling, and Alex moved throughout the hotel nursing patients and administering medicine. Chills the fever's victims suffered, and excruciating pains; they spit up black vomit, into eternity they passed.

Not only did Maffitt nurse patients. He also made time for *Oreto's* final trial in the British Admiralty Court. Alex and Stribling attended the hearings when they had the chance, never entering the courtroom together or at the same time of day and always careful not to sit with each other nor with Maffitt lest it arouse suspicions. Convened in a packed courtroom, it lasted six weeks.

Alex figured *Oreto's* freedom didn't look promising. The crew who'd brought her to Nassau, every man of them, swore under oath that she was a warship bound for the Confederacy and thus violated the Foreign Enlistment Act. Most of her officers gave similar testimony, though two of her officers and her nominal captain Mister Duguid contradicted them. When Commander Semmes arrived on the island, many thought that ship was meant for him. But new orders sent him back to England to assume command of the *290*, Stribling had learned from their former captain. Semmes said he'd rename her the *Alabama*, after his adopted home state. His sudden departure squashed that rumor.

Commander Hinckley, *Greyhound's* captain and the British squadron's ranking officer in the region, testified that he first boarded her three days after her arrival. "May the first," he said in court, "I led a boarding crew to inspect her design and cargo. She had every look of a warship. We found no guns or munitions aboard her. However, in my professional opinion, she is a ship built for war." He went on to explain how he, on another occasion, witnessed Captain Duguid assisting his crew in loading shells aboard her. Duguid, who saw Hinckley watching him, immediately ordered the shells off-loaded. This statement was previously given by a member of Duguid's crew. Hinckley only confirmed it.

Maffitt's unconcerned air kept steady. He was, after all, the captain of a blockade-runner and attended the trial out of mere curiosity. As far as everyone knew, he had no personal stake in the trial's outcome.

Other former crew members testified that *Oreto's* warlike nature was obvious. For example, they'd seen her shot lockers and powder magazines. Everything about her, they said, proved she violated the Foreign Enlistment Act. By day three, their testimony convinced Alex they'd lose her. Maffitt, however, never failed to tell someone a joke or two after a day of hearings. If he was worried, he never let it show. Too much rode on the trial's outcome.

On his way to a café during a break from his nursing duties, Alex spotted Maffitt shaking a policeman's hand. Turning south, he strolled past Alex smooth as molasses, neither of them breaking stride nor acknowledging the other.

More men testified during the trial's closing days. Policemen, shop owners, and prominent merchants all spoke in her favor. Each man said under oath, in one way or other, that *Oreto* wasn't a warship but a mere merchant vessel. At noon on the seventh day of August, the judge announced his decision: "The *Oreto*, being unarmed, did not violate the Foreign Enlistment Act. The ship is free."

The verdict was recorded and her clearance papers issued the next day, naming Maffitt's stepson Laurens Read her captain.

"Take her out of the harbor," Maffitt told him, "to the outer anchorage. My officers and I will join you in a few hours."

Laurens strode toward the harbor.

One hour later Maffitt led his officers, all wearing civilian clothes, out of the Royal Victoria. He'd made Alex and Bradford Acting Lieutenants and Stribling his executive officer. Other officers he'd met in Nassau signed on during the past month: a midshipman, four engineers, a clerk named Vogel, and an Acting Marine Lieutenant named Wyman. Laurens would serve as acting paymaster once they made it to sea. Some twenty men comprised her crew.

Aboard *Oreto*, Maffitt chuckled. "I won't say, gentlemen, that I wasn't worried about the trial's outcome. I was! Indeed I was! But if that Yankee Consul Sam bribed her original crew to testify against her and jump ship, I decided I'd bribe men to speak in her behalf. Every man who testified in our favor, gents, I bribed with my own money. That was our only chance at freedom. And it worked. Ha!" He grinned broadly. "It also helped that the island's governor supports our Cause."

Alex and his fellows laughed.

"Mister Stribling, I'm laying below to check out my quarters. You have the deck."

"Aye, sir," Stribling said.

"She is one beautiful lady, sir," spoke a sailor in a thick British accent, surveying her neat, trim lines.

"That she is, Henson," Stribling said. "That she is."

Alex thought her a far sight prettier than *Sumter*. Her brass work glinted beneath the boiling afternoon sun; sails were furled on her three towering masts. Twin stacks rose midships; above her stern bulwarks port and starboard hung a whaleboat. Her wheel stood deep inside her stern, well aft her mizzenmast, unlike other ships he'd sailed in. The brisk breeze strummed her rigging like a master guitarist.

Stribling ordered the sailors forward and down to the berth deck. To the other officers, he said, "In my wake, gentlemen." He led them into the wardroom below.

Though small, it was roomier than *Sumter's*. An oak mess table halved its center, atop a brilliant oriental rug. Overhead, two lanterns swung from each end of a skylight. A sconce on the forward and aft bulkheads allowed the possibility for more candlelight in the event of dark nights or black, stormy days.

"Gentlemen." Stribling addressed them from the wardroom's most forward section. "As Captain Maffitt's executive officer, he has told me to assign you your quarters."

The six senior officers gave Stribling their full attention. He called out each name and sent them to their staterooms port and starboard.

"I'm off to the engineers' and stewards' quarters," Stribling said once he finished. He disappeared up the companion ladder.

Alex untied his cast net from his sea chest.

Wyman poked his curly-haired head inside. "How do you like this lady so far?"

Alex slid his sea chest beneath his cot. "I think we'll do the enemy some damage. Maybe more'n the *Sumter* did."

Wyman pointed at Alex's net. "Mister Stribling told me you're pretty good at throwing that thing."

"Can you throw a cast net?"

"I've been known to throw one every now and then."

"Maybe we'll be able to do some fishing on this cruise. Ever caught a marlin before?"

"That I've never done."

"I sure would like to catch one of those big babies someday."

"Wouldn't be easy."

"Easy takes the fun out of things."

Fifteen minutes later, Stribling rejoined them. "The captain's ordered me back to Nassau to take charge of our tender bringing us supplies, munitions, and guns. Mister Jessup, you will assume my duties till I return." He hurried back up the ladder.

The following day, Maffitt called all hands to the quarterdeck. "Take a gander portside."

The men looked behind them. A ship flying a United States ensign circled them like a shark.

"That would be the USS *Cuyler*," Maffitt continued. "Our friend Consul Sam has obviously informed her captain of the court's decision.

Do I look worried, gentlemen? Of course, I don't. Why not? Because blockades are nothing to me. I've run them before, easy as a knife through hot butter. She's a mere minor nuisance. No reason to fret."

Alex awaited one of Maffitt's poetic lines. It never came.

"Sir," Bradford said, "suppose more Yankees turn up?"

"Let them," Maffitt said. "There's not a blockade known to man I can't penetrate."

Alex hoped Maffitt's words weren't mere braggadocio.

"Look what's happening," another tar, Brownleaf, said.

"A ship flying a British ensign bearing down on the *Cuyler*," Alex said.

"See what I told you?" Maffitt said. "That's the *Petrel* coming to our aid. A friend of mine commands her. Captain Watson. He'll get the *Cuyler* out of our way. Like I said, no need to worry. No need at all." He consulted his watch. "Mister Jessup, as of this second you're officer of the deck. I think it's time we test our engines."

Alex gave the order.

The engineers went below.

Since Maffitt lacked enough men to weigh anchor, Captain Watson rendered him further aid. At midnight, *Petrel* tossed him a hawser. Under Bradford's supervision, sailors secured it to a towing post directly behind her bowsprit. To prevent Yankee detection, they hugged land's shadow and sailed west till it reached New Providence's westernmost end. From here, Maffitt directed her on a southerly course.

Some ways out a schooner, her fore-and-aft sails billowing, tacked toward them. "Here comes the *Prince Albert*." Maffitt lowered his glass. "Mister Stribling has returned right on schedule."

The following afternoon, they anchored a little over a mile west of Green Cay and began the arduous task of unloading guns, powder, shot, and shells in stifling heat.

21

SPICY AROMAS DRIFTED over the square table where Locke and Upton sat. Murmurs, clattering dishes, and the dinging of silverware filled the large establishment. Comfortable in his cushioned chair, Locke held the *Daily Delta* straight out. These days, it was New Orleans's only newspaper. Not long after Butler occupied the city, he'd shut it down. Later, he let it resume publishing when some of his troops took it over.

Three days earlier, General Williams was killed in a battle against a Rebel force that had tried and failed to retake Baton Rouge. Two days ago, *Arkansas* met her end just north of Baton Rouge. Accounts of her demise conflicted. What was clear, though, was that the feared ironclad no longer existed. Her men abandoned her, and she blew up.

"All we have left to do in these parts is secure the river between Vicksburg and Baton Rouge," Upton said. "We'll own the whole Mississippi then. Maybe this war'll be over soon."

"Mobile's our next objective," Locke said.

"Lee's been whipping us pretty good back East if the papers have it right. But once we take the whole river, the Rebels this side of the Mississippi will have trouble getting beef and supplies from their states west of here."

"Lee will lose eventually, on the condition that Abe finds himself a general smarter than McClellan. Our old fanatic got us thrashed at Vicksburg. The Rebs have Lee and Jackson, and we have Farragut. None of them are geniuses."

"Why must you keep calling our flag officer a fanatic?"

Locke set down his paper. Ever since Upton's bout with malaria, he'd noticed a gradual change in his friend's conduct, speech, and demeanor. "Because as far as I'm concerned, he is."

"He's not a fanatic."

"How would you know?"

Upton got to his feet.

"Has Doctor Kirby's nonsense finally affected your brain?"

"When I was sick with malaria and thought I was dying, my life flashed before me."

"Did you die? Do I look like a ghost or something?"

"Stop it."

"The quinine saved your life, not some great big man up in the sky somewhere."

Upton thrust back his shoulders. "Like the doctor said, we're all going to die one day. We need to be ready."

"Upton, this is where you and I part company. No longer consider me your friend."

"I am still yours, but before I shove off, I'll say two things. Number one, I pity you. Number two, I doubt you ever were my friend even though I remain yours."

Locke started to mock Upton, till he spotted the waiter bringing their gumbo and iced tea. He devoured both gumbos, swilled both glasses of tea, and finished off his meal with a beer. Once he paid, he struck out for the Westcotts' home.

Locke rapped on the Westcotts' front door. No answer. Attached to the wall beside the door hung a tiny brass doorbell. He pulled its cord. No response to its ding. Someone inside moved, the shadow he'd spied through the draperies as he'd walked up the flagstone walkway. A female.

"Open up," Locke screamed. "I know you're in there." He banged the door, shook the doorknob. "Open, I say!"

"Needin' some help?" From the lawn below, Jason peered up at him beneath a floppy straw hat.

"I want that woman inside to open this door," Locke said.

"There ain't a woman inside." The man casually stuck his hands in his pockets.

"Listen, you banjo-eyed….I saw her, she saw me."

"That woman inside ain't no woman. She's a lady. I'd take it kindly if you'd refer to her that way."

Locke tacked on a gentler approach. "Forgive me. I didn't mean to insult her."

"I believe I'm needin' an apology too."

"For what?"

"For callin' me 'banjo-eyed.'"

"I did, didn't I?"

"I'm waitin'."

"My apologies." Locke came down the steep steps.

"Apology accepted."

"Actually, I'm looking for the Westcotts."

"They're upriver."

"That person inside?"

"Her name's Nancy. We're grateful to you folks for comin' to this city, but we still ain't exactly free yet, but Miss Annie, because she don't cotton to slavery, she lets us do pretty much whatever we want long as we don't do nothin' bad. The Westcotts are fine folks."

"You really believe that?"

"Oh, sho'. Greed and money had lots to do with makin' us slaves. I know that, but not a man alive among us is perfect."

Only the weak forgave. "Since they're upriver, why is it you two are living here?"

"Why, shucks. I said they let us do whatever we want. Been that way ever since y'all came into this city."

"Why is the door locked?"

The man grinned. "Sorry. I cain't answer that question." He shifted his eyes and put his finger to his lips. "Shhh. It's a secret."

Locke strode off. Since the door was kept locked, he needed to find a way inside and kill everyone in that house.

While Danny absently swept the wardroom's dust into a neat pile, his thoughts and worries ashore, Doctor Kirby poked and prodded one of *Madison's* coal heavers.

The doctor gave the coal heaver a small bottle of powder. "Take a spoonful of this three times a day and see me again tomorrow."

The coal heaver coughed, rose from the mess table, and stumbled topside.

"Would you like me to speak with her first?" Doctor Kirby asked.

"What if Nancy doesn't love me anymore after the mean way I talked to her when we took New Orleans?" Danny moved to another dusty section of the deck and started sweeping. "Her being married to that other man? Titus?"

"I'll be glad to speak with her first."

"I was awful to her. No girl deserves to be talked to the way I did. I was wrong. I admit I was wrong. Do you think that'll be enough for her? For me to admit it, I mean?"

"Danny, if you'd like me to speak with her, I'd be happy to."

"I don't wanna hurt Titus if I see him. I'm powerful scared I'm gonna do it. Powerful scared." He dropped the broom and studied his large fists. "These things, sir. I don't wanna use 'em. I can hurt somebody with 'em real bad."

A Bible tucked under his arm, Upton came down the wardroom ladder. "Here, Doctor. I bought this for you." He handed Doctor Kirby the Bible. "It's the least I can do to make up for what Locke and I did at Ship Island," Upton said.

"You men did throw my Bible into the Gulf, didn't you?" Doctor Kirby said. "Thank you, Upton."

Upton stuck out his hand. "Yates, I realize this isn't exactly Navy, an enlisted man shaking an officer's hand, but do you mind doing it with one who regrets his previous conduct?"

"I'm a colored man, sir. Are you sure you wanna shake a colored's hand?"

Upton kept his hand out.

"Well, then. I reckon it's forgiven and forgotten." Forgiving Upton came easy. His offenses didn't hold a candle to Titus's and Tuck's.

Two hours later, shouts from the Westcott house moved Danny into a sprint. He barreled through its gate, banged up its steps, and barged through its front door.

Nancy squealed.

Cringing against a wall, Nancy seized Titus's right wrist after his palm popped her cheek. She struggled against his sinewy power. Titus swatted her again with his left hand before seizing the hand seizing his wrist. He flung her onto the floor. Her dress billowed around her. Eyes welling, she moved to get up when another male servant, shorter than Titus whom Danny didn't know, lunged at the butler. Titus sidestepped him, caught his right arm, and slung him against the opposite wall. "Keep out of my affairs, Jason."

Jason sprang to his feet. "Let her go. She has a right to come here. Miss Annie's parents are dead. Cain't you at least show them a l'il concern?"

"I warned her not to come here. The woman didn't mind what I said." He clutched Nancy's forearms. "She's going back with me."

"Let her go."

"Make me, little man."

"Why don't you bully somebody your own size?" Danny said.

Titus shoved Nancy away. "Where'd you come from?"

"My ship, Stupid. Step away from my girl." His head jerked at Nancy, indicating the music room.

Nancy hesitated.

"Do like I said, Nancy. Please."

Nancy vanished into the room but poked her head into the hallway.

Danny snatched off his flat sailor's cap and tossed it between himself and Titus like a knight throwing down a gauntlet. "I don't wanna hurt you, but I will if I gotta."

"Don't make me laugh," Titus said.

Danny stepped toe to toe. "Real men don't hurt ladies. Leave."

"Nancy's my wife. She minds what I tell her."

"Nancy was my wife before she was yours. I never bullied her. Only cowards bully females."

Titus swore. "Do I look like I'm a coward? I'm not scared of you."

Like two tigers, they sized each other up and breathed hard in each other's face.

Titus swung at Danny; his fist connected and, staggering, Danny felt the blow. Titus swung again, but Danny's arms blocked the punch.

Three more swings; Danny blocked each blow before he moved in fast, landing his fist square on Titus's jaw. Titus flew back, flat on his back.

"Hurrah!" Jason shouted triumphantly. He knelt and put an ear to the butler's chest. "Still a heartbeat. I'd say you knocked him out cold."

"Grab his legs. I'll get his arms."

Together, they lifted Titus and carried him toward the open door. Nancy stood behind them, relaxed and smiling. He winked at her.

She winked back.

Once they had Titus outside the gate, Danny sent Jason to the cistern for water, which Danny poured on Titus's face.

Spluttering, Titus came to.

"Next time I catch you with my girl," Danny snapped, "I'll break your jaw. I don't wanna break your jaw, but I will do it. That's a promise."

Titus scrambled to his feet. "I'm no coward, Yates. I'll prove it to you." He ran off and kept running till he turned a corner, out of sight.

Back inside, Danny settled Nancy into a chair. Where to begin? Where to begin his apology?

"Nancy." He studied her face. Her beautiful eyes riveted on him. "Uh, I, uh, I owe you an apology for all those bad things I said to you this past April."

Nancy grasped his hands. "This chile's sorry too, for betraying you when I married Titus. I thought you and your master got killed in that ship you were traveling on last year before this ole war started."

"You knew about that?"

"Mister Ben's friend told us."

"Mister Alex."

"The ship caught fire and exploded, according to the papers, Mister Alex said. Not many people survived it. Titus, he feared he'd get sent to the cane fields or sold if he didn't treat me right. That's why he behaved when we was living with the Westcotts. He loves having power and bossing us all the time. His true self came out after we left them."

"This isn't your home anymore?" Danny said.

She shook her head. "Titus is renting a small house downriver. The owners hate slavery. Rich folks. Black folks. Black Creoles. The Brulet family. Mister Brulet, he's a doctor. The Westcotts never tried finding Titus after he left. They was all tired of the way he acted after the Yankees moved in. That's why they let him get away with leaving them."

"Are you working anywhere? Have you been able to find employment?"

Again, she shook her head. "We all still slaves down here, even though the Yankees run this town now. Mister D.H. Holmes been asking my missus for years if he could hire me." Her face suddenly brightened. "Maybe Miss Annie will let me do it."

"My Nancy, my girl, stay here tonight and ask your Miss Annie. If she lets you, go see Mister Holmes tomorrow. I'll send you my pay. No reason to keep living with Titus anymore. I don't want you around his kind."

Nancy planted a kiss on Danny's forehead. "I love you."

"Nancy, you are the only girl I have ever loved." Grasping her hands, Danny pulled her close.

Annie and Clara found Jason sitting on the top step wearing a huge grin.

"Goodness sakes!" Annie said. "What are you smiling about?"

"Shhh!" Jason put his finger to his lips. "Danny's back, Miss Annie. He and Nancy are inside."

Clara peered through the window. "Oh my word! They're kissing!"

"Come on, Jason," Annie said. "Let's leave them alone. We'll walk to Clara's. Tell us what happened."

"We've seen the end of Titus for sure, Miss Annie. Shucks. Danny made a fool out of him." Outside Clara's gate, Jason snapped his fingers and said, "Almost forgot. We had us another visitor today. A Yankee feller. Looked like an officer by his uniform."

"Why would a Yankee officer be visiting me? What did he look like?"

"About my height. A little taller, maybe. Wide, though. Not fat, but built broad in the shoulders and chest. Mostly muscle. No'm. All muscle, he was. He looked like a huge brick or chunk of rock. A boulder. Red hair and wearin' a white straw hat. Not like my straw hat. His hat was fine lookin', firm in the brim with a black ribbon circlin' it."

"Did you get his name?"

"No'm. Since I didn't know who he was, I lied to him and told him you and your family was upriver."

"His name is Locke, Mister Ben's mortal enemy. Don't let him back on our property, Jason. Never, ever again."

"No'm. No need worryin' on that account. I'll keep him away."

Farragut welcomed the news his clerk Mister Gaubadan brought him. President Abraham Lincoln, by and with the advice of the United States Senate, had appointed him to the rank of rear admiral on the sixteenth of July. Not till August, though, two days after Captain Wainwright's sudden illness killed him and a day after his funeral, did he receive this information.

Gabaudan read him Welles's letter. "Our navy has performed wonders during this war, but conspicuous above and beyond all was that of capturing New Orleans. For this achievement you well have come to the thanks and highest naval honors the country can bestow, and it gives me sincere gratification, personally as well as officially, to forward you the evidence of their grateful regard."

He wished he'd have known this while they were at Vicksburg, Farragut told himself during his clerk's reading. Then Davis would've had to do what he told him, and they might have sunk *Arkansas*. The Rebels wouldn't have humiliated him the way they did had he been in overall command.

"My congratulations, sir," Gabaudan said.

Farragut smiled. "Thank you."

"Our country's never had an admiral before, sir." Gabaudan set the letter on Farragut's desk.

Which made him its first. Farragut basked in the thought, but he couldn't let the honor swell his head. Pride always caused a man's downfall. "Send for Mister Thornton."

"Aye, sir."

Minutes later Thornton, *Hartford's* executive officer and temporary captain, reported in.

Farragut showed him his commission. "The Navy Department's made me a rear admiral."

"Well done, sir!" Thornton said.

"Dispatch an officer ashore to inform General Butler and another officer to the *Pensacola, Brooklyn. Mississippi*, and *Madison* to inform their captains of my promotion."

"Aye, sir. Again, accept my congratulations."

Farragut flashed a smile. "I appreciate it."

Minutes later, in Wainwright's old quarters, he unfolded a surveyor's map of Mobile Bay sent to him by Secretary Welles last March. Leaning close, he squinted at its markings. He wondered whether the situation there had changed and how much progress the Rebels had made in strengthening its defenses.

It'd been months since he'd seen the Gulf of Mexico. Captain Robert Hitchcock was the senior officer at that station. Tomorrow, after Farragut announced his promotion to his squadron and enjoyed their gun salutes, he'd weigh anchor for Mobile. Perhaps, by taking that city, he'd compensate for his failure at Vicksburg. Since he'd taken New Orleans, Mobile, with its vital rail center, had become the Gulf Coast's most important city.

22

WHILE SAILORS AND officers hoisted a seven-inch Blakeley gun on *Prince Albert's* derricks, death skulked *Oreto's* decks. Alex, serving deck officer duty, witnessed the first victim to fall, her wardroom steward. Onto the quarterdeck he collapsed, grimacing, shivering, slightly chilled.

"Get that man forward," Alex ordered as Maffit hastened topside.

One man grabbed the steward's arms and another man his legs. Maffitt hurried forward and knelt beside him in the forecastle, his palm on the steward's forehead. "A common fever," he said.

Common fever? Alex hoped it wasn't the Jack.

Twenty hours later, the nefarious fever hoisted his true colors and confirmed Alex's fears: Yellow Jack, come to slay *Oreto's* crew. The clerk's yellow complexion after he died two days later, the black vomit he retched at life's end—symptoms of the tropical terror. They buried him on Green Cay. Yellow Jack's tentacles crept throughout the ship. Maffitt, Stribling, and Alex kept his deadly presence between themselves.

The able-bodied labored harder, faster to load *Oreto's* stores. Maffitt threw himself into nursing the sick, laid out on the quarterdeck.

Alex barked commands at tars transferring casks of gunpowder swinging from derricks. As his father did after his sister Susanna died, he hurled himself into his work. He drove himself to exhaustion, drove fears of fever from his brain. At day's end, he shut his stateroom's door behind him and closed his eyes in the enveloping darkness. His fatigued mind and muscles dragged him into sleep quicker than he could think.

Finally, their loading ended. As the sun's lingering rays glanced off the water's ripples, *Oreto* dropped anchor in Blossom Channel.

On the seventeenth of August, she and *Prince Albert* parted ways. Southward and westward she steamed, away from the Bahamas. Alex and a handful of the other healthy men assembled midships to witness her brief commissioning. Maffitt read them Secretary Mallory's orders to "do the enemy's commerce the greatest injury in the shortest time." No longer was she the *Oreto*, but CSS *Florida*. At Maffitt's command, *Oreto's* British ensign came down and *Florida's* Confederate ensign hoisted amidst cheers.

Maffitt addressed Stribling after the ceremony. "I believe it's time we start turning the *Florida* into a real warship. Have the men who are well enough exercise the guns."

"Mister Jessup," Stribling said, "run in our guns for loading."

Alex gestured at Brownleaf and Henson. "Y'all are in my gun division. Y'all know how to run in and run out a gun?"

"We did it many a blooming time in Her Majesty's Navy," Henson said.

"Mighty fine. Almighty fine. Show me how y'all blooming did it for Queen Victoria, will you?"

Brownleaf grinned at Henson. "A mighty fine job we'll show you too, sir. An almighty fine job."

Alex chuckled to himself. Brownleaf's humor remained intact despite their fever epidemic. Alex suspected the crew had figured out that Yellow Jack had boarded to send them all to Davy Jones's locker.

Stribling screamed.

Alex clutched his head. This couldn't be happening.

Maffitt ran forward. "What's the difficulty?"

"Good heavens, Captain," Stribling said. "We are ruined! In the haste and secrecy of loading the tender, rammers, sponges, sights, locks, beds, and quoins have all been left in Nassau. The battery, sir, is impotent without these essentials, and we have no means of temporary substitution."

"Our pivot guns are complete," Maffitt said.

"But that is all, sir."

"What now?" Alex said.

"What now, Mister Jessup? We don't give up, that is what's now. One thing you gents will learn about me very quickly is that I, your captain, John Newland Maffitt, am no quitter."

Maffitt scanned the moaning men sprawled across the deck. "Yellow Jack, you vile disease, you haven't defeated me either." He glanced decisively at Stribling. "We've two engineers left who aren't sick. Set a course for Cuba. Maybe the trade winds will help us kill the fever."

"Aye, sir," Stribling said.

"Mister Jessup, send the two healthy engineers below. Tell them we're getting up steam. If they need an extra hand, I think I overheard Henson mention something about serving a short time as a coal heaver. Have him join them."

"Aye aye, Captain." Alex hurried forward. The sickness aboard, their mounting problems…his fist smacked a bulkhead on his way down the companion ladder…all these problems taxed his easygoing nature.

Noting Mobile Bay's channel markings on his chart, Farragut's brows knit. He'd arrived off Mobile Bay an hour ago and signaled Captain Robert B. Hitchcock, commander of the Mobile Squadron, aboard *Hartford*.

Hitchcock cleared his throat and bent over Farragut's chart. "Forgive me, sir, but there's something I must confess." The squadron commander straightened, cleared his throat a second time.

"A sin? I'm no priest." Farragut turned his attention to Dauphin Island. According to the cartographer, its western end was long and narrow, sand and dunes, as opposed to its much broader and fatter eastern end with a beach on its south side and piney woods on its north and near Fort Gaines. About fourteen miles long, Farragut figured, or somewhere in that range.

"Maybe not, sir, but you see, sir, I recently wrote Secretary Welles about my situation here, and Assistant Secretary Fox too. I complained about you, sir."

Farragut suddenly glanced up.

Hitchcock cleared his throat.

"And what was the nature of your complaint?"

"Well, sir, I was, shall I say, getting all frustrated because you spent most of the summer upriver, and I never could get a message to you from down here. Things are bad here, sir."

Farragut pointed at his left shoulder. "See my new shoulder straps, Hitchcock? Since I've been promoted to rear admiral, it's clear to me that your action didn't affect their opinion of me."

"Of course not, sir."

A warm smile emerged on Farragut's lips as he turned his attention back to the chart. "Forget it. It's all over and done."

Hitchcock breathed a sigh of relief.

"Let's get down to business. We need a good solid plan for taking the bay and the forts. You've been here long enough. Have you any ideas?"

"Do you prefer my honest opinion, sir?"

"That's the best opinion."

"My honest opinion, sir, is that we don't make an attempt yet."

"The reasons?"

"The squadron's morale is low, lots of enlistments have expired, but I can't release any of them yet because the Rebels have three gunboats constantly patrolling the bay and two of them carry ten guns each. They also have an ironclad ram, the *Baltic*, informers have told me. As low as my crew's morale is, sir, and with only seven ships blockading the bay and our lack of ironclads to fight the *Baltic*, our chances of victory are, in my opinion, not very good."

"Who commands the squadron?"

"Victor Randolph."

"What about the forts? Have they been strengthened?"

"Fort Morgan has seventy-nine guns and Fort Gaines thirty. There's also a company of artillerists manning three 32-pounders off Grant's Pass, about twenty-five miles from Mobile, and the Rebels have driven in pilings about a quarter-mile off Grant's Island, blocking passage. Over two hundred pilings, by my estimate." He indicated the pass and the battery on the chart, northwest of Dauphin Island. "It's too shallow for our ships anyway. It's not a natural channel. It was excavated through oyster reefs and mud."

"The Swash Channel." Pencil in hand, Farragut traced the channel markings nearly parallel with Fort Morgan's shoreline east of it. "We'd have to steam between Mobile Point and Dixie Bar, but it does bring us close to Fort Morgan."

"Most blockade-runners prefer using that channel because once they get in, we have trouble cutting them out. But my recommendation, sir, is that when we do have the forces to attack, we take the Main Channel straight through the bay's mouth."

Farragut grit his teeth. Bad news. Bad news. Steaming directly beneath the fort's guns at point-blank range, he was looking at a bloodbath far worse than New Orleans. "Who commands the forts?"

"I'm not sure of that, sir. I think his name's Powell. A deserter who recently escaped off Dauphin Island reported that to me, said he was in command of Forts Morgan and Gaines as well as Grant's Pass. Outside of that, I know nothing." Hitchcock's forefinger traced the bay from its mouth to its uppermost, northwestern side where a small grid indicated Mobile. "Sir, as you can see, the waters here, close to the city, are too shallow for our ships. The Rebels can only use schooners and sloops on account of this. We'll take the forts one day but not without an army. Might I again, sir, suggest we wait until we have the necessary ships and a few ironclads."

Farragut turned his back on the chart table, disgusted. Not at Hitchcock, but at the situation. Not enough ships; men whose enlistments had expired and who wanted to return home. He'd failed at Vicksburg. He wouldn't fail here. He loathed waiting much as he loathed losing, but Hitchcock had presented a convincing argument. "I understand your points. Better to wait and be fully prepared than risk another defeat. I'll see we get more ships down to the Gulf— Galveston, Sabine Pass, Mobile, and other ports. I'll be weighing anchor shortly and going on to Fort Pickens. If you need me for anything else, you ought to be able to contact me this time."

"Thank you, sir." Hitchcock saluted.

Farragut returned the salute, then shook Hitchcock's hand farewell. Farragut accompanied him to *Hartford's* gangway.

Yellow Jack defied the trade winds. On the nineteenth, only five men stood watch. When Alex wasn't navigating or doing deck duty, he helped Maffitt and other shipmates nurse the sick. He ached; his eyes burned; anxieties about Susan, his father, the anguished cries of the sick and the dying, their utterances of delirious nonsense, the black vomit they retched which spelled their end, robbed his rest. Sluggishly he moved. Death, death, death. It compassed him. It stank. He wondered where they went after they died. Man did possess a soul. Or did he? *Susanna, Mother, can y'all see how I'm suffering down here?* He stifled the thought.

The mainmast's masthead sang out: "Land ho!"

"Where away!" Bradford called back through the speaking trumpet.

"Four points off the port bow, sir!"

Stribling lifted his glass. "Cardenas."

Cardenas, Cuba. Alex rose from beside a sailor sprawled beneath a boat.

"We'll anchor in its harbor," Maffitt said, resigned. "Stribling, help Sinclair steer into it. Mister Jessup, have the men stand by to drop anchor on my command."

Exhausted, Alex trudged forward.

Dawn broke upon *Florida* several hours later. At nine o'clock, flying a British ensign, she entered the harbor's inner port. Maffitt dispatched Bradford to inform the authorities about their situation. Two hours later, he brought back a telegram: permission from the island's governor-general, Francisco Serrano, to stay as long as necessary.

The following day Stribling set out for Havana to contact their agent, Mister Charles Helm. His objective: bring back a physician and more men.

23

MADISON'S OFFICERS PACKED Captain Vincent's cabin, but Locke hung back, behind the others, listening to his shipmates' discussion.

"Is it true, sir?" Warren said. "We are heading back into the Gulf?"

"Pensacola will be our first stop," Vincent said. "Since we reoccupied it in May, the admiral figures it's the best place for us to make repairs. We'll also help repair its shipyard. The admiral says it needs lots of work."

"Will we be doing blockade duty after we're all fixed up nice and pretty?" Lieutenant Mandover said.

"That is a definite possibility."

"Boring."

"We do as ordered, Mandover," Zollicoffer snapped.

Blockade duty. It wasn't much time left for him to avenge that Westcott wench's insult. "Sir, when will we be departing?" Locke said.

"In a few days. Before we get underway, I'll allow each of you a few hours ashore in shifts. Your feet may not touch land again for a long time. Dismissed."

Alex witnessed it in the afternoon, expected it when Maffitt complained of a sudden chill down his back and legs. After a footbath, he said he felt better and resumed nursing his sick. Come four o'clock, about the time Midshipman Bryan assumed Alex's watch duties…"Argh!" Maffitt dropped his medicine bottle; his flushed face wrenched. Seizing his loins, he screamed. "Mister Wyman! Get Mister Wyman and Mister Floyd!"

Alex sprinted midships, where Wyman was instructing a couple of sailors on handling a musket. "Yellow Jack's boarded the captain."

Wyman thrust the weapon into a sailor's hands and darted aft. Maffitt's clerk bounded up the companion ladder. Maffitt dragged himself along the deck till he managed to sit, slouched, against the starboard bulwarks. He screwed up his face. "The fever always affects the brain."

"Sir." His clerk bent toward him slightly.

Maffitt's eyes tightened. "Everything's in my desk." His face contorted. "I wrote it down."

"What was it, sir?" Alex said, upon hearing this after bringing Floyd.

"Instructions, in case I caught the fever. How to care for the sick, the ship, me. I have it—the symptoms. Yellow Jack keeps sticking his bayonets in me. Argh! Y'all…blurry."

"What is it you need me to do, sir?" Wyman said.

"Get the sick to a hospital ashore. Find a physician."

Wyman departed quickly.

"Jessup, Floyd. Prepare a mustard bath. H-Help me below, change my clothes, and my sheets." He swallowed hard, as though struggling to beat back vomit.

Alex and Floyd, their arms twined in Maffitt's, assisted him down the ladder. At its foot, he doubled over and screamed.

"Father!" Laurens shot down the ladder and, seizing his stepfather's arm, helped lay him onto a cot.

The threesome eyed each other gravely.

"We're on a death ship," Floyd said.

"Let's hope a doctor gets here soon," Alex said.

"Not much good a doctor can do against the Jack."

"You two stay here and keep an eye on the captain. I'm topside to check on the others."

Despite every reasonable measure, Maffitt's fever worsened. He wandered in and out of delirium, and lastly, into unconsciousness. Laurens, Alex observed, never left his stepfather's side.

"Jason, you still behind us?" Danny asked, his arm in Nancy's as they walked down St. Charles Street.

"Do you got to keep on following us, Jason?" Nancy asked this from neither irritation nor anger but from amusement. She enjoyed happier times these days, making dresses for Mister Holmes's customers. The Brulets fired Titus and kicked him out of their rented house, but the Brulets and Miss Annie allowed her to remain in it. The money she earned from Mister Holmes, Miss Annie let her keep all of it for herself.

Danny was proud of her for reporting Titus. It served him right, and he told her he didn't care where Titus was or what he was doing so long as he didn't come near her again.

"Aren't you going to that Creole café, Devereaux's or something?" Jason asked.

"Best Creole café in the city, I always heard. Owned by a Creole black man, just like the Brulets," Nancy said.

"Get some faster limbs if you wanna come with us," Danny said.

Jason hurried up alongside. "When do you got to get back at your ship?"

"Ten o'clock. If I get back any later, the officer of the deck puts me on report, and that's a bad thing. We're weighing anchor tomorrow."

"How can you weigh a huge heavy anchor like your ship's got?"

Danny clapped Jason's shoulders. "That's Navy talk." During their long walk down St. Charles, Danny entertained them with stories about life aboard *Madison*, the education he was receiving, Locke's persecution, and his and Doctor Kirby's friendship.

"Evil clean through, that man Locke," Danny said.

"Watch out for him, Nancy," Jason said. "Miss Annie says he's dangerous."

"His head's all messed up," Danny said, and then he changed the subject by showing off fancy medical words and their definitions, which his friend the doctor had taught him.

"Me and Parson Silas always knew God gave you a good mind," Nancy said.

Danny smiled privately. He'd shown off those words to impress her. "When this war's over and our freedom's won, I will become somebody important."

"Being important is not that important," Nancy said. "That was Titus's problem. He always had to be the big man. I don't want you being like him."

"Humbleness," Jason said. "That's how we all supposed to act, ain't it?"

"I think my words came out wrong. I only meant I'd make something of my life. I ain't, I mean I'm not going back to blacksmithing, and I won't be staying in the Navy after the war now that I found you."

"What will you do?" Nancy asked.

Danny detected hope in Nancy's question as they crossed crowded St. Charles Street. He had a pretty good guess what she was thinking, remembering her words at Willow Wood when Parson Silas asked him to take over his preaching duties. Preaching was one thing he'd never do. Getting up in front of folks turned his spine yellow. "I don't rightly know yet."

Locke circled the block opposite Annie's house with his blue Navy cap tilted low on his forehead. Minutes earlier, he'd spotted Yates and his companions crossing St. Charles, but they didn't notice him. Probably because he seldom wore his Navy cap, and probably because he blended in with the soldiers moving among the teeming civilians. Had he worn his firm straw hat, like he usually did, he figured Yates would have spotted him instantly and thus, the reason for wearing his cap.

Each evening he'd been allowed liberty he'd come here. Always at night, always keeping across the street, but because of the army's curfew he'd not been able to stay long. So far, he'd only seen Annie, her skinny little servant boy, and sometimes their friends. He'd not seen her parents. She wore mourning clothes. Her little servant boy had lied to him about her being upriver; maybe he lied about her parents too. Maybe they were dead. He hated liars.

Seconds later, she came outside and sat in a rocker, a guitar in her lap. She plucked a plaintive tune. Into the shadows he retreated, on the perimeter of a street lamp's bright range. He watched; he listened. The wench was playing her own funeral. One hour later, she returned inside.

He moved around the street corner and studied the third story's window from across another street. Its crimson drapes were pulled back. Her bedroom, he'd discovered from previous visits. It overlooked the stables and carriage house. A light flickered on. She opened the window, undid her chignon, allowing lustrous locks to smother her narrow shoulders.

Across the street he darted, glanced left and right, and then slipped through the side gate into a garden. The gate squeaked.

"Who's there?" Annie shouted out the window. "I heard you. Who's there?" She searched the garden for movement, a rustle of a rose bush or a figure running down the garden path. Seizing her revolver from off her dressing table, she loaded it the way Jenny taught her. And this time, she got it right. She grabbed her mother's derringer, loaded it, and slipped it in her skirt pocket.

Heart in her throat, she descended the stairs. When she hit the landing, she crouched and peeked over the fainting couch, into the dark hallway below. No sign of anyone. She listened. The house's usual creaks punctuated the silence. No one coming up the gallery steps, but she most certainly did hear her gate squeak. Whoever it was, he was still outside. At the front? In the rear? Gripping her revolver till her knuckles went white, she crept down the staircase's final flight. Which way down the hall to go? Toward Prytania? Or toward the stables and St. Charles?

Steeling herself, she moved toward St. Charles. A glance behind her, out one of the front door's sidelights. No one was watching her. Maybe she was imagining it. Maybe her fear of Locke…*I did hear that gate squeak! I know I did!* She unlocked the rear door, twisted its knob, went down the steps, and entered the moonlight.

24

I NSIDE THE DARKENED stables, Locke flattened his back against the wall beside the doors. The horses in their stalls kicked up a fuss, neighed and whinnied and kicked their stall doors. *Go ahead, animals. Your ruckus will bring her to me.* He breathed easily and waited. He recalled the day she spat on him when he told her he'd killed her brother Ben during the battle below New Orleans. His lips curled. *Tonight is your night. Tonight, you will pay.*

A sound. The doors. Slowly, one door opened. He waited.

"Come out!" Annie cried.

Her voice trembles. Scared? You ought to be.

Annie entered the stables. His eyes, now adjusted to the dark, spotted her pistol. She turned toward him. He sprang upon her, clamped his hand over her mouth, and wrenched her pistol from her before she cocked it. He flung her to the ground. Faster than she could scream, his powerful legs stomped on her neck twice, breaking her hyoid bone, a small piece of anatomy he'd learned from Doctor Kirby. He lifted her limp, lifeless body and carried her out. For good measure, and to be sure he'd adequately broken her neck, he'd drop her from the top of the home's staircase. No one would see him do this. Too dark. Not many people walked the street at this hour, except soldiers.

Peering out a sidelight, Jason spotted a body at the bottom of the back steps lying sideways and dressed in mourning. Her auburn hair fanned from her head and along the grass. No blood. She didn't move. Panic launched him out the door. "Miss Annie! Miss Annie!"

He stooped and grasped her wrist for a pulse that wasn't there. Dead. She was dead! Titus did it, he knew he did it, but he couldn't say that for sure. He had to find a soldier who could maybe help him find who did it. *Her killer's got to pay for what he done. But suppose, suppose he says I did it? Suppose I get hung for somethin' I ain't done?*

"Jason?"

The question sounded from a neighbor.

"Over here, Mistah Dawson. Hurry, sah. Please, sah. Hurry!"

Mister Dawson raced to him. "What's all that screaming?"

"I didn't kill her, sah! Honest, I didn't. I…I just found her."

"Calm yourself. I know you didn't do it." Mister Dawson examined her. He lifted strands of her hair. "She might not have been murdered. I don't see any blood." He started to turn her on her back but didn't. "I'll go get the police. Wait inside. We'll be back."

Mister Dawson vouched for Jason's innocence. Ruled an accident, a stumble down the steps during the night, which broke her neck, he sent the dread news to Philippe's parents downriver and the Inchforths upriver. Next day, the Yankees let a small steamer carry her body to Monmouth for burial. The Westcotts' rector read scripture and preached a short sermon; memories of Annie's fleeting but vibrant life were shared.

The service ended and his sympathies offered, the rector returned to the boat. Annie's friends—Creole, Anglo, and slave—gathered beneath an oak tree outside the family cemetery.

"What will happen to this place?" Jenny said, sniffling.

"It belongs to Ben, that is, if he's still alive," her father said. "If not, then it goes to Moxley. Moxley also gets their Holly Oaks estate upriver."

"He's survived his wounds," Mister Dawson said.

"According to what Moxley told his father, they were serious. Moxley said he was hit twice, chest and shoulder."

"What about Moxley?" Mrs. Inchforth said. "Shouldn't we get word to him?"

"And to my Philippe?" Emerita Soileau said. "Since the Yankees have taken our city, we have received no word from him."

"We do not know where he is," Emerita's husband Louis said.

"Moxley told his father he was going to Mobile," Mister Dawson said.

"Oui. *Merci*," Louis said. "There we will journey. We have friends who live there, and also we will find him. Perhaps we shall also learn our son's whereabouts, and we can deliver him this dreadful news."

While listening to this conversation, Jason's heart was as though it carried a huge hole. *Miss Annie, you was a good lady. Nancy and me, we'll sho' miss you.*

25

FOR A FULL week, Maffitt wandered in and out of consciousness, under the care of Doctor Gilliard from a Spanish gunboat, Doctor Lacasas from Cardenas, and a gunboat's captain. With Stribling still ashore, Alex had assumed command when the clatter of oarlocks pulled him to *Florida's* starboard bulwarks.

A slender man, silhouetted against the bright moonlight, stood in a boat's stern sheets cradling a medical case. His eyes met Alex's. "Might I be correct in saying you lads need a physician's services?" he called out as the boat bumped *Florida's* side. "Me name is Doctor Barrett. I worked in Havana's hospital but since I live in Georgia, Irish though I am born, I figure you lads might need me permanently. Might I be permitted to come aboard?"

"No need to ask that," Alex called back.

"I'll take that as an aye, laddie boy."

"An aye and a thank you. Henson, the gangway."

Henson ran forward to welcome the doctor aboard.

Once Doctor Gilliard returned to his ship for some rest, Doctor Barrett devoted his full attention to *Florida's* crew, doing everything within his power and medical knowledge to save lives, and yet, despite his exhaustive efforts, Yellow Jack attacked five more souls next day.

Upon examining Maffitt, Doctor Lascasas plucked his watch from his vest pocket.

"What are his chances?" Alex asked.

"It is precisely twenty minutes after nine o'clock," Lascasas said, his air formal. "I am convinced, from careful examination, that the captain cannot survive beyond meridian."

His two peers nodded slowly, faces taut.

Doctor Gilliard and the gunboat's captain didn't nod. Instead, their faces glimmered hope.

Maffitt's eyes cracked open. "You're a liar, sir. I have got too much to do and cannot afford to die."

Alex, Wyman, and those gathered around him broke into broad smiles.

"Sir, sir. Welcome back to the living, sir," Wyman said.

"Glad to be back, Mister Wyman."

"Well, *señor*, your chances have greatly improved," Lascasas said. "Send for us again if you need us. Doctor Gilliard will take over from here."

"*Gracias*," Maffitt said.

"*De nada*." Lascasas led his friends topside.

"My advice to you, sir, is that you convalesce before you attempt any more arduous work," Doctor Gilliard said.

"That, doctor, is my full intent."

By next evening, a few hours after dark, Maffitt's mind functioned normally. His eyes shifted back and forth; he turned on his hammock, searched every face gathered near, sailors and officers; brows arched then furrowed; darkness clouded him.

Now he'd have to tell him, Alex told himself. He hated being the bearer of bad news. He searched for a way to answer the question he knew circled inside Maffitt's head.

"Where is?" Maffitt hesitated, his eyes tight with concern. "Where is my beloved son Laurens?"

Alex knelt beside him. Quiet sobs filled the cabin. A sob welled inside Alex, but remembering his father's oft-spoken words during his childhood, that crying and weeping and carrying on was something only women and children did, he held it in. He didn't judge his shipmates for crying, but hard as he might try himself, he couldn't free his own emotions. How would he tell him? "Sir." He spoke tenderly. "While you were unconscious, your Laurens, he got the fever."

"I must see him." Maffitt started to rise from his bed. Gently, Alex shoved him back down.

"He died a few hours ago, sir. We buried him ashore."

Maffitt loosed an anguished scream; it poured from the depths of his heart and filled his cabin's every corner, and as he rolled on his cot and his nose pressured his bulkhead, he heaved and he trembled.

"Please stay with him, Doctor Barret," Alex said. "We don't want him having a relapse."

Doctor Barret nodded gravely.

Alex wondered and worried if and when he'd get it. His hope heightened a little upon Stribling's return. They met with Maffitt in the captain's cabin. The top buttons in his shirt were undone, his beard unkempt. He was still weak and judging from his glassy eyes, Alex figured he still agonized over poor Laurens's death.

Stribling explained his tardiness—getting around the neutrality laws and *Florida's* predicament.

Chills gripped Alex's spine first, next his legs. The cabin spun; his head throbbed; hot pains lanced him from every direction. *Aw!* He wriggled in his chair and tried to sit upright at the same time Stribling delivered a telegram from Governor Serrano, advising him to steam to Havana because of rumors that two Federal gunboats planned to cut out *Florida* from the harbor. He promised two gunboats to escort them.

"A violation of n-neutrality laws," Alex said.

Stribling and Maffitt blurred. Alex whirled and tumbled out of his chair, screaming at the top of his lungs.

1862

SEPTEMBER

26

FEVERISH SWEAT STREAMING, pains excruciating, Alex, muttering, shivered with chills. From his brain's dusky recesses, memories drifted out, then hovered. Beneath them was a landing "over the bay," the home of his father's yachting club. Captain Hughes, Mister Obey, his father, and...

"We'll catch 'em next time, Mister Jessup. That's my solemn guarantee," Captain Hughes said.

"Maybe we can fish farther down the bay next Saturday," his father said.

Hughes stared at Alex. "You will be coming with us as well?"

Alex searched his father's face for some sign he'd allow him to go, but when he didn't detect it, he rammed his hands down his trouser pockets and shifted his feet. "No, sir. Dang it."

Mister Jessup patted Alex's head. "His mother's started complaining about us men taking too many fishing trips."

Hughes shot Alex a knowing look.

"He must study harder anyway if he expects to attend college in a couple of years."

"He ought to give the Navy a go at it, Mister Jessup. Become an officer. Why, the way he handled *Lady Amber* out in the bay today? He's a natural-born sailor, he is. I believe if I let him, he'd sail this girl clear down to Sand Island and back all by his lonesome. Even help us win our next regatta."

Alex blushed. "You've been a mighty good teacher, Uncle Will. Thank you." His eyes shifted to *Lady Amber's* white boat, where Hughes's first mate set a chest atop its stern. He started to dump its contents into the river. "No! Mister Obey! Don't do that! Leroy's still in there. I want to show him to Susan and Susanna."

His cry brought curious glances from people in other boats tied up nearby.

"Obey obeys." The first mate set the chest on the wharf.

"Since when did you give him that name?" Hughes said, chuckling.

"It just came to me all of a sudden, I guess."

"Let's put the chests on the landing." Jessup peered past him, beyond their two-masted steam yacht anchored in deeper water. "Ah, she's on her way."

The bayboat, smoke puffing from her funnel and her paddle wheels churning, slowly approached the dock to carry them, Captain Hughes, and other waiting passengers home. Mister Obey and *Lady Amber's* crew lived on this side of the bay, called the Eastern Shore. They'd not accompany them.

Hughes gave the order. Two of his men carried Leroy's chest onto the bayboat soon after it pulled up alongside.

Mary Hamilton, two years older than Susan and Susanna, clutched her doll while the twins scoured its clovers. "Silly sillies," she said. "There's no such a thing as a four-leaf clover."

"Is too," Susan snapped.

"Is not."

"Hush up."

Frowning, engrossed in her search, Susanna's fingertips brushed the clover patch.

Alex grinned. *My, oh my, that Mary's sure starting to get the looks.* He nudged his father as their wagon clattered through their wrought iron gate. "There she goes, pestering Susan and Susanna again."

"I'll speak with Mister Hamilton," Mister Jessup said, "and this time, he'd better make Mary stop."

"She'll just start up again when he goes back upriver." His eyes followed Mary, strutting around his sisters. He wondered if she'd still have the same good looks when she got courting age.

"I may be a cotton factor and he may be a client, but if you ask me, son, that man owns too many plantations. His family likes living in this city. He needs to spend more time with them. Yellow fever season will be here before we know it. We all need to be getting ready to move up to Spring Hill in a couple of weeks."

Huston dispatched a servant to drive the wagon around back.

"Mary Hamilton," Mister Jessup said sharply, "you'd best get on home."

Chin high, Mary marched down the carriageway. From her lawn next door, she observed them through her iron-railed fence's grille.

Susanna plucked a clover.

Clutching her doll by one of its arms, Susan did the same.

"Sillies! Sillies!" Mary poked out her tongue.

Susan marched to the fence. "Stop talking to us that way. There is too such a thing as a four-leaf clover, and when one of us finds it, you wait and see how lucky we get."

"Mary Agnes." This time, Mister Jessup's tone sounded a warning.

"Aw, Mary Agnes Hamilton. I'm disappointed in you. I thought you were smart." Alex's grin widened.

"I'm smart enough to know there's no such a thing as a four-leaf clover."

"How do you know there's no such a thing? Because you've never seen one before?"

"Never seen one, and my big brother told me they don't exist."

"John Stephen told you that? Aw, your brother may be big, but he doesn't know everything."

"Does too."

"Does not," Susan said.

"Aw, Mary. Don't get your dander all ruffled. What I meant was he doesn't know anything about four-leaf clovers. Let's you and me think about it. Just because you haven't seen one and somebody told you they don't exist doesn't mean it's true. Have you ever seen Leroy before?"

"Who's Leroy?" Mary said

"A sea monster I caught over near the Blakeley River today."

"There's no such a thing as a sea monster."

"Aw, now. You're only saying that because you've never seen one before, and because you've never seen one, you believe they don't exist."

Eyes twinkling, the servant whom Huston dispatched after the wagon waited at its horses.

"Come on back over and we'll show you." Alex's father waved her back to their side of the fence. "Be careful, though, honey. He bites."

"Humbug." Mary's cautious approach betrayed her bravado.

Susan and Susanna dropped their dolls and hurried to the wagon bed.

Alex and his father nudged each other. His father closed the chest's lid before he set it on the grass.

Her tense eyes fastened on the chest, Mary drew a deep breath.

Alex cracked open its lid, slammed it shut, and pulled a face. "No, sir. I can't. He'll bite Mary."

"Show me," Mary said, stammering. "I'm...I'm not scared."

"Are you sure?"

"Show me!"

Alex glanced at his father. "All right, but don't say Father and I didn't warn you." Simultaneously, he popped open the lid and Mister Jessup tapped Mary's shoulder. She nearly jumped clean to the clouds before she squealed home.

Alex's sisters burst into laughter.

"What's all this?" Mrs. Jessup called from the front doorway.

"Mary Agnes pestering our daughters again, dear," Mister Jessup said.

"That girl best quit." She hastened to them. "Both of you smell like fish. Go take your baths."

"Smelling like fish is all part of the sport, dear."

"You won't be fishing again next Saturday, will you?" she snapped. "*Romeo and Juliet.* Remember? You promised you'd take me to see it.'

His father's shoulders slumped.

Alex's spirits sagged. *Father's forgotten he'd promised to take Mother to the theater. Now neither one of us can go.*

Susanna peered into the chest. "Leroy's just a turtle. Mary's never seen a turtle before?"

"Sure she has," Alex said. "She just got so scared at all those notions father and I put inside her head she didn't bother looking at him. She just assumed this fellow would bite her if she got too close."

"You see, girls," Mister Jessup said, "Mary believes everything she hears, and I don't want my sweet daughters being that way. Make up your own minds about things no matter what other folks say because what other folks say isn't always right."

"Is there such a thing as a four-leaf clover, Father?" Susanna said.

Alex's mother rested her hand on Susanna's shoulder. She studied the yard a moment. Then brightened. "Why, Susanna, I do think I see a four-leafer." She plucked it, brought it to her eyes, and counted its leaves. "Oh, humbug! I'm mistaken. This one's a three-leafer. While our menfolk take their baths, I'll help my girls search. Four-leafers do exist, but they are quite rare."

Susan went to the fence. Hands cupped around her mouth, she shouted, "Scared the sea monster's going to bite, Mary? Scared the sea monster's going to bite? Scared the...?"

Their mother laughed.

Alex's eyes cracked open. The fiery sun pounded his head. Enfeebled, he dragged himself along *Florida's* quarterdeck to her port side. His childhood episodes evaporating from the stage of his mind, he was, thankfully, back among the living. Squinting against sunrays glancing off the dark water's undulations, he struggled as he forced himself up high enough to peek over the taffrail and ascertain their position and perhaps determine how long he'd been unconscious.

He gazed beyond *Florida's* bows. In the distance, about three miles of water separated two specks flying what looked like Confederate flags. Forts. Trees. His fever's fog slowly dissipated. *Weren't there a few trees near that fort east of me? At one time? The dunes. No more?* Westward, he recognized Dauphin Island and the speck rising from the sands, Fort Gaines, on its easternmost end. Opposite Fort Gaines, at the westernmost tip of a peninsula overlooking the bay's channel was Mobile Point. He recognized its lighthouse and the other speck rising. A giant sandhill. No. The hill was Fort Morgan. Soldiers must have cut down the trees and leveled the dunes around it. Several more specks, probably buildings, stood outside it. And that outermost island with its lighthouse, it had to be... "Sand Island. Mobile Bay. Susan, I'm home. Your smart brother's home." His face twisted. Another stab lanced his back.

"Glad you're back with us, Mister Jessup."

Stribling's strong voice prompted a grateful smile. The executive officer assisted him past sick sailors sprawled on the deck, moaning and muttering delirious nonsense and receiving Doctor Barrett's medicine. They descended the hatch to Maffitt's cabin.

Maffitt gripped his sleeping quarters' doorjamb, peered out at them, blinked back sweat as he stumbled to his desk.

Alex collapsed cross-legged before him. Stribling recounted the ship's recent adventures and misfortunes: six men dead to date; twelve more he'd recruited at Cardenas; also Doctor Barrett, who'd resigned from Havana's hospital and remained aboard. Five nights ago, they'd slipped out of Cardenas when Yankee gunboats mistook a Spanish mail steamer leaving port for them and took out after her. The next day, in Havana, a fellow Confederate named Smith told Stribling only one Yankee ship blockaded Mobile, which information he'd relayed to Maffitt.

"We couldn't find seamen in Havana. The fever season." Slumped in his chair, pale and frail, Maffitt spoke heavily, like shoveling words off his tongue. "We hugged the coastline until we reached the sea. Took us a...about four days to get here."

"We're flying British colors and pennant," Stribling said. "Unfortunately, Smith was mistaken. Two Yankees are standing off the bay. I cannot say how long our ruse will work."

Maffitt touched his furrowed forehead. "We're going in today."

"During daylight, sir?" Stribling said, alarmed. "Broad daylight? They'll blow us out of the water. We would be wiser slipping in at night. I didn't see a channel marker."

"Which is the precise reason why we're going in before sundown." Maffitt wriggled and straightened in his chair. "We'll have our ship charged with explosives, Mister Stribling, in case we have to blow her up."

"Aye, sir," Stribling said.

"Sir, I've fished this bay for years," Alex said. "I know where all the sandbars are."

"As do I, Mister Jessup," Maffitt said. "Stribling, my limbs have mutinied against me. Please assist me topside and secure me to the quarter rail. I'll direct our ship from there."

Stribling looked at Alex.

"I'll manage," Alex said.

Leaning against the bulkhead for support, Alex followed Stribling and Maffitt back into the scorching afternoon sun. After Stribling helped Maffitt to the quarter rail, he strode forward in search of a rope.

Maffitt's glassy eyes wandered toward two quartermasters slumped against the mainmast. He gestured at them. "Bellups, Sharkey, stand by at the wheel. We're charging into the bay."

The petty officers trudged to the ship's wheel.

"Well, Mister Jessup, looks like this is it."

"I wish I was healthy enough to do more, sir," Alex said.

"Jack must be a Yankee."

Alex stumbled back to the port taffrail. Stribling whipped the rope around Maffitt's body and the quarter rail, finishing it off with two half hitches.

"Mister Stribling," Maffitt said, "have the men prepared our charges as I ordered?"

Stribling nodded. "They're doing it now, sir."

"Well then, signal the engine room. 'Full speed ahead.'"

Stribling rang the engine room's bell.

Smoke billowing and her British colors flying, *Florida* steamed straight for a Yankee warship, a ten-gun vessel just over a mile away.

Alex gaped. *Aw! We're going to ram her.*

Signal flags raced up the Yankee's peak. The second Yankee ship joined the pursuit. And another one!

Captain Maffitt, you're obviously no coward, Alex thought. *Let's hope you're not a dang nincompoop.*

Soldiers raced out Fort Morgan's sally port onto her dry moat, gaining speed as they rounded a bastion. The fort's fastest runner, Moxley passed his comrades up narrow concrete steps onto an outer rampart, passed a hot shot furnace, and halted at a 32-pounder in front of the lighthouse. Other men manned batteries on the glacis and the rampart guns. Down their lines, orders reverberated: "Sponge!" "Ram!" "Wait for my order!" "Hold fire!"

Behind the battery, Captain Whittaker followed events through binoculars—a single ship flying British colors was making for the bay. "By thunder! That British ship's going to ram her! No. That big Yankee... I think...yes! She's backing up!"

To Moxley's naked eyes, the ships resembled large dots racing along the water. The vessel flying British colors kept her course, forcing the Yankee to reverse her engines to avoid the British ship charging her broadside. Two other ships steamed off the larger ship's port side.

A distant boom echoed.

"The Yank's fired a shot across her bow," Whittaker said.

Two more booms echoed, followed by a thundering salvo.

"Two more shots across her bow." Whittaker's voice crescendoed. "A broadside! Point-blank range!"

"Why doesn't she fire back?" Moxley said.

"She may not have guns." Corporal Riggs readied the cannon's sponge.

"I think I may see them aboard," Whittaker said. "Something's wrong."

Up the bay, Moxley observed other ships which had spotted the chase. *Lady Amber* he identified by her fore and aft masts, short funnel with a broad yellow band circling it, and bright red taffrails and deckhouse. They were moving in closer to watch.

Colonel William Powell, commander of the lower bay's defenses, followed events from the bastion overlooking their position.

"The Yanks are trying to cut her off," Whittaker said.

Huddled against the quarterdeck's port bulwarks, his head swimming, Alex lifted his eyes at Sinclair and Bradford running forward. They smacked the deck flat on their faces when a thundering broadside swept away hammocks and running rigging.

"Starboard helm." Maffitt's hoarse command was calm.

"Starboard helm. Aye." Stribling relayed this to Bellups and Sharkey.

Alex staggered to the ship's wheel when a shell shattered the rail behind him but didn't explode. Shots smacked *Florida's* masts. Explosions near her boats and over her deck—wood and shrapnel—sprayed like buckshot. One chunk of wood whizzed inches past his shoulder.

They'd passed the ten-gun ship, and Maffitt's order for a "starboard helm" had brought her and the second ship in line astern.

"English ensign. Haul down." Maffitt forced power into his feeble voice. "Stars and Bars, Mister Jessup. Stars and Bars."

Alex stumbled over some sick sailors on his way to the signal halyards, joined by Brownleaf and Henson. They hauled down the British ensign; the halyards slipped off their blocks.

"Reeve them again. Fast." Shrapnel hit the deck a few feet behind Alex. He stumbled to the flag locker, bent down while splinters stung his cheeks. Chest heaving, he paused, grasped a fresh ounce of strength, then broke out their country's ensign.

Steadily, quickly, Henson and Brownleaf obeyed Alex's order. Once again, the signal halyards ran up the ensign on the spanker gaff. Fort Morgan's guns boomed. Great gushes of dark spray splashed behind them and around their enemy, but despite the fort's supporting fire the Yankees tightened the distance.

"Hands aloft!" A surge of strength overwhelmed his frailness. Suddenly realizing he'd given an order without Maffitt's approval, Alex looked over at his captain, bound and slumped against the quarter rail.

Maffitt nodded. "Send every able man aloft. Loose topsails and topgallants."

Alex's knees wobbled. He crumpled onto the quarterdeck. Looking up at the sailors shuffling along the yards, casting off gaskets and loosening sails, everything spun around him faster, faster…whirling.

Yankee guns unleashed with renewed fury. Shrapnel splattered the yards and shot away the standing rigging. *Florida's* men scurried back down ratlines. One man hit the deck, writhing and gripping his wounded leg. Another man staggered forward, his shoulder spurting blood. Doctor Barrett scurried from one injured man to the next, his examinations quick.

"Stribling," Maffitt said, "every man below except officers and helmsmen. Have our wounded taken to the wardroom."

"I'll get them below!" Doctor Barrett shouted over salvos.

Stribling's speaking trumpet touched his lips. "Henson, Brownleaf, help Doctor Barrett."

The men zigzagged between explosions.

"Sharkey, Bellups, keep your station," Stribling barked again through his trumpet. "All other hands—below!"

Alex doubled over. The freshening wind increased *Florida's* speed. It was as though a thousand crabs dug their pincers into him. Eyes squeezed, he screamed. A shell smashed *Florida's* coal bunker, and Yellow Jack's fiendish fist smashed Alex's world back into blackness.

27

THE NEXT DAY, a mail steamer from New Orleans pulled in among Commodore Hitchcock's squadron blockading Mobile Bay and lashed alongside *Oneida*. Commander Preble delivered his report of the previous day's action for the admiral, presently anchored in Pensacola Bay. Since Hitchcock and his *Susquehanna* were also at Pensacola, command of the Mobile station had devolved upon him, which made him responsible for what had transpired.

In his cabin, Farragut heard the mail steamer drop anchor. He awaited Captain James Palmer, who'd assumed command of *Hartford* ten days ago, to bring him his mail.

Farragut rifled the dispatches.

"Sir, with your permission?" Palmer said.

Farragut placed the dispatches in Palmer's outstretched hand.

The first dispatch Palmer handed Gabaudan.

"This one's from Commander Preble." Gabaudan folded it in half and looked up, concerned.

"What is it?" Farragut said.

"Sir— "

"Read it," Palmer said. "Out loud."

Gabaudan unfolded the dispatch and started reading. "Sir, I regret having to inform you that a 3-masted screw steamer, bearing an English red ensign and pennant, and carrying four quarter boats and a battery of six or eight broadside guns and one or two pivots, and having every appearance of an English man-of-war, ran the blockade this afternoon under the following circumstances."

Gabaudan hesitated.

Farragut shut his eyes. "Read on."

The clerk did.

Another defeat. Farragut's spirits sank. Preble's report recounted the details: how Preble got *Oneida* underway when the *Florida* bore down on him, how he signaled *Winona* to chase her "at discretion."

"We soon neared the stranger in company with the *Winona*," Gaubaudan continued reading, "who, as we approached him, gradually hauled to the northward and westward. When abeam of him, about 100 yards distant, I hailed him, but receiving no answer, I fired a shot across his bow.'"

Shot across his bows? You were close to him, Preble. He didn't stop when you hailed him. Why didn't you fire at him? Why didn't you sink him?

"He ranged ahead without stopping, but still thinking he was an English man-of-war, I fired two more shots across his bows, and then directed a shot at him, which unfortunately went over between his fore and mainmasts." Gaubadan cleared his throat.

Yes, of course. That's why you didn't try sinking him at first. You kept thinking he was a British ship. Farragut gestured at Gaubadan.

Gaubadan resumed reading. "We continued firing at him, assisted by the *Winona* and one of the mortar schooners, but he made sail, and by his superior speed and audacity managed to escape."

Farragut lifted his palm. Gabaudan ceased reading.

"Secretary Welles won't like this news," Gabaudan said.

"George Preble's a fine officer," Farragut said. "He commanded the *Katahdin* during our operations around Vicksburg. I refuse to believe the Rebel's success was all his fault."

"Had not the Rebel been flying the British ensign, sir," Palmer said, "Preble wouldn't have hesitated."

Farragut gestured them to leave.

Elbows on his desk, his palms pressured his forehead. He hated seeing a good officer's career ruined by something like this. He would recommend a censure, but not dismissal from the service. Had she been a British man-of-war and had Preble sunk her, they might have another Trent Affair and another war on their hands—against Great Britain. He must be careful how he worded his letter to Secretary Welles. He'd think about it first before he sent for Gabaudan.

28

SUSAN SORTED LETTERS in the post office's back room. This new job didn't pay much, but she hoped it eased Uncle Will's financial burden. He seemed appreciative that she found this employment as it let him keep all the Army's salary for himself and his crew. Uncle Will needed a new cap. He'd been wearing that same old black one since she and Alex were little. Maybe she'd buy him one.

The ladies working alongside her prattled endlessly about the war, their husbands and sons and male relatives and friends and beaus. Since she'd come here, she'd heard complaints about the Postal Department's inefficiencies. Such complaints held merit. Her father's last two letters, written on both sides of old envelopes, arrived in the wrong order. The first one she received, dated the tenth of August, described a battle fought the previous day at Cedar Mountain, Virginia. They'd suffered over a thousand casualties and would've lost the fight had not General A.P. Hill's division come up in time to mount a successful counterattack. Thus far, thankfully, he'd survived every battle without a scratch.

The second letter, dated the tenth of June, recounted their victory at Port Republic in the Shenandoah Valley. "Our General Jackson's a strange one," he'd written. "Some of our boys consider him eccentric, others swear he's insane, but I guess all geniuses like him are a bit crazy. He's a religious fanatic, doesn't drink liquor or use tobacco, sucks on lemons, and lives like the lowest privates. All I've ever seen him eat is corn bread, butter, and milk. I tell you, daughter, I don't care how strange the man is. I'd follow him anywhere. He's no coward, nor does he tolerate cowardice, and he can sure whip the blue-bellies anytime, anywhere."

Based upon August's letter and newspaper reports, they'd chased the Yankees clean out of the Valley and rejoined Lee's army.

"Miss Jessup?" The postmaster poked his head through the opened door. "Someone's looking for you. He says he's your Uncle Will. Urgent, he says."

Susan hastened out the room.

The moon glow skimming dark, rippling water guided *Lady Amber* along Mobile Bay. Susan's distress shut out the yacht's noisy engine. Bitter memories swamped her while helplessness sapped her strength. That terrible day Susanna took sick, that hour she died, one month after Alex brought home that silly turtle.

"Do You see me here, God, going out to see my brother?" she said, hissing. "Well, I'm still alive, aren't I? And Alex better still be alive when we get out to his ship. Do You hear me? I'm warning You, God."

Her stateroom door opened. "Not much longer, Susan," Mister Obey said. "Captain Hughes says we'll be there within an hour. The *Florida's* anchored off Melrose. We got that piece of information from the *Morgan* earlier today."

"Thank you, Mister Obey. Leave me, please, and keep my door locked. I will not be disturbed till we reach Alex's ship."

"Obey obeys, miss."

"That's a stale joke, and this is not the time for humor."

"Of course. My apologies." Obey backed out, his footsteps fading.

Susan collapsed beside her bunk and clasped her hands beneath her chin. The whitewashed bulkhead swam before her; images flashed across her troubled mind.

Prostrate on her bedroom floor, praying and crying her heart out to God during Susanna's three days of illness. The hallway creaking beneath her pacing mother's footfalls; billiard balls smacking each other, her father working out his frustrations and fears; and Alex nervously tossing his cast net time and again across the front lawn, every night and every day for three days. Everyone, including her family's servants, all their prayers encompassed her sister. No one ate.

The mansion's doors and columns, draped in black crepe. Susanna's funeral. Somber friends and Mary Hamilton, her face twisted with agony, taking Susan's hand. "Can you ever forgive me, Susan? I'm sorry for the ways I pestered and teased you and…and…dear Su…" She choked on her sister's name.

Susan wrenching her hand free. "I hate you, Mary." Glaring at the headstones and tombs, large and small, rising around her. "You don't love me, God. You killed my sister. I'll always hate You. You had no right."

Six months passed. Her mother's constant complaints about Huston, the other servants, her need of a maid.

Fannie joining their household. Hatred brewing between them; Susan wielding her mother's whip; Fannie snatching it from her. "Want to know what a whip feels like, l'il girl? I'll show you what it feels like." She popped it.

Susan, dodging behind a chair.

Downstairs stormed her mother after a long afternoon nap, seizing it from Fannie and whipping her hard. Fannie's wincing, a little cringing and gritting of the teeth, but no wails or frightened screams, which angered her mother more.

"Alex better not die, else I'll—"

Why do you hate?

Susan started. The gentle voice touched her heart unbidden.

"Life's hard. I have a right to hate."

Everyone's life is hard.

"Not as hard as mine."

Men are dying in a horrible war while you're safe and sound at home. Do you call their lives easy?

"There shouldn't be wars. Men shouldn't be dying."

Wars are a terrible thing that ought not to be. That is true. I hate wars, dear Susan, the same as you do. But wars are fought because mankind is sinful, because I give men a choice of who they'll follow. Death is the wages of sin, my dear. My Son suffered for your sins, for mankind's sins. He didn't have to die for you, but He did because He loves You. He was nailed to a cross outside Jerusalem. He bled and died for the whole world. For you, Susan Jessup. He died for you.

"Susanna died because she was sinful?"

I love your sister. And I love you.

"Oh no, You don't. I heard all that claptrap when my father made me go to church and sent me to that awful Judson Female Institute up in Marion. He thought I needed a little religion, but it didn't work, did it? I don't believe a word your Book says. Not a single 'thee' or 'thou' either."

"Pardon me, Susan." Obey poked his head inside her stateroom. "We're approaching the *Florida*."

Susan went out onto *Lady Amber's* white deck.

Lady Amber's anchor splashed alongside the shot-riddled ship. A lantern hanging from *Florida's* bowsprit cast a jaundiced glow over the dark water; another lantern, atop a cask on her quarterdeck, flickered. By these lights and heaven's candles, Susan gasped at the vessel's damage. Only three of her shrouds, silhouetted against the evening light, appeared intact. Dark holes pocked her groaning hull; her battered masts creaked. Some twenty or thirty yards astern, another ship was anchored.

Susan squeezed *Lady Amber's* rail, whitening her knuckles and telegraphing tension clear up through her shoulders. What more would she see when the sun rose?

A man peered at them from the shattered midships rail. "I wouldn't lay in too close, mate. We have the fever on board. We're quarantined."

"I'm aware of that," Hughes called back from beside Susan. "I was here earlier, as you recall."

"Oh, the captain of the *Lady Amber*, are you?"

"Yes. You were formerly the *Oreto*, out of Nassau. That is what your Lieutenant Stribling told me upon my inquiry earlier today when I came up alongside. I inquired whether young Jessup was aboard."

"I remember."

"What is that ship astern?"

"The *Areal*, sir. Admiral Buchanan dispatched her here yesterday. She's a hospital ship. All our poor sick lads are aboard her."

"And your name, sir?"

"Henson, formerly of Her Majesty Queen Victoria's Navy."

Another man poked his head over *Florida's* rail. "Me name is Doctor Barrett, miss. Ship's surgeon. Who might your brother be?" His speech was slow and somewhat slurred, a clear sign he was exhausted.

"Alexander Jessup," Susan said.

A long pause delayed the surgeon's response. "He's still alive, Miss Jessup, but I fear he cannot talk."

Susan's heart lurched. "Can't talk? Why not?"

"He's unconscious."

"What are his chances?"

"I'm sorry, miss. I've just returned from the *Areal* for a catnap. I've been working nearly around the clock for almost a week. Me body, miss, demands rest." The surgeon tapped Henson's shoulder and they withdrew.

Susan hurried back to her stateroom and hurled herself onto her knees. If he was unconscious and the doctor didn't care to answer her last question... *God! God! God! This is Your last chance. You... let... my... brother... live.*

29

ON THE FOURTH day of September, after scoring another victory at Manassas, Virginia in late August, Robert E. Lee's Army of Northern Virginia started crossing the Potomac River and headed north into Maryland.

General Jackson's columns entered Frederick, Maryland on the sixth. Captain Randall Bartlett, Annie's former beau, and Lieutenants Billy Watkins and Richard Adkins walked Frederick's main street together ahead of their company, the Bartlett Rifles. Only half of them remained since before the war started; the other half killed or recovering from wounds in a Richmond hospital; others dead of illness.

Their tattered, hodgepodge uniforms dirty, and many without shoes, the victorious Rebels didn't look much like soldiers as they passed through the town. Pretty uniforms like the Yankees wore didn't make a soldier, these men knew. Good soldiers knew how to fight, and fighting they'd mastered well.

Randall surveyed the citizens lining the street. A handful of men scattered amidst hundreds of ladies and children. Somber, dour, defiant, indifferent, many with arms folded and a few brave souls holding Union flags. Several men sauntered across the street ahead of them. Another man pulled up alongside Adkins and spat tobacco at his feet. Three boys and two yapping dogs ran past. A cat, curled up, napped on a bench. A smattering of Confederate flags poked up through the crowd, hardly the rousing reception they'd anticipated.

"I expected we'd find recruits here," Randall said.

Saber jangling on his hip, Billy indicated a lady hurrying into a shuttered shop. "I have a sneaking suspicion most of these folks here don't much like us."

"They're Southerners," Adkins said. "They ought to be ashamed of themselves, not welcoming us."

"Fact is, they're not," Randall said. "Wherever we're going and whatever we're doing, I hope we get it over with fast. I don't enjoy being treated like this."

"It'd sure be considerate of General Jackson not to always be so secret about everything," Adkins said.

"So long as his tactics keep working, 'Old Jack' can do whatever he wants," Billy said.

"He's a general," Randall said. "He can do whatever he wants anyway." He glanced at their company behind them. Its bearing and spirit was as confident and unconquerable as Caesar's legions. Unlike many regiments in Lee's army, his men were glad to enter the state and take the fight to the enemy.

Guilt nagged Randall. Ever since Billy and Jenny's wedding a year ago, it bothered him every now and then. He'd lied at their wedding when he let it be known he'd found a new girl at Richmond and Billy and Adkins, of course, weren't in on the lie. They thought he'd gotten over the hurt of Annie's rejection, and he wanted them to keep thinking it lest word drifted back to Jenny who would tell Annie the truth. He didn't want Annie feeling badly about what she'd done. He shoved the thought to the back of his mind. Maybe this would be the day he died, or the next day or the next.

Hoofbeats lifted Randall's eyes. Colonel Jessup, Alex's father, cantered his dun horse toward them. Though not as slender as a rail, the war had shrunk his formerly great girth. He was riding toward his regiment at the column's rear.

"What news, Colonel?" Randall called out to him.

Jessup reined in alongside. "We're halting here today."

"That's all you know, sir?"

"We'll learn our dispositions soon enough." He tipped his mud-splattered gray hat. "Back to my boys, gentlemen." He spurred his mount into a canter.

30

Forehead on her forearm, draped across her bunk, Susan prayed, her tumultuous soul tossing as it once did when she'd prayed for Susanna. All night she prayed, through turbulent, sleepless exhaustion.

"I shouldn't hate You, God," she muttered between bitter laughs. "I gave You Your chance. I was a fool to hate You all these years. Why, I don't believe in You at all."

I am here.

Susan started at the firm, gentle voice, the voice which had spoken to her hours earlier.

I died for you, dear one. I died for Susanna.

Sergeant Nathan's words returned, his insistence that God did love her and the dogwood cross he made for her last year while he stayed at Miss Evans's hospital as a reminder, and that psalm she'd read. "My God, My God, why have You forsaken me?" Her voice was hoarse when she repeated the psalmist's words to herself.

I haven't forsaken you.

An image slowly took shape—a man hanging on that cross. "Jesus," she gasped.

A crown of thorns sat upon His head; blood streamed down His cheeks and His lips and streaked His naked body. Then His head moved and His kind, compassionate eyes settled upon her, and she trembled. He saw right through her, her every thought, every motive, every word. Yet it was love which came forth from Him, pure, absolute love.

Her groaning chest heaved in and out, racked by pain, washed by His love. Again and again, waves of compassion splashed over her, each splash chipping away the hardness which encased her. Small chunks fell off first, followed by larger and larger chunks. Her sins flashed through her mind, her coldness, her hate, the times she whipped Fannie unmercifully, trying harder and harder to whack the stubbornness out of her, to make her wail and beg.

I died for all men and women, Susan. It's true. Very true. All I ask is that you turn away from your sins and believe. Will you do this for Me? Will you do it for you?

"And Alex, God. What about Alex and Father?"

Her stateroom door opened.

Susan scrambled to her feet. "Uncle Will?"

Hughes raised a boisterous hurrah. "He's regained consciousness! Our Alex has regained consciousness! Doctor Barrett says he'll recover!"

Fort Morgan's soldiers spent Saturday morning cleaning their quarters for Sunday inspection. In the afternoon, they relaxed. Moxley often relaxed outside the fort, where he spent his time thinking, watching and listening to the surf wash up, observing fiddler crabs scurrying every which way save toward him, and seagulls cackling, flying, swooping. A lot of contemplation time these days, especially on weekends, especially in the afternoons, especially about Susan. He tried not to think about Notasulga's Camp of Instruction. Its training had bored him, and he was glad that part of his life was over. Since every regiment there was being sent to Mobile, he'd hoped he'd serve on one of the batteries near the city. He'd have been able to see Susan more often, but Fort Morgan also needed men. Thus, he contented himself knowing that things could have been far worse had he been sent to a military department in another state.

The day after *Florida's* dash, Moxley learned her identity. He grabbed a fistful of sand and spread his fingers, allowing it to slip down between them. He had a great big hole in his heart. He needed Susan. He regretted he didn't have a small daguerreotype of her or a remembrance of some sort.

"Westcott." First Sergeant Ferguson's shrill voice blared from the doorway of the fort's telegraph station.

On his feet, Moxley received the telegram Ferguson thrust into his hand.

"Someone in Mobile's asking to see you. They claim it's urgent."

Moxley scanned its content: "Monsieur Westcott, please meet us at the Battle House Hotel tomorrow morning. My wife and I, I fear, have news of a most serious nature. Monsieur Louis Soileau."

"I'll get you a pass," Ferguson's shrill voice continued. Shrillness was his voice's natural tone, which grew shriller when he was angry. "I'll wire them back that you're on your way. There's a vessel heading toward us from up the bay now. She'll take you to Mobile. I'll obtain Captain Whittaker's permission for a Sunday furlough, and Monday if you need it. I'm sure he won't mind, seeing this is important and all that."

"Right."

Moxley ran back to his quarters for a few things. How did the Soileaus discover he was in the Army and stationed at Fort Morgan? Had Ben died in prison? Had Philippe been killed? He refused to believe any of that.

Moxley dove through the Battle House's entrance and accidentally knocked a porter against the wall. Up the left side of a curved staircase he raced, threading hotel guests, pounding into the second floor's huge lobby. From person to person his eyes darted. The Soileaus called his name.

Emerita Soileau crossed the tile floor and enveloped him in a warm motherly hug.

"I am deeply regretful, Monsieur Moxley," her husband Louis said. *Called me Moxley? That was the first time he'd done that.* "Ben's died."

"*Non*, he has not died as far as we are aware. Your parents and your sister, I fear to say to you, they are d—"

"Don't lie."

Emerita parted from him. "We are not lying. They are— "

"Dead," Louis said.

Moxley turned away, fighting his tears, and pounded his fist in his palm.

"We might have come sooner," Louis said, "had not our carriage broken an axle in Mississippi and had not our train jumped the track. Come. Let us go outside. Let us talk."

Emerita steered Moxley back down the lobby stairs and out the door. His mind misted. His parents, Annie, Ben. Was he the only family member left alive? *Not fair!* He shouldn't have left New Orleans like a coward. He should've stayed there, defended them.

During their somber walk, Louis explained how they'd found him. Guessing he'd try to get hired by a newspaper, he'd first approached editors about him, and they referred him to Miss Evans, who told them he'd joined the Army and was at Fort Morgan. Then they recounted his parents' deaths and Annie's.

"A fall," Louis said. "That is how the authorities believe she died. Emerita and I are regretful. Sincerely so."

Moxley steeled himself. "Philippe knows about this?"

"His army is somewhere in Tennessee, according to the papers. We have received no letters since the Yankees came. A friend lives here. Their only son was killed somewhere in north Alabama. Emerita and I are staying with them. We will remain here as long as you need us."

"Shouldn't you get word to Philippe?"

"We shall tell him," Emerita said, "only after this war has passed."

"We considered taking the train and trying to find him," Louis said, "but then we decided it was best not to do it. He is burdened enough by the war. We want him back home alive."

"Knowledge of Annie's death might contribute to his death in battle," Emerita said.

"What's the time?" Moxley said.

Louis consulted his watch. "It is nearly ten-thirty."

"Y'all go on back to New Orleans." He started past them. "I'll be fine."

"Where are you going?" Emerita said.

"To a place I haven't visited in a long time. Church."

"We will attend Mass," Louis said. "Emerita and I will pray for you."

Hands in his pockets, Moxley headed the opposite direction. *One more hypocrite, on his way to hear a boring sermon with other hypocrites.* He could've stopped those Yankees from killing his parents. He could've protected Annie. Smart he was, moving here. *Real smart, Moxley, you big tomfool.* He made his way to the first Episcopal church he saw.

31

ALEX HAD A boatswain, as yet unaffected by the fever, pipe aboard *Florida* the Mobile Squadron's newly appointed commander, Admiral Franklin Buchanan. Also, Lieutenant commanding Maffitt, still weak but on the mend, early in the afternoon.

Buchanan was the former commander of the James River Squadron, his flagship the ironclad CSS *Virginia*. During the first day's fighting in Hampton Roads, Virginia, he suffered a wound that prevented him from leading the battle against the Union ironclad *Monitor* on the action's second day, but his boldness that first day won him a promotion to his current rank. The admiral's wound caused his limp.

Before the war, he was the Navy's most prominent officer. Alex had remembered tales about him at the Naval Academy. He'd been its first superintendent, a no-nonsense officer who never faltered in matters of discipline, particularly regarding drinking and smoking. It was also rumored that before Congress outlawed flogging, he'd preferred it over other disciplinary measures. Judging by his taut, downturned lips and dour demeanor, Alex didn't doubt those tales were true.

The admiral limped aft.

"Where is Stribling?" Maffitt asked.

Alex clutched the ship's logbook tighter.

"I asked you a question, Mister Jessup."

"The forecastle, sir. Mister Stribling's caught it."

Maffitt groaned as though he'd had the wind knocked out of him. "Sinclair?"

"Worse, I'm afraid."

Maffitt searched the warm, pure blue sky as though seeking a sign. His attention shifted to the forecastle where Doctor Barrett administered medicine to young Sinclair, pale and slumped against a shot rack. They hastened there. Maffitt still stumbled, but not as often. Alex thought his recruiting trip ashore might have done him some good.

"I won't stay aboard long," Buchanan said. "Captain, muster your crew. I'll address them briefly."

"Mister Bradford," Maffitt said, "have the crew mustered on the quarterdeck."

"Aye aye, sir." Bradford saluted.

"Captain Maffitt! Cap...Captain... Ma...Maffitt!" Stribling shoved Doctor Barrett's hand aside. "Help me, Captain! Don't leave me, Captain! Medicine! Med...Medicine! Captain! Captain! Where are you? I can't see you! Help!"

Maffitt dropped beside him. "It's going to be all right, Mister Stribling. I'm back aboard now." Tenderly, he lifted Stribling's head and gave him Doctor Barrett's medicine. His eyes shut and his lips quivered as though saying a prayer.

Lieutenant Wyman approached Alex solemnly. "It's my time to go on watch, sir."

Alex opened the logbook. Short of watch officers due to disease, Wyman and a few others had been forced to assume the duties. He signed off on the logbook beneath his notes.

"Signal the *Areal* to lower a boat, Mister Jessup," Maffitt said. "We'll send Misters Stribling and Sinclair to her."

Alex plodded toward the signal halyards. The eighth day of September. His birthday. He looked back at his poor, suffering shipmates. It wasn't fair, Jack attacking them. *Happy miserable birthday to me. Cheers.*

32

OXLEY MADE CHURCH too late to hear the rector's full homily. Bits and pieces of it tumbled through his troubled thoughts. Susan would listen to him; they'd spill their hearts to each other. She'd lost only one sibling whereas he'd possibly lost two and his parents.

He trudged up Susan's carriageway and the gallery steps. Before he could pull the brass doorbell's cord, she dashed out. Clasped hands uplifted, she almost glowed.

"Oh, Mister Westcott! Susanna's in heaven! My Alex, he's alive!"

Numb, Moxley stared at her.

Her hands dropped into her blue-and-white checkered hoop skirt. "What's wrong?"

"My parents and sister are dead."

"Oh no."

They sat in her rocking chairs.

Susan was different. She wasn't as cold as she'd been before. Voice choking, the Soileaus' story poured off his lips.

Susan withheld comment until he finished, but her expression convinced him she listened hard and with sympathy. She recounted her experience on *Lady Amber* once he finished. "Mister Westcott, my sister's in heaven and my brother was almost dead from the fever but God healed him."

"I have no doubt." He barely managed his skepticism.

"I'm serious. God told me."

"God told you?"

"While I was praying." She cocked her head. "I may sound crazy, but I am telling the truth. Your parents believed in God, didn't they?"

"Never talked about Him much, except on Sundays when they went to church. They did go to church and Annie, well, she liked religious books."

Susan clasped his hand between hers. Compassion, unlike anything he'd ever felt from her, passed through her gentle fingers and down, deep down inside him. He knew she'd listen; he knew she'd understand.

While Maffitt devoted endless hours aboard *Areal* nursing Stribling, Alex assumed Stribling's duties in addition to standing watches. His exhausting efforts to save the beloved officer's life hindered the captain's full recovery. For Alex, the only bright spot during this ordeal was Susan, who called up to him from *Lady Amber* one day, laughing.

He scratched his head. Susan laughing? That was odd. He'd not heard her laugh since before Susanna died. His heart leaped when he caught her mention of Susanna, but a stiff breeze muffled everything else she'd said.

Five days passed. He was on the quarterdeck a little after six o'clock in the evening when Maffitt, red-eyed and weak, stumbled through the gangway. "Lost him." His voice cracked. "We've lost Stribling."

"Sinclair?" Alex said.

"He'll recover, but Stribling." He stretched forth his trembling arm. "Assist me below. I need sleep, lots of it. We'll find a plot for him tomorrow and send his body ashore and…and bury him."

Alex swallowed hard. He whispered, "Farewell, my good friend. Farewell."

33

WHEN LEE'S ARMY rested at Frederick, Maryland local girls, ladies, and other Confederate sympathizers visited Randall's camp.

Randall observed Lucy, a youthful blond, coming toward their camp. From her previous visit, he knew she had her sights set upon Billy. But after he told her he was married, she approached Randall and blushing, gave him a delicious pound cake which he happily devoured. Every day during their brief stay, Lucy trekked one mile from town to camp. Every day, she flirted with him. Sensing Lucy's loneliness, he took it in stride.

"Two of my brave brothers died for the South," she said. "One at Malvern Hill and another one at Mechanicsville."

"Do you have other brothers?" Randall asked.

"Three more. They're all whipping Yankees under General Bragg."

Four days later, she arose hours before dawn and watched them march out of Frederick. Regimental bands struck up "The Girl I Left Behind Me." Lucy yelled Randall's name, waved her small Confederate flag, and blew him a kiss. Soldiers broke out in song.

Randall lifted his hat in acknowledgment. He hoped she'd find the love of a man she longed for, and that she'd not lose that love like he'd lost his beautiful Annie's.

Neither Randall nor Billy had any clue where they were heading, no one did except "Old Jack" himself. Only the Army of Northern Virginia's top generals—Jackson, Stuart, and Longstreet—knew Lee's grand strategy. Jackson's men trusted them. Randall and Billy and Adkins and almost every man in the army did: Lee, Jackson, Longstreet, Stuart, time and again they'd proven they could win.

They recrossed the Potomac back into Virginia toward Harper's Ferry, a small, vulnerable garrison situated at the confluence of the Shenandoah and Potomac rivers where high, hilly terrain rose on its south and north and to its west, where it sloped upward to a high plateau. After several engagements, the Confederates plugged all the gaps through which the Federals could escape. They encircled them, followed by bombarding them. On the fifteenth, 11,000 Federals surrendered, along with 73 pieces of artillery and about 13,000 small arms. Randall's unit suffered no casualties; Jackson's corps lost a mere hundred men.

Awakened by reveille hours before dawn on the sixteenth, Randall found himself on the march again. This time they headed north, back across the Potomac. Weary and footsore from days of near-constant marching, Randall and his friends forced vigor into their strides.

"I think I have it figured out," Billy told Randall.

"Figured what out?" Randall said.

"What General Lee's up to. We took Harper's Ferry so we'd deprive the Yankees of reinforcements while we're invading their territory. When we came back to Virginia, I was sort of hoping we'd stay awhile. My legs are hurting plumb awful from all this marching and river-crossing and mountain-climbing. Besides, Virginia folks are friendlier."

"So, you figure we're going back to join the rest of the army." Randall's calves ached, but unlike Billy, he never complained about such things.

"Why else would we be heading back north? Then I'll bet we're going into Pennsylvania and after that New York."

"On condition McClellan doesn't stop us first." Puffing from their rapid pace, Adkins spoke behind them.

"We'll give him a good, sound thrashing, same as we've always done," Billy said.

Dust swirled around their feet. Ahead of them and behind, thousands of bayonets glinted in the sun. For twelve miles their proud, dirty division marched, every division save one, A.P. Hill's, left behind at Harper's Ferry to receive the Federals' surrender. Their weary columns entered a small valley. It rested a couple of hours in a grove before resuming its march into a village called Sharpsburg. North of it, a ridge sloped into pastures and cornfields checkered by wooded thickets. South and east, higher, wooded ground overlooked the Antietam Creek rolling into the Potomac.

Billy glanced behind him. "Where's Adkins off to?"

Adkins had joined two other lieutenants at a small red brick house on the edge of town where a trio of brave girls, a handful of those citizens who dared venture outside, stood watching what had become an endless military parade. Most of the townsfolk, Randall figured, were likely hiding in basements or some other place till this battle ended.

"Don't worry about him. He'll catch up soon enough, else 'Ole Jack' will have his hide," Randall said.

Nothing else was spoken. They continued their march over a low hill, slower now since they'd reached their destination. They passed General Lee's headquarters, established in an oak grove overlooking the town. He stood outside his tent, shoulders square, every inch the soldier, he and Generals Jackson and Longstreet conversing and gesturing at the undulating terrain. A courier galloped past.

From across the Antietam, Yankee shells screamed after them, rending the air with terrific explosions beyond the town's center. They picked up their pace. Amidst the enemy's artillery fire, they hurried onto Hagerstown Pike, its western side bordered by rocks. It traveled past acres of fenced farmland.

"Looks like a schoolhouse on that ridge up ahead." Billy indicated a whitewashed building along the road. "Wonder when we'll halt. My legs and feet are the dickens."

Woods, mostly hickories and oaks, curved behind the building. It was a simple structure without fancy columns, though its roof did have a steep pitch.

East of this structure stretched a large pasture and about a half-mile beyond it, more woods. Randall squinted north, farther up the road. Ripened corn higher than a man's head rustled and swayed.

Yankee shells crashed around them from an opposite ridge. Explosions spurred them on, into the woods behind the schoolhouse. Randall's brigade was dispatched to the edge of the woods, on the left wing of another brigade as part of a reserve. Two other brigades in his division, Grigsby's and Jones's commands, deployed in an open field about five hundred fifty yards to their front, behind a ridge, tall grass, and a worm fence. The divisions posted in this section, Jackson's Corps, formed the Army of Northern Virginia's left flank. From here, the army stretched southward along the ridge clear down to the Antietam. Jeb Stuart's cavalry and artillery, posted on some heights northwest, was about a half-mile from the Hagerstown Pike.

Exhausted and footsore, Randall plopped down against a hickory. Thankfully, the sun was descending, and the air was growing cooler. He pulled off his battered shoes and massaged his bare feet.

Artillery rounds crashed for several hours after dark; their batteries fought back. By ten o'clock the day's shooting, for the most part, had died.

Adkins swaggered toward Randall and Billy through the dense trees.

"Finally decided to join the fun, Richard?" Billy said.

Adkins thumbed the schoolhouse behind them. "How much y'all wanna bet that building isn't a schoolhouse?"

"Go to sleep," Randall said. "The shooting's liable to be worse tomorrow. We'll have lots of fighting come daylight."

"It's not a schoolhouse. It's a church."

"No, it's not." Billy hung his gun-belt over a limestone outcropping and lay down on the grass. "It doesn't have a steeple."

"It's a Dunker Church. They don't believe in steeples and fancy buildings and all that. They don't believe in fighting either. They think war's a sin. Can you believe that?"

Randall set his sword beside him. "Thank you for that bit of useless intelligence."

Picket fire echoed in a distant pasture.

Billy's eyes shut.

"When we passed through that town," Adkins said, "I saw the most beautiful little filly standing in her doorway watching us. She told me this was her church and that everyone whose land we're on attend it. It's a German Baptist Brethren Church, a Dunker Church. She said she disapproves of slavery. Called it a sin too, and she tried converting me and a few other officers. Can you believe that? Me, an honest heathen dog?"

"So ends all your hope of flirting with her," Randall said. "Why didn't you take Lucy from me in Frederick? She wasn't pretty enough?"

"I'm not interested in mere pretty girls. Only beautiful girls." Adkins pivoted on his heel. "I still say there's the perfect, most beautiful of all belles out there for me someday. I just haven't found her yet."

"Get some sleep. You'll need it for tomorrow's work."

Adkins wandered deeper into the trees and sat down, his back against an oak. He pulled his revolver from his holster and set it in his lap.

"I can't wait to hear his stories back home after we get this war over with," Billy said, his eyes still shut.

"He'll make himself out a grand hero, I'm sure," Randall said. "He'd say anything to impress our beautiful New Orleans belles." He sprawled out on his back. Treetops rustled, clouds hovered between him and the stars, and rain approached. He could smell it.

He pulled his thin blanket over him, but it was useless against the evening's chill and would be no protection from the elements. *I hope I die tomorrow.* He drifted into fitful sleep, awakened several times by the cold drizzle falling at midnight, which kept him awake when it turned into a gushing waterfall.

A few hours later, musketry reverberated down the front lines. Randall threw off his soaked blanket; every man in every unit sprang to their feet and seized their weapons and started loading them, ripping off cartridges and ramming balls down musket barrels, and officers loading and capping their revolvers. Rainwater soaked his frock coat clean through. He stared up through the trees; heavy rain pounded his face. *Today, please, let my agony be over.*

34

RANDALL SPRINTED THROUGH knee-high fog and trees, back to the edge of the West Woods, so Adkins called it after he visited that Baptist girl. Thankfully, the rain which started at midnight had stopped. Shells roared overhead and beyond him, their explosions gouging earth. Confederate batteries responded.

Randall's brigade hastily formed line of battle.

Colonel Jessup left his regiment and strode to Randall, standing at attention in front of his company.

"Didn't you mention once that you met my son Alex?" he said.

"In New Orleans, sir," Randall said, "when he was assigned to the *Sumter.*"

The colonel shoved a piece of paper in his hand. "Here's my address. If I get killed today, write him and my daughter Susan for me. Tell them both how much I love them."

"Of course, sir," Randall said. "But suppose I get killed?" His words trailed off. No more did Colonel Jessup look at him, but returned to his regiment, his sad eyes fixed dead ahead at the fierce bloodletting unfolding beyond them.

Randall's comrades at the front endured horrific artillery rounds—enfilading rounds, rounds to their front, rounds crashing around their battery defending Dunker Church. *They're trying to turn our flank,* Randall thought.

"Fix bayonets!"

Randall echoed his general's order to his men as it reverberated down regiments and companies.

Almost in unison, the two reserve brigades in this sector of the field slid bayonets onto their muskets' barrels.

A three-gun battery supporting Grigsby's and Jones's brigades boomed round after round. His head calmly bowed as though in prayer, Stonewall Jackson, oblivious to the flying iron, sat astride his horse. Yankee shells burst over the cannons, which withdrew behind the brigades' lines.

Soldiers wearing blue advanced. Lying prone behind a ridge, Randall's comrades awaited them. Suddenly, they made their presence known by standing up and discharging a volley point- blank range. The bluecoats staggered, dropped where they'd stood, or pulled back toward the corn.

In and around the forty-acre cornfield, men on both sides dropped like dominoes, riddled by bullets or blown apart by artillery. Yankee cannon pounded Rebel cannon. Stuart's cannon blazed from the heights. Briefly, some thirty minutes after the battle began, rifle fire and musketry died, and shells smashed the woods behind Randall's men. More bluecoats advanced through the corn, thousands of men, corn stalks shattering and flying in bits and pieces....their right wheel through the corn, toward a split rail fence and the two outnumbered Confederate brigades on its opposite side. Halting, the Yankees unleashed a devastating volley. The Rebels fled, only turning to return fire before continuing their retreat toward the West Woods.

Artillery rounds kicked up dirt and rocks near Randall's position. *We're losing this one. We're falling back. Can't let them turn our flank, else our whole army's done for.*

The advancing Federals clambered over the fence, firing relentlessly, rapidly closing on their position and Dunker Church. More Rebels went down, clutching bellies and heads and legs and shoulders. Yankees...Now they started getting the worst of it.

His revolver drawn, Randall's heart pounded.

The Yankees withdrew to the rail fence. What remained of the two Rebel brigades regained their former position alongside their comrades' corpses. Fighting and dying intensified, a bloodletting the likes of which neither Randall nor his men had ever witnessed. He wondered when their chance would come.

The Federal advance's right wing charged through the cornfield's southern edge. Desperate Confederate fire failed to halt it. Determined as death, the blue wave surged forward, forcing the Rebels over the split rail fence.

Had their men lost their nerve? Randall squelched his panic.

His comrades were running along the eastern side of Hagerstown Pike, toward his position and the church, filling the air with cries and shouts or just standing in place, gripping their heads and trembling violently.

General Jackson and his staff galloped their horses toward them, shouted at them, and gestured toward the onrushing enemy. But the men kept running. Gunners seized them by their arms but were flung aside. The men kept on toward the woods and the church.

"No ammunition!"

These words, the words of defeated soldiers, rang in Randall's ears when they surged past.

A courier galloped to General Starke, astride his horse and watching the division's resolve disintegrate. "We need you, General. Our situation's critical."

Starke tipped his hat at the courier, dismounted, and turned his horse over to an aide who led the animal into the relative safety of the timber. His sword held high, he barked the command: "Advance!"

They marched through their retreating comrades toward the battle's hottest point. Another courier galloped up, frantically waving his hat. Randall caught bits and pieces of the exchange between him and Starke.

"General Jones is down," the courier screamed over shot and shell. "Concussion. General Jackson says you command the division now. He says hurry. Faster. Faster."

Starke seized a flag from a fleeing regiment. He waved it, trying to rally it when four enemy bullets struck him dead.

Without orders, the two brigades turned toward the Pike and their charging foes. Randall glimpsed Colonel Jessup, firing his revolver with cool deliberation, felling one bluecoat after the next like shooting tin cans.

Bullets whistled.

Sword aimed at the Yankees, Randall screamed, "Charge!"

His entire brigade made for the Pike and the enemy, climbing over fence rails along its eastern side. Shots popped around him. Screams.

"Jenny! I'm hit!" Billy went down, his beloved's name on his lips, a bullet in his thigh. He jerked. Two more bullets struck his chest.

"Billy!" Randall wanted to attend his friend but hadn't time. Yankees all around him.

He and Adkins stood side by side, firing their pistols fast as possible.

Adkins dropped to his knees, got a musket and cartridge box from a dead soldier, which he passed to Randall. He raced to another dead man and picked up his own. Kneeling, they and the remnants of their shattered company triggered a volley.

The brigades raced toward a hollow and a Yankee battery spewing case-shot before cutting into the corn. Randall turned back briefly once they entered the stalks. "Adkins! Where...?" He darted back out of the corn and found him on his back, a bullet in his forehead.

He ducked back into the corn and the fight. Everyone was getting killed but him.

Decimated. That's what Randall's brigade discovered as its dwindling numbers hastened behind the Georgians shooting at the Yanks. Southern corpses strewed every direction, bloody arms and legs severed from bloody bodies, dead heaped upon dead. Artillery plowed down Union soldiers in rows. Shrapnel exploded near Randall, yet he stood still as a statue. *Annie, forgive me.* Artillery boomed. *I don't know what I did that made you reject me. I want to die. Please. I do want to die.*

Yelling, screaming, shooting, he and his brigade surged past the Georgians. Rifles exploded in Yankees' hands, bullets riddled their canteens, men in blue fell right and left in piles of shattered corn.

Randall screamed at the enemy. "I'm standing right here! Kill me! Kill me!" He discharged his last bullet.

Minie balls whistled close, but as if by some miracle, they all missed. Slowly, they drove the bluecoats back toward the woods on the field's eastern side and then, from inside the cornfield, Federal artillery thundered, cutting down the brigade like a scythe through wheat. Randall stumbled and fell, still unhurt. *I'm alive? I'm alive?* He leaped up and moved forward with the remnants of his brigade.

Throughout the day, Sharpsburg's merciless madness raged along Lee's line. By mid-morning, Randall breathed a little easier when the worst fighting on his flank ended, thanks to reinforcements that routed the Yankees during their final big attempt against Dunker Church.

Late in the afternoon, he learned that the Federals nearly defeated the Rebels during an action along Antietam Creek. For three bloody hours, Rebels stymied a Union advance across a bridge till finally, the bluecoats managed to cross it and march on Sharpsburg. Only A.P. Hill's timely arrival from Harper's Ferry seized victory from disaster. By day's end regiments on both sides, exhausted and decimated, ended the bloodletting in a draw.

Next afternoon, under flags of truce, soldiers North and South moved among their fallen comrades in the Cornfield. Death's stench lingered everywhere. Randall surveyed the carnage.

"The Cornfield," Randall muttered. "The Cornfield. The Cornfield." Thousands of bullet-riddled bodies, comrades and foes who, the morning before, lived and breathed, lay across the forty acres like storm-tossed leaves, like limbs fallen from trees, mown down and snuffed out as easily as the cornstalks. He'd seen Billy's and Adkins's corpses taken to the rear on litters. He hadn't found Colonel Jessup's body yet.

His weary, aching legs carried him past a row of Union corpses, shot down where they'd stood, where they'd charged as though on parade.

"Hey, Reb." The friendly Yankee voice spoke behind him.

Randall faced the hollow-cheeked corporal.

"Got some tabaky, Reb?"

Randall shook his head no.

"I don't know about you, Reb, but me personally? I'm sorry this war even started. I'm sick of it." He extended his hand. "The name's Crenshaw. Yours?"

"Randall Bartlett." His forearm swiped sweat off his brow. "We saw more death yesterday than I ever care to see again, enough to last me a lifetime. I wish our generals would let us all go home."

"There'll be no argument from me there, Bartlett. How many men your unit lose?"

"Only seven men left in my company, including myself. I'm the only officer who made it through. Can't say for sure about all our brigades on this flank. Y'all shot us to pieces."

"We shot you to pieces? Your artillery and infantry must've destroyed half of us. There's some fine soldiers in your army, Bartlett. Some of the bravest men I've ever seen in my life. Only three men in my company left alive, including me."

"You wouldn't have any stationery on you, would you? Or pen and ink?"

"I got some back at my camp. I imagine you've got lots of folks to write."

"Yes."

"As do I. Don't go far. I'll go back and get them for you."

"Thanks, Crenshaw. For a Yankee, you're a pretty nice fellow."

"Ain't such a bad feller yourself either, Reb."

Randall ran his fingers through his hair. What had he been thinking, wanting to get himself killed as revenge for Catherine Anne's rejection of him?" *Randall Bartlett, you are a first-rate idiot.*

A familiar shriek sounded ten yards off Randall's right. He looked beyond what was left of the cornstalks and noticed two men heaving a heavy man onto a litter.

"Gently!" the heavy man screamed. "Gently!"

Colonel Jessup. Randall strode to him. "You're hurt."

"Of course, I'm hurt," Jessup snapped. "Oh. Sorry, Bartlett, I didn't recognize you at first."

"What happened?"

"These men were lifting me like a sack of potatoes. They don't care a whittle about my broken leg. Before we got into the fight, I had a strong premonition something bad was going to happen to me. I took it to mean I was fixing to get killed."

"Obviously, you were hurt, but not badly."

"No, not too bad. I tripped over a dead man and twisted my leg during the charge, and when I stood back up a shell fragment smashed my knee and broke it." He managed a chuckle. "First time in my life I've been happy about a broken bone."

"It saved your life, sir."

"That it did, my boy. To the rear, litter bearers."

Next evening, Lee gave the order to withdraw across the Potomac and back into Virginia.

Farragut paused his dictation to Gaubadan when Captain Palmer entered his quarters.

"Admiral, someone's just boarded asking for you," the captain said.

Gabaudan gathered up his paperwork. "Shall I leave, sir?"

"Whatever you like. We'll continue our work after I visit with our guest."

"I'm no guest!" the familiar voice sounded from Farragut's cabin doorway.

"Loyall!" Farragut sprang from his chair and embraced his only child. Eighteen years old, he stood an inch shorter than his father. "Your mother wrote me you were coming. It appears you made it sooner than I expected."

"Since Congress started a draft, Mother thinks I'm safer with you rather than being forced into the Army."

"Excuse us, Captain Palmer. My son and I have lots of catching up to do. Mister Gabaudan, return within the hour. You will teach my son his duties then. He'll also be my clerk."

"Gabaudan," Palmer said, "bring your work to my quarters."

1862

OCTOBER

–

DECEMBER

35

Every day Alex grew stronger. On the thirtieth day of September, he was able to stand on deck and watch as *Florida* hauled down her quarantine flag. She steamed further up the bay to Dog River Bar just below Mobile, where Buchanan ordered her crew transferred to another vessel anchored nearby. Since he prohibited those ashore from boarding her, a precaution against the fever's spread, her own men cleaned and fumigated her.

On the fourth day of October, two hours before sunset, his triumph over Yellow Jack complete, Alex visited his mother's and Susanna's graves, a promise he'd made the day he'd shipped out for New Orleans. He'd vowed he'd visit their graves upon returning home before going anywhere else, just as he'd visited them an hour before he'd reported to Commander Semmes back when the war first started.

He followed the cemetery's pathway past tombs, headstones, and obelisks. Though peacefulness permeated the acreage, his soul was disturbed. To his right was a kneeling angel; his left, an obelisk; up ahead, a leaning pillar ornately carved with lilies. Trees shaded other tombs and headstones, trees all around, alive among the dead.

At the end of the long path, he made an abrupt right. Up ahead, a giant granite angel spread upward its wide wings as though praising heaven. Unadorned pilasters marked the tomb's edges, carved between them large roses which framed his mother's and Susanna's engraved names. His mother loved roses.

Alex picked up speed. Faster he walked, faster and faster. He broke into a sprint. Puffing hard and choking back tears, he stopped at their tomb. He removed his cap, bowed his head. Brown, cracked leaves scattered over his feet.

"I'm alive." His throat caught. "Mama, Susanna, I pretty near died a few weeks ago, but your boy's still alive." He dropped to one knee. "I'm glad father's not here to see me blubbering. Men don't blubber. Remember him always saying that? Blubbering's what girls do. Well, I'm blubbering, and I wish I had died, 'cause maybe I'd see y'all again."

He scowled at the earth. Weeds! Weeds! *Susan! You promised me.* Through the calf-high grass he crawled, snatching one weed after another. *Grass needs cutting. Susan, how could you?* He moved fast around one side of the square tomb, tugging and pulling at a strong one. He pounded the earth and tugged harder. His fingers scratched around it to no effect. The ground was too hard. He tugged, he yanked, he pulled. He wept. Years of stifled grief exploded from his heart.

"I'm sorry, mister," a policeman's sympathetic voice came from outside the fence. "This cemetery will close in a few minutes. I must kindly ask you to leave."

"It's still light." He tugged the stubborn weed again. "I'm not done tending my folks' graves."

"Do come back tomorrow and finish it, sir."

"Can't you let me get this dang weed out first!" He tugged hard.

"Here." The policeman handed him a pocketknife over the fence. "Use this and be done with it, young man."

"Forgive my outburst. I won't be much longer." He worked the blade up under the weed's stubborn root. "Forgive me, Mother, for letting this happen. It won't happen again. I'll see to that."

Alex roared up his home's steps. "Susan! Susan! Su-u-san!"

Susan flung open the door. "Dear brother, welcome home."

Alex stopped short of her embrace. "Mother's and Susanna's graves are a wreck. The grass isn't cut, the weeds aren't pulled."

She smiled at him.

"I find nothing funny about the state of our family's cemetery plot. You promised me you'd tend it while Father and I were away."

"Come on, Alex. Get your body inside." She gestured for him to enter. Arms folded, Alex shook his head. "I demand an explanation."

"Explanation for what?"

"For why the grass is so high around their tomb. If you were under my command, I'd masthead you a whole day for that offense. It's inexcusable. Maybe even court-martial you."

Susan sobered and gripped his hand. "Oh, Alex. I'm sorry. I've been so excited of late, I quite forgot. We'll both do it tomorrow. After church."

Her words, her mild tone and manner, blew the anger out of him. "What's this about church?" When he went inside, he noticed she wore no jewelry. Splotches of rose bush design wallpaper clung to the hallway's walls, most of it having been used on letters to him and their father. He remembered her laughing aboard *Lady Amber*.

"I'm going to church tomorrow," Susan said.

"Why?"

"Because I want to."

Alex tugged his earlobes meaningfully.

"My earrings?" Susan laughed. "They're in my jewelry box. I don't wear those silly things much anymore. I'd just as soon give them away."

"You'd just…as soon…give…uh…give them…*away?*"

Playfully, she shoved him into a hallway chair.

"All right, Susan. Would you please tell me what's going on?"

"Don't go anywhere. I'll be back directly."

Her quick steps echoed up the stairs.

Huston, Fannie, Hulda, and Dolphus closed on him.

"Is she sick or something?" Alex said.

"Touched in the head," Fannie said.

"Ever since Cap'n Hughes brought her back from your ship," Huston said, "she's been acting peculiar. But Mister Alex, if you don't mind me saying so, I like her better this way."

"She said something about finding God or something," Hulda said.

"Ha!" Alex said. "How can she find God? No one knows what He looks like. Besides, I doubt He was ever lost."

"I don't understand it either, Mister Alex," Huston said. "I don't think any of us do."

"She's been going to church with that writer lady," Hulda said.

"Missy Evans," Fannie said.

The servants nodded.

"It's a trick," Fannie continued. "She's trying to find my—" Her jaw clamped.

Alex's eyes narrowed. "Find your what?"

"Nothing, sah. She ain't trying to find nothing." Fannie retreated toward the back door.

Something bumped the floor. Fannie turned and swiftly stepped over it, covering it with her skirt.

"Stand clear," Alex snapped.

"Mistah Alex."

"I said 'stand clear.' That means, step away."

"Don't, Mistah—"

"That's an order. Move."

"Sakes on earth." Susan came down the stairs, a thick black book tucked under her left arm. "Why all this shouting?"

"Why should that bother you, you champion of shouters?"

"Well, I don't shout anymore. It's rude."

"Huh?"

"I'll explain later. First tell me, why the shouting?"

"Fannie's hiding something under her skirt. I heard it hit the floor."

Susan scanned the floor. "I don't see anything." She erupted into laughter. "Fannie, dear, was your fife sewn in the hem of your skirt? Of all the places to hide it. I don't know why I never suspected your dress's hem as a hiding place."

"Because I've got more brains than you, Missy," Fannie said.

"Belay that back talk," Alex snapped. "Stop it, I mean."

"Oh, hush," Susan said. "Fannie did outsmart me, and had her thread not broken I'd have probably never found it. Step back, Fannie. Please."

Fannie stepped back.

Alex swooped up the toy, which Susan snatched.

She closed the maid's hand over it. "I'll never take it from you again."

Fannie shook her head and moved on. "I don't know what kind of water you've been drinking, Missy."

"All right, everyone." Susan clapped her hands. "Back. Back to your duties."

The servants scattered every direction.

"What's that you're holding?" Alex said.

"A Bible."

"What?"

"The one Stephen gave me before he left for India."

Stephen Hamilton, Mary and Amelia's brother, their neighbor the abolitionist. Alex's brain reeled. From what he remembered, Stephen was a nice enough fellow, except he was always serious about everything, more serious even than Doctor Kirby. Alex never cracked jokes around Stephen, nor engaged in silly behavior lest Stephen consider him crazy. He'd expected Stephen would move north and work with the abolitionist movement, especially after all those arguments over slavery with his father. His decision to go to India took Alex and everyone else who knew him by surprise.

Back in the parlor, Susan recounted her experiences aboard *Lady Amber*.

Patiently, Alex listened, glad that Susan seemed to have changed for the better. Her new-found religion, however, prompted concern. She seemed to have gone from one extreme to the other, extreme hatred to religious fanaticism. Envy touched him. If he ever heard God talk to him, well, he'd give up fishing and billiards for that!

"Will you attend church with me tomorrow?" she said. "Gusta's in the choir. She's singing a solo. We can tend Mother's grave after that."

"Who is Gusta?"

"Miss Evans, of course. She's a soprano, and she does sing most lovely. Will you attend? For me?"

"I have nothing against church. I'd better secure Captain Maffitt's permission first. He might need me for something tomorrow."

"I quite agree."

"I'd better be getting on back. I'll return first thing in the morning, Captain Maffitt permitting." He stepped out the door.

"Alex. There's something else."

"Later, Susan." He went out the gate.

"The Westcotts are dead."

Turning suddenly, he stepped back onto the lawn.

"Except for Mister Moxley Westcott. He's posted at Fort Morgan. His parents were murdered by Yankee deserters, and his sister broke her neck in an accident. A fall, or something like that."

"Ben?"

"Mister Westcott told me he was shot twice during the battle below New Orleans. Last time he saw him, he was a prisoner aboard a Yankee ship preparing to take him downriver to a Yankee hospital. One wound was especially serious, he said."

"Does he know who shot him?"

"He didn't tell me he did."

No, Ben didn't tell her, but he had a fairly good idea who did it.

"Will you still attend church with me tomorrow? You're not mad at God the way I used to be?"

"Me? Mad at the Almighty? That, my sister, is a foolish notion. When I get a chance, I'll call on Moxley and see how he's doing."

"He's managing it best he can."

"Hello, Alex." Mary waved at him from her lawn. "Welcome home."

"Why are you down here in Mobile this time of year? The fever season isn't over yet."

"We decided to stay here until the war ends. I'm helping out in Miss Evans's hospital. We're actually living at our Spring Hill residence for now. I just came back here for a few things." Mary hurried up her home's steps and passed through her front door.

Alex smiled at her before he hurried down the street. Images of Locke brewed, dark and dangerous. Let him see that crazy man again, he'd kill him.

Alex followed Susan into the front pew beside the Evanses. When Mrs. Evans smiled him a welcome, he returned it. The choir director announced hymn numbers; a glance behind him showed a few gray-haired men and a smattering of younger fellows. Mostly, though, ladies and children occupied the sanctuary. Numerous vacant pews testified that their occupants were off to war. He listened to the singing but remained silent. He couldn't carry a note in a bucket. Music was a gift neither he nor Susan shared. Finally, the congregational singing stopped.

During the offering, the organist moved into a rousing rendition of "O for a Thousand Tongues to Sing." From the choir, Miss Evans's voice merged with the majestic pipes, an unusually powerful voice for someone so tiny and soft-spoken, Alex thought. Her singing flowed from deep within her as though calling down heaven itself to flood the place with its glory.

Alex marveled. Writer, singer, nurse, public speaker, self-educated scholar—that's how Susan described her. Was there nothing this lady couldn't do?

The minister paced his sermon slowly, stating first one point and expounding on it, followed by the next point and further expounding. Passion buttressed his preaching. He sounded a lot like Doctor Kirby. Alex wanted to get up and leave. Out of courtesy to Susan and the Evanses, however, he forced himself to stay put.

At the end of the sermon, his noticed his sister beside him. Tears welled her eyes. Strange. What did the preacher say that made her do that?

She looked over at him and smiled. Alex smiled back. Something was happening to his sister. Could it have something to do with that voice she claimed to have heard?

36

THOUGH NEW OFFICERS were being assigned to *Florida*, Admira Buchanan had other plans for Alex. Ordered to report to him, Alex reluctantly donned his best gray uniform obtained from *Florida's* tender *Prince Albert* off the coast of the Bahamas. His trek to the feared admiral's office seemed an eternity. All the way there, he constantly thumped lint and dust off his frock coat, constantly squared his cap, and couldn't stop clearing his throat.

Standing at strict attention, he suffered the humorless admiral's inspection.

Slowly, hands behind his back, Buchanan circled him like a lion sizing up his prey.

"I understand you'd prefer to stay with Captain Maffitt. Am I correct or am I not?"

"That is correct, sir." Alex stammered his response.

"Why?"

"I like him, sir. I respect him, sir."

Buchanan grunted. "You don't like me? You don't respect me?"

"I didn't say that, sir."

"It's a good thing you didn't because Maffitt spoke highly of you, and I happen to like what he told me. He wants you to remain on board the *Florida*. He wants you aboard when she puts out to sea."

Alex stiffened. The old man's austerity reminded him of Captain Semmes.

"Over the past couple of weeks, you were one of the topics of our discussion. Do you imbibe, Mister Jessup?"

"Only on social occasions, sir."

"What are your liquors of choice?"

"Wine, sir. Champagne, claret. An occasional beer, sir."

"Have you ever gotten drunk?"

"No, sir."

"Not even at the Academy?"

"No, sir."

"But you do imbibe?"

"Sometimes, sir."

"Drink when you're at liberty ashore if you must, but I must never, ever catch you staggering around this city or on board your ship intoxicated. If I do, my wrath will blast you like a twenty-gun broadside."

"Understood, sir."

"I have been told this city is your home. Is that or is that not true?"

Alex breathed a sigh of relief when the admiral changed the subject. "It's true, sir."

"And you are familiar with the waters in the bay."

"I know them well, sir. I've fished in it often. My father owns the *Lady Amber*, sir."

"Captain Hughes's yacht."

"He worked for my father, and they sailed her in regattas before the war and used her for fishing trips. My father's serving in General Lee's army."

"Hughes is a valuable asset to both our navy and our army." Again Buchanan circled Alex; he tugged his coat and looked at his shoes. "There's mud on your shoes. Did it rain on the way here?"

Alex started to look down, but fear of the admiral stayed his neck. "N-No, sir."

"I want that mud off your shoes."

"Y-Yes, sir. Aye aye, sir. Now, sir?"

"I haven't dismissed you." Buchanan settled into a wide, heavy leather armchair. "I desperately need good officers and more men in my squadron. My best man is Lieutenant Johnston. At the moment, he's up at Selma assessing the construction of ironclads. He'll be sending me a report when his work's done there. I'm trying to build a squadron of ironclads, Mister Jessup. They're the only way we can sink the Yankees. As of this second, consider yourself in my squadron. I'll obtain our Navy Department's approval. I'm confident they'll agree."

Alex swore under his breath. *Buchanan the flogger. Great, just great.*

"If you don't like that or me, live with it."

"Aye, sir."

"Return to your ship, collect your things, and report back for your assignment. My officers will look like officers and will conduct themselves like officers and will always, Mister Jessup, always wear their uniforms when on duty."

"Yes, sir. Aye, sir."

"Dismissed."

Alex lifted his cap's bill in a quick salute. Once out the admiral's door, his shoulders slumped as he relaxed. *Well, Alex, look at the positive side of things. At least you'll be near Susan.* He bent down and thumped mud off his shoe.

37

So PACKED WAS the clattering train's car, Ben's breaths came heavy and hard, with stabs of pain to remind him of Locke's wound during their battle below New Orleans. Though he had no business riding this particular one, the ladies' car, all the others, including the baggage car, were crammed with soldiers and had less breathing space. He wasn't the only man who rode this one standing. Their bodies pressured each other single file down the narrow center aisle separating the ladies' seats. Virginia's countryside rolled past.

"That's a fine-looking uniform, son. Is it new?"

The old woman's question startled Ben out of his daydreaming. He looked down into her sweet, wrinkled face. "Yes, ma'am. The Navy Department issued it to me in Richmond. I was a prisoner at Fort Warren. I got exchanged a few weeks ago."

His attention returned to the pastureland.

"Where are you heading?"

"Mobile. I've been assigned to Admiral Buchanan's squadron. He's a stickler for uniforms and those kinds of things. I want to look my best when I report to him."

"How do you know he's a stickler? Have you met him?"

"No, ma'am, but I've heard stories. Every Naval Academy graduate has. He was its first superintendent."

"I see. Well, I shan't bother you with any more questions." She gathered the knitting in her lap.

"You're not bothering me, ma'am."

The lady's knitting needles worked slowly.

Ben's thoughts drifted deep into Dixie, to Mobile, to Susan. Today, the thirtieth of December. Barring any unforeseen eventuality, he'd reach Mobile in a couple or three days. First, he'd visit her. Then, he'd report to the admiral. Throughout his time in Fort Warren, he'd pondered his family and many hours her. Since her unpleasantness marred her natural beauty, he didn't understand why she dominated his musings. Back in New Orleans when the war first started and Alex was about to go down the Mississippi and into the Gulf of Mexico aboard *Sumter*, he'd promised Alex he'd be nice to her if he ever saw her again. He'd try hard to keep that promise. Breaking promises cut across his grain. He could caress Miss Susan forever, but only if her heart of stone had changed to one of rose petals. How likely was that?

1863

JANUARY

–

APRIL

38

WORDS SPRANG INTO Miss Evans's head and seemed to pop off her pen, dashing them across pages of brown wrapping paper. Her novel, *Macaria*, fast approached its end. She dipped her pen in an ink well, and her rapid writing resumed. Her nation's indomitable patriots sacrificing everything, even their lives, demanded her massive undertaking's completion.

Since June, she'd devoted every available hour to this literary endeavor. She'd planted herself at her desk nearly every day and worked from eight in the morning till hours after midnight, only taking time off for her duties at Camp Beulah, caring for its sick and Mrs. Wilson, Mister Lorenzo Wilson's ill wife at his nearby Ashland estate. Battling weariness and burning sleep-deprived eyes, determination fired her youthful energy. *Macaria* would silence the South's critics, persuade them their Cause was just, and encourage the brave men and boys fighting and dying on blood-drenched battlefields.

She set aside a page and snatched up another one. Down into the inkwell went the pen. She left it there. She needed more information on their nation's early victories. She'd write General Beauregard and request more details on First Manassas.

She pulled out a fresh sheet and wrote:

Mobile January 1 1863
General Beauregard

Suddenly disgusted, she shoved aside the inkwell. *The nerve of President Davis and his treatment of my Creole friend.* Davis had removed him from a field command and replaced him with Bragg, having ordered him to Charleston. Charleston's previous commander, John C. Pemberton, Davis transferred to Vicksburg. Both she and Beauregard considered Davis's actions an insult.

Her brother Howard served in Bragg's army. The papers said it was fighting up in Tennessee. Behind her, floorboards creaked.

"Gusta."

Miss Evans peered over her left shoulder. "Why Susan, darling. I didn't hear you come in."

"May I ask a question? I realize you're busy with your book and all, but I need a few minutes."

"Is that the sound of worry I discern in your voice?"

Sallie's laughter rang out in the hallway.

Miss Evans closed her study's door. No doubt, an officer had paid her sister a visit. More officers would soon follow, and the evening would grow noisy. "All right, darling. What ails you?"

"Mister Westcott." Susan drew a deep breath. "Oh, Gusta! His letters and telegrams. He doesn't quit wooing me."

"Would you prefer that he stop?"

"Oh, I don't know. I think that…he says he loves me. He's written that to me many times."

"Do you love him?"

"Possibly." Her response sounded hesitant. "Maybe not. I'm not sure. He says he has no one left in his family. His parents were murdered, his sister died in a fall, and his younger brother Ben was severely wounded in the battle below New Orleans. He, too, might be dead. The truth is, I feel sorry for him. He said in a telegram today that he's getting a furlough tomorrow. I fear he's going to propose to me, and I'm…I'm not sure of my answer."

"Then don't give him one. Besides, isn't it only proper that he first consult your father on such matters?" Miss Evans moved toward her study's door. "Be wary of your heart, my dear. It is a tragedy what's befallen him, and do be his friend. But courtship? Do not allow your heart to overrule your brain. Always remember. We girls have minds too."

"But if he asks, what do I say?"

"Why, tell him he must ask your father first. Come along. We have visitors."

One hour past sundown, the third day of January, Ben paused at Susan's gate. He cleared his throat and wondered…would she remember him? How would she receive him? Could he keep his promise to her brother Alex he'd made two years ago, that he would be nice to her if they ever saw each other again? Deep purple drapes framed a chandelier's glow which illuminated the parlor and filled the gallery. A loud, familiar voice startled him. *It can't be. Not here.*

The door flung open. With a joyful whoop, Moxley gave him an enthusiastic bear-hug.

"A handshake," Ben said, mildly amused. "I don't like being hugged by men. Or have we forgotten?"

"Not even by your brother who loves you?" Moxley said.

"The feeling's mutual. A handshake, please?"

Moxley stuck out his hand. "Handshakes it is."

The brothers' grips crunched each other's fingers.

"Did Mother and Father come with you?" Ben said. "And Catherine Annc?"

Moxley shifted.

"Are they here?"

Face grave, Moxley rested a palm on Ben's shoulder.

Ben whacked it off. "What's happened?"

"Yes," Susan spoke softly. "Something has happened. We shall tell you."

Susan sounded different, looked different. No hardness, no sharpness in her tone. *Strange.* He joined them in the front parlor. A bolt of gray wool cloth lay on the floor beside Susan's sewing machine; gray trousers draped a chair. At the fireplace, a servant nudged a log back into its crackling blaze. Warmth, scented by burning wood, traveled the room.

"Please shut the door," Susan said.

Susan was polite? What happened to his family? He didn't want to hear it; he did want to hear it. He wanted to stay. He wanted to leave. She wasn't wearing jewelry. *Odd.* Ben recalled Alex's stories about her inordinate fondness for expensive handmade jewelry.

"Mister Westcott," she said, "your family is…I fear they're…"

"Dead," Moxley said.

The news staggered him like a blow from a two-by-four. "Everyone?"

"Our parents murdered, and Sister died in a fall. Susan was trying to be tactful, but I can't be tactful. Get the truth out fast. Get it over with. Doesn't hurt as much that way."

Ben stifled a groan.

"We're sorry," she said.

Ben glared at them. "Miss Susan, will you permit my brother and me to leave you for a few minutes?"

Susan sat at her sewing machine, and the brothers crossed the hallway into the billiard room.

Ben gestured at its double doors.

Moxley pulled them shut then sat on the edge of the billiard table. Beginning with Fort Jackson's surrender, he detailed events up to his departure via a swamp road; how he came to Mobile next; how Philippe's parents found him. Since he left them behind in New Orleans, he confessed he was at fault for their deaths.

"Don't torture yourself," Ben said. "You might not have been able to do anything. Besides, if Butler had you arrested, they still would've suffered the same fate."

Moxley idly rolled a billiard ball across the table.

"Stop blaming yourself. Was Annie's neck broken when they found her?"

"That's what killed her in her fall."

"It wasn't an accident."

"How would you know?"

"Trust me. I'm sure of it. And I know who killed her."

"Impossible."

"Do you recall that little encounter you and that officer from the *Madison* had at the Head of the Passes, back before Farragut took command of the Yankee squadron?"

"Locke?"

"That's the one."

"He brought me aboard that ship so I could be interrogated. October of '61, I think it was. The man's crazy."

"My sentiments exactly. While I was at the Academy, we went on a summer training cruise. He killed a woman in Santa Cruz."

"He wasn't court-martialed for it."

"No evidence. However, I am certain he did it. He hates females, the woman was a barmaid, and I was deck officer when it happened. He got in trouble for reporting back to the ship late. Earlier, Alex saw her in a cantina sashaying around tables, teasing patrons and Locke. Later than evening, Santa Cruz's police found her at the bottom of some stairs with her neck broken, thus, they deemed her death an accident. When I learned her neck was broken, I reported my suspicions to Lieutenant commanding Craven, our captain. Locke may be short, but you've seen him. Solid muscle clean through. Built like an ox. He has the strength to do it."

"Sister might've insulted him."

"No 'might've' about it, 'specially if she believed he killed me. He knew where she lived because he'd heard me mention our street's name several times aboard the *Madison* and at the Academy. That's why I pulled my pistol on the Yankee officer whose boat picked me up. Locke and I were going at it during the battle, close quarters, and in the fog of anger and pain I mistook him for Locke. It's fortunate I didn't exacerbate my chest wound when I did that."

"Alex is back in Mobile. Serving aboard the *Selma*. Have a place to stay?"

"Not tonight. I haven't the money for a hotel room."

"Then you'll stay with Uncle Will."

"We have no Uncle Will."

"You don't. I do. Susan's uncle. Not her real uncle. She just calls him that. Captains her father's yacht, *Lady Amber*. Runs errands and delivers mail and supplies for the military here. Sure he won't mind your staying aboard her till tomorrow."

"Susan calls him uncle. I see nothing wrong with that, but what gives you the right?"

"Getting married."

"Congratulations."

"Don't get too excited for me."

"Take me to your brand spanking new Uncle Will for me, will you?"

"Jealous?"

"Me, jealous of you because you're engaged to a beautiful young thing like Susan? Don't make me laugh. She shouts a lot."

"Hasn't shouted in months. I'm the one who changed her. Never gave up on winning her. Wore down her resistance." After bidding Susan good-bye, Moxley and Ben went outdoors.

Ben cast a final glance at Susan through her parlor window, bent over her sewing machine. *Better beat to quarters, Moxley, my man. Our battle for Susan has begun.*

39

OUTSIDE ADMIRAL BUCHANAN's office, his head throbbing due to his nerves, Ben studied his reflection in a rectangular mirror hanging from a whitewashed wall. He squared his cap, adjusted his bowtie, and thumped lint off his shoulder straps. *Admiral, sir, I am here to report to you, as ordered, sir. Aye, sir. Aye aye, sir.* He lifted his fist to rap on Buchanan's door, lowered it quickly. *Admiral! Sir! Well, Ben, here we go.* He rapped on the door.

"Enter," the admiral boomed.

Ben squared his cap better, adjusted his tie better, flicked lint off his gray frock coat's sleeve. He cleared his throat. *Admiral Buchanan... er...Aye, sir. I will do that, sir. Whatever you say, sir. Aye, sir.*

"Enter. I haven't all day."

Ben steadied himself then marched into the famous admiral's office. "Sir." He saluted. He handed the admiral his papers. "Secretary Mallory has ordered me to your squadron.... Sir!"

Thin lips downturned and eyes dour, Buchanan rifled Ben's orders and service record to date. Ben recalled the tales about him, his quickness to court-martial and suspend Academy midshipmen, even for such minor offenses as smoking. It was said he favored flogging unruly sailors, but new laws passed a decade ago put an end to this disciplinary method. Thankfully, the Confederacy had the same "no flogging" policy.

"Westcott, is it? Richmond sent me a wire you were coming." Buchanan searched his face, his uniform. His hand ran backward over his bald pate. He grunted. "Good. Very good. Clean uniform, regulation and neat. Do you smoke?"

"No, sir."

"Cigars? Pipes?"

"No, sir."

"Cigarettes?"

"No, sir."

"What about imbibing?"

"As in—"

"Liquor, Lieutenant. As in liquor."

"I do drink a little, sir."

"What is your liquor of choice?"

"Claret, sir. And red wine."

"Have you ever been intoxicated?"

"Drunk, sir? No, sir."

"Let me catch you disgracing the service by intoxication, I will see you court-martialed and drummed out of the Navy."

"It won't happen, sir." Ben pitied the man who got on the old man's bad side.

Buchanan tossed Ben's service record aside. "It says you fought at New Orleans."

"I was wounded and captured there, sir."

"I'll read its details later. Since we've reached an understanding, I have an assignment for you. Our squadron's small. My temporary flagship is one slow-poky ironclad, the *Baltic*, and she doesn't count for much. Not only because she's slow, but because she's not completely armored. If the Yanks ever figure out how weak we really are, we can't whip them. Not before we're ready and not without good ironclads."

"What are your orders, sir?"

"We're building new vessels at Selma and Montgomery. Commander Johnston's up there making a report and trying to speed along their progress. Our country's draft has gobbled up practically every available man. Since you were in prison you might not be aware that this past October, the Confederate Congress amended the draft law. Men conscripted into the Army who'd rather serve in the Navy may do so. I'll see you get booked passage. Tomorrow, you will take a train to Tennessee. General Bragg's army is there, around Murfreesboro.

Seek out and recruit good seamen. What vessels we do have here are all undermanned. We'll need more after we've finished building our ironclads. Any questions?"

"Two, sir. First, sir, there is this certain girl…uh…lady who lives here, and I…uh—"

"I'll permit one day with her, Mister. I'll book your train passage for Monday instead."

"Thank you, sir."

"Next question."

"Where is the *Selma*, sir? I heard my best friend's on her. Alex Jessup, sir."

"I like your friend. He seems competent."

"He is, sir."

"She's anchored in the Mobile River. She and the *Morgan* and *Gaines* take turns helping Fort Grant guard Grant's Pass. She's not far from the Battle House."

"Thank you, sir."

"I expect you to bring me back some good sailors, Westcott."

"Aye, sir."

Headache subsiding, Ben strode out Buchanan's door. He'd learn more about Moxley and Susan's courtship from Alex. After uncovering as many details as he could, he'd stop it.

When Ben first saw *Selma*—a low, black side-wheeler minus bulwarks and boarding nettings—tied up at a wharf in the Mobile River, he instantly recognized her. Her original name had been *Florida*, a mail packet built in this city back in '56. In New Orleans, Captain Rousseau seized her, cut down her sides, and converted her into a gunboat. Her deck they'd plated with iron to protect her boilers. Midships, she carried huge paddle-boxes; a long deckhouse filled her midships deck; a black funnel pierced it. Four pivot guns armed her, two of them being powerful bottle-shaped Dahlgrens which were situated forward and two aft.

Within hailing distance, an officer stepped forward. Speaking trumpet touching his mouth, he shouted, "Identify yourself, Westcott."

So, Alex hadn't lost his sense of humor. Ben cupped his hands around his mouth: "Lieutenant Benjamin Westcott, sir! Request permission to come aboard!"

"Why? So you can eat the load of fish we have on board?"

"I hate seafood."

"I know."

"May I come aboard?"

"I'll take that under consideration, lousy fish hater." Alex disappeared behind the big Dahlgren. Seconds later, he returned within view. "I've considered it. Permission not granted."

"Not granted! You're out of your mind!"

"Shove off, Westcott. That's an order."

"Why?" Ben said.

"Because I'm officer of the deck and I said so."

For crying out loud. "Are you serious?"

Alex backed away.

Slapping his cap against his thigh, Ben turned to leave. Alex's uproarious laughter exploded. Ben wagged his head. *A born clown.*

Lieutenant commanding Murphey invited Ben into his cabin till Alex's forenoon watch ended. Ben judged him to be over sixty years old, yet not quite seventy, perhaps. Curious regarding the battle below New Orleans, Murphey said he distrusted newspaper accounts.

Ben recounted his part in the engagement, except for his and Locke's quarrel. That was a private matter. He described his wounds, how he almost died, and life in Fort Warren followed by his recent exchange.

"Permission to ask a question, sir?" Ben said, once his story ended.

Murphey nodded.

"How are our defenses here?"

"We're working on them," Murphey said. "Our army's erecting earthworks around the city and batteries on the rivers. General Bragg moved his army through here this past July. He took over what had been General Beauregard's command. Most of our squadron's men aren't Southerners. They're Irish and British, and we have a few French. The *Selma* has twenty or so Northerners and only five or six Southerners. Troublemakers, the lot of them. The admiral once told me he wished our government would let him hang a few of 'em. Every time we stand off Grant's Pass, some manage to desert despite my best efforts to stop it."

Ben started to ask what sort of efforts the captain made so that he might offer some suggestions but thought better of it since this was the first time they'd met.

"What are your orders?" Murphey held out a box of cigars.

"No, thank you, sir."

"Not a smoker?"

"No, sir." He started to add "poker and billiards player," but refrained from that. The less Murphey knew about him, till he knew more about Murphey, the better. To get in a fix with the admiral or to have the captain report him…that wouldn't do at all. "The admiral's dispatching me to Tennessee to recruit men from Bragg's army. He believes it has sailors who'd like to sign on with us."

"Let's hope the generals cooperate."

"Admiral Buchanan doesn't go in for much foolishness, the scuttlebutt I've heard."

"Not much of a sociable animal, but I tell you one thing certain. He's earned my respect. He definitely gave the Yanks a good licking in Hampton Roads. What's more, our soldier boys here respect him. He's the ranking officer."

Everyone respected him. That was a good thing, but respecting and liking were two different birds. Did he intimidate everybody the way he'd felt intimidated? "Who's in command of the army?"

"Brigadier General Simon Bolivar Buckner. Before him, General Mackall and before him General Forney and before him…" Murphey whistled, long and low. "I tell you, Westcott, it seems this city's seen more commanding generals than a dog's seen fleas."

"And the navy?"

Murphey eyed the clock on a small shelf attached to his port bulkhead. "Forenoon watch is minutes from over. I imagine you'll want to catch up on the news once Mister Jessup gets relieved of his duty."

"Yes, sir." He had only one question for Alex, and his friend better give him a straight answer.

Ben and Alex cradled warm cups of coffee at the mess table.

Alex lifted his and caught a whiff. "Ah! Real coffee, courtesy of a blockade-runner that sneaked in through the Swash Channel day before yesterday. Haven't enjoyed real coffee since the *Sumter* days when we'd confiscate it off prizes."

"Al—"

"Shhh! I, sir, am a coffee connoisseur." Alex sipped the coffee and smacked his lips. "Not bad. Have you seen Susan yet?"

"That's what I need to discuss."

"Have you… heard…about…your…fa—?"

"Yes."

Alex's face clouded. "A tragedy."

Alex's regret was sincere. Not only was his friend sad for him, but Ben suspected Alex pitied himself. Could it be he still grieved over his mother's and sister Susannah's deaths? All these years he'd known him, he'd never once betrayed a hint of the blues. Positive, easygoing, sarcastic, that had been the Alex he'd always known. Or maybe: "Have you heard from your father?"

"He's still alive, far as I know."

So it must be his mother and Susannah. "I'll get my revenge. I have a strong suspicion Locke killed Annie."

"There wasn't any proof, Moxley says."

"The circumstances of her death and the way she died are similar to Rosalita's. When this war's over, I'll find him and I'll kill him. I wish I'd done it that day we fought our duel."

"Suppose you never find him again. But then, I suspected he'd killed you, and I made a similar vow."

"I tell you, Alex, I'll spend my life hunting down that man." Ben dumped four spoonfuls of sugar in his coffee. "When did Moxley and Susan get engaged?"

Alex gagged on the liquid going down his throat. "They're about as engaged as a possum and a polecat. Where'd you hear that nonsense?"

"Moxley."

"Why am I not surprised?"

"He was at Susan's house when I saw her. I think she was making him a uniform."

Down went Alex's coffee cup. "Your brother has gotten some foolish notions of late. Why are you asking me that question?" A toothy grin spanned his face. "Oh, yes! I see it. She has sparked your interest, hasn't she now?"

"She appears to have changed for the better."

"She's changed an almighty lot. Funny thing, though. Your genius brother gives himself credit."

"So he told me."

"When I was on board the *Florida* this past September, at death's door from yellow fever, she was alongside me on the *Lady Amber*, praying for me. She claims God spoke to her then, and that it was God who restored my health. I fear she's turning into a fanatic."

"I never considered the doctor a fanatic. Religious, yes, but not a fanatic, not in the sense of his being crazy like ole John Brown was. In fact, he's one of the most rational, intelligent men I've ever known."

"Well, she's turning into a fanatic. I'm writing Father about it. Maybe he'll have some ideas about what to do."

"If she's turned religious fanatic, trust me, my self-centered heathen dog brother had nothing to do with it."

"That is correct, sir."

Ben looked over his shoulder at the officer behind him who'd spoken those words, sitting on a stool and reading a book. He peered up over it.

"I'm glad you agree," Ben said. "Who might you be?"

"Acting Master Walker, Lieutenant," the officer said.

"Walker's our ship's theologian and self-appointed chaplain," Alex said drily. "Another Doctor Kirby in our midst."

"The admiral's sending me on a recruiting mission tomorrow," Ben said. "When I return, we'll play some billiards."

"For pleasure," Alex said. "I'm not in the mood for any wagers right now."

"Agreed."

Alex held his hands as though holding a cue stick. "Number six ball in the right corner pocket." He pretended to strike the imaginary ball. "Got her in there." He squinted. "Dang it. It was the cue ball I sunk." He laughed.

Ben glanced behind him again and noticed that Walker had resumed reading. He almost invited him to join their future game until he thought better of it. Likely, he wasn't interested. At least, he didn't seem like he was.

40

THE CLOP-CLOP OF hooves on oyster shells, the occasional pop of a rider's crop, the winter sun casting long shadows of animals and wagons between the limbs of magnolia trees, people traveling the Shell Road afoot, and among this busyness, Susan and Ben rode horses while the Evanses' buggy kept pace. A Sunday stroll was what Susan wanted after church. With Captain Hughes down the bay and her father at war, the Evanses were their chaperone. Ben hated chaperones as much as Annie did, though he understood that Susan considered their outing as one between friends. He wouldn't make Moxley's mistake by jumping to conclusions about things.

"I enjoyed today's sermon," Susan said.

"It was a fine one," Ben said.

"Do you believe it?"

"What kind of question is that?" Ben wished she'd end her interrogation. He felt like he was on trial. Determined to uncover more information regarding hers and Moxley's relationship, he changed the subject. "My brother's a fine individual."

"He's persistent."

"He's mule-headed. He doesn't quit or get discouraged easily."

"I admire that in a man."

"I'm glad you admire him." *Ben, you liar.*

"How can I not? When I was evil and rude and tried to force him out of my life, I think it made him like me more. He told me he doesn't care what others think, and he's proven it time and again. Nor has he ever complained about not being an officer, never complained about anything. At least, not in my presence. I like men who don't complain. If we all had it easy, life wouldn't be interesting."

"It's good that you've gotten over your sister's death."

"Oh, yes! She's fine now. She's in heaven. What greater place is there to be other than heaven?"

"I can't think of any better place than that. Where are we going?"

"To my home in Spring Hill. I'd like you to see it. I have some things to collect there."

"We aren't on the Spring Hill Road."

"We're going a different way."

Ben caught Mrs. Evans smiling at them. *All right, Ben, my man. Time's come. Watch Susan's reaction.* "I'm leaving for Tennessee tomorrow."

His and Susan's eyes locked.

"Recruiting duty. Admiral Buchanan's sending me there."

"Then I pray you'll have a safe trip and find success."

"Thank you." Ben unlocked his eyes from hers and stared dead ahead. Susan's tone and reaction betrayed nothing of her thoughts, other than she wished him well. Well, he was as mule-headed as Moxley. He'd prove it to her and his idiot brother soon as he returned.

41

"**P**IG KILLER." HANDS on her hips, blond brows knit hard, Amy Hamilton blocked her gate.

"I'm sorry," Susan said. "It was wrong what I did."

"Wrong won't bring him back."

"No. It won't."

Susan moved to open the gate. Amy yanked it shut.

"Don't come on our land," Amy said. "We don't like you. We think you're strange."

"Amelia," Mrs. Hamilton shouted from an open window. "Step aside, or else I'll have your father give you a spanking when he gets home tomorrow. I invited Susan here."

"I hope you get bit by a dog."

Susan ignored the insult. The poor dear was still upset over that time she'd made Huston kill her pet pig because she was starving and so she could eat him. She must find a way to make it up to her.

A butler let her inside. Unlike her home, its wallpaper remained intact. Camellia bushes and magnolia trees and a vast cotton field filled it. She hadn't been in this home since she was five. Because the Hamiltons had no family member fighting in this war, they had no one on the front lines to write. Mrs. Hamilton was an only child. Her five siblings all died young. Mister Hamilton's brothers were planters up around Tuscaloosa and Opelika. Their sons fought on various fronts; occasionally, they'd receive letters from them.

"Forgive Amy," Mrs. Hamilton said. "She's got a temper."

209

"I understand," Susan said. "That's one thing I truly do understand. I'll make amends one day. That's a promise." She followed Mrs. Hamilton into the dining room on the right, where Mary sat at its long table mending a pale blue bonnet.

Mary paused her needle. "Good morning, Susan."

"Morning, Mary."

"Have a seat, dear." Mrs. Hamilton pulled out a dining chair. She sat opposite Susan, next to Mary, laced her fingers on the table, and smiled. "I guess you're wondering about our invitation."

"Yes, ma'am," Susan said. "I guess I am."

"I'm sure you've noticed my friends filing into my house every Saturday. Perhaps you've read about our work in the newspapers."

"Isn't it a Soldier's Aid society or something like that?"

Mary set down her bonnet. "We'd like you to join us, Susan, that is, if the post office doesn't keep you too busy."

"Me? Why me? My reputation is— "

"Forgiven and forgotten," Mrs. Hamilton said.

"The city's doing all it can to help the poor folk in our community," Mary said. "I'm not working at Camp Beulah anymore. Mother and I aren't going upriver with father anymore either. At least until the war's over. I believe helping mother is what I'm supposed to do."

"Our city's Free Market certainly can't do enough," Susan said. "That's obvious from what I've read in the papers."

"It helps, but you're right, it can't do enough. It's not the Market's fault."

"My husband's a member of the Mobile Supply Association," Mrs. Hamilton said. "They purchase supplies and sell them at cost."

"We are starting to suffer a severe supply shortage," Susan said.

"It's liable to get worse. Will you join us, Susan?" Mrs. Hamilton unlaced her fingers. "We need you."

"I can't help you, work at Camp Beulah, and the post office too."

"Quit Camp Beulah," Mary said. "Gusta has plenty of ladies helping her."

Susan considered it for half a minute. "I'll do it. Mary, will you accompany me to her house so I can tell her?"

Mary reached across the table and clasped Susan's hands. Susan realized that as of today, their feud was over.

"Let me get my cloak and gloves," Mary said. "I'll meet you at your house."

"I'll be waiting." Susan walked to her side of the fence to get her reticule.

While Dolphus drove her carriage toward Georgia Cottage Susan sat opposite Mary, her hands crossed in her lap. She was glad Lieutenant Westcott had survived his wounds. His survival, though, complicated her situation. Confident Gusta wasn't the sort to reveal a person's secrets, Susan trusted her not to divulge anything personal. Mary, though, could she trust Mary to keep her mouth shut? She wasn't sure, and because she wasn't sure, she kept her feelings to herself. Sometimes, Mary talked too much.

"It's wonderful news about Mister Westcott's brother," Mary said.

"I agree," Susan said. "At least Mister Moxley Westcott has one family member who remains alive."

"I hope I can meet Lieutenant Westcott when he returns from his recruiting trip. What sort of person is he?"

"I don't know him well, but what I do know and what Alex has told me about him, he seems polite. He and his brother love each other as siblings should. That's a good thing."

"Is he handsome?"

Susan nodded absently, again and again, half-hearing Mary's conversation. And therein was her predicament. Her head told her to accept Mister Moxley's persistent efforts at courtship, but since Lieutenant Westcott had returned her heart was tugged toward him. Head, heart, head, heart. *Oh, let them line up on one gentleman only. That will settle my problem.*

Miss Evans took Susan and Mary aback. Dark rings circled her red, watery eyes; she moved at a creep and yawned constantly. Susan feared she bordered on exhaustion.

The author leaned her head against her study's doorjamb. "Forgive me."

"Gusta," Mary said, "you really must get some sleep."

She shut her eyes. "I can't."

"But you must."

"I haven't time." The author yawned loudly into her fist. "Forgive me."

"Make the time."

"I don't have the time, and neither will I make the time. What I'm writing is too important." She returned to her paper-strewn desk.

"How much longer before you finish it?" Susan said.

"It's finished." Miss Evans plopped in her desk chair. "I'm in the process of revising it before I send it to my publisher."

A diamond-studded pen caught Susan's interest.

Miss Evans handed it to her. "General Beauregard gave it to me. He told me he used it to write dispatches during First Manassas."

Mary took it from Susan, who returned it to the author's desk. "It's lovely."

"Susan," Miss Evans said, "I have written a letter to my publisher in Richmond. Since you work at the post office, will you see it gets delivered?"

Susan received the letter, written on brown wrapping paper and folded in half, a wax seal affixed to it. "We know you're busy so we won't keep you long. I won't be able to work at Camp Beulah anymore. I've joined the Soldier's Aid Society. I'll be helping Mary and her mother."

Miss Evans perked up. "That's a capital idea, Susan."

"Thank you, Gusta, for understanding."

"We're all doing what we can for the war effort. Forgive me, please. I'm afraid my friends have caught me at a bad time."

"Of course," Mary said. "Let's go, Susan dear."

Miss Evans leaned over her tall stack of pages, her pen moving swiftly, jotting changes and corrections. And yawning, continually yawning.

Do what Mary says, Gusta, Susan thought as she and Mary left her room. *Get some sleep.*

42

DANNY'S HAMMOCK SWAYED him gently, midnight moonlight streaming through the skylight overhead. Several shipmates shuffled around the berth deck preparing to go on watch. Others snored. *Madison* creaked.

During muster several weeks ago, Captain Vincent announced that President Lincoln had signed the final version of the Emancipation Proclamation. A few days after Antietam's battle in September, he'd announced a preliminary version of it. Now, with his signing the final version, it could be enforced. Danny whispered a "thank you." Now all the slaves were free. When "hurrahs" rang out across the deck, Danny believed most of them sincere. Locke, though, kept his mouth shut, as did several enlisted men he knew.

Danny remembered his last master, Hickory Yates, telling him the war would end slavery. Danny reckoned he'd be smiling right now from heaven's portals.

His thoughts drifted toward shipboard rumors. Mobile would be taken next, most everyone believed, and yet, Admiral Farragut had ordered their ship back up the Mississippi, most likely to join him at New Orleans. Another ship relieved them of their duty at the river's mouth.

Throughout January and February, the West Gulf Squadron suffered disasters on top of humiliations. Union forces easily captured Galveston in October and as December wound down, Farragut ordered General Nathaniel Banks, Butler's successor, to occupy it, but he didn't occupy it long. The Rebels recaptured Galveston on the first day of January.

When the admiral sent Commodore Bell's *Brooklyn* along with five or six gunboats to retake the town, Semmes's new commerce raider, *Alabama,* lured one of Bell's ships into a nighttime ambush and sank her inside of fifteen minutes. A mere handful of men escaped capture, having lowered a boat minutes before *Alabama* identified herself and opened fire. They rowed hard toward *Brooklyn,* reported the disaster, but by then, the raider was gone. During the predawn hours of the sixteenth, *Florida* escaped Mobile Bay. With these two cruisers prowling the Gulf, *Madison* joined other ships on various stations keeping a lookout for them.

Danny turned on his hammock. "I hope I'm gonna have time to visit Nancy."

"Go to sleep," Juniper mumbled from the hammock beside him.

"I can't."

"Try."

Bundled in his pea jacket, Danny hugged his body. People streamed out of D.H. Holmes's store, climbing into carriages and coaches or swinging into saddles. He'd considered going inside, but since he'd arrived near the time Nancy got off work, he waited at the entrance despite winter's cold. He was grateful Miss Annie let her start work here before her poor mistress was killed.

He peeked through the window, crouched, spotted her chattering with two white ladies. A purple hat was tilted low on her forehead, ribbons of pink lace falling from it, flowing over her mass of dark curls. She tossed back her head and laughed. He sure liked hearing her laugh. Did a soul good, hearing it.

She glanced his direction.

Lower, on his left knee, he sank.

No sooner was she outside than he jumped up and flung his arms around her and hefted her high. She squealed, till she realized it was him. She burst into giggles.

"Who on earth is this man, Nancy?" a white woman said.

"Only my husband." Nancy winked at him.

"So, this is the Danny you've always been bragging about," the other white woman said.

"I hope I am." Danny grinned.

"He's my one and only, Lillian," Nancy said.

"Well, I must declare. He is as broad in the shoulders as you said he was."

"And his heart's just as broad."

Danny clasped her gloved hand.

"Danny, I want you meeting two of this chile's new friends. They also sew clothes for Mister Holmes's customers. This here's Lillian, and this other lady's Julia."

"It's nice meeting you," Danny said. "I'm glad you're her friends."

"We're glad Nancy's our friend," Julia said. "She's taught us all sorts of things about making lace. Let's be on our way, Lillian. See you Monday."

"Bye!" Nancy waved at them.

"White friends, Nancy? Since when did white Southerners start befriending us black folks?"

"Wasn't Mister Hickory your friend?"

"He was that, and a good friend."

They headed up the street.

"I reckon you know about Mister Lincoln's Emancipation."

"Humph. It don't do us no good in this chile's town. He's exempted us since the Yankees took us before he did his emancipating."

"Exempt?"

"Means he didn't free us down here, what I heard. And them slaves up in Kentucky and such, they ain't freed either because they stayed in the Union."

"But with Miss Annie—"

"I made myself free, Danny. With Miss Annie dead and Mister Moxley gone to Mobile and poor Mister Ben probably dead, the Brulets pretend like I'm their slave and give me a pass whenever I need one, but they don't treat me like a slave. They just give me the papers I need so I don't get in trouble. They even lowered the rent on my house."

A buggy rattled alongside. Its driver, a well-dressed black man wearing a top hat, reined in his horses. "Could you use a ride?"

"No." Danny pulled Nancy into a faster walk.

"I don't mind." He whistled at his two horses. His buggy kept pace. Two jagged scars crisscrossed the man's left cheek. His eyes were small, his brow narrow.

Danny wasn't sure he trusted him. "We don't need a ride, sir."

"The walk is a long one. Plenty of room in the rear seat."

"We'll get there. And I thank you not to ask us again."

"Oh, Danny!" Nancy jerked him to a stop.

"Get in," the driver said, smiling.

"No," Danny said.

Nancy shoved him into the vehicle.

"Thank you kindly for the ride, Reverend Dotson." Danny assisted Nancy down from the buggy, having quickly overcome his initial embarrassment upon learning who he was. "I apologize for my previous conduct."

"Protecting one's self and one's wife is not a sin. It's something to be commended." The pastor climbed out behind them. "I don't live far. Walking distance." He tipped his hat at them. "I'll leave my old buggy here and go fetch my wife. After all the stories Nancy's told us about you, she's been wanting to meet you."

Danny led Nancy toward her narrow wooden house. Since he'd been down at the passes these past few months, he'd received all her letters. In many of them, she'd mentioned the reverend.

"He's Baptist," Nancy said. "Is that all right?"

"Makes no matter to me, my Nancy-girl."

"He's a good man. A good preacher too. He has that same fire in the belly Parson Silas had. He pretty near has the whole Bible memorized."

"Maybe if my reading gets better I can start memorizing it."

"He knows Greek and Hebrew. He says those are the Bible's original languages. His wife is a good friend. I met them outside Mister Holmes's store four months back, remember what I wrote you? She's the one who invited me to their church."

"Esther, I think you said her name was."

Inside her house, Nancy lit the gaslight. "Reverend Dotson says Esther means star. She twinkles all the time, he says to me." Nancy chuckled.

Danny hung his sailor's cap on a wall peg. A faded blue sofa, two Windsor chairs, and a simple square table fronted a small fireplace. He'd been here before, after he got rid of Titus. Black people, poor white people, and others of lesser means lived in this district.

"Big fancy homes like the Westcotts owned don't make for happiness." Nancy handed him her hat.

He hung it beside his.

"That's one thing this chile's learned."

"Are you truly happy here?"

Nancy twined her arm around his. "This chile's the happiest girl in this whole wide world. I have you, I have this house, and—"

"What's happened to the coffee?" Reverend Dotson boomed from the entrance. He stepped aside, allowing his wife's entry.

"Rev'rend. Be patient." Esther said with mock indignation.

The pastor smiled at Danny.

Danny smiled back.

"Mister Yates, permit me the privilege of introducing you to my lovely wife, Queen Esther the Twinkler!"

"Shush that nonsense." Mrs. Dotson, no taller than four-feet nine and her dark hair bound in a chignon at her nape, offered her tiny gloved hand. "Nancy's told me a lot about you, sir."

Danny held it briefly. "Yes, ma'am. It's good meeting you as well."

"Nancy, let's us ladies slip into the kitchen so our menfolk can have a sit down by themselves in private. We'll make my husband his coffee."

"With lots and lots of sugar," Nancy said.

"And more sugar," Esther said.

Laughing, Nancy and Esther went straight back through the doors.

Once Danny and Reverend Dotson made a fire in the fireplace, they pulled up chairs.

The pastor drew a small Testament from his coat pocket. "Nancy tells me you've been a Christian a long time."

"Since I was a boy. Nancy and me have been married since we were, I reckon you'd say we were in our youth. I don't exactly know when I was born. Nobody bothered telling me."

"What are your duties in the Navy?"

Danny described them quickly. "Doctor Kirby, sir. He's our ship's surgeon. He and the kind quartermaster Mister Appleton have been giving me a good education. If it wasn't, I mean weren't, for them, I wouldn't be able to read and speak nearly as well as I do now."

"Umm." The pastor flipped through the Testament's pages. "Do you plan on staying in the Navy after the war?"

"When it's over, I wanna do something different. I don't wanna go back to blacksmithing. I'd like my life to count for something on this earth. That's why I asked Doctor Kirby to help me get a better education."

"There's not a thing wrong with blacksmithing. It's an honorable way to earn a living."

"I didn't mean it that way exactly. I meant, I wanna do more, I wanna help folks more."

Reverend Dotson looked up from his Testament. He urged Danny to continue.

"I'd love being a doctor, 'cause doctors help folks, but I can't see myself doing that. It takes lots of studying and education, and my being born a black man and all."

"Have you asked God about it?"

"About what I wanna do?"

"His plans for us are better than our own. Before the Yankees came, it wasn't easy for me to be a colored preacher down here. Esther and I have always been free-coloreds, and before the war we felt called to move down here from Virginia. After much prayer, and hesitation I might add, we did it. Trying to start a church in this city..." Reverend Dotson shook his head. "At the time, I thought it was impossible. You see, police often broke up our meetings. I spent quite a number of days in jail because I held public meetings, and that was against the law for us free- coloreds. All I wanted to do was preach. I got so sick and tired of the way we were persecuted I nearly quit the ministry."

Danny sat on the edge of his seat, eager to learn more about the pastor's story.

"It wasn't two days after I'd decided to quit that I met some white folks who, although they owned slaves, thought we ought to be allowed to have a church building. They even gave me the buggy you saw me driving. It wasn't new when they gave it to me, but it serves my purposes. They arranged with the city to let us meet for two hours every Sunday afternoon. We still had to have a police officer attend our meetings. You see, Mister Yates. Deep down inside I knew God called me to preach, but it wasn't an easy thing. Not in New Orleans, but He helped me even when things got tough. God may want you to do something difficult, at least from your point of view. But He'll help you and provide a way. He always does. First, you must ask Him to show you. He'll lead you in the right direction." He slapped his knee. "Well, that's my sermon for today."

Danny reached down and picked up a splinter which he flung into the fire. "I can't see it happening. I can't ever see me becoming a doctor."

"Coffee!" Mrs. Dotson trilled as she brought in a tray bearing two steaming cups.

Danny reached for a cup. He could go back to blacksmithing after the war, yet with all his heart, he hated doing that.

43

ROM *HARTFORD'S* QUARTERDECK, Farragut observed his ships steaming the Mississippi on a course upriver from Baton Rouge. Tars swarmed decks and masts, their battle preparations confirming rumors. Another fight awaited them on the bluffs up ahead, against Rebel earthworks and Rebel cannon and Rebel troops at a tiny garrison called Port Hudson.

Anchors splashed near Profit's Island, the late afternoon's sunlight playing between the slight gaps of its thick forest. The island's bank, perfect for running up boats and offloading supplies, had no trees. Beyond this island, on the eastern bank of a 150-degree bend, rugged bluffs gently sloped up as high as eighty to one hundred feet. Gunboats were lashed to the port stern quarters of Farragut's men-of-war—*Albatross* secured to *Hartford, Genesee* to *Richmond, Dolphin* to *Madison, Kineo* to *Monongahela,* and his slowest ship, the side-wheeler *Mississippi,* brought up the rear.

Early next morning, blanketed by heavy fog, they slowly steamed to the head of the island where the ironclad *Essex,* two gunboats, and six mortar schooners awaited them. The admiral signaled his captains aboard for a final conference.

"Gentlemen." Farragut planted his fist on the chart table. "Everyone has read my General Order. I want to review it once more before we advance and if there are any questions, now is the time to ask. Commander Caldwell, give us your report on the Rebel defenses."

Commander Charles Caldwell, *Essex's* captain and commander of the mortar flotilla between Port Hudson and New Orleans, lifted his intense gray eyes. "It will be a bloodletting, make no mistake about that. They have batteries all along the river's east bank. Maybe some on the west bank, but I'm not certain about that."

"Guns? Batteries?" Commander Alden, *Richmond's* commander, asked.

"I wouldn't swear on how many," Caldwell said. "There's also five Rebel ships."

"I saw them. They're lying off the town. One of them is the *Queen of the West.*"

Farragut winced. That struck a nerve. Thanks to his acting rear admiral foster brother David, who'd replaced Davis as commander of the Mississippi Squadron, the Rebels captured that ship and the ironclad *Indianola* the previous month. David was sending his ships downriver one at a time, and the Rebels were picking them off. His failures defeated any effort he might make to assist them, but he'd best keep such thoughts to himself. "We'll retake the *Queen of the West.* We passed Forts Jackson and St. Philip. I imagine we'll pass Port Hudson even easier."

The captains' expressions flashed concern.

"General Banks's troops will soon move into position in Port Hudson's rear. He'll create a diversion while we pass. Our main objective is to stop the Rebels from using the Red River to bring in supplies and beef cattle from Texas." He indicated the river's mouth on his chart, a few miles above Port Hudson and winding all the way through Shreveport, in north Louisiana on the Texas border. "We need vessels above the Rebel garrison and others patrolling the Red. Our second objective once we pass is to assist General Grant's efforts to take Vicksburg if he needs us. As we steam around the bend, each ship will keep a very little on the starboard quarter of the one next ahead. This will allow our chase guns free range without risking damage from a premature explosion. We want to pass with as little damage as possible to our ships."

"Once we pass the Rebel batteries, the gunboats are to break off and proceed up the Red's mouth," Vincent said.

"That's correct." Farragut leveled his gaze on the gunboat captains. "Gentlemen, capture anything and everything you can in the Red."

Those captains nodded.

For thirty more minutes, Farragut reviewed his plan detail by detail. His *Hartford* would take the lead. "Commander Caldwell," he said at the conference's end, "have your schooners test their range on the Rebel batteries. If they're not close enough, see that you move them closer. We'll need your covering fire when we pass."

"Aye, sir." Caldwell squeezed back between two other commanders and left Farragut's quarters.

"Mister Farragut," the admiral called.

Loyall poked his head in the cabin.

"Get the memorandums for me. Distribute them to each captain."

"Aye, sir."

"Our signals are listed in them, gentlemen. Read them. Memorize them if necessary."

Loyall returned, memorandums in hand. As they filed out, the captains took them.

When Vincent's cutlass jangled up *Madison's* poop deck ladder and he stepped onto the quarterdeck, Locke turned toward him. It was just a few minutes before ten o'clock. Silence, cold and thick as a tomb, saddled her sailors. The whitewashed deck silhouetted men against the black evening. Oak buckets in hand, Hoag and Roscoe delivered cartridges to each gun division. Until he went off deck officer duty, Ensign Rawlins commanded his midships gun division.

Hartford and *Richmond* lay to up ahead, their consorts lashed to their sides. He considered requesting liberty when they returned to New Orleans. No one suspected his role in Annie Westcott's death. He could walk its streets for years, and no one would be the wiser. He could get away with anything.

"We're in position, sir," Buckley said. "Behind the *Richmond* and *Genessee* as ordered."

"Very well," Vincent said.

"I can't say that for the *Monongahela* and *Kineo*." He tilted his head aft.

"Don't tell me they haven't moved into position yet." Vincent whipped his night-glass to his eyes. "What's wrong with them? The old *Mississippi* doesn't look like she's moved either."

"No, sir."

"Mister Locke," Vincent said, "signal the admiral we're in position."

Before Locke gave the order, blaring lights and piercing whistles bearing down on *Hartford* screamed.

Vincent jerked his night glasses to his eyes again. "She looks like the *Reliance.*"

The captain's assessment proved correct. She steamed past the column, down to the three straggling vessels. Soon they closed up, and soon, *Hartford* hung two red lanterns over her stern.

"Finally," Vincent said, observing the flagship's signal. "Two red lanterns off our stern, Mister Locke."

Locke relayed the order to the signal officer nearby then dispatched an ensign to the assistant engineer who stood by the engine room's bell. Steam up, *Madison* and her consort *Dolphin* proceeded upriver.

"Ow!" Danny jerked up his right foot and hopped back against the wardroom's bulkhead. "What'd you do that for?"

"'Cause you're in my way, Coal Tar." Roscoe snatched his bucket and darted through another door and down a ladder leading to the ship's aft magazine.

Danny set down his aching foot. "That boy, dropping his bucket on me." He limped into the wardroom.

"They'll learn better one day," Doctor Kirby said.

Danny shook his head. "I can't see it, sir. I'm sorry, but I can't see it for them, or for Mister Locke."

"There's always hope."

"Did you see hope for me?" Upton spoke from the mess table's farthest end.

"No, sir," Danny said.

"Well, doesn't that prove the doctor's point?"

The surgeon's steward, John Shoot, a stout man with light brown hair recently assigned to *Madison*, set aside the chloroform.

Roscoe darted back up the ladder.

"If we weren't moving into a battle, I'd make him apologize to you," Doctor Kirby said. "I'll make him do it later."

"Apologies don't mean nothing, sir, unless a man changes. I'd rather him do it on his own. That way, it'll be more, uh, uh…."

"Sincere," Shoot said.

"That's the word."

From his station on *Madison's* quarterdeck, Locke watched a Rebel signal rocket streak up from the west bank. He and his fellow officers heard *Hartford's* first shot. Flashes, thunder, and smoke from *Essex's* guns below the Rebel batteries. Mortar boats followed her fire; their arcing bombs smacked Rebel positions.

Dolphin's men ran out her port guns and *Madison's* men her starboard. Artillery blazed from the east bank. Up ahead, smoke enveloped *Richmond* while she returned fire. Along the west bank, flames flared from piles of pitch pine, making their ships an easy-to-see target.

"We're approaching the batteries, sir," Buckley told Vincent.

"Very well," Vincent said. "All divisions, open fire."

Buckley dispatched an ensign forward to relay the order.

Madison shuddered beneath her first broadside.

Up ahead, a terrific explosion punctuated the gunfire. Locke strained to see what happened but made out nothing on account of the thick smoke. *Madison* suddenly stalled; her engine hissed.

"Crazy fool. Our pilot's run us aground." Vincent bounded down the ladder to the ship's wheel to speak to him and the quartermasters at the wheel.

Shells exploded overhead. Shrapnel littered their deck. From the west bank, musketry erupted.

Roscoe and Hoag and other boys raced up and down the divisions carrying leather bags filled with gunpowder. Sailors ran out their guns and ran them in time after time, jerking lanyards, broadside after broadside, oblivious to whistling Minie balls and explosions.

Through his speaking trumpet, Vincent shouted at *Dolphin's* quarterdeck to reverse her engines. The assistant engineer standing at *Madison's* engine room bell rang it three times, the signal for reverse.

A shot shattered the hawser securing the vessels.

"Captain!" Locke screamed through his speaking trumpet as he pointed to the hawser.

Vincent looked up from the deck below, where he and the pilot were talking. His speaking trumpet to his lips, he shouted back, "Get another one!"

Shrapnel sent them diving for cover. For the moment, every man on the quarterdeck lay prone. Locke gripped an ensign's ankle, the same one whom Buckley sent forward earlier. "We need a fresh hawser!"

The young man sprang to his feet and bounded down the ladder.

Locke gained his feet and resumed his station.

Morning revealed the squadron's disaster. Every ship, save *Hartford* and *Albatross*, repulsed. *Genesse's* and *Richmond's* hulls were holed, and *Richmond's* cabin windows were also shattered. They'd managed to anchor west of Profit's Island. *Monongahela's* bridge no longer existed, and *Kineo* nearly got blasted into oblivion after she cast loose from *Monongahela* and grounded opposite the enemy's batteries. Another shot split her rudder post. She, too, drifted downstream to the island.

As *Madison* and *Dolphin* had backed off the shoal, Rebel batteries dismasted *Madison's* foremast, killed two Marines, smashed her funnel, and holed *Dolphin* below her waterline. *Dolphin* might have sunk had not a fresh hawser been secured to her, which enabled *Madison* to bring her down to the island. Hammers and saws raised a racket while carpenters made repairs.

The Rebels destroyed the old *Mississippi*. Her officers and crew abandoned her; some drowned, others escaped to shore or in boats rowed to *Essex, Richmond,* and the gunboat *Sachem*. An inferno, her timbers buckling and crackling, the side-wheeler drifted downriver. Her unmanned guns delivered a final broadside, shells exploded, and she drifted past her injured sisters.

Boats resumed picking up survivors.

44

Miss Evans set her pen in her inkwell and rose from her cluttered office desk, her letter to General Beauregard finished. He'd responded to her previous letter in which she'd requested more details on First Manassas. This time her letter was, for the most part, a "thank you." Scheduled to dine with Admiral Buchanan this evening, she gathered up a small stack of mail and headed out her office.

"Shall we be on our way, Sallie?"

"Way to where?" Sallie set down her book.

"The post office."

"Major White was supposed to visit me."

"If the major requires your company bad enough, he'll wait."

"I'll let him know you'll be back, Miss Sallie," Elkanah said.

"We won't be gone long," Miss Evans said.

The author and her sister climbed into their buggy. The two horses drawing it started forward. Thanks to General Beauregard's letter about First Manassas, *Macaria's* revision fast approached completion.

"Have you noticed our defensive measures lately, Westcott?" Corporal Riggs' knife jabbed a slice of beef. "No way those Yanks will get past us."

A seagull alighted on one of Fort Morgan's cannon in a nearby casement. Another one soared overhead.

"The citizens of New Orleans would disagree," Moxley said.

"Ain't no way Mobile will end up like that city." Private Peterson Persons wagged his head vigorously.

"I most heartily agree," Moxley said. "Too shallow close in. Pass our forts like they did Forts Jackson and St. Philip, then capture our forts guarding the entrance to the bay. Do that, they'll isolate Mobile. Don't need to take the city to do it in. Take us, no more blockade-runners'll get through." Moxley bit off a small corner of the worst excuse of a piece of meat he'd ever put inside his mouth. "That's my wager. Tell you what, Riggs. They get past us, I'll take that fancy bowie you're wearing."

Riggs leaned back and drew his bowie knife from its leather sheath. He twisted its blade back and forth, admiring it. "It's a fine blade. I'd sure hate losing it." He handed it to Moxley. "But I won't. You'll give me those fancy boots of yours after you lose."

"Friends," Moxley said to Persons and his two other messmates, "you've all born witness to this wager." He handed Riggs back his knife. *Ironclads, Riggs. All they need do. Attack us with ironclads. Those ironclads Buchanan's building won't stop them. Not the Tuscaloosa. Not the Huntsville. Not the Tennessee. We'll be outnumbered.*

"A telegram's arrived."

Moxley reached up behind him and received it from Sergeant Ferguson. "Susan says my brother'll be back in a couple of weeks. Promised to wire me again when he arrives."

"Let's hope he's found our admiral some sailors," Ferguson said.

"Let's hope he stays away from my sweetheart."

A bugler blew drill call.

On the twenty-eighth day of March, Ben returned to Mobile. Rather than report to Admiral Buchanan straight away, he struck out for Susan's house. Large wooden signs nailed onto stakes and posted on street corners blared at him in large black letters: "Bread or Peace."

Approaching Dauphin Street, an elderly woman flung one of them out of her parked wagon.

Curious, Ben approached when she suddenly whipped out a large revolver from her battered, faded blue skirt pocket.

"Ma'am?" Ben gestured at the pile of signs in a small wagon. "May I ask what all those things are about?"

The elderly woman puffed her iron-gray tendrils. "Quit standing there, whoever you is. Is you or is you not a gen'lman? Is you or is you not going to hep me with this here thing, eh?" She stooped to pick up her sign. Ben snatched it quicker.

"Where do you want it?" Ben asked.

"Where lotsa folks can see it, eh? That there's where I want it."

Ben scanned their section of banquette. "Ah. The perfect spot." He carried it to a hitching rail at a small shop.

The woman's beady eyes flashed. "Its owner's a Jew. See that there name painted all nice and purty on the winder? Rubenstein Saddlery. He's a Jew. A stinking, thieving Jew." Her crooked grin displayed jagged, yellowed teeth. "Good spot you chose, whoever you is. All these here rich high-falutin' Jews need to see what they're doing to us poor folk. If'n they got a smidgen of conscience, they'll quit it. Stick that sign right yonder, against that there rail. Eh?"

Ben held the sign flat against it. Pulling a large nail from her skirt pocket, the woman hammered it in place with the butt end of her revolver. "Carryin' a concealed gun's against the law in this here state, but I don't give a care. Don't tell nobody I carry me a gun."

"I won't."

She offered him her veined, olive hand. "Agathena Mott."

"Lieutenant Benjamin Westcott." He briefly accepted her hand.

"And you was asking?"

"About the signs. I've been away on navy business these past few months. I don't know what all's been happening since I've been away."

"We're suffering, Westcott, and ain't 'nough being done to help us poor folks. It's the Jews to blame. The Jews and the war."

"It's the war, ma'am. Only the war and the Yankee blockade."

Agathena reared up on her toes. "The war *and* the Jews!" She puffed her dangling tendrils. "Them Jews raise their prices more'n they oughta be."

Ben almost responded to that false accusation but voted against it. The war and the blockade was the short answer as to why Mobile and other cities and towns suffered shortages of food and paid high prices for goods. The longer answer was more complicated, and he hadn't time to argue with a woman whose mind was already dead-set against Jewish people. "Well, a pleasure meeting you, Mrs. Mott." He tipped his cap and resumed his walk.

Ben peeked inside Susan's keepsake box. Atop a neat stack of telegrams and folded letters, he found one from Moxley.

"Those are personal," Susan nearly shouted from the hallway.

The lid dropped over the correspondence. "How many are from my brother?"

"I told you he was persistent."

A flash of the old Susan. "Aren't we glad to see me back?"

"Oh. Well. I'm sorry. I'm still working on my temper. Sit down, please. How did your recruiting trip go?"

"The generals refused to cooperate with my efforts."

"No sailors came back with you?"

"No sailors."

"What will Admiral Buchanan say?"

"Nothing he can say, I hope. I tried, tried hard. Men wanted to come with me, but their commanders forbad it. They told me those men wanting a transfer out of the Army were only trying to get out of military service and since they outranked me…" He shrugged. "What else could I do?" He noticed clothes piled on the music room's floor. "What's that all about?"

"I'm delivering them in a few minutes. Will you accompany me?"

"Where?"

"To a lady's house not far from here. She lost her husband in battle two months ago but only learned of it yesterday. She has six children. I'm doing what I can to help her and others. I'd appreciate your company."

"It will be my most excellent pleasure." Ben escorted her into the adjoining room.

Susan called for Dolphus. Fannie and Hulda stayed out back, washing dishes.

Ben drove Susan's landau while Susan sat on the seat behind him, its roof folded down. Dolphus followed in the wagon.

"Look, Miss Jessup. Another one. Two points off our starboard bow." Ben pointed out a "Bread or Peace" sign on their right and mentioned Agathena.

"Most of the ladies I've been helping in recent months know her," Susan said. "She's popular with a lot of them, but many others dislike her."

"She has no great affection for Jews."

"Didn't take long to discover that, did it?"

"Do you like her?"

"Not her opinions. She does have one worthy point, though. Despite Mobile's Free Market, poorer citizens are suffering horribly from a lack of food. It's a supply issue. The city lets them go there to get free food, but even that's not enough to cover their needs."

The horses pulling their buggy clopped past the sign Ben had seen.

"Agathena's not alone putting up those signs. A lot of women are doing it. They're desperate. Turn at this next block."

Ben steered the buggy's team onto it.

"Lieutenant Westcott, if the situation isn't fully solved, I fear Agathena and her friends will one day make trouble. Here we are. This is Mrs. McTighe's place. Stop here."

Ben halted the horses at a small frame house enclosed by a rotting white picket fence and flanked on either side by two larger, nicer brick homes. Black crepe wound around two of its narrow, square columns on its front porch; more crepe draped its entrance. Not only did its fence need repair, its faded whitewashed sides indicated it hadn't seen paint in years. He pitied these poor people. All his life he'd socialized with the rich and in the Navy, though some of his officer friends weren't rich, they at least came from middle-class families and were well-educated. He could only imagine what poverty felt like. He was proud of Susan for finally getting out of her selfishness and helping these folks.

Up and down the street, people mourned loved ones—black crepe hung on practically every house, except the two flanking this one.

Dolphus halted the wagon at the widow's gate.

Ben swung off his buggy seat and moved swiftly to Susan's side.

"Get the clothes, please," Susan told Dolphus after Ben helped her down.

Dolphus gestured at two boys sitting on the wagon bed.

Mrs. McTighe emerged from her front door. "Miss Jessup."

"It is I, Mrs. McTighe."

Her arms outstretched, the widow rushed through the gate and enfolded Susan in a huge hug. "A godsend, dear. You are a godsend."

More wagons and buggies pulled up before other crepe-draped homes. Susan broke from Mrs. McTighe's embrace. Because she wore a heavy black veil, Ben couldn't see her face; her quivering voice, though, exposed her misery. Ladies climbed down from the other buggies and wagons while their servants heaved down trunks.

"Those are my friends." Susan gestured at the activity. "We're all here to do what we can."

A tug on Ben's sleeve caused his eyes to wander down to a tiny, blond, curly-haired girl with a dirty yet smiling face. She appeared no older than six years.

"Are you two married?" the girl said.

"Hattie!" Mrs. McTighe drew the child close. "Don't ask questions like that."

"Mommy." Hattie buried her face in her mother's heavy black skirt. "I want—"

"It's none of your business."

Ben darted a glance at Susan out the corners of his eyes. She was blushing. He pulled in his sudden grin.

"This is Lieutenant Benjamin Westcott," Susan said, stifling a stammer.

"I am her friend." Ben wasn't about to assume he was her beau. Not yet. "I am her very good friend."

Hattie's siblings, two older brothers and three younger sisters, came running out of the house. They surrounded the trunk which Dolphus set on the ground. Ben took its key from Susan. "Are you ready, children?"

"Ready!" they cried.

"Here we go."

Key in the padlock, Ben twisted it open. Once he looked up, he glimpsed a handsome red-haired beauty a few houses down. Her soft gaze wandered to his. Her eyes gleamed.

When Ben reported his failure to recruit men, he anticipated the worst end of Buchanan's wrath. Instead, the admiral discharged his ire a different direction.

"I've written our secretary of war," Buchanan said. "I sent him names of men who applied to me for duty. I expected you, and other officers I dispatched to Polk's army and the conscript camps, would bring them back. Do you think that man has responded to my requests?" He snatched his pen out of an inkwell. "No, sir. It's not your fault, Westcott. Nor is it mine. It's the Army's. They don't understand our need. The *Tennessee, Tuscaloosa,* and *Huntsville* were towed down while you were away."

"Yes, sir."

"They aren't finished yet, and we have a long way to go till they are. I haven't determined a permanent assignment for you. For the time being, you will be on temporary duty until those vessels are complete."

"Aye, sir."

"I'm ordering you to the *Selma.* Captain Hughes will take you there."

"Aye, sir. Thank you, sir."

Buchanan grunted. "Thank me for what?"

"For letting me serve with my closest friend."

The admiral resumed writing his reports.

Taking that as Buchanan's signal to shove off, Ben did.

General Grant's early efforts to take Vicksburg failed. Not only was the city well-defended by troops and cannon, it was also protected by the terrain itself—towering bluffs along the Mississippi on its west, nearly impassable swamps on its north; and batteries guarding its southern approach forced enemy armies to march through Louisiana's delta to get around them. A railroad linked the soldiers in Jackson with Pemberton's troops.

Grant tried several flanking maneuvers through swamps and bayous, but nothing succeeded. Then he hit upon a different tactic. He'd send his army down the Mississippi's western bank, through Louisiana swamps well below Vicksburg, and Porter's squadron would pass Vicksburg's batteries, along with four of the general's transports. Once below them, he'd ferry Grant's troops across the river to its eastern side. This would also enable Porter's squadron to relieve Farragut, patrolling the Red and Mississippi Rivers north of Port Hudson and thus allow his return to New Orleans.

At midnight on the sixteenth of April, Porter's squadron weighed anchor. To avoid being noticed by the enemy, they drifted single file rather than steamed. But the Rebels did spot them, and their guns did open up, roaring and flashing, and the pop-popping of muskets from rifle pits on the bluff at point-blank range.

Shells smashed a transport's hull; flames lighted the sky. Back and forth the stricken ships swerved, cannons thundering; the river's swift current carrying them. After a two-and-one-half hour fight, every one of Porter's ships, except a transport, had passed. Exhausted, Grant rejoiced. The garrison was his. He could feel it.

Late Saturday morning, the sun pounding their heads, Moxley, Riggs, and Persons rounded Fort Morgan's citadel. No dress parade this day, not like those held every weekday morning. A day of leisure for the garrison.

"Still fancy your bowie knife," Moxley said, reminding Riggs of their wager a few months back.

"So do I," Riggs said.

"Yanks'll come right through the front door, right beneath our guns. If the rumor's true, Admiral Buchanan's competent and aggressive, the perfect adversary for a man of Farragut's talents, but he won't be able to stop it when that day comes." Moxley halted. "Well, well, look what the crabs brought in." His baby brother was entering the sally port and coming straight at him. Carrying something, was he? *My, my, how he's swinging that right arm. Why, I'd say he's angry, isn't he?*

Ben slapped the brown leather book against Moxley's chest.

Moxley opened it and found lined pages, no words.

"It's an old journal Susan never used. She asked me to give it to you when I came back down the bay. So there, I've done it and you have it. She wants you to start writing your chicken scratch again."

Moxley flushed. "Who called my writing chicken scratch?"

"Me."

"Bah!"

"Do you see my shoulder straps, Private Westcott? They mean I'm an officer."

Moxley snapped to attention, clicked his heels, and snapped a smart salute. "Please accept my deepest apologies, Lieutenant Benjamin Francis Westcott, Confederate States Navy. I will never, ever address you by your first name again."

"See that you don't. See that you don't visit Susan again either."

"That's an order?"

Ben jabbed his forefinger at his shoulder straps, about-faced, and stalked out the fort.

Moxley grinned at Persons. "*Lootinant* Baby Brother thinks he's winning."

Her fore-and-aft sail thumping in the salty breeze behind him, *Selma's* cutter lazily tacked across the bay's mouth. Ben turned his eyes southwest, toward Sand Island, its beauty marred by mounds of bricks and shattered wood, what once had been the island's lighthouse and surrounding buildings. Soldiers from Fort Gaines had destroyed them because Yankee blockaders often used its lighthouse as an observation post.

Up ahead, Fort Gaines. He'd visited it the previous week. Five-sided, with five projecting bastions like its counterpart across the bay's mouth, it wasn't the perfect pentagon Fort Morgan was. Its landward side extended longer than the others.

Susan's image nudged a smile as the cutter tacked northwest, toward Shell Island, Grant's Pass, and *Selma*. When he gave Moxley her journal and pulled rank on him, he'd launched his plan. Even if he'd been an admiral, Moxley wouldn't care. Nothing would stop his pursuit of Susan. Only one thing could and would stop him—Susan herself.

True, Moxley had known her for nearly a year, but they'd never actually courted and Susan's change was a recent event, about eight months according to Alex. If she liked Moxley as much as she claimed, why didn't her interest in him seem more serious? She talked about him as though he were a friend. Moxley's infatuation blinded him to this. His efforts at courtship failed repeatedly. Naturally, that didn't deter him. Let him propose marriage to her instead of just courtship. Let him do that, she'd reject him outright. That would end their friendship. And though Moxley may not stop his pursuit, she'd turn him a cold shoulder permanently.

Therefore, he'd pulled rank to convince Moxley that he feared losing her to him because she'd become attracted to him, and thus provoke his brother into proposing marriage with such urgency, to be so demanding at last, that she'd give Moxley a final and definite "no." After she did that he'd make his move. Not even Alex knew his plan.

Ben didn't know much about Martha Massingale and Alex's stupid "k" word. He promised Susan he'd discover what Alex meant. *In time. In time.*

His boat reached *Selma* by noon mess.

Susan paced her hallway, rereading her father's letter dated October past, many months late like all his letters thanks to the postal department's inefficiency. He'd penned it on stationery obtained from an officer in his brigade, Captain Randall Bartlett, who'd acquired it from a friendly Yankee during a truce at some town called Sharpsburg, up in Maryland. While she read his account of that battle's events, her heart thumped. It sounded worse than the newspaper reports.

Sharpsburg had been a fierce, bloody fight. Had it not been for his suffering a broken leg early in the battle he might have been killed, he said, because most everyone in his regiment had been shot to pieces or severely wounded. He remained whole, recuperating in a Richmond hospital. He expected he'd return to the field as soon as his leg mended.

She folded the letter in half, took it into the parlor, and set it in her keepsake box. Moxley's unmistakable footfalls banged up the gallery's steps.

Hastening into the music room, she sat at her mother's harp. She strummed it once, twice, plucked several strings. Unlike her mother, Susan's tone deafness stole any musical skill she might have possessed, but Moxley didn't know that. She stifled her twitter. In matters of love, her heart remained unsettled between him and his brother.

Moxley eased up behind her. "Miss Jessup?"

"Yes?"

"No more games. My brother delivered me your journal last Saturday. Thanks."

"I'm glad he did."

"I'll write in it like you wish. Poems greater than Robert Browning's. Love poems, Miss Jessup. Love poems I'll address to you. I'll be your Robert Browning and you, my Elizabeth Barrett."

She tensed. She wished he'd stop this nonsense. She'd given him her answer time and again.

"Know what Brother also did when he delivered me your journal? Ordered me to quit seeing you."

Susan turned suddenly. "Then you've disobeyed his orders."

"Bah! Never listen to him. I'm older and smarter. No one and nothing will separate me from you. I love you. Can't you see that? You're the only girl I've ever known that I can honestly say I love. Deep down inside my heart. Truly. Colonel Powell approved my furlough so I could come here and ask. Will you do me the pleasure of becoming my wife?"

"Mister West— "

"Put me off with excuses, that's what you've done. No more of this trifling 'wait till my father gets home' or 'talk to my Uncle Will' if he doesn't. Not talking about courting anymore. Need an answer today. Yes or no. Will you be my wife?"

"Susan. Oh, Susan." Mary banged through the front door waving a letter.

Susan breathed a sigh of relief. Maybe she wouldn't have to answer him yet. "It's all right, Mary. What's that?"

"A letter from Stephen."

Moxley stepped back. The ladies met at the center of the room.

"How did you get it?"

"He's in England raising support for his work. He managed to slip this letter on a ship bound for the Bahamas, which made it onto a blockade-runner which ran into Mobile. Susan, he's inquiring about you."

"Will you write him? Will you tell him what's happened to me?"

"Who's Stephen?" Moxley said.

"My brother," Mary said. "He's a missionary in India."

"He's quite good looking," Susan said.

"Married?" Moxley said.

Susan and Mary burst into giggles.

Moxley stormed out of the house.

1863

MAY
–
JULY

45

"**T**HEY'VE QUIT." CAPTAIN of Marines Julius Meire, Buchanan's son-in-law, uttered the words with contempt.

Buchanan slammed down his pen. "What's this noise?"

"Our carpenters, sir. The scoundrels quit work on the *Tennessee.*"

"Where are they?"

"In irons in the guardhouse."

"How many quit?"

"Ten, sir."

"The same ones who did it several months back?"

"Not all the same ones, sir."

"Bring them to me, Julius. Every last man of them."

"Aye, sir."

Buchanan resumed writing. Since General Danville Leadbetter's engineers were planting torpedoes off Grant's Pass and in the Spanish River, he needed to warn his captains about it. *Gaines,* down the bay, had already been warned, but his captains closer in needed to be aware. Mountains of problems, military and personal, were piling on top of him like a stack of bricks. The last thing he needed was for one of his ships to blow up.

Outside the Custom House, which housed the post office, Ben repeatedly opened and closed his watch. With *Selma* anchored in the Mobile River several blocks away, he had a two-day pass, the second two-day pass he'd gotten since he'd returned to the city. He'd tried visiting Susan the last time. She wasn't home. Glad the war was softening her heart and turning her into a generous person, he nevertheless joined Moxley and Alex in being skeptical of her so-called religious conversion. Her righteous busyness interfering with their relationship disappointed him. So busy was she, in fact, she ignored her servants, who'd consequently slackened off on their chores. He suspected they neglected their work more out of spite than laziness. He'd considered dressing them down like he sometimes did sailors. He'd have made them work.

Sailors. The Mobile Squadron had few true sailors. Some men understood how to work a ship. Not many, though. His ship, *Gaines* and *Morgan*, all suffered the same disease. Desertions. Every time they went down to Grant's Pass, a tar or two inevitably jumped ship. Yankee vessels outside Mobile Bay stood ready to receive them.

Buchanan was correct. The only way they could whip the enemy was by using ironclads. He'd seen men in the shipyard working on *Tennessee*, *Huntsville*, and *Tuscaloosa*, except they didn't appear to be working very fast or very hard.

His left hand clutched his watch. There she was, moving out another door. Susan wouldn't get away this time. He called her name and followed her onto the street.

She glanced his direction; a sudden smile suffused her face.

He smiled back.

"Isn't he adorable!"

She crossed the street.

"Miss Jessup!" the postmaster yelled after her from the Custom House's door. He took out after her.

Baffled, Ben watched. Susan was at the Battle House, a policeman and the postmaster on one side of her; and a lady and a dusty pig on the other side. He crossed over.

"Woman, you can't be letting your livestock run loose like this," the policeman said.

"It wasn't my fault he got away," she said.

"I'm fining you five dollars, and if I see him waddling around this city again, I'll impound him, and you can pay twenty dollars to bail him out."

"Well, I'm sorry. It won't happen again."

The policeman wrote a ticket.

"Please return to work, Miss Jessup," the postmaster said, pleading.

Susan gathered the animal into her arms and thrust him into Ben's.

"What do you think you're doing!" the lady screamed.

"I'm paying your fine and buying your pig," Susan said.

"No deal," the pig's owner said.

"Twenty-five dollars. Thirty?"

"He's my food."

"Think about all that food you can buy with thirty dollars."

"Forty."

"Miss Jessup." The postmaster huffed, clearly annoyed. "Please, miss. Will you please return to work?"

Ben struggled to contain the wriggling, grunting pig. His eyes shifted up and down the street and at the Custom House's windows. He hoped Admiral Buchanan wasn't watching him from his office. It'd be an embarrassment. This animal was soiling his best civilian suit.

"Forty it is. Lieutenant Westcott, please take him to my house."

So the beautiful lady finally acknowledged him. "May I ask why?"

"My neighbor's little girl needs a new pet. This adorable little pig is it."

Ben made no move, wondering why she'd started treating him like an afterthought, the way she'd treated him when they first met a little over two years ago.

"Stay right here," she told the former pig owner. "I'll go back inside, get the money, and pay the fine if you and the kind policeman will wait."

She and the exasperated postmaster headed back across the street.

Ben, holding the squirming pig, fumed.

"Take him." Ben deposited the wriggling swine on Susan's front lawn.

Snout to earth, he waddled around a camellia bush, up to Dolphus, and sniffed the servant's trousers.

"Pardon us for saying so, sir, but we don't want him," Dolphus said.

"Miss Jessup ordered me to bring him here. All right. I brought him. Look at my clothes. They're a mess. If I were wearing my uniform I'd be in real trouble." The pig sniffed Ben's shoes. "I blackened them this morning, varmint. Touch 'em, I'll be eating you for supper." His toe nudged the grunting pig toward an oak tree.

Laughter rang out behind him.

Pivoting, he spotted a red-haired lady and a young girl beaming at him from Susan's gate. The beauty he'd spied at Mrs. McTighe's.

"My pig! My pig!" The child raced to the animal, dropped to her knees, and threw her arms around his thick neck.

The lady strolled to him. "You must be the Lieutenant Westcott I saw with Susan that day we delivered clothes."

"Miss Susan's mentioned me to you?"

"I am her neighbor, Mary Hamilton, and the little girl playing with the pig is my sister Amelia."

"My name's Amy," Amy said.

"All right, Amy," Ben said. "It is a delight meeting you, Miss Hamilton. I'd best get going."

"So quickly?"

"I must return to my ship and change clothes."

Amy looked up at him; concern flashed from her dark eyes. "Did my pig make your clothes dirty?"

Ben patted her curly head. "It's all right." One day, he hoped he'd have a houseful of daughters.

"I'll get my mother's coachman to drive you back," Mary said.

"Thank you. I'm obliged."

Ben's eyes followed Mary walking over to her house. He regretted they hadn't met sooner. He liked red hair; he liked handsome ladies with red hair. Clara Dawson, his neighbor back in New Orleans, was a handsome redhead, and he might have considered her had she not had so many freckles. As for Mary, her skin possessed no such blemishes.

Admiral Buchanan didn't acknowledge the rattling shackles. His pen crept across his stationery, line by line, composing a letter to Commander Catesby Jones, his former executive officer aboard *Virginia* and the new commander of the Naval Ordnance Works in Selma. He updated him on affairs at Mobile: his tests of *Huntsville's* and *Tuscaloosa's* engines this past April. Too slow, he told Jones. He could only use them as floating batteries, but he needed guns. *Tuscaloosa* was already plated over with iron. Much more was needed for his other ships. Since *Tuscaloosa* and *Huntsville* were too slow, he'd exert all his energy arming, armoring, and manning *Tennessee*. On the Tombigbee River other vessels were being built, as well as another one, *Nashville*, in Montgomery. But numerous problems and delays hampered progress.

One prisoner coughed.

The admiral kept writing.

Two more prisoners coughed.

Buchanan set aside his pen and opened his desk drawer. "Go get him, Captain."

Meire clicked the door shut behind him.

The prisoners' shackles rattled.

Let the rascals squirm. Buchanan set another page of stationery in front of him and resumed his correspondence. This time, a letter to his wife Ann. He'd received word several days back that their house had burned down. The letter came through enemy lines under a flag of truce. Fortunately, his family had escaped. This letter would have to find its way to her via Nassau or Bermuda aboard a blockade-runner and smuggled into Maryland.

One hour later, Captain Meire returned with an army lieutenant.

At last, Buchanan confronted the prisoners. Thin lips downturned, he glowered at one particular individual whose grayish-brown hair fell halfway down his back in a tangled mass. *Brickman.*

"Admiral, I…" Brickman faltered.

Buchanan limped up to him. "What did I tell you when you and your friends went on strike in Selma and came down here looking for work? Does your feeble brain recall?"

"Admiral, we want more— "

"More money? That same old noise again?"

"Sir." This from a man with a ragged black beard, Brickman's friend Haynes, another of those Selma carpenters who'd gone on strike a few months earlier. "Please, sir. We're only asking for a small raise. Times is hard, sir."

"A small raise so you can patronize saloons and purchase more liquor and get drunk out of your minds?"

"Y-Yes, sir. N-No, sir. I have a family, sir. All the saloons is closed at this moment, sir, on account of the blockade."

Buchanan's eyes signaled the lieutenant.

The lieutenant stepped forward smartly and thrust some papers in his hand.

His ire swung back on the ten malcontents; he set the papers on his desk, gestured the lieutenant behind it. What these rascals needed was a good flogging. A pity the law deprived him of the privilege.

The malcontents fidgeted; their chains rattled louder, like knees knocking or teeth chattering.

"You know what those papers are and who the lieutenant is, don't you, Brickman."

"Admiral," Brickman screamed.

"Silence." Buchanan leaned into Brickman's frightened face. "I'm sure you recall that promise I made a few months back. I'm a man who keeps his promises."

"But sir."

Buchanan handed the lieutenant a pen. "The lieutenant here is a conscription officer."

"Admiral."

"Silence. My word is my bond. My orders will be obeyed. As for the rest of you rascals, watch and learn. If any of you dare go on strike again, Captain Meire has my permission to deliver you to the lieutenant here. Haynes, you and Brickman are in the Army now. Lieutenant, sign them up. General Maury informs me that he needs more men."

Slumping as though the wind was knocked out of them, the carpenters signed the enlistment papers.

Buckner no longer commanded the District of the Gulf; his subordinate, Major General Dabney H. Maury, did.

As Meire marched out the others, Buchanan returned to his squadron's problems. He didn't doubt the day would come when Farragut would attack him. The only question was: when? He needed his ironclads finished so he could sally forth beyond the bay and scatter the enemy's blockaders before his old friend made his move. After that, he'd recapture New Orleans.

Calling the pig to follow her, Amy sauntered a circle on Susan's front lawn.

"Do you like him?" Susan said.

"I do! I do!" Amy sat on the grass and patted the ground. The animal waddled to her.

"See. I promised I'd make it right."

"That was a sweet thing to do, Susan," Mary said.

"It was the least I could do after I broke her heart last year."

"He's a fine-looking animal, Miss Amy," Huston said. "What's his name?"

"I'm not sure yet," Amy said.

"What about Missy?" Fannie spoke from the gallery's steps. "As in Missy Susan."

Susan ignored her. No one would upset her happiness over Amelia's joy.

"He's not a sow," Amy said. "He's a boy. He needs a boy's name."

"Well, we all figure you'll come up with a good one," Huston said.

"I'm sure you will," Susan said.

"Miss Jessup, do you have a rope? Mama says she doesn't have one I can have."

"Why do you need a rope?"

"For a leash. For my pig."

"You might choke him if you use a rope," Mary said.

"Not if I make a slipknot."

"Where on earth did you learn about slipknots?" Susan said.

"Lieutenant Jessup showed me how to make them the other day when he was here playing with his fishing poles. He made one with a fishing line."

The pig nosed Susan's dress. She didn't have a rope, but she did have…she recalled Stephen Hamilton's arguments against slavery. He loved his Southern roots but hated his region's "Peculiar Institution." Inside her house was a symbol of that institution, and it was time to change that part of her life. Amy gave her the perfect opportunity. "Wait here, dear. I'll be back quick as a flea."

Huston sidestepped Susan as she darted into her house and seized her whip from off a hallway table. Back outside, she thrust it into Huston's hand. Befuddled, he stared at it.

"Is he supposed to whip your little spine, Missy Susan?" Fannie sat in the rocking chair.

"Huston, cut it off at the crop. The long, thin part of it will serve as a leash until Amy can find something better."

Amy scrambled up. "But…but I can't make a slipknot. I only saw Lieutenant Jessup make one. I thought maybe…maybe you could make one for me."

"I don't know how either. I think that may be something only sailors and such know how to do. Maybe when he or Lieutenant Westcott visit me again, or perhaps Uncle Will, one of them will do it for you. Meanwhile, I'll think of something we can use for a leash." She gestured Huston, who took the whip around back.

"Lieutenant Westcott ain't coming back." Fannie's air was triumphant.

"Of course, he will."

"He was sore angry. That pig ruined his clothes."

"Oh, goodness. I wasn't thinking."

"It'll be all right," Mary said. "We met when he brought the pig here. After he saw me, he calmed down. He'll be fine. He'll come back."

"To see you or to see me?"

"To see both of us, I assume. I think he likes me."

"Like Alex likes you. He's always liked you, even when we were children."

"Even that day when he teased me with that sea monster turtle?"

"Even then. He's just scared to admit it. Alex only teases people he likes."

"Why is he scared?"

"Something about a 'k' word. Don't ask me what it is. I have no idea. He mentioned this to a Mississippi lady he met in the Bahamas before he came here."

"Well, come along, Amy." Mary gestured to her sister. "Let's you and Mister Pig get on back home."

"Mister Pig," Amy said brightly. "That's a good name for him."

"I'll send Huston over with the leash when he's done," Susan said.

"It's a dad-burn puzzle, it is." Ben's slow-stirring spoon halted. He sipped his coffee.

Alex, seated at the mess table opposite him, sorted his fishhooks. "My 'k' word? Martha Massingale, that girl I met in the Bahamas?"

"Susan Jessup. Mary Hamilton."

Walker, seated at another table reading a book, cleared his throat.

Alex held up four large hooks. "I hope I can buy some bait tomorrow. Live minnows would be nice. Captain Murphey's given me permission to go fishing. Uncle Will's taking me."

"Stop it, Alex. This is important."

"My 'k' word happens to be privileged information." He picked up a short, thin wire. Squinting at the hooks' eyes, he carefully slipped the wire through them then tied it tight.

"I'm not talking about your dumb 'k' word." Ben battled back his irritation. His friend could be frustrating at times. "Nobody can find it in a dictionary. It's a made-up word. It doesn't exist."

"Yes, it does."

"Al—"

"I wrote Martha last week, first time in months. Does that tickle your insides or what?" Alex wrapped a longer wire around the hooks' shanks, carefully adjusting them so that their barbs faced outward like the four points on a compass, and then wrapped it several more times before tying it tightly. He held it up for all present to see. "Spanish mackerel, redfish, speckled trout, flounder, all caught on the same line. Ain't I a genius?" Puckering his lips like a fish, he made a sound that resembled loud kissing. "Here, fishy, fishy, fishy."

"I believe Mister Westcott's talking about your sister and her friend." Walker lifted his eyes from his book.

"That's exactly who I'm talking about, your dad-burn complicated sister and her equally complicated friend Mary Hamilton."

"All females are complicated, worse'n a riddle wrapped in a puzzle. That's why I'll never get married."

"I thought it had to do with your 'k' word."

"It does, and if it weren't for my 'k' word I'd marry Miss..." He flipped open his wooden tackle box and dropped his invention inside it. "Never mind."

"Marry who?"

"Nobody."

"Who? Who?"

"Miss Nobody, dang it."

Walker shut his book decisively. "Do you two realize how little sense either of you is making?"

"I'd like Alex's sister to consider me her beau," Ben said.

"Maybe she already has a beau," Walker said.

Alex went topside.

"Know something, Walker?" Ben said. "Ever since he's been home, all Alex ever thinks about is fishing."

"Fish is your friend's favorite food source."

"I was born on the Gulf Coast just like him, but I prefer beefsteak and potato pones."

Alex came back down the ladder. "Better strap on my pistol before I go on watch. What's this you were telling me about Mary Hamilton?"

"Her father's home. I offered to ask his permission to let us court but just like Susan, she declined. She was nice about it, but she still declined."

"Good."

"Huh?"

"Good thing I'm going on watch." Alex vanished into his stateroom. He came back out wearing his holstered revolver. "Riddles wrapped in a puzzle. The whole lot of 'em." He exited the wardroom fast. He poked his head back down the hatchway. "Mary's father agrees with me. Riddles. Riddles. They're all a pack of riddles!"

Rain clouds gathered. Miss Evans leaned back against her buggy's leather seat, her eyes closed. Done. *Macaria.* Her novel, finished. Sent to a publishing company in Richmond, and she was on her way home from the post office. "I hope my book will prove successful," she muttered.

"It will be," Caroline, who sat beside her, said. "There's no one who can write better than you, Gusta. Pshaw! You're the most famous author there is."

"Fame is fleeting. I only want my book to do its work for our Cause, to mean something important, to encourage our poor, brave boys fighting for us, to convince those who question the righteousness of our Cause that they're wrong. Wake me when we arrive home." Drizzle sprinkled Miss Evans's face; she drifted into sleep.

June passed into July, bringing Confederate disasters. The Army of the Potomac stopped Lee's second invasion of the North on the outskirts of a small town called Gettysburg on the third; on the fourth, General John Pemberton formally surrendered Vicksburg to Ulysses S. Grant after a long siege.

On the eighth, Port Hudson surrendered, and thus, the entire Mississippi River returned to Union hands. By the second day of August, Farragut set sail back to New York, his flagship in sore need of repairs after her long campaigns. Mobile's capture, though, played heavily in his thoughts, for with its capture went the South's last stronghold on the Gulf of Mexico.

1863

AUGUST
–
DECEMBER

46

NANCY DOVE INTO Danny's embrace. "My handsome sailor's home!" Laughing, Danny hefted her high then set her back down on the porch. Kisses smothered their cheeks and lips. "Nary a wound nor a scratch."

"And still as fine a looking man as this chile's ever seen."

"I might have gotten back sooner after Port Hudson surrendered, but we pretty near ran out of coal after we got on up to Vicksburg a spell. Had to wait for a supply ship to bring us some."

Nancy grasped his hand. "How long will you be staying?"

"Captain Vincent's letting me stay overnight so you and me can go to church tomorrow. I gotta report back to the *Madison* by two o'clock. We're leaving again at sunset."

"This chile doesn't much like being a sailor's wife. You're always home a spell and gone for too long a spell. Your Navy work is done, isn't it? Why must you go?"

"Because my ship's been through lots of fighting. She's worn out, Nancy. She needs lots of fixing up."

"Can't you do that here?"

"Doctor Kirby says we're going to New York. It has a shipyard that has everything we need to get us back into good fighting shape."

"That's a long way away."

"I don't much like our being apart so long either."

"Hello, there, Sailor."

Danny darted outside and shook Reverend Dotson's hand hard. Grinning, Esther followed him back inside, undid her flowered bonnet, and handed it to him.

"Nancy?" Puzzled, Danny looked around the small room, suddenly realizing she was gone. "Now, where did my wife get off to?"

"I think she has a surprise for you, Mister Yates," Esther said. "Darling, I'll let you two visit. I'll go see if I can help her."

The pastor and Danny sat a small table.

Reverend Dotson turned suddenly grave. "Nancy hasn't told you yet."

"Told me what?" Danny said.

"About Titus and Jason."

"No, sir."

"They were at Port Hudson. Their Native Guard regiment was almost wiped out. They were charging an impregnable Rebel position, from what I read in the papers. They were ordered to take a high piece of ground the Rebels held. Practically every man was killed. Titus and Jason were among them."

The news struck Danny like a shot smashing midships. His fists drove against his knees as he stared at the low ceiling, swimming it seemed, as his eyes pooled. *Guilty. Guilty as charged.* "I'm to blame."

"You didn't kill them."

"I might as well have." He rested his forehead on the wobbly table. "I hated Titus, sir. I tried hard to forgive him. I should've gone to him. I should've told him. My anger at Titus, sir. I was so mad I never even bothered."

"There's no guarantee he would've listened to you. He hated you also, I imagine.'

"Sir, it would've at least given him a chance."

"Certainly, Mister Yates. You are very much right."

"It ain't worth it, hating folks, white men or black. I always knew that in my head. Now, now…" Danny swallowed hard. Words abandoned him.

After a long silence, Reverend Dotson spoke again. "Mister Yates, you can start forgiving them now. Tomorrow, I'd like you to speak in my church. Introduce yourself. Tell my congregation a little about your story."

"Me, sir? Speak?" Danny's eyes widened a little. "Do you mean in front of a whole passel of folks?"

"I'm not talking about a sermon. Just get up and spend a few minutes telling everyone about yourself."

"No, sir. I can't do that."

"The matter's settled. Tomorrow, then… Ah, Mrs. Yates." Reverend Dotson arose with Danny.

When he set his eyes upon Nancy beaming in the doorway, Danny stood transfixed. She was decked out in a bright blue gown with tiny, dark red ribbons sewn across the top of its bodice and intricate white lace decorating its numerous flounces. He opened his mouth to speak, but all that came out was an awestruck gasp.

"Danny? Danny?" Nancy said. "I made it myself."

"You are…where'd my words go?"

Everyone burst into hilarity. Fears of public speaking niggled in the back of Danny's mind.

Reverend Dotson's church occupied a third of a block, five blocks downriver from the French Quarter. It was a red brick building with a short white steeple atop its pitched roof.

During his walk to the church, Danny nervously buttoned and unbuttoned his black vest. He and Nancy followed the long line of people through the church's whitewashed double doors.

Nancy always wanted him to be a parson, ever since their younger days on that Willow Wood plantation in Georgia where they were married. He cleared his throat three more times before they entered the building. He buttoned his vest a final time before he shot up a quick prayer. *Help.*

Angled toward the congregation and a simple pine pulpit, Danny sat in an armchair on a platform beside Reverend Dotson. Behind them, a large square opening within a brown-painted wooden wall; inside this opening, a tub where they baptized folks, Danny assumed.

After a long prayer, the pastor's palm gestured upward. Rustles followed as the congregation stood. On his feet, Danny's thoughts wandered elsewhere.

Nancy and Mrs. Dotson sat directly in front. He avoided Nancy's proud gaze. Mouthing the spirituals he knew well, watching the congregation dance and wave their arms skyward, their voices ringing the rafters with joyful songs and hymns, his heart would've been more into worship had he not been so nervous. His fingers thumped his thighs; his foot tapped. The joyful singing continued on and on.

Warm surf rolled over Moxley's feet. Wind whipped a page over his writing hand. He slapped the page back and resumed writing, fast and furious. Sunday inspection over, he sat on a camp stool in his usual spot. Susan had written him numerous times, even explained that her neighbor's brother, Stephen, was married. He withheld a response, though he did write almost every day in this journal she gave him.

Anger spewed from his pencil, vented itself on the page. Beaten, defeated. First by a stupid looking, cock-eyed Yankee general named Butler, who'd shut down his newspaper and burned down his house after he refused to publish the general's orders upon his occupation of New Orleans. Fearing arrest, Moxley had fled that city.

And now, a beautiful belle had defeated him. He'd had it! She could take him or leave him, he was who he was, and that was that. He didn't give a cat's meow what anyone said. He would not join a church and become a hypocrite like everyone else. He also doubted Ben's chances these days, unless he suddenly turned all religious on him.

Danny's eyes shifted to the double doors down the center aisle. Everyone's gaze riveted on him. Curiosity? An eagerness to hear him? How many out there, fanning their faces in this hot sanctuary, had been free before the war? How many, slaves? He should've asked the reverend. Sweat popped out of his arms, his neck, his forehead. The words leaped off his tongue. "My name is Danny Yates. I was born on a plantation in Georgia. It was there that my beautiful wife Nancy and I met when we were very, very young." Numerous memories flooded him; off his tongue they rolled, like a creek overrunning pebbles, the good and the bad, the day he began to learn blacksmithing and Nancy started learning to nurse white children under the tutelage of the mistress's mammy.

He recalled all the plantations on which he'd served, his numerous escape attempts to find Nancy after she was whisked out of his life, and how he'd gotten his last name from Hickory Yates, who hated the institution with every fiber of his being. The beatings he'd endured to find his beloved, long hot days locked in cages like a wild animal, the brands he bore on his shoulders and back, every kind of physical and verbal mistreatment imaginable. "It was all worth it." His warm, loving gaze rested upon Nancy. "It was all worth it to find my beloved. And now, we're all free." By the time he finished, he was sweating profusely not just from the heat, but also from his nerves.

His eyes caught the stern policeman standing at the church's entrance as he stepped off the platform and took Nancy's hand. *Oh!* He'd forgotten. Nancy told him many in this city were still slaves! Those slaves in the congregation only attended with their owners' permission. *Oh!* He'd misspoken. He'd failed.

Reverend Dotson gestured everyone to rise. They moved into a spiritual, swaying and clapping and raising their hands.

Danny shrank in his pew. He took too long a time. The reverend didn't get a chance to preach his sermon. The reverend was mad at him.

The song ended and people headed out. Though some friendly parishioners crowded Danny, others left quickly. The policeman who'd stood in the doorway, and several other policemen, checked the slaves' passes from their masters and monitored their leaving. Within minutes, the sanctuary turned quiet.

Esther crooked her hand around Danny's elbow; Nancy grasped his other arm. They steered him into a pew while the pastor disappeared through a rear door. Reverend Dotson soon returned holding a thick envelope which he tossed in Danny's lap.

"These are my notes on the Gospel of St. John," Reverend Dotson said. "I spent a year studying it, verse by verse. Take it with you. I want you to study it for next time you visit us."

"Won't you need it for your sermons?"

The pastor pointed at the pulpit. "Mister Yates, what I heard today was the makings of a preacher."

"Not me, sir. No, sir."

Reverend Dotson smiled. "Yes. You."

47

WHILE SUSAN WORKED in the post office, it happened. Agathena Mott and her friends, determined as pit bulls, pretty near caused a riot. Thousands witnessed it. When she returned to her home up Spring Hill, Mary and her parents visited her and described what they'd seen.

"They came marching down Dauphin Street," Mary said. "Hundreds of poor, angry women carrying hatches and brooms and axes and Agathena out front, waving her revolver and hammer."

"Screaming and carrying signs," Mrs. Hamilton said.

"Agathena kept screaming 'Bread or Blood.' She screamed louder than you ever did."

Mister Hamilton chuckled. "Pretty hard screaming louder than you used to do, Susan."

Concern restrained Susan's smile. "Did anyone get hurt?"

"No, thank goodness," Mrs. Hamilton said.

"We all kept watching, holding our breaths, and waiting to see what they'd do next," Mary said. "Their hatchets and brooms and axes and hammers, they smashed windows and doors with them, looting the stores."

"I can't believe no one tried to stop it."

"The truth is, Susan," Mister Hamilton said, "all of us watching them felt sorry for them. I started to go get Mayor Slough, but soon as I turned to leave I spotted him arriving on the scene. He promised he'd help them if they all went back to their homes. Fortunately, this brought an end to it."

"We must try harder to help them," Susan said.

"We will," Mary said. "Mother and I promised the mayor we would. So did all the other charities in the city. He's going to form a Special Relief Committee to deal with the problem." She put her hand around her father's arm. "Father's staying here to help out."

"As long as I am able," he said, "till I have to tend to my farming business again." He eyed his wife and daughter. "Edith, Mary, I need a word with Susan in private. After we're finished, we'll go pick up Amy."

Mrs. Hamilton and Mary returned to their carriage. Susan knew that Amy had been visiting a friend who lived not far from her home here, their refuge from the fever.

Mister Hamilton narrowed his eyes at her. "You have certainly changed."

"It was God who changed me, sir," Susan said.

"Stephen would most likely agree. I'm glad he's not involved in this war."

"As am I," Susan said.

"I'm also glad you and Mary have finally become friends."

"What is it you wish to discuss, Mister Hamilton?"

"I know I've not been much of a father or husband, seeing how I'm gone from home so much. I will try to do better. I trust my overseers will be able to handle things without me since I plan on staying here for a longer time than usual. Where is Alex?"

"Down the bay. At Grant's Pass. He'll be there all this month. Our gunboats take turns guarding it."

"Well, then, it looks like I won't be seeing him for several weeks."

"No, sir." Susan wondered what he was trying to say.

"Even though Alex was a bit of mischief when he was little, I've always liked him. Does he like my Mary?"

"I think he does. During your last visit, sir, when you and Mary were outdoors in Mobile, I caught him in his bedroom upstairs watching you and Mary through his window. I asked him what he was doing."

"And?"

"He said nothing. He fled downstairs."

"Still shy, is he?"

"Perhaps."

"My Mary won't wait for him forever. Next time you see him, please let him know I'd be proud for him to court my daughter."

"I'll do that, sir."

Mister Hamilton stretched forth his hand, which Susan took. He set his other hand atop hers. "I am praying for your father's safe return."

"Thank you, sir. I thank you very, very much."

On Dauphin Island's western end, Alex and Walker strolled its beach. Alex carried a fishing pole and a bucket of shrimp on ice; Walker, a fishing pole and a bucket for their catch. On the island's Gulf side and well out of range, three Yankee gunboats bobbed on dark undulations. Two days ago, those boats steamed in close and engaged their batteries at Grant's Pass, a six hour duel that inflicted zero casualties. Alex figured they were testing their position's strength.

Screaming gulls dove for fish.

"I figure this is as good a spot as any," Alex said.

Walker set down the bucket.

Alex reached for a shrimp and proceeded to bait his hook. "Ever caught whiting before?"

"I've done most of my fishing in rivers and lakes."

"Grab yourself a shrimp. It's high time you did some real serious fishing. Saltwater fishing's a far sight more challenging, far as I'm concerned." He set his pole on the sand, rolled his trousers up above his knees, and waded into the warm surf.

Walker baited his hook. "I wouldn't be so sure about that. Makes no matter to me what size they are or how hard they fight, long as they're good eating. Isn't it sort of odd, Westcott being born on the Coast and not liking seafood?"

"Everyone has their oddities. Many people think I'm strange because I have no desire for marriage and think about fishing and billiards all the time. Westcott's a mighty good billiards player. We played that game we talked about after he got back from his recruiting trip. He won every game."

"Sounds like you're content."

"Like a hog in mud." Yet when Alex uttered this, he privately admitted it was a half-truth. Content in his bachelorhood...*Mary*... He groped for a jest. Nothing funny came. *Leroy, Susanna, Mary, I*....Dashing aside this memory, he concentrated on the surf.

Alex raised his pole behind him, waited longer, watched the waves. He cast his line smack into a trench those waves made, where the whiting were. Whiting ate sand fleas, which explained their swimming close to shore. He waited a few minutes, no tug, he poised his line behind him for another throw. Out the corner of his eyes, he watched Walker.

No! No! No! Alex waded to him. "Look here, Walker. For starters, you're not likely to catch any whiting casting that line the way you are. Don't cast your line into the waves. Cast it into the dip, where the waves break, because that's where the fish are."

"Wait. I have something." Walker yanked his line out, bringing up nothing save the dead shrimp dangling in the breeze.

"You caught a giant chunk of air! Ha! My, ain't it a big one! Ha! About four, five feet long, I figure." Alex pulled a comical face and laughed. "Call it trash fish, er, trash air. Next time, cast your line in the right spot."

"But I felt a pull, like something was nudging it."

"Aw! It was only the waves. Fish in salt water as much as I have, you'll soon learn the difference between wave action and a bite." He sloshed back to his fishing spot. He loved fishing because it gave him an escape from his every day cares and yet…for a reason he couldn't explain…he didn't feel fulfilled today. It was all an act. All these years, he'd tried filling it with humor. Humor and fishing and billiards. These helped him handle his grief over Susanna and his mother. He'd crack a joke or two, other folks maybe laughed, and then his fulfillment fled. He jerked his line out of the water and tossed it carelessly into the waves. Thinking about his mother and Susanna…Now he didn't care if he caught a fish or not. *Alexander Dunwoody Jessup, you're crazy.*

Standing on *Selma's* quarterdeck, Ben groaned. Alex wasted their entire supper discussing whiting recipes and Hulda's special way of baking them. He'd give anything for a few potatoes on board. He observed Fort Grant against the full moonlight. Its three-gun battery's short range offered scant hope of striking enemy vessels farther out. Such was proven a few days ago when the guns opened fire. Not a shot or shell one came close to hitting those Yankees who'd opened on them.

Their outer defenses were nearly finished, the wharf at Fort Grant was up, Fort Gaines sodded, yet work continued on the city's interior lines.

Alex sure was proud of his and Walker's catch. Ten fish they'd brought aboard, five of them smothered in ice in a special compartment below and kept for tomorrow's supper.

Stinky ole fish. Annie's words penetrated that thought. Ben imagined her crinkling her nose the way she always did when something amused her.

He asked himself what she would've thought about Susan. She probably wouldn't have liked her at first. Her rudeness, her coldness was a far sight different from Annie's friendliness and gaiety. Maybe since she'd changed, Annie might have liked her better. Or perhaps she might've liked Mary most.

He started. Someone was swimming in the starlight. He focused his night glasses. *About fifty yards off, the dark figure, swimming toward Dauphin Island and Mississippi Sound. One of ours. One of Fort Grant's?*

"Sir, what is it?" a young acting midshipman said.

"Get Captain Murphey and Mister Jessup," Ben snapped. "Find Hanlin and bring him here. Double-quick."

The midshipman darted down the hatch.

Within the minute Murphey, Master-at-Arms Hanlin, and Alex joined him.

Ben handed Murphey the glasses.

"He's too far away to make out who he is," Murphey said.

"Sir," Hanlin said, "let me lower a boat and go after him."

"Mister Jessup," Murphey said.

Alex's coat and shirt were off before Murphey gave his order. He slipped over *Selma's* side.

The deserter swam faster. Alex made gains.

"Is Jessup a strong swimmer?" Murphey said.

"He has great endurance, sir," Ben said. "I've seen him swim three miles in a race during our Academy days."

"Did he win?"

"Came in third."

"Let's hope he comes in first this time."

When Alex reached shallow water, he stood thigh-deep, chest heaving, gulping air. *Aw! Not again.* Alex yelled, then pursued. Waves slapped him. He sloshed after the deserter who'd scurried up, over, and down a dune. A Yankee boat might be awaiting him on the island's Gulf side. If he expected to catch him, he had to do it now.

On the beach, Alex darted up the same dune he'd seen the man go over. The man collapsed in the sand, head hanging, winded. But when he spotted Alex, he took off across the sand and over more dunes.

Alex raced between the dunes, glancing every direction searching for him. Something clutched his ankle, yanked him down, backward onto the sand.

It smacked his face—knuckles, a fist. Alex seized it when it flew at him a second time. The fist struggled to break free; sand stung Alex's face. Spluttering and spitting, Alex's grip briefly relaxed enough for the deserter to break loose. Before he realized what happened, Alex found himself jerked into a choke hold. Coughing and kicking, his hands moved to his foe's forearm pressuring his windpipe. Tighter, the deserter squeezed. Alex's struggle....to get free...to breathe...air...

Ben and Doctor Hays, *Selma's* surgeon, scrambled out of the boat they ran up on Dauphin Island's beach. The orange-red sun blazed over the horizon.

"Alex!" Ben cupped his hands around his mouth and screamed louder. "Alex! Alexander Dunwoody Jessup! Answer me! Where are you?"

"A fairly sizeable island," Hays said. "No telling where he could be."

"We better find him. I fear something has happened. It's not like him not to return to the ship." Ben dropped a kedge anchor on the sand and forced its flukes in deep so their craft wouldn't drift away. He strode the beach, pausing every now and then to shout Alex's name. "Let's head farther west. That's the direction their boat was heading."

"I sincerely hope he's not dead."

"Cold, doctor. That was cold."

Alex's voice rose from behind a dune.

Ben led Hays between two smaller dunes where, a few yards off, Alex had knelt, eyes squeezed, head hanging, mumbling.

"What's he doing?" Hays whispered.

They flanked him.

Alex squinted up. "Ben. Doc. How y'all doing?"

"We're all fine and dandy," Ben said. "Why didn't you come back to the ship?"

"I lost him. I tried catching him, but he got away."

"We've lost men before."

"What's that on your neck?" Hays bent down and examined the red marks. "A bruise. Where'd that come from? Did McDougle try to strangle you?"

"McDougle, was it?" Alex said.

"He's the only man we discovered missing during muster," Ben said.

Standing, Alex massaged his neck. "He did come mighty near strangling me. I passed out. When I came to, he was long gone. The Yanks out there probably sent a boat for him, same as always."

Ben kicked sand over the two indentations Alex's knees had made. "What was all that mumbling about?"

"Ben, you may not believe this, but I was praying."

"Right you are. I don't believe it. I thought you only prayed in church."

"I'm not crazy. This was the second time in this war I nearly died. Yellow fever first, now strangulation. Susan told me it was God who rescued me from the fever. Maybe He saved my life again this time. I was asking God that if my good luck was actually His doing, to make it clear. I wasn't planning on leaving till He did. I want God to tell me something like Susan claims He did her."

"Don't tell me we're starting to believe all that craziness."

"Maybe I do, maybe I don't. I want to find out. I really need to know."

"God exists, Alex. We both believe that. Isn't that enough?"

"No. It's not. Y'all want me to get back to the ship. Well, let's get the lead out of our britches and go."

Ben and the surgeon swapped worried glances.

"Well," Alex said, almost a shout. "Shove off, men. Move it. Move it. Double-quick."

When Colonel William Powell, commander of Mobile Bay's lower defenses, died toward the end of September after a lengthy illness, Alex's concerns about his soul mounted. Through the weeks of

October, he devoted every free hour aboard *Selma* pondering his spiritual state. He devoured Walker's copy of Spurgeon's sermons. He sensed Ben and other officers watching them, listening to his and Walker's religious conversations mingled with a little fishing talk.

"I wonder what's become of him." Alex spoke this one evening around the mess table.

"The colonel's dead. That's what's become of him," Lieutenant Bradford said.

"That's not what I meant."

"He meant his soul, sir." Walker sipped hot tea, courtesy of a recent blockade-runner.

"Quit letting Walker's sermons get to you, Jessup," Bradford said.

"Has God told you anything yet?" Ben asked.

"No, and it's mighty frustrating."

"Susan just imagined it."

"I'm keeping an open mind." Alex quickly cut up his salt pork.

"God speaks to us in many ways," Walker said. "We're sailors. We've seen the sea's power, its tremendous waves, its strong winds. The birds, my friends. Seagulls and egrets and why, even the whale. Have any of you seen a whale before?"

"In the Azores," Alex said.

"Only an all-powerful God can create such marvelous creatures."

Alex slammed down his fork. "Either God will speak to me, or I'll become an atheist. For life!" He stormed into his stateroom and slammed its door behind him.

Shivering in the wintry November air, Ben stopped at the Hamiltons' gate as Amy hurried across their front lawn toward him.

"I like you," she said, opening it.

Ben wiggled her tiny nose. "I like you too."

"My sister told our father about you. He thinks he may like you."

"I haven't met your father. I hope he likes me. Where is he?"

"He's gone to the bank. He owns a plantation."

"I see."

Amy's chin tilted up. "He owns three plantations. We're rich."

"How is your pig?"

"He's asleep."

"Have you decided on a name?"

"My sister suggested I call him Leroy. Where are you going?"

"Next door."

Amy scrunched her brow. "My sister's inside. Want to see her again?"

"I would, after I visit Miss Susan."

"Susan's not home." Amy grasped Ben's forefinger. "Come on. My sister wants to see you again. She says she likes you."

"Well, Miss Amelia— "

"My name is Amy. I don't like Amelia. Mama calls me Amelia when she's mad."

"Please accept my apologies, Miss Amy. Lead the way."

"I am." Amy led Ben toward her pillared house.

Alex surveyed the Methodist Episcopal Church's vacant pews. Cold the sanctuary was; winter seeped beneath its front doors. *I'm here by myself, I think.* He sensed a presence. Was it someone watching him? No one knew he'd come here, not Walker, not Susan, not Ben, not Miss Evans, not Captain Murphey.

"I must know the truth." Exasperated, he threw up his arms. "All right. Here I am. Speak to me, God. Shout at me louder than You did to Susan! God, I already believe in You. I'm a good person, and I try to do the right thing. I've never whipped a slave. I've never spoken to them harshly. Isn't that enough?" He folded his arms. "All right, God. Show me. Show me right now. Either what Susan said is true or it isn't. Show me. Show me. Sho-ow me!" His shouts echoed throughout the sanctuary. He dropped to his knees and stared straight ahead. He had a two-day pass. He'd spend all night in this same spot if necessary.

From a rosewood sofa facing a window opening toward Susan's house, Ben received a cup of tea from the Hamiltons' butler. Mary and her mother sat opposite him. Amy's laughter, interspersed by Leroy's grunts, sounded outdoors.

Mary's calm brown eyes assessed him.

He squirmed.

"I apologize for my little sister," Mary said.

"Why?" Ben said. "She didn't do anything."

"Ever since you brought her that pig, she's taken a shine to you," Mrs. Hamilton said.

"She's trying to play matchmaker." Mary moved from her seat to the marble fireplace. "I think you already know my answer, though."

Such is my life and luck, unfortunately.

Mrs. Hamilton set her tea on a saucer. "Susan's spoken highly of you."

"That a fact?"

"She likes you a lot," Mary said.

"As much as, or more than, my brother?"

"She hasn't seen or heard from your brother in months. She's written him, sent him telegrams, but he's ignored her. She feared she'd hurt his feelings and was trying to make up for it, but when he didn't respond back, she got hurt as well. Those are my thoughts, for what they're worth."

"How is she coping?"

"She's getting over it."

Ben tugged his chin. *Hmm.* The winds of love had started shifting in his favor.

Mrs. Hamilton pointed at a portrait above the fireplace, set within a large gilded frame. Its subject was a young man wearing thick, curly black hair and a heavy black mustache. "That's my son Stephen. He's not fighting in the war."

"He's a missionary," Mary said. "He's been in India since a few years before the war started."

"Several months ago, we received a letter from him," Mrs. Hamilton said. "Your brother happened to be visiting Susan when Mary showed it to her."

"I commented that Stephen had inquired about her," Mary said. "Susan called him handsome. Your brother asked whether he was married."

"Is he?"

"Very much so, to an English girl, but before we could answer he stormed out of her house never to be heard from again."

Ben downed his tea and got up.

"Please sit," Mrs. Hamilton said.

"I'll be back when Miss Susan returns. I've enjoyed our little sit down, ladies." With a tip of his cap, Ben departed.

Morning hit Alex fast. When he got up off his aching knees, the sanctuary barely held enough light for him to find his way out. "All right, God. I've made my decision." His shout echoed. "As of this minute, this moment in time, I am an...an...an...a heathen dog atheist. You don't exist."

He pivoted and marched out onto the street. He'd return to his ship, grab his pistol, and blow his brains out. No sense going on living with his pain, suffering over his mother's and sister Susannah's deaths, pretending he was easygoing and carefree when he wasn't.

Whistling, Alex stuck his loaded revolver in his trouser waistband and left his stateroom, his demeanor cheerful as ever. Strolling down her gangplank onto the wharf, he was glad his ruse worked. No one asked questions.

He made his way to the nearby Battle House. At its desk, he inquired regarding a room. All rooms were occupied, he was told. Alex thanked the desk clerk, laughed, and left. He might as well laugh. His life had played him for a fool. His whistling ceased.

The Pattison House said the same thing, unless he wanted a roommate, which he didn't.

All he wanted was a private place where he could put a pistol to his temple and trigger a bullet in his brain. No God existed, so no hope existed. That's all there was to it. Whatever happened to his mother and Susanna, he wanted that too. A strange happiness flooded him. His grief, almost gone for good. He started whistling again.

Aimlessly, he wandered Mobile's busy streets, but he avoided Government Street as best he could. He desired no reminders of Susan. Her dramatic change, he couldn't dispute. Perhaps she was pretending. Except, Susan never pretended about anything. She claimed God spoke to her.

He reached inside his coat and gripped his revolver. Passersby curiously studied his move; out came his hand; the pistol stayed hidden. He wanted to hear from God. He wanted to change. Whatever happened to Susan, it didn't happen to him. Death, it was the only solution to his grief.

Upon thinking this, he found himself wandering into his mother and Susanna's cemetery, up a long path toward an iron fence on its farthest end, past headstones and mausoleums. Winter hung heavy; his fingers were numb.

A GOOD PLACE TO DO IT.

That suggestion blared in his mind.

LOOK AROUND, ALEXANDER. SEE. NOBODY'S IN THIS CEMETERY. IT'S TOO COLD FOR FOLKS TO BE OUT HERE. YOU'RE ALL ALONE. DON'T YOU MISS YOUR MOTHER?

"Yes."

DON'T YOU WANT TO JOIN YOUR DARLING SISTER SUSANNA AND YOUR MOTHER? DON'T YOU WANT TO KNOW WHAT HAPPENED TO THEM AFTER THEY DIED? THERE'S ONLY ONE WAY TO FIND OUT. DEATH IS FUN. IT'S AN ADVENTURE.

"Like my cruise on the *Sumter*."

YES! YES! EVEN MORE FUN. GO AHEAD. YOUR MOTHER'S PLOT IS UP AHEAD. THAT'S A GOOD PLACE TO DO IT. IT'LL END YOUR HEARTACHE. GO ON. UP AHEAD. SEE?

Alex fastened his gaze upon the angel atop his mother's tomb. "Brrr!" He shivered in the cold. "Angels are a myth."

YES. THEY ARE.

Through tears, he read his mother's and Susanna's names. He glanced around.

SEE, ALEXANDER MY FRIEND. I TOLD YOU NO ONE WAS NEARBY. IT'S TOO COLD. SEE HOW BROWN THE GRASS IS? IT'S DEAD. IT DOESN'T NEED CUTTING THIS TIME OF YEAR. YOU'RE ALL ALONE. IT'S PRIVATE. NOW GRAB YOUR GUN AND KILL YOUR PAIN. QUICK. IT'S THE ONLY WAY OUT.

Trees rustled; doves strutted. The revolver, heavy. Loaded and ready, he touched its cold muzzle to his head. "Father, Susan, forgive me." He squeezed the trigger.

48

"**H**EY, MISTER. GOOD thing that's a single-action revolver. You forgot to cock it."

Alex gaped at the tall black man who climbed down from his wagon on the street side of the cemetery fence. "Go away."

"Now why would I be wanting to do that?" Smiling, he approached.

"Because I said so."

"Because you're white and I'm black. Reckon that makes you think I'm a slave."

"Leave me alone."

"Jedidiah's my name. I'm free-born in this city. My pappy was a carpenter, free-born, and I'm a carpenter like he was. My mammy free-born, my grand-pappies on both sides of my family and my grand-mammies, free-born, all of us was, so I reckon I won't do like you tell me. I'm my own man, same as you."

"Well, watch and enjoy the white man's blood and brains splattered everywhere."

Jedidiah's smile vanished. He rocked on his heels. "Just going to cock that hammer back this time, and…boom!"

"Boom."

"Right into eternity."

"There is no eternity."

"Since when did eternity quit being eternity?"

"There's never been an eternity."

"What makes you so sure?"

"Leave me alone. You're becoming a nuisance."

"Not till I hear why you don't believe in no eternity."

Alex raised his pistol back to his temple and cocked the hammer.

"Supposing you're wrong?" Jedidiah said. "Eternity is forever, that is, on condition it hasn't quit being eternity. Is it smart to gamble with your soul that-a-way? Hell's not a fun place, that is, supposing hell's real."

"There is no eternity, there is no heaven, and there is no hell." Alex's finger caressed his pistol's trigger. He quivered. He eased down the hammer and lowered his pistol halfway. He'd still kill himself after he got rid of this, this…. He stomped to the fence and in his most authoritative naval officer voice, said, "For the last time, *GO!*"

"If I leave, you'll kill yourself?"

"Yes."

"Then I ain't going nowhere, not till you stop this foolishness."

"I'm wearing civilian clothes because I have a short furlough. Want to know the truth? I'm a naval officer fighting to defend the South and—"

"Look at me. I'm colored." Jedidiah shrugged and laughed.

Alex glared at him. "I don't like you. Get."

"Why don't you like me? I like you. And the good Lord loves you."

"Why would a colored man care about me?"

"Supposing I explain it more directly. See, this poor old man hates slavery worse'n anything on this earth, but he don't hate nobody in particular. It's the institution he hates, not the folks like you doing it. Hating never did no man no good. Way back in my younger days, I was cougar mean. Back then, I got in my share of fights and such. Then one day, a gentleman happened to see me prowling the street. I tried to fight him, even threw a punch or two at him, but he refused to fight back. He wasn't a coward. He just said he'd given up fighting, that the good Lord had changed him. Judging by his size, I'm sure he could've handled me. His refusal to fight and what he said about the Lord Jesus, well, it just got me to thinking. After a while, I forsook my evil ways and decided I'd go on the straight and narrow like him. I didn't want to ever be known as Cougar Jed again. I haven't been in trouble with the law in years."

Recognition flashed through Alex's mind. *Cougar Jed? The infamous Cougar Jed?* He'd heard about him before the war. He'd knocked his father's friend unconscious because his friend refused to buy him a drink at a saloon near the waterfront. Liquor was illegal for black folks. Though he'd never met Cougar Jed till now, he'd heard stories.

"I'm from this city. I've heard many tales about you," Alex said. "Read a few in the newspapers too."

"I'm sure of that. Now, sir, would you please put your gun away? It frightens me to think what you're trying to do to yourself. There's always hope in this life. What would it do to your family if you were to kill yourself? Don't you figure they'd be upset, depressed for the rest of their lives even?"

Alex hesitated. Susan flashed before him. If he killed himself, her emotional life might go out of control again. And his father, up in Virginia, it'd tear his heart to pieces.

"May this colored man pray with you?" Jed said.

Alex nodded. As they prayed, peace washed over him. God had answered his prayers. No voices like Susan heard but in the form of a kind man named Jed.

"I thank you, Miss Jessup." Ben slipped his arm through his left frock coat's sleeve first, followed by his right. Earlier, he'd ripped off a button to give him an excuse for visiting her.

"There's nothing that difficult about sewing on a button," Susan said.

"What's the latest from my dear brother?"

"He doesn't write anymore."

"I'm sorry. Have you written him?"

"Several times, but he never writes back."

"Not a telegram either?"

She moved to her sewing machine.

"Allow me." Ben gripped its sides. "Where do you want it?"

"Over next to that window."

He lifted the heavy machine chin high, hoping to impress her with his strength, and set it down where Susan indicated.

She confirmed what Miss Hamilton told him, and since he heard no regret in Susan's voice, he concluded that Moxley had lost interest in her and she in him. He'd not lose this girl like he'd lost others. "Miss Susan, I'd greatly appreciate it if you would agree to be more than my friend. I'm an honorable man. I don't approve of the way some men treat ladies. I'd never embarrass you or do you harm or court another lady behind your back."

"I'm flattered. Ask my father first."

"He's in Virginia."

"Well, I guess you'll have to wait."

"Is that a no?"

"A maybe."

They turned toward Alex's shout. He came running through the front gate, yelling his lungs off. Susan and Ben met him on the front lawn while curious servants gathered round. He told them about his secret grieving over his mother and Susannah and how he had to put on a bold face because of his father, his attempted suicide, and Cougar Jed. "I would have died myself if Jedidiah hadn't talked me out of it."

"Is that a fact?" Ben said.

"Dang right it's a fact."

"Are you skeptical, Mister Westcott?" Susan said.

"No, no," Ben said lightly. "I'm glad our grieving's over, my friend. Come, let's shoot some billiards."

And then, Mary came through the gate.

Alex shifted. "Mary, I see your father's coming toward us."

"Mister Hamilton told me he likes you, Alex," Susan said.

"He enjoyed the pranks you used to play on me." Mary giggled. "Remember the time you and Gideon Deshler brought me that rat snake and told me he was poisonous?"

Alex chuckled. "Well, your parents told my father rats were getting into their stable. Since I couldn't find a cat to do the job, I figured a rat snake was just as effective. Fun times, back in those days."

"How did you come across that snake?"

"Gideon found him over in—"

"Uh, I'm leaving," Ben said, interrupting them, but no one seemed to hear. "If you've found Susan's brand of religion and are happy about it, Alex, I'm happy for you," He passed Mister Hamilton on the way out. Maybe his love for Susan, perhaps, maybe it wasn't real after all.

49

ONCE AGAIN, *SELMA* steamed down to Grant's Pass, which allowed the gunboat *Morgan* to join *Gaines* at Mobile. Though Ben still considered himself Alex's friend, he distanced himself. Alex and Walker spent more time conversing like he and Alex used to do. Since Ben questioned the genuineness of Alex's conversion, he mostly listened and waited for him to return to his old, sarcastic ways.

Work on Mobile's key ironclad, *Tennessee*, pressed ahead. Her guns were being cast at a gun foundry in Selma. But what good was an ironclad without a crew? Buchanan's struggles recruiting capable seamen continued while he sought a competent officer to command her.

During *Madison's* repairs in New York, Danny learned *Hartford* had likewise gone there, which led him to seek out Tuck. He'd survived every battle thus far, Danny learned. But where he'd gone, no one he'd met from that ship knew. Many of her men had received furloughs; others were discharged.

Madison's repairs were completed in New York by mid-November. By mid-December, she steamed for the Gulf after receiving her officers and crew, including Danny. Some personnel had changed. Commander Vincent, promoted to captain, assumed command of a sloop-of-war hunting Rebel commerce raiders. Buckley, *Madison's* newest captain, now wore shoulder straps edged in gold with a silver anchor in the middle flanked by gold leaves, the newly-created rank of lieutenant commander. Lieutenant Warren, formerly *Madison's* second lieutenant, served as his executive officer. An ensign, Samuel Whitehurst, also came aboard. Like Buckley's new rank, Congress had also created the rank of ensign this past year. Lieutenant Jonas Birdwell and an assistant surgeon, Doctor Michael Youngblood, rounded out the ship's newest officers.

Her workday ended at the post office, Susan met Miss Evans and Sallie outside the Custom House. They sat in their buggy preparing to leave when Susan asked if she could join them.

"Certainly, darling," Miss Evans said.

Deftly managing her battered hooped dress, Susan sat opposite them.

With a crack of the driver's whip, the buggy moved out.

"Gusta's mailed a letter to a friend in Columbia," Sallie said. "Her book's printer had to move there from Charleston."

"Which has delayed its publication," Miss Evans said, a hint of annoyance in her tone. "I'm having to go there myself. Problems must be resolved before it gets published. I've asked my friend Rachel Lyons if I could stay with her or at a private boarding house rather than a hotel. I may have to stay there for a month or more. I will if I must. I cannot tolerate any more delays with *Macaria's* publication. Evans and Cogswell have had my manuscript in their possession since the first day in June."

"What sort of problems?" Susan asked.

"Matters pertaining to punctuation and proofreading. I'm going to have to revise all the proof sheets myself."

"When will you be leaving?"

"In a few days."

Susan sensed the author's impatience. In Miss Evans's opinion, her book was of extreme importance to the Confederacy's cause. Her sense of urgency probably accounted for her attitude.

1864

JANUARY

—

AUGUST

50

O<small>FF</small> P<small>ENSACOLA</small>, F<small>ARRAGUT</small> received his newly appointed commander of the Mobile Squadron, Captain Thornton A. Jenkins. Together with the admiral's new fleet captain, Percival Drayton, they conferred in Drayton's quarters aboard *Hartford*. Drayton, wearing a short beard, towered over his five-foot-six superior. Farragut's new clerk, Alexander McKinley, jotted notes.

"Things don't look promising, Admiral," Jenkins said. "Since your absence, the Rebels have almost finished their ram, and deserters informed me that Buchanan considers her more powerful than the *Merrimac*. Sir, we all remember what the *Merrimac* did to our wooden ships in Hampton Roads."

Farragut, squinting and leaning over the chart indicating the bay's defenses, massaged his chin. The news of *Tennessee's* completion boded ill for Jenkins's squadron. He glanced at Drayton, whose grave eyes analyzed the chart. Like himself, Drayton was Southern-born, a native South Carolinian. He possessed a quiet temperament, a keen intellect, and great competence. They'd met during his recent stay in New York where Drayton had been doing shore duty. He'd offered Drayton a post as flag captain, which Drayton eagerly accepted.

"Frank Buchanan and I served together on the *Franklin* way back during our midshipmen days," Farragut said. "Did I ever tell you that?"

"No, sir," Jenkins said.

"That's when I was serving with the Mediterranean Squadron. He's the South's best naval officer. I believe I can whip him. Give me a few monitors and attack before he does, we can hold his gunboats and ram in check in the shoals. What say you to that, Drayton?"

Drayton withdrew from the chart. "We'd best get started acquiring them, sir."

"I'm topside to my quarters. Admiral Porter has monitors. I'll write him for a couple or three. Meanwhile, we'll go to Mobile and investigate matters there ourselves."

While parishioners filed out of Reverend Dotson's church, Danny gripped each passing hand, looked each person in the eye, and thanked each one for coming. Unlike the first time he spoke, a mere smattering of folks attended this meeting.

This morning, he'd used Reverend Dotson's notes on John 17 as well as things he'd gleaned from his own study. Unity in Christ's church, that the Church would be one—that was Christ's prayer.

From the moment he opened his mouth, power and confidence surged through him like something he'd never before experienced and to such a degree that he startled himself. His words flowed like a bubbling stream in a lush valley. Reverent silence permeated the sanctuary, everyone's faces lifted to where he spoke from the pulpit's platform. Doctor Kirby arrived a few minutes late. He'd told Danny he'd planned to attend. He slid into the back pew beside an elderly couple.

After everyone left, Reverend Dotson and Esther disappeared through a rear door.

"A capital sermon," Doctor Kirby said.

"Thank you, sir." Danny pulled Nancy toward him. "This is my wife."

"Mrs. Yates, it is indeed a pleasure. Last night he showed me our ship's name you embroidered on his cap. He tells me you have a special talent for making garments."

"I try, Doctor." Nancy's grin spanned her gentle face. "I don't think I married me a blacksmith. I think I married me a parson."

"Mebe Parson Silas."

Aghast, Nancy clutched Danny's arm. "Tuck."

A little grayer in the hair, wrinkles etching his beetle brow, dark eyes like pebbles, but the same Tuck, Danny thought. Not much different than when he encountered him that day on Ship Island.

"It is me, mebe. I escaped Willer Wood a few years after your Danny got hisself sold. Made it North. Joined the Navy."

"I saw the *Hartford* anchoring off the city two days ago," Danny said. "I tried getting some liberty to talk to you, but I couldn't get away till this morning. How did you find me here?"

"That feller friend of yours, Juniper Jones, told me where you was when I got some liberty and went to your ship looking for you."

Danny unlocked Nancy's nervous fingers clawing his arm. Bidding everyone good-bye "for a short spell," he and Tuck walked down the street. "Tuck, I got something to say."

"Me, first. What I done to you at Willer Wood's been gnawing on me fer years. I kept hoping one day me and you would meet."

"Listen—"

Up went Tuck's palm. "Ain't done. Been carrying a load of bricks on my chest fer a long time." And then, he told his story. He didn't mean for Nancy to get sold, but rather Danny, when he planted Phineas's watch on him. After Danny's three failed escape attempts and his finally getting sold, Tuck decided he'd make his try for freedom. With the help of several free blacks and a few friendly whites, he succeeded. He had no conscience about what he'd done to Danny. That came later, he said.

"I made it clean up to Pennsylvania and right into Philadelphia. I'm sorry for what I done to you and Nancy. Powerful sorry."

Danny brought Tuck to a sudden halt. "I was going to apologize to you for hating you all these years."

"You're forgiven, mebe."

"Maybe?"

Tuck laughed. "No mebe about it no more."

"Danny," Nancy yelled from Reverend Dotson's stopped buggy. "What are you two doing?"

"We're making amends."

Nancy got down from the buggy's back seat and gave Tuck a hug. She handed Danny a thick envelope. "Reverend Dotson's notes."

"Study them." Reverend Dotson spoke from the buggy. "Nancy says she's married herself a parson. Esther and I quite concur."

Study? Danny gulped. He wasn't going to be a parson, never ever. A glance over at Tuck—Tuck was all grins.

51

SUSAN CALLED ON Miss Evans shortly after she'd learned that she'd returned. Certain she'd finished proofreading her novel, else she wouldn't have come back, she was eager to know its publication date.

Upon her arrival in the late afternoon, she discovered Miss Evans had another visitor. Judging by his spotless gray naval uniform, the silver tufts circling his large bald head, he was Admiral Buchanan. He matched Alex's description perfectly. An aura of command saddled him, and he might have put the scare in her had he not risen when she entered the parlor. His downturned lips lifted slightly, what she took for a smile.

"Admiral, may I introduce you to my dear friend, Miss Susan Jessup." Miss Evans pulled her closer toward him. "Her brother serves aboard the *Selma*."

" 'Tis a fine pleasure, Miss Jessup," Buchanan said. "Your brother has been conducting himself well."

"I am pleased, sir," Susan said.

The admiral escorted her to a chair.

"I hope we don't bore you," Buchanan said. "Miss Evans and I were just discussing my squadron's problems."

Ignorant in military matters, Susan listened throughout their conversation. The author never ceased to marvel her. An admiral discussing naval concerns with a lady, why, it was almost unheard of, yet Miss Evans commanded everyone's respect. Her friendships with politicians and generals and admirals, her correspondence with them, their letters back to her—Freely they discussed with her issues men generally discussed only among themselves.

Their conversation concerned the soon-to-be-finished *Tennessee*. Buchanan recounted workers' strikes, Mobile's lack of a dry dock, iron plates rolled out at the ironworks in Columbiana, Alabama—two-inch iron plates and one-inch iron plates, to be bolted atop each other across her thick oak and pine casemate. Three plates deep total, since the two-inch ones consisted of two layers. However, their bolt holes didn't always match.

"Those errors caused unnecessary delay," Buchanan said. "It forced me to ship them back to Selma for redrilling."

Like most everyone in Mobile, Susan knew the ram was in the Mobile River. Her thoughts trailed off to the Westcott brothers. Maybe neither one of them was meant for her. Perhaps she'd meet another man after the war, a man with whom she'd fall in love and marry.

Alex told her Ben had lost interest in his new life and that his and Walker's religious discussions wearied him. Ben wasn't antagonistic toward it. Merely uninterested. He'd started developing closer friendships with other officers.

Regarding Moxley Westcott, she missed his visits. More than she missed his brother's? She missed them both. She prayed they both came to a deeper faith, the kind of faith she now possessed.

"I've bombarded our Navy Department with requests for men, Miss Evans. I've sent six-hundred and fifty applications to Richmond. Only a mere twenty men have been approved."

The admiral's statement pulled Susan from her thoughts.

"We must find those officers and crew, Admiral." The author's voice rose. "Dulius built Rome's navy in three months and won a great victory over Carthage."

"Sadly, we have no Dulius in our government."

Susan perked up when a solution to the crew problem struck her, then her mouth clamped quickly. How could she suggest it? She was a nobody, Miss Evans a somebody.

Buchanan's eyes slid toward her. "Were you about to say something, Miss Jessup?"

"No, sir. Yes, sir." Susan averted Buchanan's quizzical stare. "Sir, I'm no expert on much of anything. An idea about how you might obtain a crew has occurred to me. Will you permit me to suggest it?"

"All right, miss. Let me hear your idea."

"Well, sir, what I was thinking was that maybe our army, the one here in Mobile, General Maury might—"

Buchanan's eyes lighted. "Yes, Miss Jessup. Yes, yes, yes. You, Miss Jessup, have given me a splendid idea. Thank you."

Ben's hackney clattered toward the moored vessel. She was almost as long as *Madison*, over two hundred feet he estimated, and rusty gray; an awning spread across stanchions spanned her iron-plated casemate's hurricane deck, her armored pilothouse situated atop its forward end. Its sloping sides reminded Ben of a breadbox.

The vessel sat low in the Mobile River, her freeboard barely visible. Aft, two boats hung from davits and her ensign fluttered. How many gun ports did she have? One aft, he spotted, and four on her port side. Their shields were closed. He assumed she had four gun ports on her starboard as well and perhaps another one forward. Ten in all, he figured, though he wasn't sure. Occasionally, he'd watched her undergo construction. Finally, she was finished and finally, he was transferred to her, CSS *Tennessee*, commissioned the previous day. Whether or not he'd enjoy serving aboard her was an open question. He'd get Bradford's opinion. Assigned to her as her executive officer, Lieutenant Bradford had likewise been transferred from *Selma*. An officer named Comstock replaced him on board that ship.

The driver reined in his horses at the mooring.

Sea chest in hands, Ben climbed down. At least he'd not hear anymore religious talk. That wasn't an open question. He feared Alex's newfound religion was driving him mad.

Ben saluted Lieutenant commanding James D. Johnston, *Tennessee's* captain, upon entering the captain's cabin.

"How do you like our little clad so far, Westcott?" Johnston said.

Johnston's spacious whitewashed cabin was situated aft, adjoining the wardroom built over the vessel's two engines. A simple oak desk and two pine chairs occupied its center. No rugs, no pictures or paintings, though there was a keg on the starboard side holding six large paper rolls tied with brown string, what Ben assumed were nautical charts. Ben could observe their boilers, controls, and other gears because the wardroom lay open to her engines. Winter air cooled them through ventilators overhead.

"I'd not exactly call her little, sir," Ben said at last. "It makes me feel kind of like a trapped rat."

"There's no clad afloat more powerful than our *Tennessee*." Johnston's hand threaded his receding brown hair. "Our Brooke rifles can deal with their Dahlgrens easy enough. The admiral and I agree on that point."

"I'm glad for that." Ben tempered his doubts. Johnston hadn't experienced battle yet, not against a man of Farragut's skill and daring.

"Well, I do believe you are acquainted with my executive officer, Lieutenant Bradford. I'll send for him. He'll show you around and assign you your quarters."

Ben set his chest beside his stateroom's cot.

"Yellow pine and oak, that's what this casemate's frame is made of," Bradford said.

"How thick is its iron?" Ben asked.

"Five inches. Captain Johnston says they laid six inches across her forward shield."

A lieutenant wearing a sprig of blond beard and a wisp of a mustache came down the aft hatch, Kentuckian Mortimer Benton. Ben had met him and other officers when he first came aboard. Benton was *Tennessee's* second lieutenant, and Ben, her third. Few enlisted men had reported yet.

"We can't fight anyone so long as we wallow in this blame river," Benton said. "We can't get across Dog River Bar. A couple of lighters came alongside yesterday with fire engines. We lashed them alongside us, port and starboard, ran poles from them and through our gun ports. The engines pumped hard as they could, but they only lifted us about twenty-two inches higher."

"Why keep the guns on board?" Ben said. "It's reasonable to me, having them off-loaded would've lifted her higher."

"According to Captain Johnston," Bradford said, "the admiral didn't care to risk the Yankees coming into the bay while we were aground. Without guns we'd be defenseless. Besides, don't you realize how difficult it is to load guns onto a vessel at sea without the right equipment to do it? We can only find such equipment on docks."

"Jessup told me the *Florida* loaded her guns at sea."

"We're an ironclad, Westcott. It's harder doing that sort of thing on an ironclad."

"Well, we can't do much of anything without sailors. No landlubbers who get seasick at the first rock on a wave."

Bradford led the way back up the hatch, into the eight-foot-high casemate. Shafts of sunlight spilled through the iron gratings cut into its top. They passed the smokestack piercing the casemate. At the large windlass, they halted.

The fore and aft Brookes, set on wooden slides, could be pivoted to fire broadside. The other four were strictly broadside guns. Though smaller than the Yankees' 15-inch Dahlgrens, the Brookes were rifled. This gave them a longer range. "They might give us some advantage," Ben said.

"What?" Bradford said.

"I was thinking aloud."

"Something about our Brookes?"

"Yes. I was thinking that their long-range rifles might be an advantage over Farragut's guns." He made himself sound confident. Their wooden gunboats, *Selma, Morgan* and *Gaines,* stood no chance against him. It would be up to this ironclad alone to defeat Farragut. Despite their advantage in range, they'd be massively outnumbered. Also, once Mobile Bay fell, if it did, the entire Gulf Coast would be the enemy's. Ben recalled his and Moxley's argument back in '61 when Moxley read him and Annie that poem he'd written, "Dixie's Doom," or something like that. It pained him to admit it, but Moxley's warnings about this war and the South's chances of winning may have been right.

He went to a starboard gun port's shield, lifted it along its tracks, peered out its narrow slit, and up at the cloudy sky. "These ports won't let us elevate our guns very high."

"The idea is to sink the enemy, isn't it?" Another officer had wandered into the casemate from below, followed by two others.

"Mister Smith, our ship's gunner." Bradford referred to the stocky officer who'd spoken.

"I fought Farragut below New Orleans," Ben said, "and if he does here what he did there, holing his ships below the waterline won't be easy. He bolted chains across her broadsides before he steamed upriver. They were, in effect, ironclads."

"Let's finish showing our new lieutenant around," Bradford said.

"Do you play billiards?" Ben asked Benton and Smith. They went down the forward hatch to the galley and crews' quarters.

"I'm a tolerably decent player," Benton said.

"Smith?"

"No, sir."

"Perhaps we'll have an opportunity to play a few games before we get down the bay. I know a good saloon with billiard tables. I found it after I quit playing at Jessup's house. If it's open for business, are you in for a wager, Benton?"

"Why, yes," Benton said.

"That's good to hear."

"I don't know the captain's opinion of you gents gambling," Bradford said, "but don't let the admiral find out."

"So long as you don't report us, sir," Ben said.

"You know me better than that, Westcott," Bradford said. "Let me know who wins."

52

Dᴜʀɪɴɢ Fᴇʙʀᴜᴀʀʏ, Fᴀʀʀᴀɢᴜᴛ bombarded Fort Powell. Formerly Fort Grant, it was renamed to honor the late commander of the bay's lower defenses. Unable to cross Dog River Bar, *Tennessee* stood by helplessly while *Huntsville, Tuscaloosa,* and *Baltic* went down to Grant's Pass to assist.

Mobilians panicked. General Sherman and Admiral Farragut were coordinating an attack against them, they assumed, till nothing more came of it. Farragut's only purpose was to discourage Maury from sending troops to reinforce General Leonidas Polk against Sherman, who'd captured Meridian, Mississippi, torn up its railroads and for five days, with ten thousand men, leveled its buildings. Farragut still had no ironclads to deal with *Tennessee,* nor did he have troops to capture the forts. On the last day of February, he called off the attack.

Meanwhile, desertions steadily shrank Buchanan's muster rolls, at least his gunboats'. Thanks to Susan's idea, *Tennessee* fared differently. The admiral wired Richmond a request for soldiers to be transferred from Maury's army, which it approved. Not sailors, most weren't, but the admiral would turn them into seamen. He'd also get the mighty *Tennessee* over Dog River Bar and into the bay before Farragut attacked. Since his first attempt failed, he'd try again. Neither Buchanan nor his old shipmate Farragut were quitters.

By the last day of February, her port anchor splashed down five fathoms, the guns of the Spanish River battery bristling from its parapet due south, a mile away.

Meanwhile, camels underwent construction, special camels Buchanan ordered designed to fit *Tennessee's* hull to raise her over the bar. He raced against time, against Farragut, to get her into the bay before his old messmate made his move.

He'd never been a general before, much less a soldier. Nevertheless, the Confederate War Department appointed Richard Lucien Page to that rank, brigadier general in command of Mobile Bay's lower defenses. Formerly a captain in the Confederate Navy, he assumed command in March, making Fort Morgan his headquarters just as his predecessors had done.

His neat, close-cropped beard was white as cotton, his posture erect as a ship's mast, and when he walked it was with long, confident strides like the commander of a man-of-war pacing the quarterdeck. During an assembly on the fort's parade ground, Brigadier General Page introduced himself and addressed the men. He recounted his long years in the Navy, summarized his Confederate naval service, and ended it by voicing his determination to sink Farragut's ships once they steamed close. He expected every man to do his duty, that his orders would be obeyed, that he would run a "tight ship," and after all this was said he pinched his cap's bill in a naval salute, quickly lowered his hand, and snapped his fingers against his forehead Army style. He and his staff headed out the fort for a vessel waiting to take him across the bay to Fort Gaines.

"He's been in the Navy too long." Riggs knelt at a cistern, one of four inside the fort, and dipped a tin cup in its water.

"He'll learn the Army's ways soon enough," Moxley said. "Didn't take me long. Still wearing that fine-looking bowie, I see."

Riggs downed the water and sent his cup into the cistern for a second drink. "Dandy boots you're still wearing." He offered Moxley the cup.

Moxley shook his head no.

Riggs stood. "Since we got us a naval officer in command of things down here now, he'll know better than any real general how to handle Farragut." He downed his water. "Even if I do lose our wager, there is one particular I have full confidence I'd win."

"Wager on it then."

Riggs set down the cup. "I don't make wagers on affairs of the heart."

"What the blazes are you talking about? Miss Jessup no longer interests me."

Riggs cocked a brow.

"Quit looking at me that way. Speaking the truth."

"The more you deny you no longer love her, the less I'm inclined to believe it."

"You're crazy, Riggs."

A bugle summoned them to artillery drill.

News of *Tennessee's* progress and lack thereof reached across the waters to *Selma* and other vessels in the Mobile Squadron. Ben wondered if that much-needed ironclad would ever get into Mobile Bay. On the first of April, Lieutenant commanding Johnston was promoted to commander and on the third, the camels undergoing construction for *Tennessee* caught fire, three of them destroyed.

By April's end carpenters, crew, and slaves scurried around *Tennessee* in boats and on her fore and aft decks. Huge chains attached to the wooden, boxlike devices called camels were dragged across the ram's exposed decks and bolted into place. Six camels total, three per side, perfectly aligned with her hull and half-filled with water. Once this task finished, engines on barges started pumping the water out and gradually, the vessel rose.

On the seventeenth of May, Buchanan boarded her while she was underway, towed by the steamer *Magnolia* and followed by *Morgan*. Later, *Morgan* cast her hawser aboard *Magnolia* and joined the towing. At 6:00 P.M., *Tennessee* anchored near the Spanish River's battery not far from its obstructions, pilings driven two fathoms deep. The admiral returned to Mobile.

Next day, *Morgan* and *Magnolia* towing her, *Tennessee* cleared the Dog River Bar. Propeller churning and still under tow, she headed down the dark, calm, rippling, sun-streaked bay into deeper waters.

For the next two days carpenters, crew, and slaves worked off the camels. They moved about the ram's exposed fore and aft decks, banged about her casemate's grating on her hurricane deck, and worked from boats alongside till they'd unlashed all the camels' chains.

Ben and Benton drilled sailors and a detachment of Marines.

"The Marines performed fine," Ben told Bradford that evening over wardroom cocoa coffee. "It's the sailors who concern me."

"They're improving," Bradford said.

"Not fast enough." Ben frowned. "I still don't like the way our gun ports were designed."

"Listen here, Westcott. It's too late to do anything about the gun ports. We hit the enemy below the water line or send a shot through his engine room, we'll sink him. Blasting his masts won't do any good."

"I don't like the way their shutters are designed either. While my men were working their guns, withdrawing them for loading and closing the shutters, I imagined an enemy shot hitting us. The way they're made, if the Yanks hit them when they're closed they could get jammed shut."

Bradford leveled his hard stare on Ben.

"Is the admiral aware of all this?" Ben said.

"Captain Johnston says he's due to come aboard tomorrow or next day. Ask him, Westcott." He sipped his coffee. "That's an order."

Ben quieted and shoved his cup and saucer aside. Why couldn't he keep his mouth shut?

Next day, the camels were towed back to Mobile and *Tennessee* took on coal.

The admiral wasn't piped aboard till the evening of the twenty-first, when the side-wheel gunboat *Gaines* brought him alongside. Ben's head throbbed during his deck officer watch; back in his cramped stateroom, he tossed and turned on his cot. Hot and stuffy, it drew sweat out of his pores despite its ventilation, and the odoriferous coal from the nearby engine room, engineers' chatter, his worries about questioning the admiral, these things kept him wide-eyed most of the night. No doubt, Buchanan would muster the crew tomorrow and make a speech. He'd have to voice to him those same concerns he'd voiced to Bradford.

But Bradford was the executive officer. That was his duty, or Captain Johnston's. Bradford thought his ordering him to ask the admiral amusing. It wasn't funny by a long shot. Why did he fear that old man so? He tumbled off his cot, smacked the deck on his face, and winced. His nose hurt.

53

Glass in hand, Farragut descended *Hartford's* poop deck ladder early next morning, his young flag lieutenant, J. Crittenden Watson behind him. He'd seen the Rebel ships up the bay. Rumors about "Buck" had proven true. He was coming down in *Tennessee.* He spotted her, along with three other ironclads. Reports claimed she was the most powerful ironclad ever built. She did look formidable from his vantage point. To deal with her, he had a mere handful of wooden ships. He'd written Washington requesting ironclads, but Washington denied his request. Well, if Buck did come out, he'd amuse him.

Before he entered his cabin, he studied Fort Gaines and the pilings obstructing his approach, then shifted to the Main Channel where boats worked.

"The Rebs keep on planting their torpedoes, sir." Drayton eased up alongside, his binoculars focused on the activity.

"Those infernal things might give us a serious problem, sir," Watson said.

"We'll worry about it when the time comes," Farragut said.

For several minutes, they observed the Rebels. They worked from a launch. Containers, such as large barrels with an oblong shape and others made of boiler iron, had chains and anchors attached to them. Lowered into the water, they disappeared beneath the surface, probably not very deep.

Every time he'd passed a fortification, he'd not had these torpedoes and other well-placed obstructions to deal with. *A serious problem,*

Mister Watson? You are entirely correct. This time, passing the forts won't be easy. Soon as I get my ironclads, it will be done. He just hoped Ole Buck didn't come out first.

The boatswain's shrill whistle scurried sailors into *Tennessee's* casemate. Shoulder to shoulder by divisions, on her starboard side, they assembled for morning muster, a mass of men in white frocks with black silk neckerchiefs, white trousers and white caps. Officers and Marines wore gray.

Silence permeated the divisions. Buchanan limped between the ranks. His speech stirred Ben and likely did his fellow officers. Battle was nigh at hand. "Every man will stand by his guns. No one will surrender. Never! For the eyes of the people of the Confederacy are turned upon us and they expect much."

Three hurrahs followed the admiral's short speech.

He cracked a slight, rare smile.

At least he's pleased, Ben told himself.

Johnston had Bradford dismiss the men.

Throughout the day, the low tide immobilized the ironclad. Ben battled his nerves. He only found relief during gunnery drills, when he could think about things other than the admiral. Numerous times the admiral, in Johnston's company, crossed through the casemate, going up the ladder to the pilothouse and back down into the wardroom. He hoped he discovered the same troubling things he had. Maybe then, he wouldn't have to say anything. He didn't want to talk with the admiral anymore than necessary.

For a few hours, he rested easier when the admiral left to inspect other vessels.

Shortly after supper, Ben stepped out onto the aft deck for fresh air. Clouds dark as iron gathered overhead. Outside the bay, Farragut's ships rocked and tossed on white-capped waves. Eleven, twelve of them, he estimated. Their force was growing larger, a sure sign Farragut intended them his next target.

"Have you told him yet?" Bradford ducked out the gun port.

"No."

"Why not? Scared?"

"No. Yes. Yes I am. All those tales I heard about him, the way he looks at everybody...the man, he's—"

"I'm what?" Buchanan said.

Ben's veins turned to ice. The admiral spoke from the hurricane deck. Two pilots, judging by their civilian clothes and having seen them brought in from Fort Morgan, flanked him. The awning overhead popped in the strengthening wind.

"Sir, I...I'm—"

"Scared of me. I want my men and my officers scared of me. It makes for good discipline."

"Yes, sir."

"What's this noise about the gun ports?"

"Sir, I'm not trying to be disrespectful or anything sir. I don't want you to think...." Ben hesitated.

"Say it, man. What's on your mind?"

"Well, sir. It's... the way the gun ports are designed, when we pull them down to reload our guns, they might get jammed if a Yankee shell hits them the right way."

"See where you're standing, Mister," Buchanan said.

"Sir?"

"At your feet. The tiller chains."

Ben realized what Buchanan was talking about, and its gravity hit him harder than did the gun ports. They stretched across open grooves, an easy target for a Yankee gun. One shot severing them, they'd no longer be able to maneuver. "Yes, Admiral. I understand."

"Westcott, I am more aware of the strengths and weaknesses of this vessel than are you. More than anyone else, with the possible exception of Captain Johnston. I am working to remedy those weaknesses. Bradford, have all hands mustered on the gun deck."

"Aye, sir."

Before he reentered the casemate, Ben studied the clouds, the seas rolling harder and faster. They were in for some rough weather.

Inside Johnston's quarters, Buchanan felt the ram rocking while *Tennessee's* crew scurried inside her casemate one deck up. They started clearing it of all unnecessary things so they could fight their pending battle. He'd promised them a foray outside the bay tonight. He'd sworn to raise David Farragut's blockade. At their last muster, Johnston had read them his fighting order. The admiral grunted, displeased by the worsening weather.

The two pilots entered behind Johnston.

"Give me the verdict, Henley," Buchanan said.

"Sir," the first pilot, Henley, said. "The wind's blowing hard from the southward and westward."

"Simpson?" Buchanan addressed the second pilot.

"My opinion is this, Admiral," Simpson said. "And Captain Johnston agrees with my opinion. And my opinion tells me the weather's going to get worse before it gets better. I think a bad squall's coming on soon."

Buchanan's eyes cut Johnston's direction. Johnston nodded.

"Sir," Henley said, "it may be wise to call off the attack. Tonight isn't a good night for it."

"That is, in our opinion, sir," Simpson said.

Buchanan limped to Johnston's desk. They were right, of course. Steaming outside the bay in this foul weather and the seas getting higher and rowdier and *Tennessee* with so little freeboard, the waves might sink them.

"I'm disappointed, Johnston," Buchanan said, "but you and the pilots have given me wise advice. Lay topside and inform Mister Bradford I'm calling off the attack due to inclement weather."

"Aye, sir. Right away." Johnston left.

54

MAJOR GENERAL EDWARD Richard Sprigg Canby matched Farragut's strides through the admiral's cabin doors. In his late forties, square of jaw with a large nose and ears he, like Farragut, wore no beard. Two of Canby's aides followed them.

A West Point graduate, Canby had served on the frontier before the war, fought Indians and Mexicans, and had commanded the Department of New Mexico soon after the war started, where he'd fought Rebels before being ordered East. Banks's recent fiasco up the Red River led to Canby's replacing him in May. The ill-fated expedition created numerous administrative problems. Canby's well-known administrative talents earned him a promotion and a new command— the Military Division of West Mississippi. Banks, though, retained authority within New Orleans.

"Forgive me, Admiral," Canby said. "I haven't much time. I must get back to New Orleans by tomorrow morning. I've inspected my new command all up and down the Mississippi. I have a good feel for our strategic situation as it stands." He took a letter from his aide and gave it to him.

Farragut passed it to his clerk, Alexander McKinley. "My eyesight isn't what it used to be."

"Sir," McKinley said, "it's from General Sherman."

"He's advancing against Atlanta," Canby said. "He's asked me to make either a strong feint or a real attack against Mobile from Pascagoula, with your assistance, of course. General Grant likewise approves."

Grant, now a lieutenant general and commanding all Union armies, was fighting Lee in Virginia. The day before, he'd received a report that Grant was attacking him around Petersburg. Farragut stifled his mounting eagerness. Finally, they'd take Mobile. "How many men will you have?"

"General Sherman's promised me ten thousand troops."

"Mister McKinley, have Captain Drayton bring his chart of Mobile Bay. I need Watson too."

"Aye, Admiral."

Not many minutes later, Drayton and Watson gathered around Farragut's desk. Drayton rolled open his chart.

"Gentlemen." Farragut rubbed his hands together. "General Canby has called upon us to help him conduct either a feint or an actual attack against Mobile."

Drayton and Watson smiled.

"I've been thinking on this moment ever since we took New Orleans," Farragut continued. "General Canby tells me General Sherman's promised him ten thousand troops for an overland campaign."

"I may be able to get us twenty thousand," Canby said. "My Nineteenth Corps, in Morganza, Louisiana, is already standing by for orders."

For the next few hours the commanders hashed out their plan's general details, but more work remained before they put it into effect.

"I'll need ironclads," Farragut said near the end of their conference. "The Rebels have a powerful one inside the bay ready to tear us apart with her long range Brookes. The *Manhattan* is on her way, but I need more. Would you be able to help me acquire two or three, General?"

"I'll write Admiral Porter and request them," Canby said. "Since General Banks's river campaign is over, he ought to be able to spare a couple or so."

"Do it."

On June's last night, leaden clouds smothered the moonlight. A hard slap on his thigh awakened Moxley. Rolling sideways, he spied Sergeant Ferguson's shadow dashing from man to man. "Get up. Get up. Grab y'all's muskets. Double-quick."

"Huh?" Moxley rubbed sleep from his eyes.

"A blockade-runner's aground off the Swash Channel."

Moxley sprang off his bunk.

"Captain Whittaker's outside," Ferguson said. "Riggs, you and Persons and Davidson go with Lieutenant Ashboth for the wagons. We're unloading her cargo before the Yanks sink her."

Other soldiers stirred from their bunks, many throwing on shirts before grabbing their guns.

Within the minute, Moxley's company ran along the shadowy beach paralleling the channel.

Havoc accompanied the dawn. Heart pounding his head, Moxley clambered up the iron-plated runner's side and through her gangway. It seemed every ship in Farragut's squadron unleashed the fury. Screaming shells kicked up a fuss, exploding over her paddle wheels or smashing sand behind them. A nearby battery boomed its reply. Fort Morgan's cannon cut loose at long intervals.

Moxley stumbled down the forward hatch behind his comrades and sailors.

Ferguson screeched orders. "The hold, men! The hold!"

They bolted down another ladder, into the shaft of sunlight dancing off the compartment's center. It flickered off rows of casks and crates crammed and stacked atop each other along each bulkhead.

"Single file," Ferguson screamed over the din. Standing nearest the ship's bows, he reached up high and worked down a crate, which he thrust into a soldier's hands. Quickly it passed from man to man, soldier to sailor to soldier. Moxley received it last and thrust it up the ladder to others waiting a deck above. Soon as he turned back, another crate came at him. Another. Another. Another.

He quivered, that same quiver he'd experienced when Locke aimed his sword at him that day at the Head of the Passes. Except this time, he sensed his situation was more serious. He was in the bowels of a stranded ship unloading her cargo with nowhere to run and no enemy to see. Only hear. Hear…and worry.

Captain Whittaker passed the order from topside: "Abandon ship."

"For now." Ferguson gestured the men to turn back. They scurried back up the ladders single file.

Farragut and Drayton observed the bombardment from *Hartford's* quarterdeck. Six of their gunboats thundered at the grounded runner; six other vessels, including the admiral's flagship, weren't engaged. Wagons waited at the runner while soldiers and the runner's crew heaved barrels and casks and crates of all sizes and shapes into them. Many fled amidst the shells landing in their midst. Farragut wondered why Buck never came out and fought after the weather cleared. Since so many of his wooden ships were converging on the bay, perhaps he figured his squadron had grown too large to challenge.

"It doesn't appear we're inflicting much damage, sir," Drayton said.

"It's likely they'll have all her cargo off by tonight." Farragut wished Buck would come out. He was tired of watching his friend. Iron versus wood. Let it be settled in one big battle, once and for all. "Signal the *Glasgow*. I'm going in for a closer look."

"But sir—"

"Those are my orders, Drayton."

"Aye, sir."

Upon the admiral's return, he told Drayton that the Rebel ship had not suffered any significant damage.

On the first day of July, a mail steamer pulled up alongside *Hartford*.

"Admiral." Watson saluted before placing a letter in Farragut's palm. "I think this one's from General Canby, sir."

"Thank you. Drayton, keep me abreast of any developments in the bombardment. I'll be in my quarters. Watson, send McKinley to me at once."

"Aye, sir." Watson saluted and left.

McKinley joined Farragut in the admiral's cabin.

"Blast it! Our attack's been cancelled," Farragut said once the clerk finished reading aloud the general's correspondence.

"I'm sorry, sir," McKinley said.

"Guess it can't be helped. Grant and Lee are stalemated at Petersburg, Early's raiding the Shenandoah Valley and with the President's reelection chances, with all this happening and General Canby's being ordered to send every man he can spare to Virginia, and his Nineteenth Corps in particular. Return to your other duties." Farragut donned his cap and went out. The thunderous firing had subsided but would soon pick up again. Since he couldn't attack Mobile, he'd do everything he could to sink that blockade-runner.

For five days the runner endured Farragut's heavy shelling, but her iron hull remained intact. Obsessed with her destruction, Farragut's frustrations mounted.

On the late afternoon of the sixth, Farragut called Watson into Drayton's quarters to discuss his newest plan. He gestured at a chair. The young man sat.

Before speaking, he studied his flag lieutenant's youthful features. He'd been a master aboard *Hartford* at the war's start and had served with him in every campaign. His plan might lead to the young man's death, but there was no officer aboard whom he trusted more, both him and Captain Drayton. He took a deep breath. *God forgive me if this young man gets killed.* "How are you this fine afternoon?"

"I'm well, sir," Watson said.

"Are you in the mood for a fight?"

"I'm always in the mood, sir."

"It's a dangerous assignment."

"I'll do it, sir. Whatever your orders are, I'll do it."

"That's why I'm giving you this responsibility."

"Does it have something to do with the blockade-runner, sir?"

"It does. Tonight, under cover of darkness, I want you to take a crew and three boats to her. I want you to board her and set her on fire. I also want you to plant a keg of gunpowder in her and blow her up before the Rebels spot you."

Watson licked his lips like a cat who'd just finished off a bowl of milk. "The runner's good as kindling, Admiral."

"Mind you, Watson. Choose your men wisely."

"I'll get it done, sir."

Raucous seagulls kept Moxley awake while he stood guard. The night was cool, calm. His attention returned to the side-wheeler fifty yards away. Though they'd finally off-loaded her cargo, they guarded her against more Yankee attempts to destroy her. *Ivanhoe.* Her crew had told him her name, and he liked it since it bore the name of his favorite novel.

Because no one had been injured or killed thus far, his fear of death subsided. He and his comrades slept with their muskets every night while always having one man standing watch. He respected Farragut. In some ways, the man was like him—stubborn.

A boat. Three boats. Off the Ivanhoe. He seized his musket and strode along the sand past his fellows to Ferguson, snoring. He shook him awake.

"Shhh." Moxley's finger touched his lips. "Sergeant. Three boats. At the *Ivanhoe.*"

Ferguson stood, yawned, and scratched his balding head. "I see 'em." He kept his shrill voice at a whisper. "Wake the others."

Moxley ran from man to man, shaking each man awake. His attention back on *Ivanhoe*, he watched the enemy hurry down her side into their boats. He rammed cartridge and ball down his musket's barrel, brought it up against his shoulder, and squeezed its trigger.

A rattle of musketry from his comrades followed.

Flames spewed from the runner.

"She's on fire." Riggs sprinted toward the vessel.

"Wait. Come back." Moxley lit out after him.

The Yankees discharged a salvo as their boats pulled away. Moxley stumbled, fell, got up to run, stumbled again. He gripped his thigh. Warm blood spurted between his fingers. His artery. He yelled for help.

Riggs raced back, dropped on his knees, and unbuttoned his shirt. With his Bowie knife, he ripped off a sleeve. "Steady there, friend. I'm making you a tourniquet."

Moxley winced; his strength waned.

"Davidson! A litter!" Captain Whittaker's voice.

"He's dying." Person's, fading.

"Dead." Ferguson's, barely audible.

Moxley turned his head on his thin feather pillow. Breeze whipped through his room's opened window, his bed beside another man's, who was rolled over on his side snoring up a squall. Male nurses walked past his opened door pushing wheeled carts which looked like they held medicine. Also, a man hobbled about on crutches and a bespectacled doctor, indicated by the stethoscope dangling from his neck, jotted notes. He was in a tomfool hospital. He didn't have time to be here. "Doc!" he yelled at the note-taking physician. "Want out of this place!"

The doctor stepped into the room. "We shall discharge you when you have recovered."

"I've recovered. Lemme out." He tried scooting back and sitting up against his headboard, but collapsed onto his sheet. "Doc!"

The doctor swooped on him. "Be quiet, Mister Westcott."

The snoring soldier rolled on his side toward Moxley. His eyes barely cracked open. "Shut up, idiot. I'm sleeping." Then he rolled back toward the opposite wall and within seconds, lapsed back into snores.

"Can't sit up," Moxley said.

"That is quite understandable. Your leg was amputated at Fort Morgan before you were brought here, to the hotel in Point Clear."

"I know it was amputated. Give me some crutches. I want out of this place. I hate lying around doing nothing."

"Not until you have recovered." The doctor left.

"I want out!" Odd, that sensation of still having his right leg. He stretched forward slightly and touched his bandaged stump. Was that a splint the doctor put on it?

The snoring soldier awakened again. Without turning he said, "He'll discharge you when he's ready. Now will you please shut up so I can sleep?"

"My goodness, what's all this fussing about?" Susan came straight through the door.

"Leg's gone," Moxley snapped. "Doctors stole it."

"They had to else you might have died."

"How'd you find out I was here?"

"Uncle Will was on his way back from the forts when he noticed a steamer's boat bringing you here. He was getting in one of *Lady Amber's* boats at the time and recognized you being brought out on the wharf on a litter. He sailed her to Mobile and told me. I came soon as I could."

Moxley looked away. Susan was still beautiful. But…*ah!* He didn't love her anymore. He smacked down his flipping heart.

"Did you know Miss Evans's book has finally come out in print?" She handed him her copy, its words printed on wrapping paper, its binding made of boards and its cover, wallpaper which bore the title, *Macaria, or Altars of Sacrifice,* and her name, Augusta Jane Evans. "It's made quite a stir. Everyone's talking about it."

"Not me."

Susan set it on the bedside table. "Miss Evans told me she smuggled one copy aboard a blockade-runner to her publisher up North. Maybe it'll get published there too."

"Hurrah. I'll never have a novel published."

"Why, I cannot believe what my ears hear. Of all the people to talk the way you do, the man who never gives up."

"Lost my leg. Can't be a burden on Baby Brother. Can't be a burden on you."

"Your brother? Me?"

"Since I'm out of the picture finally, since the doctors stole my leg, expect you two will get married."

"I'll marry the man I love."

"Who is?"

Susan left fast.

Half-man. That's me. Right. Life's over, a beggar on the street I'll become. Can't do much else, not without my leg.

55

THE THIRD DAY of August, at 10:25 A.M., *Madison* anchored a few miles off Mobile Bay, her dreary duty off Galveston done. White-capped waves rolled and splashed a host of vessels—sloops-of-war, gunboats. Also, three monitors, one single-turreted and the other two, double-turreted, anchored inside Sand Island. From the quarterdeck's weather side, Locke observed the most distant fort. It resembled a giant white ant hill, its Rebel flag fluttering. He recalled that day he and Westcott dueled each other amongst its dunes, back in January of '61, the flesh wound he suffered, Jessup's sarcasm which followed. Jessup's family lived in Mobile. He wondered what Jessup's sister looked like. Once they passed these forts, he'd pay her a call and kill her like he did Westcott's sister. For no reason, really, except he hated Jessup.

"Mister Locke."

He turned at Warren's demanding voice.

"Were you listening to me?"

Scowling, Locke nodded. Warren's promotion to executive officer had swelled his head.

"I'd say you were daydreaming."

"Sir, I—"

"Forget it. Captain Buckley's told us to strip for action. The others have obviously stripped for it. We're going in soon."

Ensign Whitehurst, *Madison's* signal officer, bounded off the mizzenmast's ratlines after he scrambled down them. He went straight to Buckley, who was observing the bay through his spyglass.

"Sir," Whitehurst said, "the admiral's hoisted signal two-one-three-nine, sir. All captains to report aboard."

"Mister Warren," Buckley said, "the deck is yours. Locke, I need my gig lowered."

He needs his gig lowered. He needs his gig lowered. Locke fumed. *His precious little gig.*

Alongside Lieutenant Bradford, Ben peered through the slit in *Tennessee's* pilothouse atop the forward portion of her casemate. Like dots on bounding waves, boats pulled madly toward the large steamer anchored almost center among her sisters.

"I'd say Farragut's captains are off to their powwow," Bradford said. "How many ships did you count out there, Westcott?"

"Twenty-five," Ben said.

"Try twenty-six."

"Twenty-five, twenty-six. We're still outnumbered."

"Admiral Buchanan's sending the *Baltic* back to Mobile. She's too slow to do us much good."

"So it'll be our single ironclad against his three."

"Counting our three little gunboats, that's twenty-six against—"

"Long odds."

"Our *Tennessee* has her ram, and we've torpedoes in the Main Channel."

Ben backed out of the pilothouse and descended its ladder into the casemate. "I still say long odds, sir!" he shouted back up at Bradford. He disliked the recent developments. They should've attacked last May before things started looking bad. He thought Buchanan was aggressive. Now, he had doubts.

Hartford's wardroom pulsed. No time for small talk this day. Serious business was at hand. Farragut was determined to get it done and get it done right.

"Our gravest concern, gentlemen?" Farragut said to his assembled captains in *Hartford's* wardroom. "I will tell you what our gravest concern is. The Rebels' torpedoes and obstacles. Since May, their boats have been planting them. That black buoy we see at the torpedo field's eastern end marks the Main Channel they've kept open for blockade-runners. The channel's the only way we'll get past those infernal devices and other obstructions. Above everything else, we must stay east of that buoy."

"Sir," Buckley said, "my apologies for speaking out, but that will put us directly beneath Fort Morgan's guns. We won't have much space for maneuvering."

"Let me repeat," Farragut said. "We are going in through the Main Channel. We'll be within two hundred yards of the fort's water battery. The closer we are to it, the safer we'll be. Captain Buckley, I issued an order several weeks ago. Since your arrival, you must also do it. The same thing we did in New Orleans. Drape sheet chains over the *Madison's* sides and sandbag your engines."

"Aye. sir."

He shifted some boat-shaped blocks, made by his ship's carpenter, on a table to illustrate his plan. "Once you're opposite the torpedo field, gentlemen, stop your screws and let the current carry you past. I don't want your propellers getting tangled in the ropes the enemy's laid out for us. The paddle-wheelers lashed to your ships will keep moving under steam. Their paddles are less likely to get tangled."

Moving the blocks different directions, he detailed other aspects: seven ships would remain in the Gulf and six in Mississippi Sound to assist the army's landing on Dauphin Island and behind Fort Morgan on Mobile Point. The rest of the fleet would steam in, in a column, the wooden ships lashed together.

The admiral also assigned the captains their order of battle, which ships would be lashed to which. The ironclads *Winnebago, Chickasaw,* and *Manhattan,* the slowest vessels, would take the lead and steam off their starboard. They'd keep the fort's gunners busy till every ship passed. Then *Winnebago* and *Chickasaw* would follow them while *Tecumseh* and *Manhattan* dealt with the Rebel clad *Tennessee.* During his explanation his wrath rose, but quickly he squashed it. These men weren't to blame that the one ironclad he'd been expecting, *Tecumseh,* still hadn't reported in. He'd go in without her if need be, but he'd prefer not to. The most powerful of his clads, her battery of two huge Dahlgrens could fire 440-pound projectiles, and he'd planned on her sinking *Tennessee.* But he'd suffered too many delays already. He was done waiting. *Tecumseh* was at Pensacola, and Captain Jenkins of the *Richmond* was there trying to hurry her captain, Commander Tunis Craven, to Mobile. Craven claimed he didn't have enough coal nor enough men to load his vessel's coal bunkers. Excuses, excuses! He hated excuses for inaction.

Later, Farragut's mood soured even more as he surveyed his fleet, their topmasts taken down, their unnecessary rigging removed, sheet chains draping every wooden ship's sides, their decks sanded and girded for battle. Canby's troops would land on Dauphin Island this afternoon and yet still, no *Tecumseh*.

He entered Drayton's quarters.

"Mister McKinley, I'm writing Jenkins."

The clerk got out his stationery.

Farragut paced a tight circle, dictating his words, struggling to contain his ire. McKinley's pen scarcely kept pace with his rapid, quivering speech. "I have lost the finest day for my operations. I confidently supposed that the *Tecumseh* would be ready in four days, and here we are on the sixth and no sign of her, and I am told has just begun to coal. I could have done very well without her, as I have been without her, and every day is an irretrievable loss.

"The soldiers, by agreement, are landing today back of Dauphin Island, and could I have gone in this morning, we would have taken them by surprise. Four deserters came off from Fort Gaines last night, and they do not expect any landing there; but they are working like beavers on Morgan....

"I send the *Bienville* to tow the *Tecumseh*....I can lose no more days. I must go in day after tomorrow morning at daylight or a little after. It is a bad time....I have the wind just right, and I expect it will change by the time I go in."

A hard pause ended Farragut's dictation.

"Sir," McKinley said. "Today's the third, not the sixth."

"Huh. So it is." Steadying his voice this time, Farragut resumed pacing. "I need another letter to General Granger. He needs to know I won't be able to go in till the fifth, with or without the *Tecumseh*." He resumed his dictation.

On the fourth of August, late morning, *Winnebago*, one of the three monitors inside Sand Island, turned her two turrets on Fort Gaines while Rebel reinforcements disembarked boats. Booms reverberated. The fort answered, its shells striking water around her.

Meanwhile, Farragut and his captains conferred a second time. Once the conference ended the admiral, anxious for *Tecumseh's* arrival, dictated a letter to his wife. He expected Mobile Bay would be his bloodiest battle. Ole Buck was no fool, and the Rebels had done well with their defensive measures. Should he be killed, he wanted to assure her and Loyall that he loved them, that he did his duty. "...if God thinks it is the proper place for me to die, I am ready to submit to his will, in that as in all other things...."

"Admiral." Drayton hurried through Farragut's doors at the sound of a naval gun salute. "Captain Jenkins has returned."

"The *Tecumseh?*"

"He's signaled us she departed Pensacola about ten this morning."

Farragut clapped McKinley's shoulder. "She ought to be here by sundown. Drayton, signal all captains of ironclads and consorts aboard. We need one final conference before we go in. I'll brief Captain Craven upon his arrival."

In Buckley's cabin, Locke stood beneath a flickering bulkhead sconce and listened, not just to Buckley, but to the thunder, to the rain. *Madison's* officers gathered around Buckley's desk along with two army signal officers whom Farragut assigned to their ship, Lieutenants Lyman and Quest. Locke didn't budge. One day, Buckley was going to find an excuse to court-martial him. He'd be glad to get transferred to another ship, one with a captain who shared his opinions before that happened. Stupid Buckley had developed a respect for Yates. Most everyone on board had come around to that. Yates, an ignoramus undeserving of respect. Locke caught Buckley's hard glance. The whole crew, respecting a black man. *A disgrace!*

"Would you care to join us, Mister Locke?"

Locke ambled to Buckley's desk where Buckley unfolded a chart of Mobile Bay. He'd penciled the order of battle for the wooden ships with plus signs, the four ironclads inside Sand Island Channel with large dots, and for the Rebel vessels, he'd simply drawn short, vertical lines, *Tennessee's* line the longest and thickest.

Winnebago continued her distant firing. *Madison* creaked and tossed.

"Tomorrow morning," Buckley said, "we're going in. This time, it's certain."

Hurrahs resounded around the cabin.

Locke silently counted Buckley's marks. Fourteen wooden ships and four ironclads against one Rebel clad and three gunboats. An uneven match, except the Rebs' torpedoes gave them a slight advantage. Unpredictable, they were the deadliest weapon in the enemy's arsenal. He disliked the notion of dealing with them.

The excitement subsided.

Buckley resumed speaking. "A victory here means the end of all major naval conflict along the Gulf Coast. It will hasten the war's end. Our consort is the *Seminole.* Her captain is aboard the admiral's ship receiving his final orders. As for us, we'll be stationed behind the *Richmond* and her consort, *Port Royal.*"

"What about the torpedoes, sir?" Lieutenant Caldwell spoke with a flat, nasal voice.

"The admiral dispatched his flag lieutenant to investigate them last night. He dragged a grapnel through the channel, but that squall that hit us ended his efforts. He found nothing that one time he searched."

"So, we don't know for sure whether or not there are torpedoes in that channel," Locke said loudly. "We're stupid to steam through it without being sure."

"The admiral's tired of waiting, I'm tired of waiting."

"We're all sick and tired of waiting." This from Zollicoffer.

Locke glowered at the Marine.

Buckley reviewed the plan in detail, what to do in the event certain unexpected things happened, and all the instructions passed down from the admiral. *Tecumseh* and *Manhattan,* he said, would fire a shot at Fort Morgan's water battery and then steam in to engage *Tennessee.* The other two ironclads, the double-turreted *Chickasaw* and *Winnebago,* would blast away at the Rebs' batteries to distract them from the fleet's wooden ships while they passed. "Since Navy signals differ from the Army's, our army signal officers will communicate with Canby's troops on shore," he said, bringing his discussion to an end. "The admiral has assigned such men to every sloop-of-war."

Clean-shaven Lyman, petting his bushy black side-whiskers, furrowed his brow and studied the chart.

"We'll also communicate with the army signal officers on the other sloops," Lieutenant Quest said.

"Naturally," Buckley said.

"I assume the brave admiral's ship will lead us in," Locke said.

"He'll be second in the column," Buckley said.

"Why is that, sir? He is our gallant admiral."

"He wanted to lead us in, but we all insisted against it. The *Brooklyn's* taking it, and the *Hartford* will follow. Besides, the *Brooklyn* has sweeps to catch torpedoes and four chase guns to explode them. All of you, dismissed. We're forming line of battle at sundown. One more wisecrack from you, Locke, I'll see you miss this fight."

Locke smirked, about-faced smartly, and marched out of Buckley's cabin. Buckley was looking for an excuse to get rid of him. He knew Buckley and his kind.

Buchanan followed Johnston down the pilothouse's ladder, the rain having ended and the waning sun beating through the casemate's gratings. Sailors sat cross-legged against gun carriages and the windlass, oblivious to their presence and concentrating on scribbling letters to loved ones. He and Johnston stepped through the aft gun port. Scattered about the aft deck, sailors also sat and wrote and enjoyed the cool breeze which followed the squall.

Buchanan considered the rapidly developing situation. He and Johnston had just finished assessing things from atop the pilothouse, fully aware that a fourth monitor, single-turreted, had arrived.

He'd learned from General Page, who'd received a signal from Fort Gaines' commander, that Yankee troops were advancing across Dauphin Island and that the battle there was underway. Julius had reinforced it with his Marines. He prayed his son-in-law survived that fight. Sponges and rammers in hand, men awaited developments on Fort Morgan's bastions and ramparts.

Once Farragut advanced, the torpedoes and other obstructions would force him beneath Fort Morgan's guns. He'd be steaming a nearly straight line through the Main Channel. No doubt, the monitors would join him. The lighthouse battery and the fort's cannon would have an easy range. If he did everything right and his captains performed their duty, he just might defeat Farragut despite his more numerous ships.

Gaines, Morgan, and *Selma* anchored behind him were stripped for action. He'd line them across Farragut's column just north of the torpedo field, their broadsides facing his fleet. *Tennessee,* he'd position in the channel's clear section, her ram targeting the vanguard vessel, thus "capping the 'T.'" He noted the still-exposed chain cables. They should've been covered. Too late for that now. Since the Yanks had moved against Fort Gaines, naval battle was imminent.

The sun's final red blaze skimmed the bay. At *Selma's* wardroom mess table, Alex joined Walker in prayer for God's protection, for success in the pending battle, for Ben and for Moxley.

Walker ended the prayer then consulted his watch. "Almost time for us to go on duty."

"I hope we don't run from the Yankees," Alex said. "Do you think Captain Murphey's the running type? He's never been in a real battle before, I don't believe."

"I have no idea. But then, you've never been in a real battle either."

"True, but I've been shot at while serving on the *Florida.*" Alex laughed. "And we ran faster'n a jackrabbit!"

"I can't fault you for that since you couldn't fire back. That was some feat of bravery Captain Maffitt performed."

"I really like that man. He has a keen sense of humor and laughed as easily as his courage came to him." He leaned forward. "Say, I'll let you in on a secret, Walker."

"That 'k' word?"

"Naw. No one will ever figure that one out. Before—"

Selma's bell cut short their conversation. "Time to go on watch duty. I'm officer of the deck now. We'll talk more later." Alex headed up the ladder.

Every afternoon since he'd been bedridden, Susan had visited him. She'd talk animatedly, always positive, always teasing and laughing and trying to lift his spirits. The deep disappointment he'd felt regarding her previous spurning, his bitterness at losing her love, all evaporated. From the inside out, her beauty glowed. Always positive, always confident of his full recovery, and though her faith was intact, she wasn't the flamimg, wild-eyed fanatic many had accused her of becoming.

The doctor was planning on making him a wooden leg after he'd healed, she'd said. He'd be able to walk again, though probably with a limp.

"How are you today, Mister Westcott?" Susan fluffed the pillow behind his head and helped him sit upright.

"Better."

She fluffed the pillow again then her fingers touched him briefly. "Are you more comfortable now?"

"Yes, ma'am."

"Good." She pulled the top sheet up tighter beneath his stubbly chin, her knuckles touched him. His heart bubbled.

"Sure wish I had my limb. Perhaps we could then…"

Her finger touched his lips. "Shh. I wished you had it too. But a man is still a man with or without a leg. It's what's in his heart that counts." She turned away and muttered something as she left.

Did she mutter what he thought she did? Was it something like, *I love you?* She loved him even though he didn't have a leg? If he could've jumped out of bed and danced a jig, he'd have done it right then.

Battle of Mobile Bay

August 5, 1864

Union Squadron

Commander: Admiral David Glasgow Farragut
Flagship: *Hartford*

Ironclads/Monitors in Order of Battle
Tecumseh
Manhattan
Winnebago
Chickasaw

Screw-Sloops/Consorts in Order of Battle
Brooklyn/Octorara
Hartford/Metacomet
Richmond/Port Royal
MADISON (Lackawanna)/Seminole
Monongahela/Kennebec
Ossipee/Itasca
Oneida/Galena

Confederate Squadron

Commander: Admiral Franklin Buchanan
Flagship: *Tennessee*

Ironclad
Tennessee

Gunboats
Gaines
Selma
Morgan

56

USS *Madison*

HOURS BEFORE DAWN, Danny awakened to the sound of boatswain's pipes shrilling throughout Farragut's squadron. He jerked his hammock off its hooks, balled it under his arm, and hastened topside with his shipmates. Shouted orders directed them to their vessel's wheels instead of the hammock nettings. Groping through the mist, he and his fellow tars stacked their hammocks beside the wheels to protect them; sandbags and sails followed. Every direction men moved, phantoms in the haze, sanding decks and setting out water casks and tricing up whiskers.

Danny and Juniper helped spread nets along *Madison's* starboard side to catch splinters. They leapt the chains being dragged over her machinery as they moved aft to help lower a starboard boat, thus allowing greater room for firing their starboard gun. Blocks and tackle squeaked. Wind whistled. *Ghostly sounds on a ghostly night*, Danny thought.

Within two hours a gunboat approached, the fog swirling around her lights and masts, her engine a racket. *Gotta be the Seminole.*

The boatswain's pipes shrilled again, and *Madison's* crew rushed portside to receive her.

"Yates," Upton said. "The doctor needs you."

Danny followed the paymaster down three decks, into the hold, the new sick bay Buckley had assigned their division.

He recognized Lyman and Quest by lantern light. They'd been aboard two days. He held a favorable opinion of Lyman, who stood about his height. Quest, a head taller and wearing a blond goatee—Danny had formed no firm opinion on him yet.

"These men will assist us during the battle," Doctor Kirby said of the army officers. "Yates, get Jones and have him help you bring down that table from the wardroom. Find Roscoe and Hoag. Tell them I said to bring down that small table in the dispensary. I'll need it for my medicines. Oh, and let Shoot know I'll need every bottle of chloroform in our inventory down here."

"Make it fast," Doctor Youngblood, *Madison's* assistant surgeon, said. "We're liable to need it all."

Danny made a quick exit and relayed Doctor Kirby's order to Surgeon's Steward Shoot, who was gathering medicines from the cabinet, then he darted up the next ladder.

Topside, he glimpsed Roscoe hurrying aft carrying an oak bucket toward the aft guns. "Roscoe. Wait a minute. The doctor— "

"I ain't taking no orders from you," Roscoe said.

"They're not my orders. They're the doctor's."

"Let him do it." Roscoe disappeared into the fog.

"That's no way to talk!" He went searching for Juniper.

CSS *Tennessee*

The fog evaporated before dawn's soft breeze. The sea barely rippled. From *Tennessee's* pilothouse Buchanan, Johnston, their pilot, deck officer, and a quartermaster at the wheel observed Farragut's ships steaming into a staggered column, smaller gunboats lashed to sloops-of-war. Ensigns streaming from mastheads, they slowly swung their bows toward the Main Channel and its bar.

Buchanan handed Johnston his spyglass. "Look over at Sand Island, Mister Johnston."

Johnston surveyed it. "The fourth monitor we observed arriving yesterday is taking her position in the van. The main fleet has started its advance." He shifted his glass to Fort Morgan. "General Page's guns are all trained on the Channel, sir. Shall I signal our gunboats?"

"Very well. Get under way."

"Aye, sir."

An hour later, when Fort Morgan and the lead Yankee man-of-war swapped shots at long range, the admiral gave Johnston the order: "Signal our gunboats to follow our lead. You know where we're all to be stationed to receive the enemy."

"Bows on in the Main Channel, sir. The gunboats beside us, broadsides aiming over the torpedo field. Cap the 'T.'"

"Do it."

"Aye aye, sir."

In the gun deck below, every sailor in the casemate snapped to attention when Buchanan's feet hit it. Wearing neat uniforms, all present turned their eyes upon him. His determined gaze roamed from one gun division to the next. His officers looked smart and professional in their gray uniforms with their cutlasses buckled round their waists. The hour of decision had come. Westcott, at strict attention with his first division, followed him with eager eyes.

After clearing his throat Buchanan launched into his brief speech, ending it with the words: "whip and sink the Yankees, or fight until you sink yourselves, but do not surrender."

Orders for loading and running out the guns echoed down the lines. Carriages trundled.

Climbing back up the ladder to the pilothouse, Buchanan peered at Fort Morgan's fluttering flag. *A westerly breeze. Not good.* Smoke from Farragut's guns would get blown into its cannoneers' faces; it'd hamper their accuracy.

USS *Hartford*

Farragut raised his spyglass to observe the action in his column's van. Smoke from *Tecumseh's* thundering guns drifted over Fort

Morgan's cannoneers, who answered the ironclad before targeting the approaching *Brooklyn*. The Rebel cannoneers took careful aim; their cannon fire slow, steady. The monitors steamed way out front, some two thousand yards from the fort.

Within minutes, *Hartford* became the prime target. The first shot fired at her flew fast and hard…a boom…a shriek…the smash and crash which followed when it struck her foremast. A second shot shattered her port netting, a third soared across the deck and smashed her consort *Metacomet's* sandbagged wheel.

Farragut's attention shifted to *Metacomet's* captain, Lieutenant-Commander James Jouett, standing on his side-wheeler's starboard paddle-box following the action much as he and his aides were doing it from *Hartford's* poop deck. Since they were still too far from the fort to inflict much damage, *Hartford's* starboard broadside kept silent.

Farragut noticed the great gap between *Brooklyn* and the monitors. She was going in too slow. They couldn't keep a concentrated fire if they didn't keep close order. He waved at Watson. "Signal *Brooklyn:* 'Go on.'"

Watson seized the flags—six, six, five—from out of the flag locker, darted down the poop deck's ladder, and ran forward to have them, the general signal for "Go on," hoisted from one of *Hartford's* fore-yards.

USS *Madison*

Danny set down the small dispensary table he'd told Roscoe and Hoag to get several minutes ago, but which they refused to get despite Doctor Kirby's orders. He'd prayed hard for them over the recent months.

"Roscoe and Hoag, those lads are the genuine dickens," Lyman said after Danny moved away from the table.

Shoot began arranging medicines on a tray atop it.

"A constant thorn in our sides," Doctor Kirby said.

"Well, I wouldn't have gone up and gotten that table," Quest said, "not if I ordered them to do it. You should've made them get it, Yates."

"Yes, sir," Danny said. Maybe he should have, but he didn't much like arguing and giving orders.

"Yates got it and it's done." Doctor Youngblood rolled up his sleeves.

"If those boys stay in the Navy, they won't rise very high," Quest said. "I doubt either one will become a petty officer."

Doctor Kirby planted his fists on the table. "No man is without hope, Lieutenant Quest. No man, no boy, no lady, no girl. I forbid such negative speech in my presence."

Quest flashed a disdainful look.

Danny cocked an ear. "Doctor. The engine."

"I don't hear it anymore either," Doctor Kirby said.

"It's stopped." Upton got down off the crate.

Danny and his shipmates kept listening, wondering and worrying about what was happening. It was a terrible, helpless feeling, not knowing what was going on topside.

Topside, Locke glared at Zollicoffer's Marines, crouched at their Parrott rifle gun they'd run out *Madison's* starboard bow port. Smoking cannon roared from the fort's ramparts. *Richmond,* firing her starboard guns, had swerved close to shore.

Locke's face burned. *Richmond's* position hampered their approach. It looked like confusion up there, white smoke enveloping *Hartford,* and *Brooklyn* being so far ahead. Red flashes through the smoke, thunder and ear-splitting whistles and roars. Next in line, they'd ceased steaming and were letting the current carry them into the fight, though *Seminole's* paddle wheels kept churning.

Marine Sergeant Kite, Zollicoffer's first gun captain, raised his fist, barked a command, and the bow gun recoiled as it discharged its first shot. Fort Morgan responded. Explosions raged over their heads.

CSS *Tennessee*

Ben, commander of *Tennessee's* first gun division, peered out the ram's forward bow port. In the vanguard of the wooden ships, two monitors steamed toward their line while the other two blazed away at the water battery. So far, they'd let Fort Morgan deal out destruction. Dense, swirling smoke obscured the approaching wooden ships. Shots bounded off the ironclads' turrets. He searched for *Madison*. If Locke, that murderous, sorry excuse of humanity was aboard her, he'd die... today. Thick battle smoke swirled; splashes disrupted the calm water, explosions and...the two monitors neared.

Johnston eased up alongside him. "The monitors are going to try and grapple us. When they get in close, find the best target...either the gun ports or the turret where it touches the deck. Don't pull the lanyard till our vessels touch. Admiral's orders."

"Aye, sir." Ben relayed this to his gun captains.

He peered out the gun port while his crews loaded the Brookes. *Here she comes. The lead monitor. Come on. Come on.*

Johnston stood among the forward gunners. "Remember. Hold your fire until our vessels make contact."

"Aye, aye," Ben said.

Boom!

Every sailor on board dashed to Ben's gun port to glimpse what happened. Inside of a minute, the lead monitor careened to her port, her bow plummeting while men scrambled out of her hatches and her turret's gun port, diving into the black water. Her stern shot up, facing the sky while her propeller spun. Then, she plunged beneath the swirling surface and as she sank, the last thing they saw was that propeller, still spinning its final farewell as the vessel carried her crew to their eternal grave, their underwater tomb. Sunk by torpedo.

Stunned whispers passed from man to man.

CSS *Selma*

"Hurrah!"

"Huzzah!"

Alex joined the cheers ringing up and down *Selma's* deck. Her four pivot guns, two forward and two aft were swerved broadside, banging away at the enemy. *Morgan* and *Gaines* cut loose deafening fire. *Selma* shuddered beneath each boom. After that monitor sank, they'd caught the Yankees in a crossfire between Fort Morgan, *Tennessee,* and them. One enemy boat pulled swiftly toward the sunk monitor's survivors. Using a boat hook, a crewman snatched them and yanked them into it. Other Yankees swam to shore; a few madly rowed one of the clad's boats.

In command of *Selma's* two bow guns, Alex sighted one of them on the fourth ship drifting into the battle. He leapt; his throat caught. He'd targeted *Madison,* grand-looking as ever

"Fire when she moves in closer." He then gave his gun captains the order. The first shot landed short, the second one closer.

USS *Hartford*

Farragut directed the battle from the mainmast's ratlines beneath the futtock shrouds, a rope secured around him so he wouldn't fall. His pilot, Martin Freeman, was in the maintop directly above. Orders passed from Farragut to Freeman, who relayed them to Drayton on the poop deck below by means of a speaking tube. From *Metacomet's* starboard wheelhouse, Lieutenant Commander Jouett tracked the battle's progress with absolute calm.

Marines worked *Hartford's* bow guns, the only ones that could bring to bear while explosions boomed around her. Running men slipped on her blood-soaked deck, fell port and starboard; their shell-ridden and bullet-ridden corpses were laid out on her port side, and those wounded taken to the surgeon below.

The gut-wrenching cries of wounded men and the mangled bodies sickened Farragut. Stalled directly beneath Fort Morgan, turkeys in a turkey shoot edging toward disaster, his crew was getting decimated. And why? He'd signaled Captain Alden of *Brooklyn* three times to "Go on," but the man disobeyed.

"Mister Freeman!" he called up. "What is the matter with the *Brooklyn?* She must have plenty of water there."

Brooklyn had reversed her engines; she was backing toward them! Up ran her signal flags: "Our best monitor has been sunk."

Farragut called up to Freeman. "Have Drayton reply to *Brooklyn:* 'Tell the monitors to go ahead and then take your place.'"

Too late. The distance between *Hartford* and *Brooklyn* shortened rapidly. A collision and humiliating defeat threatened within minutes. Up here alone and above the fray, while below guns thundered and men died. *What must I do?* He shot up a quick prayer.

A gentle, yet decisive voice responded: *Go on.*

USS *Madison*

Danny helped Sanders and Bridges bring two wounded Marines into *Madison's* sick bay. Blood gushed from one man's left shoulder; the other man's right, crimson forearm dangled by a sinew.

Gently, while *Madison* lurched during the battle's give and take, Doctor Kirby helped them lay the Marine with the mangled forearm on the table.

Upton helped the other Marine sit against a row of barrels. Shoot grabbed a roll of bandages from off the dispensary table and started bandaging the wound.

Sanders puffed hard. "There's more, Doctor. Lots more."

"Shot right through our broadside," Bridges said. "More'n a dozen down."

He and Bridges disappeared up the ladder. Two more sailors brought down two more bloodied men.

"Go help them, Yates," Doctor Kirby said. "Everyone else, stay here and assist me." Tourniquets in hand, Danny hurried up the ladder and sprinted down a short passageway linking the engine room to the wardroom, and up the wardroom ladder to the spar deck and forward, slipping on blood through flying balls, where mangled men lay sprawled on the forecastle. Rebel sharpshooters peppered the gunners. Another man fell, Minie ball in the forehead. Another down, struck in the leg. Danny stumbled before he knelt at a fallen man. His blue eyes were open, his stare blank, and his chest still. He touched his wrist for a pulse. He laid his ear on his chest for a heartbeat. Nothing. Danny offered a quick prayer for the man's family.

Then turning, he saw Roscoe go down. Not hit. On his knees. Sobbing uncontrollably at Hoag's side. Hoag... sprawled in blood. *Dear Lord Jesus.* Danny's prayer rose from deep within his broken heart.

Shells exploded around him. Minie balls whistled past. He got up and rushed to the boys. Vainly, he felt Hoag's wrist for a pulse. He wanted to say something to Roscoe, but this wasn't the time. He sprinted forward and helped bring down more wounded men.

USS *Hartford*

From his rigging station, Farragut observed *Brooklyn* and *Richmond* turning with him into the torpedo field. Speaking tube in hand, Jouett kept his post on *Metacomet's* paddle-box. For the third time he called up to the admiral: "Sir, cut me loose! Let me at them, sir!"

"Wait a little longer, Jouett!" Farragut shouted down at him.

A shell exploded off their port sides.

"Please, sir!"

"A little longer, Captain! A little longer!" Farragut liked Jouett's cool-headed aggressiveness, but the timing in casting his ship loose had to be perfect. Observing *Tennessee's* ponderous approach, like a powerful, lumbering bear, Farragut decided Buchanan had determined to ram him.

Shots from the gunboats rained on his ship. One vessel in particular gave him trouble, the gunboat in the deepest water. Her four guns raked his deck, sending men diving for cover. Then, his men leaped up and quickly reloaded and ran out their guns.

Hartford sped around *Tennessee's* bows point-blank, delivering a broadside and receiving fire from the Rebel's bow guns. *Tennessee* changed course, back to the Main Channel to engage *Brooklyn* and her consort. The Rebel gunboats dealt death to *Hartford's* men.

Farragut waved at Jouett. "Stand by to cast loose!"

"Aye aye, sir!" Jouett sprang off the paddle-box onto *Metacomet's* deck. Her sailors raised a cheer.

CSS *Tennessee*

After lumbering in a wide starboard turn, *Tennessee* made her second full-steam, six knot charge at the next ship in line. The Yankee's shots glanced off her casemate. Ben's ears rang. He glimpsed the enemy ship when his gun port opened again for firing. She had eluded them. Their gunboats stood no chance if the Yankees crossed the torpedo field. Buchanan, commanding the gun deck since their wounded pilot forced Johnston to direct the vessel's movements, ordered them to fire at the next ship crossing the torpedo field.

Men scrambled to reload *Tennessee's* guns. The Yankee's broadside cut loose, musketry erupted from her forecastle, Minie balls flew through *Tennessee's* open ports, her gunners dodged for cover.

Ben's heart became ice when the next ship approached within range. *The Madison.* Locke had best be on board. "I'll do it." He shoved aside the first gun captain and carefully sighted her. He'd hit her midships. Maybe he'd kill Locke if he still commanded that gun division. Lanyard in hand, he stepped back from the gun and waited till she came within range. He sighted the gun a second time. *Closer. Closer.* He stepped back. *Fire!* A jerk of the lanyard. A roar. The gun port shut for reloading.

USS *Madison*

Locke turned from observing *Hartford's* blue pennant snapping proudly in the breeze while *Madison's* anchor, along with *Hartford's* and four other ships' anchors, splashed in the Lower Fleet, Mobile Bay's deepest pocket. White smoke smothered shot-riddled decks and masts. Except for the distant gunfire, quiet prevailed. Overhead, darkness spread. For over an hour they'd fought the Rebels and though bruised and battered, *Madison* remained intact. *Metacomet,* along with three other gunboats, were pursuing *Morgan* and *Selma.* Holed during the recent fight and sinking, *Gaines* had limped to safety beneath Fort Morgan's cannon. The Rebel ironclad *Tennessee* stayed a serious threat.

Sailors laid out their dead along *Madison's* port side while in her galley, a cook prepared breakfast.

Locke went below. Lacking their wardroom table, *Madison's* officers sat in chairs or on stools outside their staterooms. Not a man among them had been killed, and only Lieutenant Underwood had received a minor wound in his hand.

Locke smirked. "Buchanan thought he could kill me."

"Well, since we're finally in the bay, I wonder when he'll surrender." Underwood rested his bandaged hand in his lap.

"He'll attack us tonight," Zollicoffer said. "It's too shallow for us to proceed further up the bay. We're trapped here."

"How many lads did you lose?" Chief Engineer Edges asked.

"Too many," Zollicoffer answered.

"Well, two of mine are dead meat," Locke said. "I got a broadside right at my gun, like someone on that ram meant to kill me directly." He slapped his knees and laughed.

Zollicoffer leveled his scathing glare on Locke.

Want to rip me apart, Zolly? I dare you.

"One day, Locke, you'll quit making light of death." Turning to Edges, Zollicoffer said, "I lost a dozen men. Good, brave souls. And poor Hoag got killed. Excuse me. I must check on my wounded." He headed through a door that led to the ship's hold.

"Where'd Hoag get his?" Locke's amused glances darted from officer to officer. "The head? The heart?"

Not a man one looked at him. Locke's temper stirred. Danny emerged from the same door through which Zollicoffer had passed.

"Don't ignore me!" Locke screamed. "Yates! Where are you heading?"

Danny kept walking. "I'm helping the doctor in the ship's hold, sir."

"Come here."

Danny shook his head.

"Yates! Yates! Come back here! That's an order!"

"Yates is heading topside to console Roscoe," Underwood said. "He has a huge heart, Locke, which is something you've never had, and something you'll probably never get."

As he emerged on deck, Danny coughed as he whiffed the stench of blood. Lookouts manned the crosstrees. Mandover, the deck officer, scanned the bay for *Tennessee*. In the forecastle, sailors stuffed arms and legs in canvas sacks for tossing overboard. Juniper had brought two similar sacks below for the limbs the surgeons amputated. Roscoe stood beside Hoag's body. Danny went to him.

Roscoe's tears were no more; his ashen face, stunned. Danny lifted up a prayer. No words came to mind, so he remained silent. His hands clasped, he studied Hoag's face. It wasn't peaceful, yet it wasn't terrified either. Death showed no favorites.

"I wish it was me. I wish I'd been killed," Roscoe mumbled.

"Why is that?" Danny said. "I mean, if you don't mind my asking."

"My going to sea was my parents' idea. I didn't want to go. I wanted to stay home with my friends."

"Why did they want you to go to sea?"

"They thought the Navy would make me behave better. They claimed they loved me." Roscoe's knuckles wiped the tip of his nose. "I don't believe it."

"Hoag was your best friend on board."

"Uh-huh."

"Did he like the Navy?"

"He told me he'd rather been home playing baseball. I can catch a ball real good. Did I ever tell you how good a baseball player I am?"

"I can't play much of any game very well."

Roscoe's and Danny's eyes met. No longer did Roscoe belittle him or talk down to him. Because of Hoag's death, he'd become... suddenly... serious.

"What is it about you, Yates?" Roscoe said. "Did you come up here just to see me? Shouldn't you be helping the doctor?"

"He gave me permission to find you."

"After all the hard times I gave you and the name-calling I did?"

"I have no right to hate anyone. This is something I learned the hard way, two years ago when I was really angry about something and taking it out on everybody."

"Roscoe," Mandover said. "Lay below. The cartridges!"

"Wait, Mister Mandover," Danny said. "I'm not finished talking with him."

"Give me another order, Yates, I'll clap you in irons for insubordination."

The ship's drummer beat to quarters. Roscoe and Danny darted below. Officers and crew swarmed to their stations.

"Buchanan's a fool," Locke muttered as he stood near his division's starboard gun port soon after beat to quarters.

"He is that, sir," Locke's gun captain said.

Colors flying and ignoring every other Yankee in the Lower Fleet, *Tennessee* bore down on *Hartford* bows on. *Monogahela*, upon casting off *Kennebec* and after a brief engagement with Fort Morgan and the ram, was steaming slowly up the bay when she received *Hartford's* signal to run down the Rebel ironclad. *Ossipee,* also coming up, and *Madison* received and answered the same signals.

Locke dispatched several men from his division to replace Zollicoffer's losses. Outnumbered and outgunned, and in broad daylight, Buchanan had lost the second bout before he'd fired his first shot. They were gaining on him; he on them. Within minutes, *Monogahela* closed on the clad.

And Locke grinned. Another glorious victory was near at hand.

CSS *Tennessee*

Ben reeled from the blow when their sides scraped. Two Brooke rifle guns loosed a broadside. The Yankee's shots banged and thudded harmlessly against *Tennessee*. A second strike rocked them briefly. Men tumbled onto the deck.

Another ship. Ben scrambled to a gun port, but he couldn't identify the enemy vessels. Too much smoke. A second glimpse before his men ran out their gun, the flash of a shattered bow. The vessel...*is she backing up?*

A jerk of the lanyard. The Brooke thundered and smoked.

USS *Madison*

Sailors, prostrate on *Madison's* deck, scrambled to their feet as she reversed from *Tennessee*. Another broadside smashed her. Shells exploded below. Locke fired his revolver into the enemy's open ports. Several in his division lay sprawled behind their gun, one dead and three others wounded.

A third explosion below and aft.

Someone leaped up and bumped him. *Rawlins. What....?*

"The magazine's on fire! Yates!" Rawlins hollered at Danny, who'd been tending the wounded when smoke billowed out of the wardroom hatch.

Dodging gunfire and explosions, they darted down it.

Danny sprinted ahead, coughing in the smoke stinging his eyes. He sprang down the ladder leading to the hold and barged into the aft magazine.

A flame sizzled along a powder trail toward barrels holding twenty tons of gunpowder. He stomped on it time and again till it snuffed out. Breathing a sigh of relief, he turned back. Pale, Rawlins and those in the powder division stared at him, their mouths agape.

"That was too close," Rawlins stammered.

"Yes, sir," Danny said.

"We've put out the fire, sir," a sailor said.

Rawlins nodded absently.

Guns raged.

CSS *Tennessee*

Through the pilothouse's slit, Buchanan observed the enemy monitor approach. Puffing hard, Johnston joined him after a quick inspection below.

"Sir," Johnston said, "we've started shipping water at six inches an hour. That second blow we received did us some serious damage."

"I will sink David Farragut's ship." Buchanan shifted his attention from the monitor to the enemy's flagship steaming at them bows on. "We will ram and sink the *Hartford* or go down in the attempt. Is that understood?"

"Aye, Admiral."

Buchanan hastened back down the casemate ladder to resume his self-appointed battle station. For a few seconds, he stood beside Ben before peeking out the forward gun port. The monitor moved between them and *Hartford.* Slowly, her turret revolved; her two 15-inch guns targeted them from her gun ports. Buchanan limped toward the windlass. "Fire, Mister Westcott."

"Stand clear!" Ben shouted to his men.

The monitor fired first.

Tennessee rocked hard starboard when the ironclad's shell smashed her casemate. Another hard hit from another ship rocked her again. As Ben peered out a gun port, above the dense, swirling smoke, he recognized *Hartford* as the ship which struck them after the monitor fired. Aloft, in *Hartford's* mizzen-rigging was an officer. *Who is he?* Their eyes met. He cocked his Colt.

One of *Hartford's* Dahlgren's roared. Muzzle smoke blocked his aim. He released the trigger and searched for another target. A cry cut loose behind him. Someone killed or wounded.

One of the ram's broadside guns delivered a powerful shot smashing *Hartford's* hull. Explosions and triumphant shouts.

Ben raised a silent hurrah at the havoc *Tennessee* caused. Sailors closed her ports.

Their ships grazed each other; *Hartford's* shots caromed off her casemate. More shots pounded her starboard to no effect.

At Buchanan's command, the starboard gun ports went up. Ben glimpsed the ships that had pummeled her. *Brooklyn and Richmond, is it?* He remembered them from New Orleans. They kept coming, and two monitors and…"Fire!"

His gun captains jerked their lanyards; guns discharged, and her gun ports closed for reloading.

Nearly surrounded, *Tennessee* fired her every gun with deadly desperation, booms echoing and rocking her.

USS *Hartford*

"Captain Drayton." Farragut, back on the quarterdeck and unaware how close he'd come to getting killed by Ben while he was in the mizzen-rigging, spoke from the mizzen mast. "We'll try again."

Drayton relayed the order to an ensign, who bounded down the poop deck ladder and raced to the ship's two quartermasters steering her.

The quartermasters leaned into the flagship's huge wheel, steering her starboard, bows on toward the ironclad for another ramming attempt. The admiral didn't see it coming when he delivered the order. She was behind them, and its suddenness and speed...none could stop it...the jolt, the crash, the sound of timbers buckling beneath *Madison's* power just forward of Farragut.

"Save the admiral!" Cries echoed up and down the deck.

"Lower the port boats!" a boatswain shouted over the din.

Panicked sailors dashed to them. Calmly, Farragut climbed onto the starboard mizzen rigging and peered down. *Madison* had holed *Hartford* severely, her bowsprit and bows deep inside her mangled hull. Had she struck lower they'd be sinking.

Madison's engines reversed her prow out of *Hartford.* And *Hartford* forged ahead while monitors continued their long-range fire. For reasons no one understood, *Tennessee's* guns stayed silent. They hadn't fired within the last quarter hour.

CSS *Tennessee*

Buchanan limped aft, toward the sound of shots repeatedly striking the stern port-shutter. Men struggled to open it, and Bradford vainly tried working out the pin around which it revolved.

"It's jammed," Buchanan said after a hasty examination.

"Shall I send for Silk, sir?" Bradford said. "He'll get it working."

"Do it."

Bradford dispatched a sailor below to get John Silk, one of their machinists.

Tools in hand, Silk plopped down beside the shutter and slowly backed out its pin. A shot smashed its edge. His limbs and insides exploded, blood and gore spewed every direction like shrapnel.

Iron splinters followed, felling a seaman and striking Buchanan's knee. The admiral screamed, collapsed. "Ugh." He struggled to stand but his leg, twisted under his body, prevented it. "Mister Bradford."

"Sir." Bradford hurried to him.

"Tell Captain Johnston I have need of him. I think my leg's broken."

Bradford hastened up the ladder to the pilothouse.

Johnston reported within seconds.

Buchanan grimaced. Severe pangs lanced his injured leg. "Well, Johnston," he said in a quiet voice, "they've got me. You'll have to look out for her now. This is your fight, you know."

"All right, sir," Johnston said. "I'll do the best I know how." While he headed back to the pilothouse, the ram careened so sharply beneath the blow of a ship that it threw him off his feet.

Ben slammed his fist in his palm. Four shutters jammed shut, and not one gun could fight the enemy.

Johnston returned from the pilothouse a half hour later. "Was the admiral taken below?"

"Yes, sir," Ben said. "How is it out there?"

"They've shot up our tiller chains."

"I feared something like that would happen. We can't maneuver."

Johnston disappeared down the aft hatch.

Men cowered behind the ram's big windlass, ducked beside gun carriages or wide-eyed, dove for nonexistent cover. The constant pounding took a toll on their morale and fighting spirit. They'd opened one of the still-working shutters to fire, but Farragut's wooden vessels stood out of range. The enemy's three monitors hammered them. Helpless, surrender wasn't many minutes away.

Ben now battled boredom. Always priding himself on his professionalism, he never lost his composure. Get the surrender over with, get the war over with. He was ready to go home, to visit his parents' and Annie's graves, and then, find and kill Locke.

1864-1865

SEPTEMBER

–

MAY

57

ON THE DAY *Tennessee* and *Selma* surrendered, around midnight, the Rebels evacuated Fort Powell. *Morgan* eventually made her way back to Mobile, and *Gaines* sank near Fort Morgan. Two days later, Fort Gaines surrendered; Fort Morgan fought till the twenty-third when, after enduring Farragut's bombardment and Canby's batteries, it hauled down its flag.

Ben, Alex, and Captains Johnston and Murphey were sent to Fort Warren. In October, they returned South in a prisoner exchange. Ben and Alex were assigned to the James River Squadron, Raphael Semmes's command.

During an epic battle with the USS *Kearsarge* off the French coast in June of '64, Semmes's famous cruiser *Alabama* met her end. With the help of a friendly British citizen who'd witnessed the fight from his yacht, he'd been rescued and eventually returned to his beloved South. Promoted to rear admiral, he received command of the squadron.

As Lee's battered army began its retreat from Petersburg, the Confederate government evacuated Richmond. Ordered to burn all his vessels, Semmes did so. From Richmond, where news of Lee's surrender at Appomattox Courthouse reached them, Semmes's command traveled south by railcar, a mere four hundred or so men. Mallory made Semmes a brigadier general, and Ben and Alex became soldiers in Semmes's small brigade. They marched toward Joe Johnston's army, which surrendered to General William T. Sherman on the twenty-sixth of April.

Ben and Alex headed home. But Ben didn't go straight home. He stayed at Mobile instead. On the morning of April 11, 1865, General Dabney H. Maury finished his evacuation of the city after fighting General Canby in a siege Maury had no hope of winning. On April 12, the city surrendered, the South's last major city to be captured by Union forces.

Since the Yankees occupied it, Ben hoped he'd find Locke there and finish their business the same place it started—amidst the dunes a few miles east of Fort Morgan. If he didn't encounter him within the next few weeks, he'd inquire of the naval authorities and learn his whereabouts.

1865

JUNE

58

STUDYING HIS NEXT shot, Ben tapped Colonel Jackson Jessup's billiard table with his cue stick. The colonel had recently returned from Virginia where he'd served with General Robert E. Lee's army.

Hmm. Ben tapped the billiard table again. Number six ball, closest to the far right corner pocket, but the eight ball sat about a half-inch behind it after Jessup's last shot. If the cue ball struck number six, number six might strike number eight and number eight might drop in first.

"Quit taking so long," Colonel Jessup said.

"My apologies, Colonel." He leaned over the table, his cue stick's tip inches from the cue ball. Suddenly, his eyes lifted toward the window facing Mary Hamilton's house. He set down the stick and watched, for Alex was outdoors holding a small wooden crate, his eyes fixed upon her house as well. When his friend turned past them, he headed around front and through Mary's gate. "Well now, do my eyes deceive me? I can't believe it."

Amy led him up the steps onto their gallery.

"He's going to show Mary Roy," Colonel Jessup said.

"Who's Roy? A snake?"

"A turtle he found over near Dog River early this morning." Colonel Jessup turned back to the billiard table. "Don't let Alex know I said this, but he's always fancied Mary. He never admitted it. His mother noticed it before I did. Every time he saw her, there was this special gleam in his eyes mingled with a little mischief. Until recently, he never had the nerve to do more than tease her and gawk. He was in his room this morning mustering up courage to call on her. I guess he's using the turtle to help him. A humorous incident that goes back to their childhood."

"This bachelor till I die business then. All talk, Colonel?" Ben waggled his cue stick.

"I think he was trying to convince himself he wanted to be a bachelor when he really didn't. Don't know why. Certainly, you realize how much my son has changed. My son and my daughter."

Back at the billiard table, Ben made his shot. The cue ball brushed the six ball aside, but stopped shy of the eight ball like he'd planned. He set the stick in its rack. *Enough playing.*

He'd observed a further change in Alex during their brief service under Semmes's command. Unlike their time in New Orleans, where Alex often complained about Semmes's "stick in the mud" personality, never once did he speak ill of the man. In fact, he'd been happy when he was assigned to the James River Squadron and now, his formerly lady-shy friend had taken the initiative to call on one of them. His curiosity was aroused.

Jessup set aside his cue stick. "I never imagined I'd be enjoying such peace and quiet when I came home. My Susan's quit shouting, and my son's finally found his courage regarding females."

"They claim God changed them. Moxley says the same about himself."

"They want me to attend Miss Evans's church with them, but I'm a Baptist. Not a very devout Baptist, but a Baptist nonetheless. They claim there's not a lot of difference between the two, except that Methodists have bishops and such things like that."

"I'm Episcopalian. I'll always be Episcopalian."

"Sounds like you're as devout as me."

"Sir, I'm glad my brother's marrying Susan. He'll make her a better husband. Susan and I would be arguing pretty near every day over my playing billiards and cards and such."

"Most likely true, unfortunately. My wife didn't mind my billiards playing. She even went to horse races with me when I was a member of a jockey club here. Why, I even owned a horse farm once and raced a few Thoroughbreds. But she was always nagging me about my fishing and yacht racing and duck hunting. We argued a lot, but I still loved her. Miss Evans seems to think your brother will make a good newspaperman. She's promised to help him find a job here."

"What about Alex?"

"I'm getting back into the cotton broker business. He'll work with me. Have you made a decision?"

Ben flipped his cap from off a wall hook. "I'm paying Miss Evans a call. Moxley said he was going there."

After the battle in the bay, *Madison* underwent repairs in Pensacola's Navy Yard. Since October, she'd cruised between Mobile and Galveston. On the first week of June, she anchored in Mobile Bay's Lower Fleet. The second week in June, Buckley permitted Danny and several others a twenty-four hour liberty ashore. Northern soldiers roamed everywhere, walking streets, riding horses, visiting sympathizers who welcomed their victory. Buckley denied Locke's request for liberty, though, to Locke's great disgust.

Madison was leaving for New Orleans tomorrow. Danny was on his second and final trip to talk sense into Fannie and Hulda. From the depths of his soul, prayers welled. Those two worried him. The war was over, God had freed them, yet still, their cup of hatred was full. The previous week, Fannie told him she and Hulda quit working for Mister Jessup, said they'd found work with the Yankee soldiers occupying the city as well as a new place to live.

He found where they lived easily enough, thanks to friendly Yankee corporal. They were employed by a regiment camped on the city's outskirts, washing the men's clothes and cooking and similar things. He found them sitting on stools, taking a break from their washing chorers.

Fannie's lips curled. "'Scuze us for not standin' up."

"No need apologizing on that account." Danny tipped his cap.

Hulda spat.

He had no idea what made it happen, but a sort of wall shot up between Danny and them. A spark, sizzling sort of, repulsive, something he didn't care to be around or touch. Their attitudes. So hard, so cold were the two. He wanted to leave; he couldn't. Not in good conscience. Not till he made one last attempt to persuade them to change.

"It hasn't been an easy life, us having been slaves," he said. "I'm glad we don't have to worry about that anymore."

"White folks better worry," Hulda said. "Yankees are liable to be in these parts for a long time."

"I had a hard time forgiving my masters, especially the one who stole my Nancy from me. It took me nearly thirty years to find her."

"They ain't worth forgiving," Fannie said.

"I must forgive. The good Lord Jesus commands me to. Hatred does nobody no good. Is there no forgiveness in your souls?"

Tossing back her head, Fannie delivered a scathing laugh. "Missy Susan came here the other day and tried apologizing, said she'd been thinking a lot about what Mister Stephen Hamilton had said about slavery's sins and how God was going to judge the South. Know what we told her?"

"Get lost," Hulda said. "That's what we told her."

"Hee, hee. She turned pale as a ghost. Now you get out of our lives, preacher man. We don't need your sermons."

Danny swallowed his anger, pivoted on his heel, and strode back down the street. Fannie screamed insults at him. He couldn't bring himself to look back. His eyes moistened as he thought about them—two poor souls sold out to evil.

Two men seated in chairs on Augusta Evans's front porch greeted Ben. One wore a rumpled white shirt, its sleeves rolled up above his elbows, and faded gray trousers, remnants of a Confederate uniform. The other man, also coatless, wore dusty black trousers and a rumpled gray shirt. The man in the white shirt rose as he approached; the man in the gray shirt kept a blank stare.

Ben stuck out his hand. "My name's Benjamin Westcott, late lieutenant of the Confederate States Navy."

"Vivian Evans," the man in the white shirt said, "late of the Confederate States Army."

Ben went to the other man, who looked at his hand, befuddled. Then his right hand grasped Ben's left. "Howard Evans."

"Benjamin Westcott."

Howard's left arm appeared locked against his side.

"The Yankees got him at Atlanta," Vivian said. "His arm's paralyzed. Which sister have you come calling on today?"

"Actually, I came to see my brother," Ben said.

"Mitchell Westcott!" Howard cried. "You are Mitchell Westcott's brother!"

"No, Howard," Vivian said gently. "His brother's name is Moxley."

Howard grinned, embarrassed. "I had a fever…a…a…."

"Typhoid fever," Vivian said. He whispered in Ben's ear: "It's affected his memory."

"I understand."

"Let's go inside."

Ben followed Vivian.

Randolph and Virginia drew pictures on wrapping paper in the dining room, too involved in their art to give him notice. Caroline and Sallie, wearing raggedy dresses with torn sleeves, were in the front parlor reading. The war and the South's defeat took a toll on most everyone in Dixie. Almost everyone in Mobile wore worn-out clothes these days, because almost everyone, like himself, had gone broke.

Sallie looked up from her book. "Welcome, Mister Westcott."

"Afternoon, Miss Evans," Ben said. "Is my brother still around?"

"He and my sister are on the back porch."

"Thank you."

Vivian joined his younger siblings.

Ben continued down the hall and out the back door. Miss Evans and Susan arose from a rectangular table. Moxley remained in his chair, a crutch laid across his lap. Ben pitied him, having to use that crutch and hobble around everywhere on a wooden leg, but at least he'd survived the war. He hated himself for his plan, but it was the only thing he knew which would prove the genuineness of his brother's so-called change of heart.

Susan picked up four pages and handed them to him.

"He is a superb writer," Miss Evans said.

"Is that a fact?" Ben studied Moxley, whose thin brown mustache twitched. His brother owned one point of sensitivity when it came to other people's opinions: criticism of his writing. He considered himself another Washington Irving. Well, if he flew off in a rage or got defensive, well, his recent spiritual awakening would be proven false. He scanned the four pages slowly, the words drifting past him while he made a pretense of reading. He set the pages back on the table. "It's bilge."

Moxley lips twitched before he broke into a broad smile.

"It's poorly written. I say you have no talent."

Moxley kept smiling.

Pull in that grin!

"Alex told me you weren't a reader," Susan said, annoyed. "You're not qualified to be a critic."

Moxley picked up the pages. "Don't get your dander all ruffled, Susan my dear. Perhaps my brother's right. Miss Evans, I think this needs more work."

"Editing and revision are the heart and soul of all good writing," Miss Evans said.

"Yes," Ben said. "Well, er, it's been a pleasure seeing you again, Miss Evans." Ben tipped his cap, strode around the house, down its tree-lined lane to Spring Hill Road, turned left, and headed toward Mister Lorenzo Wilson's recently-finished streetcar line. Its cars would carry him back into town.

On Government Street, Ben encountered Danny when he spied *Madison's* name embroidered in gold thread on the black silk decorating his cap.

"Avast there," Ben said the moment their eyes met. "I see from your cap that you serve on the *Madison*. Is Vincent still the captain?"

"He got promoted two years ago," Danny said, "and got command of a ship looking for the *Alabama*."

"Bully for him! Who's her captain now?"

"Lieutenant Commander Buckley."

"Johnson Buckley?"

"Yes, sir. And if you don't mind my asking, who are you, sir?"

"I served aboard the *Madison* before the war. I was a passed midshipman back then. What's your name?"

"Danny Yates."

"Humph. My mammy's husband was named Danny. They got separated when they were younger, and she kept believing he'd find her one day. I kept hoping that myself."

Danny's eyes widened slightly. "Is your name Mister Benjamin Westcott?"

"What! How'd you know my name?"

"I heard stories about you. Yessir. All kinds of stories, I sure enough did. And I met your sister an—"

"Wait. Don't tell me." Brows arched, Ben raised his forefinger. "You're Nancy's husband. You didn't get killed, after all, when that packet you and your former master were aboard caught fire."

"No, sir. The good Lord spared me and brought me back to my Nancy, just like I'd always believed He'd do."

"Yes. Well."

During their trip back to Jessup's house, Danny recounted how he'd found Nancy, and Ben told him stories about her he'd not heard yet. He asked Danny to inform Buckley that he planned to come aboard that evening. Since Danny told him *Madison* was weighing anchor for New Orleans next day, he wanted his old ship to take him there and, he told himself, to see Locke's expression if he remained aboard. He chuckled at the thought. Locke thought he'd killed him at New Orleans. Soon, he'd die for certain. That is, if he remained aboard.

59

PHILIPPE SPLASHED IN the puddles down the muddy path leading to his parents' mansion south of New Orleans. Dirty and wet after a hard rain, he welcomed the sun bursting through the afternoon's gray clouds. Relieved that he'd survived the war, he longed to marry his Mademoiselle Catherine Anne and return to a peaceful life. His friend Paul Morphy had been wise to stay in Europe during the conflict, though he was eager to learn how his chess matches played out. War, it was no longer a grand adventure. He loathed it. War. Murder. The words, they were synonymous. Had he not planned to marry he might become a priest like his Uncle Edouard did after his wife passed away.

Shiloh, Perryville, Murfreesboro, Chattanooga, Chickamauga, Atlanta, so many battles under so many generals, places and names indelibly etched on his memory. Last December was the worst. At Nashville, their army was broken and shattered thanks to General Hood's recklessness. He was glad to get captured, glad to stay a prisoner till the war ended, and glad the war ended only four months after this. Never did he want to fight a war again. Never, ever. *Non.*

A ship brought him and other former soldiers here, stopping at various Southern ports along the way to disembark its passengers. He shielded his eyes from the sun. Up ahead, his family's pale red mansion. A thrill rippled through him at the thought of it. Reuniting with family, but concern about what his father would think when he learned he'd taken the oath of allegiance before his release dampened his joy.

Not too many steps farther had he taken when his parents barged out their front door, rushed down their staircase with shouts triumphant, their kisses smothering his face.

"Alive," his mother said in French. "My son, my son." She kissed his cheeks again and praised all the saints.

When she parted, his father kissed his cheeks once more. He pulled back and studied him. "Are you not wounded, my son?"

"*Non, Papa. Non, Maman.* A few bullets nicked me, but nothing so serious. A few close calls, but me, I am fine in body. But I am tired."

His mother put her arm around him. "Then we shall go inside, and we shall let you rest."

"We must talk after that," his father said. "A lot has happened here since your absence."

His arm in his mother's, Philippe went toward the house. "The Yankees? The news. It is about them?"

"More than the Yankees. Not now. Rest. We will tell you everything after supper."

"*Oui, Papa.*" And with those words, Philippe went to his old bachelor quarters beside the house. He wanted to plop on his bed, close his eyes and sleep; he wanted not to sleep, too; he wanted to hear what his father had to say. Whatever had happened, it sounded bad. His father's tone and his manner were grave.

Backslaps and boisterous cheers welcomed Ben aboard *Madison* at sunset. Officers he'd known from before the war mobbed him. Doctor Kirby gave him a hearty "welcome back." Warren seized his left hand and nearly shook it off his wrist.

"Are we still slurping coffee?" Ben said, a jest.

Warren laughed. "I've become executive office. I can do whatever I want. With Captain Buckley's permission, of course."

"Well, I'm a civilian now. I can do whatever I want without anyone's permission."

"Not on my ship." Chuckling, Buckley wedged between the others and gripped his hand. "Welcome aboard."

"Thank you, sir." Ben searched past Buckley, over the heads of his friends. Locke, on watch duty, glanced at him from the poop deck;

his gunmetal eyes flashed. *See me, Locke? You didn't kill me. See how I survived the war? I'd give anything to know what's going through that sick head of yours.*

"Let's go to my quarters," Buckley said. "We'll swap war stories and catch up on news. Jones!"

Juniper stepped forward.

"Bring us some coffee."

"Aye, sir." Jones started toward the galley hatch.

"Jones!" Ben barked.

Jones looked back, his expression quizzical.

"Great seeing you again."

"Yes, sir," Jones said. "I'm glad you survived this war."

"That makes two of us."

"Yes, sir."

Again scowling up at Locke, Ben followed Buckley.

This time Locke ignored him, but Ben read death in his demeanor. And this time, one of them would die.

Danny caught Ben's and Locke's angry looks. *The eyes never lie,* he told himself. He remembered the story he'd heard about their duel not far from here. He regretted Mister Upton wasn't aboard so Mister Westcott could see how much the good Lord Jesus had changed him. A month ago, Upton received word that his mother was seriously ill, so he was given a furlough home.

Roscoe set down plates around the mess table two hours later; Bridges placed a chocolate cake between the seated officers.

"Permit me." Wielding a long knife, Warren carefully sliced the cake. He took Ben's plate, placed the slice in it, and held it high. "Gentlemen, having no prior knowledge of our friend's safe return, I ordered this cake made earlier today. It was meant for our personal enjoyment. But tonight's enjoyment has become a celebration. The bloodletting has ended. Our friend has returned. If only Mister Jessup were amongst us."

Claps erupted.

"Allow me." Warren set the first slice of cake before Ben.

Bridges continued cutting it.

"Have you seen Mister Jessup?" Doctor Kirby said.

"He fought you in the bay, same as me," Ben said. "He was on the *Selma*, and I on the *Tennessee*."

"Sarcastic as ever, I imagine," Edges said.

"He never lost his sense of humor," Ben said.

"He always could liven up a conversation." Mandover poked his fork in his cake. "We all missed him, much as we did you. He lives in Mobile. Why didn't he come on board?"

"Nothing personal, that I assure you." Ben chewed and swallowed a bit of his cake.

"Busy fishing, would be my guess," Doctor Kirby said.

"Not that, either. Y'all may not believe me when I say this. I'm not sure I believe it myself. But I think he's found himself a lady friend."

Laughter exploded.

"A lady friend!" Locke cried. "Good ole Alex, the bachelor till I die man. Ha!"

Ben made no response, yet Locke's friendly overtures aroused Danny's suspicion. For a man who claimed to hate Ben, who appeared startled when Ben came on board and whose eyes had flashed a threat...Locke's sudden change...It wasn't real... Everyone who'd known them from before the war knew their history, and still, no one seemed concerned. They were taking Ben home tomorrow, and they were overjoyed to transport him there.

Something's gonna happen soon as we get to New Orleans. Was he the only man who suspected it? If something bad was about to happen, he had to stop it. He couldn't let anybody get killed or hurt.

60

P RYTANIA STREET. HOME. Ben rushed through the gate and up the flagstones. He cupped his hands around his mouth to shout: *Father! Mother!* He lowered them suddenly. Why shout? No one was inside. Why rush through the gate? To be welcomed back. By whom?

From the outside, the house looked clean. The second story windows, not a smudge nor a crack, their dark green shutters perfectly aligned with their frames. Not a speck of dust did he detect. It looked recently whitewashed. *Curious.*

The small stable and carriage house around back also looked whitewashed. He looked up at Annie's bedroom window. For several seconds, he imagined her smiling down at him, crinkling her nose at some joke or tease. He smiled back at the image. Someone must be living here now. *It's my home. It's…it's…it's…It's empty.* Someone took care of it during his absence.

Arms rigid at his sides, his fists clenched. He knew Locke killed Annie, but he needed proof and once he found it, he'd confront Locke whom he hoped was awaiting him at Monmouth. That's where they'd agreed to finish what they'd started back in '61. They did this in the wardroom, when he flicked a tiny, folded note, the challenge, under Locke's cot shortly after their little party when no one was looking.

The gate squeaked. A freckled girl wearing a pale pink flared dress came through it.

"Clara," he said.

Clara clasped her hands, her dark lashes aflutter. "Mister Westcott! You're alive!"

"Of course I'm alive."

"But, but I thought you'd been grievously wounded. I didn't doubt for a minute you'd pull through. Not me. Mother and I tried to keep the house up for you and your brother. Jenny and her mother helped us when they were in town. We wanted you to find it all nice and tidy when you returned." Her excitement subsided. "Did you…hear about…?"

Ben took both her hands. "My parents and Annie. Yes. I was posted in Mobile after a prisoner exchange. The Soileaus told Moxley. He told me."

"I'm sorry."

"Is your father home?"

"Would you like me to get him?"

"Please. I have a few questions."

Clara hurried back out the gate and down the block.

Ten minutes later, her father joined him. Mister Dawson detailed what he'd seen and told him everything he knew, which wasn't much. Annie was buried alongside their parents at Monmouth. He led Ben around to the back of the house to the spot where Jason discovered Annie's body.

"She was sprawled out," he said. "Her neck was broken."

"Moxley said the police believe she stumbled down the stairs in the dark."

"I tend to agree. Then again, I am no policeman."

"Did they search the yard thoroughly?"

"For what?"

"Evidence that someone might have been lurking about or lying in wait for her."

"The stable door was open."

"Father always made sure it was closed before he went to bed. Annie would've done

the same."

"Unless she'd gotten careless. They found nothing unusual in the stables that night, nor did anything indicate a struggle."

Same with Rosalita. No sign of a struggle.

"The police assumed Annie either forgot to close it or was going outside to close it when she stumbled."

"That a fact?"

"That's a fact."

For Locke to have killed her, she must've mocked him, similar to what Rosalita did. He wouldn't put it past Locke to visit their home and brag about killing him.

Ben entered the stables. Saddles and riding tackle hung along its far side; buckets for oats and water were on a bench near Trotter's stall. He imagined Locke crouching somewhere, behind a bale of hay or in a dark corner, stirring up the horses perhaps, and waiting for her entrance when he sprang on her and killed her. He'd visit Nancy next. Maybe she could add a few details.

"I hope you'll join us for supper tonight."

"Tomorrow night would be better, sir. I'm leaving for Monmouth this afternoon."

"Tomorrow night it is then." Mister Dawson waved bye and left.

Ben went up the steps. At the door, he hesitated. The place would be lifeless. Nice of Clara and Jenny to do what they did. Good friends to Annie, they were. He wasn't sure if he could bear the silence inside. No music from Annie's guitar, no whirs of his mother's sewing machine, no laughter, no...

"Mister Westcott?"

He peered down at the gate. *Danny and Jones. Great. What do they want?*

"May we come on your property?"

"Your decision."

Danny passed through the gate, Juniper behind him.

61

PHILIPPE GRASPED THE rosary inside his pocket. Squeezing it hard and muttering prayers, he descended the levee and crossed the road toward Monmouth's picket gate. Beyond its mud-splattered picket fence, beyond its alley of oaks, stood its white mansion. Its formal gardens, on both sides of the alley, were shades of brown and gray, the yellow flowers wilting, every plant dying from neglect. Beyond the garden on the right, inside a smaller white picket fence, three marble tombs stood side by side.

He went through the gate. Up the alley he trudged, turned right down another road. His prayers quickened; his chest thumped harder. Approaching the small cemetery, he muttered words of love and farewell to his Catherine Anne in French.

"You! Halt there!"

Philippe spun toward the booming voice. A short, powerfully-built man in a Yankee navy uniform emerged from behind a double-story brick building, what Philippe took for either Ben's or Moxley's private quarters. His features were rugged and his lips cruel; a revolver was holstered round his waist.

That man, he intends harm. Philippe hung his rosary around his neck and started unbuttoning his coat. He fought best in his shirt sleeves.

The man swaggered to him.

Philippe draped his coat over the cemetery's fence.

"Your name, Monsieur?" Philippe said. "Me, I have never seen you before. This land, it is not yours."

"Me?" the man said, mimicking Philippe's French accent. "I am here to kill someone. No?"

Philippe almost seized the man's collar till he remembered his pistol. "Who is it you intend to kill?"

"Ben Westcott. Heard of him?"

"He is my friend. He has survived the war?"

"He'll die today. We have some unfinished business. He came back on my ship, his old ship, and told me to meet him here. Our captain gave me a day's liberty. Decent of him, isn't it?" He pointed at Philippe's rosary. "I like your necklace and the little cross hanging from it."

"It is a rosary."

Locke snickered. "You're one of those fanatics. Ain't that a joke."

"Locke. That is your name. *Non*? Benjamin, he told me about you."

Locke stepped closer. So did Philippe.

"Your captain, he had no knowledge of your intention?" Philippe took one more step to within arm's reach. His hand crept toward Locke's revolver.

"Don't know, don't care. I acted as though I let bygones be bygones. We both did so we could finish our unfinished business." Locke's fiendish eyes shifted to the cemetery. "I broke his sister's scrawny little neck. She mocked me."

Philippe seized the butt of Locke's revolver. Locke fought Philippe for it, slinging his arm left and right with a strength equal the Creole's till he jerked his pistol free. Then Locke's fist plowed into Philippe's stomach.

Philippe staggered.

Locke quickly holstered his pistol.

Philippe's fist smashed Locke's face.

Locke tottered; his fingers wiped his bleeding mouth. Next, he unbuttoned his gunbelt and frock coat and tossed them aside, along with his white straw hat. "Fisticuffs, is it? I have only enough bullets in my revolver for killing Westcott. For the great big giant standing before me, I have my fists." Crouched slightly, he charged Philippe. Philippe sidestepped him and brought his fists down on Locke's back like a hammer.

Locke collapsed face first.

"You are the man who killed my Annie!" Philippe raised his foot and plunged it toward Locke's back. Locke rolled clear. Like lightning, the Yankee scooted behind him and clutched Philippe's ankles.

Up Philippe flew, down he fell, smacking earth. His jaw ached.

Back on his feet, Locke kicked Philippe's sides...kidneys, liver, spleen, chest....

Pains pierced him. Philippe screamed.

After another instant, Locke quit. "On your feet, Frenchie! Let's have it out the right way! Fists only!"

Philippe scrambled upright, panting hard and aching, determined to avenge Annie's murder and save his friend Ben. He raised his fists.

Crouched in a boxer's stance, Locke also raised his. "I prefer fisticuffs to kicking. Come at me, Frenchie. I dare you."

The man, by his stance, he is experienced. But my arms, they are longer. Me? I will pummel him till he collapses. I will keep out of his reach.

"Come at me I said. Or are you chicken guts?"

Philippe's right fist flew toward Locke's head. Locke weaved, avoiding it. Another jab, another, another. It grazed Locke's jaw when he sidestepped it.

Locke danced back and forth on his toes. "What's the matter, Frenchie? Can't hit me anymore?"

Fists flying, Philippe charged like a wild bull. Locke smashed his chest—one, two—Philippe staggered back, recovered, and plowed a left hook into Locke's head. A right hook followed fast. Locke stumbled during his retreat. Bruised and bloodied, he glowered at Philippe. Despite Locke's efforts to parry and weave, Philippe's rapid jabs found him again. Another jab missed. Locke lit out toward the stables.

Philippe took a moment to recover his wind, then pursued. Locke halted suddenly, whirled on him, grinned, and feinted left. When Philippe moved to counter, Locke rushed in and combined a grazing uppercut on Philippe's jaw with a fierce punch in his stomach. Philippe's arms dropped to his sides; he tottered. More blows followed, too furious and too fast for him to counter. His torso, his stomach, his liver, his shoulders, his arms.

Philippe tried shoving back Locke to give his long arms more room to punch and jab, but Locke kept it up, moving in range to land a blow as swiftly as he moved out of range of Philippe's exhausted, heavy arms.

Wearing down and in pain, Philippe's arms moved up when Locke moved inside and, with all the strength he could muster, they closed around his adversary, this time quicker than Locke's overconfident retreat. He shoved Locke onto the dirt and straddled his legs, Phillipe's immense size now working in his favor.

Seizing Locke's hair, Philippe banged his head time and again into the dirt. Locke clenched his eyes, writhed, spat, screamed. Philippe's right fist jabbed Locke's nose and mouth. Locke spat out blood and teeth.

Philippe started another punch, which halted halfway to his head. "*Non*. I will not kill you. It would be murder." Philippe moved off him while keeping a grip on Locke's wrists. "When I stand, you will stand. I will not kill you, but neither will I release you. I will tie your hands and take you to the police."

Groaning, his bloody nose broken and chest heaving, Locke shot him a menacing look.

Exhausted, Philippe slowly stood, pulling Locke up with him, but before he could twist Locke's right arm behind his back Locke's left foot slammed Philippe's. The man broke free and sprinted toward the stables.

Philippe forgot his fatigue and gave chase.

Within seconds Locke came outside the stables, a pitchfork in his hand.

Panting, Philippe gaped.

Pitchfork poised over his shoulder, Locke aimed its curved prongs at Philippe's chest and shrugged. "I've changed my mind. I won't kill you with my fists. I'll use this." He hurled it hard and fast. Philippe dodged, scrambled toward the weapon lying just beyond him. Locke seized it the same instant he did. Locked in close quarters, they grappled.

"I think it's around the bend." Buckley, perched halfway up the mizzenmast's ratlines, hit *Madison's* quarterdeck hard.

"Jones's and Yates's suspicions were correct, sir?" Doctor Kirby said.

Buckley went to the starboard rail. "Unfortunately. I think I recognized Locke on Westcott's land, but I'm not sure. We're still quite a ways from it. A man in a blue uniform is fighting a big fellow, and I saw Westcott and Yates on the road together, walking that direction. There will be a duel, unless the big fellow kills Locke first. Or unless Yates talks Westcott out of it. I'm not holding out much hope for that, though."

The doctor stepped up alongside him. "The man in the blue uniform must be Locke."

"Get your medical case. I'll be lowering boats soon."

"Aye, sir."

"Was I right?" Roscoe looked up from his sweeping when Doctor Kirby entered the wardroom.

"That you were," the doctor said. "Good thing you found that note Mister Westcott slipped under Locke's cot. You did right to report it to Captain Buckley."

He went into his room for his medical case and hurried back up the ladder and forward where tars readied the port and starboard boats for lowering. Zollicoffer and Kite were issuing arms to two squads of Marines. He climbed into the starboard boat just before the sailors lowered it.

"Belay that talk. I'm sick of hearing it." Ben's strides lengthened, his effort to move ahead of Danny futile.

"How do you know for sure he killed your sister?" Danny said. "Why fight your duel all over again? It doesn't make sense."

"I didn't invite your company."

"No, sir. But I'm gonna stay with you and keep talking till you get some sense in your brain. You're about to break the sixth commandment. 'Thou shalt not kill.'"

"That's all I've been hearing since we left New Orleans."

"And you're gonna keep hearing it. And I'm gonna keep telling you, you gotta forgive your enemies."

"I'll forgive him after I kill him."

"That'll make you a murderer."

"So God will forgive me after I kill him."

"Hatred is the same as murder."

"I'm a cold-blooded, heartless killer then." Ben's hard eyes never wavered from the road ahead. They approached a bend.

"No, sir. I don't think you're that coldhearted. Nancy told me stories about you. She likes you and your brother. You're hurt and you're angry, sir, same as me before I learned to forgive."

"I suppose you'll report me to the sheriff after I'm done with Locke."

"I'm gonna have to."

"Suppose I kill you next?"

"Then I'll be far away in a better place and away from all this world's cruelty and madness."

"Nancy would hate me if I killed you."

"She'd pity you, sir, same as I do."

"I don't need your pity."

"Mister Ben—"

"Up ahead is my home. Locke will be waiting, and I will kill him. You stay here."

Ben passed through the gate. Heart hammering, he cautiously moved up the dirt lane, eyes darting back and forth. On either side oak trees and yellowish-brown garden hedges stood sentinel. He searched through their branches for Locke. That man might be planning on ambushing him.

The gate squeaked behind him. *Go back, Danny. You're liable to get hurt.* Eyes shifted straight ahead, he surveyed the square columns for Locke hiding behind them, then the dusty windows on the mansion's upper and lower galleries. Cobwebs spanned one corner of the upper gallery; the crimson drapes behind each window were drawn. *Anyone inside? Locke?* He looked for the drape's movement. Saw none.

Pistol drawn, he went up the front steps and nudged open his front door. "Locke! Locke!"

His voice echoed throughout the mansion.

"He's not inside?" Danny spoke from the lane.

"He's somewhere around here," Ben said. "He's hiding, waiting for the right moment. Stay put."

He searched each room on the first floor, the dining room and parlors, the ballroom. Loneliness filled him. Gone, the gaiety in this house. His mouth went dry; he shuddered. Dread. Every wall pulsed it, every piece of dusty furniture. He hurried out the back door. Danny, who'd gone up to the second floor, called to him from atop the curved staircase outside. "He's not up here! I searched every room!"

"He's around!" Ben yelled back. "Quit following me!"

"I can't!" Danny yelled back. His eyes lifted toward the stables. "Over yonder!" He stretched forth his arm.

Ben turned his head the direction Danny pointed. His heart lurched. A figure was sprawled on the dirt, a pitchfork stuck in his chest. Was it...*it is!* Philippe's large frame was unmistakable. He ran toward his friend; a shot rang out from his bachelor quarters.

62

WHILE BEN DARTED behind a small outbuilding opposite the mansion, Danny raced down the curved staircase and jumped backward, onto the lower gallery. He flattened himself against a column. *I gotta stop this. It's going too far.* He spotted Locke crouched behind an open window inside Ben's quarters, on the second floor. Had Locke seen him accompanying Mister Westcott? Had he heard him yelling from the staircase?

Ben darted from behind the small building to a longer building.

Locke fired again; the bullet kicked dirt.

Two shots. That's two. He's got four left. Staying on the gallery while trying to keep out of Locke's view, Danny crossed it and went down several steps. Another glance up at Locke, another quick prayer. He sprinted across a short tract to Ben's quarters. He flattened himself against it.

"I saw you, boy," Locke screamed. "Come through that door down there, I'll kill you, too. Westcott, you yellow dog, come out from behind that smokehouse and fight me."

"You come outside," Ben yelled back. "We'll fight our duel the right way. No hiding behind windows and buildings."

"Dead, Westcott. You're dead."

"Shoot me then."

During this exchange Danny eased along the building, his back still flush with its side. A panel door was up ahead. Another shot sounded from Locke's window.

"I thought you were a good shot." Ben's laughter was mocking. *Three bullets left.*

Glancing up, he made sure Locke hadn't come to the window overhead. He reached for the doorknob.

Doctor Kirby's boat, packed with Marines, pulled away from *Madison*, stranded on a shoal about a half-mile short of Monmouth's wharves. Her engines were loud, smoke poured out of her funnel, and her masts and hull quivered while she labored to free herself from her predicament. Her grounding was the least of his worries. It delayed their arrival. Since his boat's oarsmen had to work harder against the current, he doubted they'd arrive before someone else got hurt.

Another boat, moving swiftly alongside them, carried Kite and more Marines. They approached a river bend.

"Poor fellow," Zollicoffer spoke from beside the surgeon. "I wonder who he was."

"A friend of Mister Westcott's, my guess," Doctor Kirby said. "Run through with a pitchfork, Mister Buckley said when he came back down the ratlines."

"He's not the only one who witnessed it. Our captains of the main and foretops also saw it through their glasses. We have him, Doctor. Locke will be court-martialed and hung for murder, and I'd say it's about time."

"We're rounding the bend."

"The wharves." Zollicoffer stood in the boat, legs braced. He gestured to Kite in the other boat. "The first wharf, men!"

"I heard shooting, sir!" Kite hollered.

"Move it! Move it!"

The boats bumped the wharf at almost the same time.

Two bullets left. Danny crept up the narrow staircase, hesitated when the steps creaked. Did Locke hear the sound? He kept on, nowhere to run now, nowhere to hide on this narrow stairway. The door to Locke's room, a few steps higher, closed. *He might be waiting for me. Nancy,*

I love you. Mister Westcott, I don't want you to die and I don't want you killing nobody. He reached the second floor's small landing. *I know where I'm gonna be. I'm gonna be with the good Lord Jesus if Mister Locke kills me. So kill me, Mister Locke, and don't kill nobody else. No, sir.* Arm outstretched, he stepped aside and away from the door best he could and eased it open.

Locke fired.

Danny charged into the room.

Locke's bullet struck him, creasing his left arm.

"That's all your bullets, Mister Locke." Danny gripped his bicep where the bullet nicked him. "Why must you go on killing folks, sir?"

Locke backed behind the bed blocking Danny's approach. He glanced out the open window from where he'd been shooting. "Westcott's coming. He'll kill me."

"No he won't, sir. I'll make sure of it. Didn't we see enough killing during the war?"

Ben's rapid steps sounded outside.

Closer Locke edged toward the opened window. Another glance out. "Zollicoffer and the doctor are on their way up the main lane."

"Sir," Danny said, his voice filled with pity. "You're a sick man, sir. But the good Lord Jesus loves you, sir. He'll forgive you, sir. He wants to help you."

"I won't forgive him." Ben came through the door. "Thanks to Danny here, I've decided not to kill you. I figured I'd make you use up all your bullets before I made my move. I'm taking you to Zollicoffer soon as he gets here. I'll enjoy watching a lady-killer get strung up."

Locke's eyes went wild— pupils dilated and eyeballs rolling. Pitching his revolver at Ben, he shrieked, leapt on the bed and shoving them aside, practically flew between them. He tripped and stumbled down the stairs, rolling and bumping on the steps till he hit the first floor. Sprawled on his back, his arms and legs almost perfectly outstretched, his movement ceased.

Doctor Kirby rushed forward and examined him.

"Is he dead?" Ben's tone was casual.

"His neck's broken," the doctor said.

"He killed himself. I didn't do it. I'm coming down, Zollicoffer. Check out my revolver. I never fired a shot."

"No need for that." Zollicoffer dispatched four Marines to return to the boats for cots. "No holes in his body I can see."

Back outside, Ben led Doctor Kirby, Zollicoffer and other Marines to the stables. "Philippe was my friend, Doctor, almost as close as Alex, and would've been just as close had I not been away so long in the navy."

"We saw him from the ship, fighting Locke," Doctor Kirby said.

"I wish he'd won."

"Shall I inform his parents for you?"

"I'll do it. Since I am his friend, I fear it is my sad duty."

When they reached Philippe's crimson-stained corpse, Ben looked skyward and squeezed his eyes. After four years of bloodletting, this noble man returned home whole and yet died defending him and avenging his sister's honor. A man who loved deeply. *I wish I was more like you, my dear friend.*

1875

MAY

63

CLASPING HIS YOUNG son's hand, Alex led Stephen up the cemetery's paved path to his mother and Susanna's tomb. The granite angel atop it, its wings spread wide, looked beautiful now. And in a sense, the cemetery was pretty, its bright green grass thriving beneath a brilliant sun, its oak trees rustling their giant limbs in the reverent silence. Pigeons strutted across their path. Doves perched in treetops. He brought Stephen to a halt, knelt at the tomb, and tugged his son's trousers.

Stephen knelt beside him. "What was my grandmother like, Father?"

Though Alex's mother had many faults, she was still his mother. He'd never told Stephen the bad about her. Only the good. Stephen always asked the same question: what was she like? Perhaps that had something to do with his being nine years old. He wasn't sure. This fatherhood business was something he was still struggling to figure out. He gave his son the same answer he'd always given in some version or other: "She'd have been very proud of you."

"My Aunt Susanna?"

"She'd have spoiled you." He took some shears out of his coat pocket and started trimming the grass around their tomb.

"Momma said you wouldn't marry her at first because of a 'k' word or something."

Laughing, Alex led Stephen down the path to a simple stone marker. "What does the name on that headstone say, Stephen? Can you read it?"

"It says…" The boy hesitated; his smooth brow crinkled. The words came slowly. "William… Kettle…uh.…"

"Hughes. He's your Uncle Will and he never married. My 'k' word was 'kettle', 'cause I was about the only person who knew his middle name."

"Why?"

"We were close and it sort of embarrassed him." Alex chuckled. "Don't know the answer to why on that one. It made him feel like a tea kettle or something, I guess. Said it was his mother's maiden name. He always told me never to get married because if a man got married, his life wasn't his own anymore. I believed that for a very long time. Too long a time." He led Stephen back to his mother's and sister's graves and resumed snipping grass. "Don't tell your mother our little secret."

"I won't."

Alex chuckled silently. *Just tell a child not to do something, and watch him do it. Wait'll I see Mary's expression when she finds out.*

Another minute passed before his son asked, "Why did you marry Momma?"

This was a new question, but he had a ready answer. He set down the shears and looked his inquisitive son square in the face. "Well, you see, Stephen. I love your mother. I loved her for a very, very long time. But actually, it all started many years ago, with Leroy."

"Who's Leroy?"

"Who's Leroy? Why, he was a turtle. One day many years ago, when your grandfather and I returned from a fishing trip.…"

The warm summer sun streamed through a window in Monmouth's office, dancing lightly off Moxley's ledger. Outside, beyond the small building, a handful of men worked the cane fields. These days, he barely earned enough to pay them. Had he not sold his parents' homes in New Orleans and Holly Oaks, their bankrupt plantation outside Baton Rouge, he'd be in even worse financial shape. His own home in New Orleans, Butler had burned to the ground.

Mister Inchforth had worked hard to manage his plantation, along with Monmouth and Holly Oaks after Annie's death, as a favor to him and Ben till the war ended. And yet, when Moxley finally returned home he discovered the sugar house a wreck, along with other buildings, and a handful of laborers, black and white, working the fields for poor wages. Raising capital demanded a herculean effort, and sugar cane plantations required far more capital than those raising cotton. He barely staved off having to sell and subdivide his land, like many sugar cane planters had done.

He studied his ledger's numbers. Debits exceeded credits far beyond what they should. He tugged his hair. He'd expected Ben to take over the farm so he could pursue his newspaper writing, but it never happened. He also hated having to give up this place, which was why he'd reluctantly quit his newspapering in Mobile so many years ago. His parents and Annie were buried here. *Ben, where are you? I need you here, helping me.* He took a swig of condensed milk, picked up his pencil, and traced it down the credit column.

Booming laughter reverberated from the big house's gallery. Susanna, his six-year-old daughter, giggled and squealed.

Moxley hobbled outside on his wooden prosthesis. Its back door was flung open and Danny, bent low, tickled her. Nancy squeezed past the pair, a brown-wrapped package tucked under her left arm.

"Sorry to bother you, sir." Danny looked up from Susanna. The child owned Susan's black, curly hair.

"My work's boring anyway, Reverend Yates," Moxley said. "Y'all have given me a good excuse to stop for a while."

Nancy patted Susanna's head and winked at her. "Let's us skedaddle upstairs. This chile here's got a present for you."

"For me?" Susanna's blue eyes widened.

"'Specially for you. Come along."

"You didn't have to do that, Nancy," Moxley said.

"'Course I didn't," Nancy said.

"We're friends now. No longer are we master and slave."

Nancy sighed deeply. "Mister Moxley, please stop telling me things I already know. Why, I love this chile much as I did Miss Annie, like she was my very own granchile. Can't a friend do a good deed for another friend?" She gestured at Susanna. "Come along now, Suzie."

Susanna skipped behind her, up the curved outer staircase to the second floor.

Moxley and Danny walked around to the front. Soon after his return to New Orleans, a few months after he and Susan were wed, he'd run into Danny strolling Canal Street still in the Navy, and from him he'd learned how Locke almost killed Ben, about Philippe's death, and Locke's ultimate fate. The last time Moxley saw his brother was ten years ago, that day he'd tried making him angry at Miss Augusta Evans's house. He and Susan wanted to send him a wedding invitation, but they had no idea where he was. All these years, Ben's whereabouts had been a mystery.

"I reckon you still haven't heard from Mister Ben."

"Lord knows, I'd give anything to know where he is or what he's up to. I hope he's still alive. I realize I'm not supposed to worry, that I'm supposed to trust God, but when you love someone as much as I love Ben and all my family...we were close once. We played hard every day in this yard when we were children, even in the rain. Annie tried to play the games we did, but that made our mother angry. Annie was supposed to be the perfect lady at all times, never sweat and never get dirty and always wear gloves outdoors, but if Ben and I got dirty, well, we were boys and boys were being boys, so that was fine. How is the church doing?"

"Since Reverend Dotson died, I've been having my share of troubles with certain members. Not everybody. Just a few. But the deacons asked me to take his place, so seems like Nancy and me will still be in New Orleans a while." He smiled slyly. "The wife and me had a squabble yesterday. She wanted me to change the sign at the front of the church. Instead of 'Reverend Danny Yates', she wanted me to change it to 'Reverend Daniel Yates.' She said 'Daniel' sounded more dignified."

"Did you do it?"

"Indeed not. I don't care much for sounding dignified. All this putting on airs and pretense and such is not my way. I told her that after our little spat. That satisfied her then, just fine."

The deep bellow of a steamboat's whistle announced it arounding a bend.

"Coming up from New Orleans," Moxley said. "Maybe Susan and Jenny are returning."

They moved down the front lawn's center lane to the picket fence. The steamboat eased up alongside their landing. Minutes later, the two ladies crossed over the levee. No longer did Jenny wear mourning. She'd remarried in '67; her husband was a fellow named Hastings. He held some important position with the Jackson Railroad.

Moxley recognized the manuscript Susan held.

"I'm sorry." Susan handed it to him at the gate.

"This is the fourth time it's been rejected," Moxley said. "Maybe I'm not supposed to be a writer."

"I declare!" Jenny cried, slapping her hands on her hips. "Of all the words coming out of your mouth, I never thought I'd hear that one."

"Oh!" Susan reached inside her skirt pocket and handed Moxley a telegram. "I almost forgot. Do you happen to know someone named Randall Bartlett? Clara said it was sent to her, and it's from him."

"Known him for years. Attended our wedding. Have you forgotten?"

"He's the nice gentleman Annie spurned," Jenny said.

"For another nice gentleman who died defending my brother," Moxley said.

"The Creole."

"The Creole. Yes. Randall's living in Shreveport, last I heard. Went to work for his cousin who owns some type of business. Can't remember what his work is." Moxley devoured Randall's news: *I have found Ben. He is in a sore state and desperately needs our help. Find Moxley and tell him to come up here at the double-quick. My address is....*

Moxley lowered the telegram.

Susan touched his arm. "What is it?"

"Ben's finally been found. Randall says he needs our help."

"Is he hurt?" Danny said.

"I don't think so."

"Mother! Father!" Susanna skipped down the lane wearing a frilly turquoise dress with a pink lace bodice. She did a quick spin. "Nancy made it for me. Isn't it beautiful?"

Moxley managed a smile. "My daughter is the prettiest little girl in the whole wide world."

Susanna hugged his leg and beamed up at Nancy.

"Thank you, Nancy," Susan said.

Moxley thumped the telegram. "Go pack. We're all going to Gabriel, Texas. We're bringing my brother home."

End of Book Two

AUTHOR NOTES

After the Civil War, Augusta Evans's poverty was short-lived. Concerned about Howard's wound as well as his mental health, a consequence of typhoid fever, she took him to New York in the late summer of 1865 to be examined by a prominent physician. During this time she visited her good friend Mister J.C. Derby, who'd published *Beulah*. He told her that *Macaria* had been published by a Northern publisher named Doolady, and that he and Doolady had reached an agreement whereby he'd been holding that book's royalties in trust for her until the war ended. A lot of money it was, too, for *Macaria* had been a bestseller in the North.

By 1868, Howard's memory returned. In this same year she married sixty-year-old widower Lorenzo Madison Wilson, whose name came up several times throughout the book.

I engaged in a bit of artistic license with the Evans's servant, Minervy. Minervy was a real person, a servant with whom the author felt especially close. She accompanied the Evanses on their trip to Texas when Miss Evans was a child. She was old at this time, so she was probably deceased by the time my book opened, but since I couldn't be sure of this, I decided to include her.

Augusta Evans Wilson continued her literary career after the war. Though not as well-known today, she ranks alongside Harriet Beecher Stowe, Louisa May Alcott, and other great nineteenth-century American female writers. Many of today's scholars are rediscovering her life and works. In 1909, one day after her seventy-fourth birthday, she died of a heart attack and is buried in Mobile's Magnolia Cemetery alongside her brother Howard.

A particular detail in this book may seem contrived, but factually, it isn't. This is when Moxley is sent back to Mobile after his period of instruction at the conscription camp in Notasulga, Alabama. Until October 1863, Notasulga and Talladega conscripts were being sent to Mobile. This I learned from the *Official Records of the War of the Rebellion*, volume 128, in a letter Brigadier General Gideon Pillow sent to Colonel Benjamin Ewell, General Joe Johnston's Assistant Adjutant-General. At the time, Pillow commanded the volunteer and conscript bureau headquartered in Marietta, Georgia. In a message dated October 1863, Pillow wrote: "The conscripts from camps at Talladega and Notasulga have, per General Johnston's orders been sent to Mobile, Ala. Orders have been given to send conscripts from Alabama in future to the Alabama regiments in Army of Virginia...." Thus, this fact played perfectly into my plot.

Though Farragut's efforts to destroy the Rebel blockade-runner *Ivanhoe* exacted no Rebel casualties, I engaged in a bit of artistic license here as well. Since Moxley Westcott is a fictional character, I allowed him to be the only one who suffered injury. This enabled me to let it play a part in his salvation and renew his love for Susan.

Regarding the Battle of Mobile Bay, I loosely based *Madison's* experience on the historical sloop-of-war *Lackawanna*. Aboard *Tennessee*, Ben's character replaces the real commander of her first division, Lieutenant A.D. Wharton.

I am indebted to many books and authors throughout my research. Emma Martin Maffitt's book, *The Life and Services of John Newland Maffitt* (New York and Washington: The Neale Publishing Company, 1906), proved especially helpful, as did Royce Shingleton's biography, *High Seas Confederate: The Life and Times of John Newland Maffitt* (Columbia, South Carolina: The University of South Carolina Press, 1994).

Other helpful sources were *Official Records of the Union and Confederate Navies in the War of the Rebellion* (Washington: Government Printing Office, 1899), William Perry Fidler's biography, *Augusta Evans Wilson: 1835-1909* (University, Alabama: University of Alabama Press, 1951) and *A Southern Woman of Letters: The Correspondence of Augusta Jane Evans Wilson*, edited by Rebecca Grant Sexton (Columbia, South Carolina: University of South Carolina Press, 2002). I'm indebted to

Jack Friend's masterful study of the Battle of Mobile Bay, *West Wind, Flood Tide: The Battle of Mobile Bay* (Annapolis, Maryland: Naval Institute Press, 2004), and to Craig L. Symonds' excellent biography of Franklin Buchanan, *Confederate Admiral: The Life and Wars of Franklin Buchanan* (Annapolis, Maryland: Naval Institute Press, 1999).

Many other sources could also be cited, but space will not allow it.

ABOUT THE AUTHOR

John "Jack" M. Cunningham, Jr. grew up in Mobile, Alabama and lived in New Orleans, Louisiana for twenty-five years. He's a graduate of the University of Alabama with a degree in history, a former history teacher and a lifelong student of the American Civil War.

He's written professionally for thirty years, his work appearing in numerous Christian magazines and various other publications. He's also a speaker at writers' groups, a freelance editor, and a writing instructor.

Other books Mister Cunningham has written are:

Southern Sons-Dixie Daughters Book 1: *Vengeance & Betrayal*

Squire, A Mascot's Tale

Reflections of a Southern Boy: Devotions from the Deep South

Visit his website at theauthorscove.com.